A DIAMOND IN THE SKY

Also by Margaret Pelling

WORK FOR FOUR HANDS

A DIAMOND
IN THE SKY

by

Margaret Pelling

HONNO MODERN FICTION

First published by Honno in 2011
'Ailsa Craig', Heol y Cawl, Dinas Powys,
South Glamorgan, Wales, CF64 4AH.
1 2 3 4 5 6 7 8 9 10

The Author would like to stress that this is a work of fiction
and no resemblance to any actual individual or institution
is intended or implied.

A catalogue record for this book is available from the British Library.

Published with the financial support of the Welsh Books Council.

ISBN 978-1-906784-28-7
Cover Images © Lovenfree
Cover design: Steven Goldstone
Text design: Elaine Sharples
Printed in Wales by Gomer

To Chris, as always

Acknowledgements

I am grateful to Robert Bourne, Tom Brown, Radmila May, Gavin Lloyd, Susan Iles, Gillian Butler and Pam Peirson for advice on legal procedure and the treatment of psychiatric cases; to Jeanne Gurr for tips on etiquette in Oxford University's central offices; and to Franco Basso, Michele Lucchesi and Claudia Kozeny-Pelling for supplying a few lines in languages other than English. Any errors of interpretation are entirely my own.

One

Dora pushed the button, and the sun and the moon and the stars and the planets began to revolve gracefully in their orbits. Their smiling faces turned towards her and away again as they moved to the tinkly music:

> *Twinkle twinkle little star*
> *How I wonder what you are*
> *Up above the world so high*
> *Like a diamond in the sky*

Round and round they went, those smiles that never changed. How little it took to amuse a baby. She turned aside and carried on sorting through the jumpsuits. What a pile she had, anybody would think there'd be several weeks' worth here. Anybody who hadn't had a baby, that is. Such colours! Everything the rainbow could offer, and more. Yellow with navy edgings, red striped with turquoise…none of that girly pink and white nonsense. You had to have mimsy colouring to wear mimsy colours. Why were girl babies always assumed to have blonde hair and blue eyes?

Pity about the orange one. She should have asked for it back, she really should. Too late now.

The sun and the moon and the stars and the planets, and the tinkly music, slowed and came to a stop.

'Again?' Once was never enough, it only made the listener want more. Not that Jo was in any position to give a clear yes or no, but Mummy wouldn't mind watching another few turns of the mobile she'd spent such a time tracking down, the only one that could possibly go with this room. She pushed the button. As the heavenly bodies began to dance to the music of the spheres, she twitched the space rocket rug a centimetre or so closer to the cot. She'd have to hoover that rug tomorrow. The rest of the house could go hang, but no dust could be allowed to rest on that. Or on anything else in here.

She ran a finger around the edges of the nappy changing table. Not a speck of dust. But how could there be, considering how often she wiped it.

The grinning little-green-man-from-Mars clock caught her eye. She could hardly blame him, he'd been trying to get her attention for the last five minutes. 'Twenty past ten, get going or you'll be late,' he was saying.

'OK, OK,' she muttered. Couldn't he see she just didn't feel like an hour at the ice rink followed by lunch at the rowdiest pizza place in Oxford? Hm. Well, even she was allowed to be ill from time to time. But it was perhaps a bit late for ringing and pretending she'd got a cold, and Jim and Jenny would be disappointed if their Saturday didn't happen as normal. And if she let her nephew and niece down this time, she might let them down next time, and then where would it end?

'OK Jo, time to go.' She lifted the midnight blue tin out of the cot and held it up at eye-level. A stuck-on 'J' made out of silver stars came into view as she turned it slowly around, then an 'O'. Other stars shone in the background, a coloured universe of them arranged in swirly, galactic shapes. Not bad for one who'd had less artistic ability than an armadillo when she was at school.

'Right then, I won't be long. Be good, and I might read you a story when I get back.'

She kissed the tin, put it back in the cot, and tiptoed out.

Dora turned away from the window. If she didn't answer her brother's question soon, the air in this room would solidify into lead.

'Yes, Steve's coming for lunch tomorrow,' she said at last.

'Ah,' he said.

'"Ah," what?'

'Just "ah."'

'An "ah" from you is never just an "ah", Syd. Especially when it's about Steve.'

'Oh, Dozza, Dozza,' he said, putting his hand on her shoulder, 'you know you're going to let him come back. Do it now and get it over with.'

'The room, Syd, the room. Jo's room gives him the creeps, remember?'

'Yes, I know, I know. But can't two people who still care about each other sort something out, for God's sake?'

'Syd, look, we've said all this a million times. Go and see what the kids are up to, will you? We'll miss the bus at this rate.'

He grunted something. She couldn't make out whether he was commenting on the time his children were taking to get ready to go skating, or the state of her life, but he did go to the door into the hallway and shout upstairs to Jenny and Jim.

You can't go on like this. Funny that Syd hadn't said that, the one thing she might have expected him to come out and say.

Three years, five months and five days since Jo died. Long enough for many people to 'get over it'. Sensible people, like Steve. But for others, time didn't move on in a sensible straight

3

line, it did strange relativistic tricks. Backward somersaults, for instance. *It could have happened to anybody. It wasn't your fault.* Christ, if she had a pound for all the times she'd been told that.

She turned back to the window. Syd was lucky, having this view of Port Meadow, not to mention the odd drowsy spire. Still, he only really got his view in winter. By summer the leaves on the tree next door would be blocking most of it. Not much of winter left now, with February almost over. It would soon be summer and the wasps would be waking up. Bugger summer, with its wasps and leafy trees. And birds.

That bird that morning. *That bird in the chestnut tree outside the bedroom window, singing its bloody little heart out while she sat on the floor waiting for the ambulance. Waiting, waiting, milk pouring out of her, spreading in huge stains all over Steve's old DIY shirt. And with something in her arms that wouldn't respond to the kiss of life, just wouldn't respond. She was doing it wrong, she must have been, she did everything wrong. Oh God. Oh God God God—*

Her arms were wrapping themselves around her so tight that she was having trouble breathing. Having a photographic memory was bad. Having a photographic memory was very, very, bad. She breathed in, breathed out, let her arms drop to her sides – and then the sound of a couple of elephants thundering down the stairs hit her ears. Jim and Jenny were coming. Thank God for Jim and Jenny, the two people in the world who could drown out any thoughts she'd rather not be thinking.

She didn't break children, not running, jumping, laughing children who had a firm hold on this world, she only broke babies. And only babies she'd given birth to.

She breathed in and out again. She was doing a lot of breathing, for a Saturday morning.

'Dozzaaa!' Jenny's warning cry as Dora went into the hall reached her just in time. She parried Jim's rugby tackle, and all

4

three were wrestling on the floor, Jim's head in Dora's pretend arm-lock, when Syd appeared from the kitchen.

'That was Tommy on the phone,' he said.

'Oh? I didn't hear it ring.' But who would, when they were taking a trip down memory lane?

'Well, it did. She's going to try to get to Astronomical Club tonight, and – wait for it – she just might be bringing the brother.'

'Ah, so the leprosy's cleared up.'

'Leprosy's nasty, it doesn't clear up,' pronounced Jenny.

'Has Tommy's brother got lepossy?' said Jim, his eyes round. Then: 'What's lepossy?'

'Miss Ross to you,' said Syd. 'She's your teacher, don't forget.'

'I was only joking, Jim,' said Dora. 'It's just that for all we've seen of this brother since he's been staying at Tommy's, you'd think he'd got some terrible disease. Or that he was a pretend brother, like that little friend you used to have.'

'Bernie's *real*.'

'Yes, of course he is, sorry. He's gone to live in America, hasn't he.'

Jim nodded, a stern look on his face.

'You are coming tonight, I take it? According to the forecast, visibility's going to be great.'

'I don't know, Syd. I'm feeling a bit provisional, I might be coming down with something.' *God, Syd, don't try to take me out of myself, please!*

'Well, don't decide now, see how you feel after skating and lunch.'

'OK, OK.' *I know how I'll feel, Syd. I know.*

'So, these friends of yours,' said Tom, swigging down the last of his coffee, 'what have you told them about me, exactly?'

'I've given them the line we agreed, of course,' said Tommy, fixing him with one of her elder-sister looks. Fond though he was of her, those looks were a bit much sometimes from one who was his elder by only ten minutes. 'You resigned from teaching at a school in Uxbridge before Christmas and you're staying with me for a bit, while you see if there's a future in writing teaching manuals,' she went on as she began to stack her breakfast things in the sink. 'You can't think I've told them any more than that, surely.'

'No, I don't,' said Tom, suppressing a sigh. The 'line we agreed' was the truth, after all, at least in the sense that none of it was false. He looked into his empty mug. Did he want more coffee? Not really. Then again, maybe he did. Jesus, should it be this hard to make a decision about coffee? This astronomical club tonight, on the other hand, that was an issue maybe worth dithering about. Did he want to stand in a field with these friends of Tommy's? The divorced teacher – why were there so many teachers in the world? – and the sister who was in some sort of admin job with the University? Capella would shine just as brightly from Tommy's garden. Oh hell, he couldn't skulk at Tommy's indefinitely, never meeting any of her friends, especially this Syd Clayton and his sister who were practically Tommy's neighbours.

'Hey, you'll be late for the bus,' said Tommy. 'Or are you changing your mind about going skating?'

'No, no, I'm going,' he said, getting up.

As he was leaving the kitchen, Tommy shot after him: 'You are *going* skating, are you? You're not sneaking up to Uxbridge by any chance?'

'I'm not a complete fool, Tommy.'

He didn't wait to hear what she might reply to that.

The bus was late. There were restive mutterings in the small queue, but at the head of it, a woman and two children, a boy and a slightly older girl, were playing I-Spy. 'I spy with my little eye something beginning with…M,' said the boy.

M. Of all the letters in the alphabet, he had to pick that one.

'M for…mud,' said the girl, pointing at the gutter. The boy shook his head.

'M for mist?' said the woman.

That was pushing it. The morning mist had all but cleared.

'M for me' turned out to be the answer, to the groans of the girl and the woman. At that moment the bus appeared.

The bus was pretty full. Tom had to take a seat next to the woman. The two children were immediately in front. He felt like tapping the boy on the shoulder and saying, 'Actually, it's M for Melanie.' What you could see in your mind's eye didn't count, though, only what was actually around you. He put his hand in his jacket pocket and fingered his mobile phone. What if he phoned Mel and suggested meeting? There was nothing stopping him taking the London bus up to Uxbridge for an hour or so, despite what he'd said to Tommy. Tommy wouldn't even need to know.

No, he couldn't. Two months it might be, but it was still too soon. If they were seen, rumours would start to fly. Things could become difficult for her. That was the whole point of his being here and not there, damn it.

'Stop that, both of you,' said the woman, leaning toward the children, 'or I'll make one of you sit here.' What the children had said or done hadn't registered with Tom. The woman turned to him: 'Sorry, do you mind swapping seats so that I can be next to the aisle? It might make it easier.' She jerked her head towards the children by way of explanation.

'Not at all,' he said, getting up. Striking woman, he observed as they changed seats. As they sat down, though, he couldn't help noticing the state of her fingernails. They were chewed right down to the quick.

For the remainder of the journey, from his new vantage point by the window, Tom looked out at the passing streets of Oxford. Was he right to have come here, to be staying with a teacher sister and be faced with meeting her teacher friends? He could have gone back to St Andrew's, back where he could walk for miles without seeing a soul. He could have slipped back into boyhood, to the time he'd first discovered that astronomy was the perfect antidote to the manse, the dour house that he was forced to call home. He could have gazed up at Capella, the perfect star, the one who looked down at you from the heights of heaven when you looked up, straight up, on the coldest, darkest nights of winter.

But St Andrew's would have been so far from Mel…

Where were they heading? An A-level student and a thirty-seven-year-old man who should only ever have been her teacher: what in the name of God was going to come out of all this?

Dora never went anywhere without a book in her bag, the sort of book that could take her far, far away. This morning it was the latest Terry Pratchett, and she pulled it out after plonking herself down in her usual spot in the middle of the spectator area on the town side of the rink. She didn't open the Pratchett straight away. Instead, she let her eyes be filled with the twirling and whirling of scores of bodies. 'Sort something out,' Syd had said. What he meant was do what Steve wanted: redecorate the room, get rid of the outer space stuff and do a completely new theme, like the teddy bears' picnic or God knew what, so that they could have another baby.

It would be good for you. No, to be fair to Syd, he'd never said that, and neither had Steve. They'd thought it, though. Everybody had. *Do it now before it's too late*, they were all thinking.

Forty-three last birthday. Still fertile, just. But not much time left.

Jim went by, racing a boy from his class whom he'd met on the way in. 'Not too fast, boys,' she called, but with the noise in here there wasn't a hope of their hearing her.

8

Where was Jenny? Ah, there she was, with a couple of other girls, watching that older girl in the tutu practicing pirouettes. What made a person want to subject her eyeballs to that much centripetal force?

'Can you see yours?'

Dora jumped. A woman had materialised two seats along, a perky-looking woman some years younger than herself, in immaculate jeans and a bright red parka. On the seat right next to Dora was a car seat. A baby car seat, the smallest size, with a carrying handle. So that make was still on sale. With a sleeping baby thrown in? Or had the stork brought this one.

The baby's red grobag was spotless. Not the slightest gob of milky dribble anywhere. It went well with the navy and red cover of the car seat.

Breathe normally, Clayton. There are countless millions of babies in the world, this is another of them. None of them are your responsibility.

Three years five months and five days. It might as well be three weeks, three days, three seconds.

'I can never see mine – oh, there they are,' said the woman. She waved at two girls who were going slowly past, holding hands, the smaller one barely lifting her skates from the ice. 'Be careful, Katie! Hold onto her, Lauren!'

I can see mine, too. Day and night, I can see her.

A white oblong object, baby-sized, in the arms of a woman in a blue nurse's overall. 'Here's your daughter to see you, Miss Clayton.' A catch in the woman's voice.

Here's-your-daughter-to-see-you. Wrong way round? Or right way? Think about it some time.

This white object. How clean it smells as it's placed in her arms, all soap and baby powder. She'd never got Jo as sanitised as this. Always a bit shitty, always a faint whiff of milky dribble. What they've brought her is dressed up like

9

somebody's idea of a baby. White nightdress, little white bonnet, towelling nappy. *What have they done with her orange jumpsuit.*

The nurse shows her where the buzzer is, rests a hand on her shoulder for a second, then melts away.

So this was Jo. Is Jo. Was. Is.

She put out a finger and touches a foot. The finger draws back, comes waveringly forward again, tries a toe. And another, and another. Five toes. Perfect toes. Amazing, unbelievable.

But the toes are nothing, compared to the lower lip. And the lower lip is nothing, nothing, compared to the row of tiny lashes over each closed eye.

She bends her head. Her lips brush the forehead, then each cheek. Like kissing a wren's breast.

The milk's leaking again. It's soaking through her shirt onto the white nightdress. Bugger.

She's always felt a bit of an idiot singing lullabies. But now, it comes out without effort, so naturally. 'Twinkle twinkle little star, how I wonder what you are, up above the world so high, like a diamond in the sky.' It comes out of her as if she'd been singing it all her life.

Well. She's done the cuddling, she's given the kisses, she's sung the lullaby. That must be it, then. Only thing left to do now is reach for the buzzer.

And phone Steve in Manchester.

That nurse, calling her 'Miss' Clayton. Still, hardly the time or place to insist on Ms.

A whimper. A baby's whimper, what…? Ah. The car seat. The car seat with the spanking bright red grobag.

'Oh God, I thought we were safe for a couple of hours. I fed her just before we came out. Look, do you mind?' said the woman beside her, the woman from another planet.

'Of course not. Go ahead.'

'The other two had better timing. My luck's run out with this one,' the woman went on, unzipping her parka and undoing the baby's safety harness.

'She's beautiful. What's her name?' Got to do it. Got to get through this, saying the things women say.

'Abby,' said the woman, hoiking out a blue-veined globe of breast and attaching the baby to it. 'She's six weeks old today.'

'Hello, Abby.' Six weeks old. Six weeks. Of course, what else would she be.

Abby began feeding lustily, making little gulping noises punctuated by snuffles and snatched breaths. Dora's breasts began to tingle. She folded her arms across them, tight.

Now what? Abby might be going for the full ten minutes a side.

Abby's mum was gazing at Abby. Not the talkative sort when she was feeding a baby, it seemed. More a contemplator of the miracle of new life. OK. Fine. Good.

Dora gazed at the eddying skaters. She would count them, see how many she could get in twenty minutes.

Moving people weren't the easiest of objects to count, though. She counted three men in black sweaters before realising they had identical thoughtful faces under longish brown-gold hair, and were either triplets or the same man. She had a feeling she'd seen him before, or somebody like him. Abby finished feeding, was burped and settled back into her seat, and then there was a commotion on the ice, some way away. Somebody seemed to have fallen over or been knocked into. 'God, it's Katie,' said the woman, jumping up. 'Can you keep an eye on Abby for a minute?' She raced off before Dora had a chance to say, 'Of course.'

'Keep an eye'? Well, no need to take the woman literally. Dora rivetted her gaze to the rink. But she couldn't avoid seeing the car seat out of the corner of her eye.

Don't look. But it was like telling her pores not to sweat.

Abby was waving her arms. And she was having a good kick. Either that or she had a family of energetic mice hidden in that grobag. And – by God – she was smiling. *At six weeks she will try to grasp. She will smile, kick, wave her arms.*

Aah. Sweet.

Dora's shoulders began to shake. She shoved a fist against her mouth. She couldn't laugh, not here. Not the kind of laugh that would have the attendants calling the police.

Steve I can't do it. I can't have another, I'd kill it too.

Just for a change, maybe she should say it as soon as he came through the door tomorrow, not wait for it to 'come up' when they were making the coffee. Then he could get his sad, wistful, sideways look over with and they could talk about the things they'd drifted back into the habit of talking about. Work, people, the Government's latest cock-up, DIY. The things people who were still vaguely married talked about, people who still cared, sort of. She did care, didn't she? He seemed to, if she was any judge. Poor old Steve, saddled with a murderer for a wife.

Oh God, how *would* she do it if she had another one, a sweet smiling one like Abby here, what kind of culpable negligence would she commit? Leaving another baby in a hot room with the window closed because she hadn't got around to doing anything about a wasps' nest would be a bit samey. Maybe she'd wait until toddlerhood, there were so many more possibilities. Like forgetting to close stair gates, or not moving pots on cookers out of reach, or going for walks beside busy roads. No telling what she might do. No telling at all.

A yelling. A howling. What… Ah. Mum was back. And Katie was feeling sore. So was Lauren, by the look on her face.

'Oh, Mu-um, I've only had ten min-utes!' whined the sulky-looking girl.

'God, who'd have kids,' sighed the woman. 'We're going home. Next time their dad can bring them.'

How in hell have you managed not to kill them, how the bloody hell? 'I'll look out for Abby,' she said. 'A minute longer and I'd have taken her home with me.'

The woman's eyes widened for a second, then she laughed. It was just a joke. Only what women say.

Dora watched them make their way towards the exit. Tempers seemed to be fraying fast. She could almost hear the 'No!' as they passed the vending machines.

Not one child, not two, but three. And all alive. How, for God's sake?

Oh shit. She couldn't have a day of thinking like this. She couldn't sit alone in that house tonight like this. She pulled out her mobile. 'Syd? I've decided about tonight. I'll come. Yes, fine, I'll stay after I've brought the kids back and play snakes and ladders with them. Yes, yes, I'll have supper with you too. Bye.' As she put her phone away, a fast-moving blur of people pulled her eyes back to the rink. Another collision?

Christ, look out, Jim!

Tom grabbed the boy's arm and swerved sideways, pulling him out of the path of the teenager who'd taken it into his head to dart out and perform a flashy manoeuvre to impress a crowd of giggling girls. 'Are you all right?' he said. The child looked shaken.

'Yeah. It was his fault. He should've looked where he was going.'

'Maybe, but that wouldn't have helped you if you'd ended up flat on your face,' said Tom. Wasn't this the boy from the bus? The lad didn't seem to be recognising him, but they hadn't really made eye contact. That lower lip jutting out – the boy was trying so hard to not cry in front of his friend. 'What I always do is expect everybody else to act stupidly,' Tom went on. 'That way I don't get hurt.' He gave the friend a share of his smile. It wouldn't do any harm to include him in the lesson. 'Hey, is that somebody's mum over there, looking worried?'

'It's his auntie,' said the friend.

'It's Dozza – er, my Aunt Dora,' said the boy Tom had rescued.

Tom raised a hand to the small woman with the big eyes and the dark cropped hair who was standing behind the barrier, a hand up to her mouth. This must be the boy from the bus, because that most certainly was the woman he'd been with.

'Thanks,' she called, raising a hand too. At least, he supposed she must have thanked him. She might only have been exercising her jaw muscles, for all he could hear above the noise in here. There was something about her. What was it, exactly?

'OK, off you go then,' he said to the boys. 'Tell you what, I'll race you to the end of the rink.' An identical grin broke out on each upturned face, then both boys shot away. Tom left it a couple of seconds before following. He'd make sure he got there a metre or so behind them.

'What I always do is expect everybody else to act stupidly.' And to think he was never going to speak a hypocritical word to a child.

That girl back there in the middle of the giggling crowd: blink, and you'd think she were Mel. And this other one he was passing right now, she was Mel too. This whole rink must be full of Mel look-alikes, brought here this morning for him to skate around like the obstacles in some slalom race. That woman just now, Aunt Dora, wasn't it obvious what he'd noticed about her? There was something of Mel about her, of course – or Mel as she'd be in twenty years or so. Same height – lack of it, rather – and same dark hair in a boyish cut, but it wasn't so much anything physical, as a sort of aura. Touch this kind of female and you might get an electric shock. He knew that better than anybody.

14

Two months of being apart, as of tomorrow. Two months of furtive phone calls, texts and emails. They couldn't go on like this. A non-stupid person would say they couldn't go on, full stop. That they should never have started. Nobody ever listens to non-stupid people, though. Not when their fourth, or was it fifth, girlfriend has just left them because they're an uncommunicative moody bastard, and they're too bruised and battered to know the difference between up and down.

Little Mel Baines. Always there with a cheerful smile on a Monday morning after one of his break-ups, when all he wanted was to nurse his post-crisis hangover. Always ready with the penetrating remark about the text the class were studying, reminding him why he'd rather be doing this job than any other, hangover or no, break-ups or no. She'd never know how much he owed her. She'd been getting older, though. Moving from GCSE to AS and now to A-level. Yes, getting older all the time, getting more mature. Not a little girl any more, but a student whose remarks could make him think: best of his bunch, best of any bunch he'd had, for that matter. On course for one of the top universities, for sure. Living just around the corner from him, so what could be more natural than for him to give her a catch-up tutorial on *Hamlet* at his kitchen table on a Saturday morning when she'd been away from school the last day or so with a cold?

A buzzing sound. He looks up and sees a wasp hovering. No, two wasps. They must have come in through the open kitchen window. Well, it's the time for them. It is September, after all.

'Aah!' she cries. 'They're bloody targeting me, they always do!' She jumps up – and knocks her coffee over, sending it lapping around the pile of Year Ten poetry projects he was marking before she arrived. He jumps up and grabs the pile of marking before it's engulfed.

15

'Oh shit, shit!' she wails, hand up to her mouth. 'I'm so sorry, I'm really, really, sorry, I—'

'It's all right, Mel. No damage done.'

'But it's gone on the Year Ten stuff!'

'Not much, only the edges. It'll improve them.'

The coffee's dripping on the floor. The wasps are struggling in the brown pool. She's watching them drown, her face beetroot.

'I can't stand wasps either,' he says, fetching the J-cloth from its hook by the sink. 'If I had a pound for all the times I've done something like that, I'd have a very large pension fund by now.'

'Now I know what it means when people say they wish the ground would open up and swallow them,' she says, folding her arms and hunching her shoulders.

'It's OK, Mel. Really it is.' He begins to mop up the coffee. What can he say to make her feel better, to make sure she doesn't go to her room when she gets home and spend the rest of the day lacerating herself? 'Pity about your coffee. Shall I make some more?'

'Not for me thanks. God, I've never felt such a complete plonker.'

He puts down the J-cloth. 'You're not a plonker, Mel,' he says, going towards her, 'so there's no need whatever to feel like one.' He lays a hand on her shoulder for a second.

'Thanks,' she murmurs, eyes darting towards the place where his hand had rested. 'Well, I'd better be going, you're busy.'

'Don't go on my account, Mel. If it's a choice between reading Year Ten's witterings on Hughes and Plath and talking to you, there's no contest.'

Stop, you fool! But this girl's not looking embarrassed any longer, she's looking – she's looking—

Oh Christ.

He puts a hand on each of her arms, brings her close to him, and kisses her.

16

The end of the rink was coming up. He had to reconnect, haul himself back to now. 'Well done,' he called to the two boys. 'Dead heat. You both beat me, anyway.'

'I was first,' said the boy he had saved.

'No, I was!' said the friend.

'You were both first. Well, cheers. See you here again sometime.' He glided away, weaving around the swirling knots of skaters. Wasn't movement supposed to get you off your mental treadmill? Well, it wasn't working today. That tutorial: the first of many. Mel had 'liked' him, it seemed, since the day AS levels finished and he'd given the class an impromptu party at his house. Yes, she'd liked him, but hadn't dared show it, so that day she'd chatted and laughed with the boys instead. And he'd noticed, and felt something in him very close to jealousy, as close as a man should get who was still trying to understand and be understood by someone else.

Those tutorials. Almost a whole autumn term of them, and some of the time even spent talking about books. Until the Head found out: *I've met some hare-brained fools since I've been a headmaster but you, Ross, you take the biscuit.* He'd have the Head's words engraved on his hare-brain until he died. It was a wonder he wasn't hearing them in his sleep. *Best teacher I've got. I despair, I really do.*

'I despair.' I despair, you despair, he/she/it despairs. We despair, all of you despair, the whole world despairs. The simplest conjugations were the truest.

Two

'Wow, this sky,' breathed a woman's reverent voice somewhere on Dora's left. 'I've never seen it so clear. Look, you can even see Orion's bow.'

A man's voice said something about the Winter Hexagon putting on the show of the year tonight, but the rest of his words drifted past Dora.

Oh bloody hell. Of course, the Angel Gabriel. That was who that man was, the one who rescued Jim this morning. That was where she'd seen him before: on a thousand Christmas cards. The hippy golden hair, the pensive, slightly downcast gaze... So she'd seen not only a tiny baby this morning, but the Angel of the Annunciation. Not bad going for what should have been just another Saturday.

'How often do you see Jupiter and Saturn that close?' said the woman who'd been so impressed by the lack of cloud cover tonight.

In February though, clouds had their advantages over clear skies: they kept your feet warm. The temperature had to be five below, if not more. Her feet were turning to ice, she had a crick in her neck, and all for the sake of some bits of old rock and blobs of gas however many millions of miles away.

You can't go on like this. Ah, but how else can I go on?

'So, what do you think, Dozz?' said a voice at her side, Syd's voice.

'About what?'

'About what I just said. About calling it a night before Jim runs completely riot and I'm drummed out of the club.'

'I thought we were supposed to be meeting Tommy.'

'She only said she might come. It's past nine, she's not going to make it now.'

'OK, you round up Jim, I'll carry on contemplating the mysteries of the universe for a moment.'

Off he went. Good old Syd, what would she ever have done without him?

'What's that one up there, Dad?' said a small girl's voice from just in front of her. A man said something, but she didn't catch what it was. 'No, not that one, *that* one,' said the child, pointing straight up as she stepped back onto Dora's foot.

That one? Don't look at that one, kid, choose any star but that.

Capella. The one star she'd been trying to avoid looking at all evening. The one star she always avoided looking at.

'That one's Capella,' said another man's voice, a voice from immediately beside her.

She jumped. Where had he come from? He wasn't there a moment ago.

She took a step away from him. Personal space was personal space, even in the dark. Especially in the dark. And especially with people who could identify Capella. Where was Syd? It was time they were off.

'Capella, in the constellation Auriga,' the trespassing man went on.

Capella. Capella, in the constellation Auriga. God, the way he'd said those words. Somewhere in the universe, a gear seemed to have shifted. Or was it that a door had blown open, a magic door behind which was – what?

She felt the man turn toward her. Had she parroted those words of his out loud, then? Damn.

She didn't turn toward him, she turned slightly away. Not that her face would be anything more than a vague corporeal outline on a moonless night like this, but still.

'What's Owriga?' piped the child, stepping on Dora's foot again.

The magic door slammed shut. She wriggled her shoulders, she had to be careful. If she started fantasising about magic doors, she'd be away with the fairies.

'Auriga's the charioteer,' said the man. 'Look at him driving his chariot across the sky. Where's he going, do you think?'

Ah, that voice. Leading you far, far away, to the unfathomable depths of the universe… If you weren't careful.

She edged a step or so farther from the man. Please, no more, or else she was off to the other side of the field. Where was he from, though – Scotland? Ireland? If she weren't so tone deaf that all she could recognise were nursery rhymes, she might be better at placing accents.

'That's not a man in a chariot,' said a familiar treble voice. So Syd had caught Jim, and about time.

'What do you think it looks like?' said the man.

'It's a boy on a scooter.'

'Yeah!' said the child with the wayward feet.

'Tom, where are you?' called a woman's voice, a voice not hard to place, the voice of Tommy Ross. 'I've got your gloves, you left them in the car.'

'Ah, she's made it,' said Syd.

So she had. And now they'd have to stay.

'Over here,' called Auriga's spokesman.

This one? *This* was Tommy's brother?

'Oh, are you the brother who's staying?' said Syd. 'Hello, I'm Sydney Carton and this is my sister, Dora Spenlow.'

'Syd's brain goes a bit Dickensian after he's been catching

up with his marking,' she said. 'Actually, his name's Clayton. So is mine.'

'Dickensian, moi?' said Syd. 'Our parents, surely.'

You bet, Syd, but let's keep that to ourselves, shall we?

'Catching up with marking?' said Tommy, coming up to them. 'God, tell me about it.'

Dora gave her social smile a rest – it was pretty damn useless in the dark anyway – while Tommy and Syd bantered away about how many hours was it to go before half term was over, and God-don't-mention-it, and was there a bear with a sore head suddenly loose in this field, and if so had it paid its annual subscription to the club.

Tommy's brother wasn't saying anything, but he did seem to glance in her direction a couple of times. *Had* she come out with something about Capella just now? Hm.

'Well, Thomas and Thomasina,' said Syd. 'How, er, neat.'

'Our parents took the literal approach to naming twins,' said Tom Ross.

As a brother of Tommy, he must be Scottish. He'd kept his accent, she hadn't. A political statement? Well, that was his business.

'And ours took the literary approach,' said Syd. 'Hey, guess the odds against finding two pairs of twins in the same Oxfordshire field on a Saturday night in the middle of February.'

'Syd teaches maths and science,' she said, in the vague direction of Tom Ross. If only she could say she was tired, and go. If she'd come here in her own car, she could have. Christ, was this the moment to beat herself up yet again about not having the balls to drive any more?

'And football,' said Syd. 'At least I did until my knees started giving out – Jim, will you *stop* that!'

'My nephew's got a thing about drilling,' she said. 'Take your eyes off him for a second and before you know it he's drilled himself to Australia.'

'Tasmania,' said Jim. 'I want a biscuit.'

'"I want a biscuit…"?' said Tommy.

'I want a biscuit *puh-leeze*,' said Jim with a sigh.

'In a minute,' said Syd.

'I want one *now*. I'm starving.'

'All right, all right,' muttered Syd. 'I'll take him into the hut. It is a far, far better thing…'

'Can't Dozza take me? She'll let me have two.'

'Give her a rest, Jim, she's had a whole day of you.'

'I'm so punch-drunk, another ten minutes hardly counts,' she said, putting in a mock-sigh for good effect. 'Come on, Jim.'

'I've just realised I should have worn thicker socks,' said Tom. 'Do you mind if I come too?'

Ah. Not a question with a wide choice of acceptable answers. 'Be my guest,' she said, beginning to walk. 'You won't find the hut much warmer than out here, though,' she went on, as he fell in beside her. 'Schoolboy footballers and windows…well, you can fill in the rest, I gather you used to teach until recently.'

For a moment or so he didn't reply. Then he said, 'Yes, I can fill in the rest. Until Christmas I was teaching English and Drama at a West London comprehensive. I hadn't expected to be walking across a school playing field again quite so soon.'

Oh? By the sound of it, he was one of the ones who couldn't wait to get out of teaching. 'The club meets here courtesy of the Head, who happens to be a founder member. Syd's the secretary. He keeps nagging me to take over, and I keep saying he must be joking. The hut we meet in is the changing room – stay upwind of any old trainers you might see in there.'

'Come on, Dozz,' said Jim, tugging at her sleeve.

OK, OK, Jim. Sometimes conversation has to be made, as you'll discover long before you're my age.

'So, Tom, are you staying at Tommy's for long?' she said.

'Syd holds the club record for the Pleiades count, I gather,' said Tom, in the same moment.

She laughed. He laughed.

'Tommy wants to improve her score,' he went on. 'She's got eight. She'll go home happy tonight if she collects one more.'

'What's your score?'

He laughed again. 'I'm not really a collector, I'm afraid.'

Jim left them without a backward glance as soon as they went into the hut, and shot off in the direction of the refreshments table. 'Coffee or soup to thaw out your feet?' she said, turning to Tom. 'Oh – hello. I mean, hello properly, now that I can see you.'

The Angel Gabriel. Well, Syd, calculate the odds against that.

'Hello,' he said, then his smile wavered and reformed into a stare.

'Yes, I'm the one with the nephew who wasn't filleted this morning, thanks to you.'

'Hey, it's you!' cried Jim, galloping towards them with a chocolate biscuit in each hand. 'Can we have a race again next Saturday?'

'Jim, don't forget I can't take you skating next weekend, I'm in Wales,' said Dora.

'Oh…nyagh! The Saturday after, then?'

'I'll be there, Jim. Will around eleven be OK?' said Tom.

'*Yess!*' said Jim, beginning to caper around them.

'Eat your biscuits, Jim,' said Dora. 'Now, where were we. Oh yes – coffee or soup?'

This man's face. That dark gold hair curling around it, the serious eyes – brown, were they, or green? It was unbelievable. The jeans and parka didn't detract one bit from the angel look. If anything, they emphasized it.

'Soup, please,' he said.

He was still staring at her, why? Ah. The fact that she was

staring at him might have something to do with it. She turned aside, ladled out two mugs-full, and handed one to him. 'It's tomato, by the look of it. By the smell of it, it's tomato plus a fair dash of additives.'

'It'll do. Thanks.' He took a sip.

'Cheers.' She took a sip, making it last. This Gabriel didn't seem exactly full of celestial joy. Maybe he wasn't enjoying the annunciation business. Maybe he'd had one too many assignments recently where the woman had had to outlive the child.

'You were on the bus this morning,' he said.

'So I was. And so were you,' she said, staring at him again despite herself.

'Do you take the children skating every weekend?' he said.

'Pretty well, Syd has access most weekends. After skating I give them lunch at one of the pizza places, it's Aunt Dozza's Saturday treat. Then later on we come here – Jim does, anyway. Jenny's at a friend's watching DVDs tonight, she's already interested in a different kind of star.'

'You don't skate yourself?'

'No, I don't skate. I like to stay upright. Don't tell me it's easy once you know how, I've tried it.'

'So you watch.'

'That's right. I'm good at watching.'

And not all that good at standing upright, even though she didn't skate. 'Upright' was how he was standing. Not army-sergeant-stiff, just upright. Not many people could stand like that. It made him look like the tallest man here, and he couldn't be more than five feet ten.

He was a good skater, even she could see that this morning. Smooth, flowing, perfectly balanced style, without being in any way show-off. With a body like that, people would take him for a dancer. Which might explain why he could stand so well. She shifted some of her weight from her right foot to her

24

left, but it was almost as hopeless trying to stand properly as to stop thinking about something once you'd started.

A round red object with a tuft of green hair flew between them, hit the wall, and gave an hysterical laugh. Then a blue one with red hair followed it, and groaned as if it had heard that laugh once too often.

'D'you like my Gigglers?' said Jim,

'I gave him those for Christmas,' said Dora. 'Sorry.'

Tom knelt down and picked them up. 'I wish somebody would give me something like these for Christmas,' he said, and handed them back to Jim.

How would she describe the look in those brownish-greenish eyes? Hunted, wistful? Just plain sad? It was a safe bet that he hadn't had many presents he liked this Christmas. The Angel Gabriel wasn't happy, he wasn't happy at all. He was doing a spell of duty in purgatory, if not hell itself. She should know.

'What were you talking to Miss Ross about, Dad?' said Jim as he struggled into the pyjamas with the glow-in-the-dark skeleton on the front, the rest of Dora's Christmas present to him.

'Your behaviour,' said Syd. 'She was telling me that if she has you in her class a week longer she'll jump out of the window.'

'But – but Declan Potter's much worse than me! And Lee Bishop's *appalling.*'

'He's joking, Jim,' said Dora, giving Syd a look. 'They'll have been talking about teaching, it's what teachers talk about. They keep coming back to it, they can't keep off it. Like ex-convicts can't keep from going back to prison.'

'Can I have a taste of that?' said Jenny, eyeing the remains of Dora's left-over Christmas scotch.

'You had a taste last weekend,' said Dora. 'Ask me again in ten years.'

'Ten *years?*'

'Go to bed, kids,' said Syd, swigging his own scotch. 'Jen, ten years'll go just like that. You'll wake up tomorrow and it'll be ten years' time. Trust me.'

What a business family bed-time always was in this house. Well, who was she to criticize, considering the time she took over night-time rituals. *Night night, sleep tight.*

Ten years. Sleep-walk through it, or keep your eyes wide open and experience every day, every hour, every second: which would she choose?

When, finally, the room was quiet, Syd leaned back in his chair and massaged the back of his neck. 'So,' he said.

'Not a "So," Syd. I'd rather have an "Ah" than a "So" any day.' She took a sip of her drink.

'Let me know how it goes with Steve tomorrow lunchtime.'

'I might.'

He gave her a wry look. Then he took a sip of scotch and flexed his shoulders. 'What did you think of Tommy's brother?'

She didn't want to say, 'He's miserable.' And she didn't know why she didn't want to. 'Oh, he's OK.'

'Did you get any idea of how long he's staying?'

'I didn't, I'm afraid.'

'Really?'

'Yes, I know, if I were still head-hunting I'd have got the name of his favourite breakfast cereal out of him just now, not to mention all his childhood pets. Not the smallest nook or cranny of any human being went un-interviewed. But as a matter of fact, he spent a lot of the time talking to Jim. So, he's good with kids, that's one thing I found out. Right, I'm off home. There's no need to run me back this time, I'm not so decrepit I can't walk around the corner.'

'Sure? I've trained the kids not to burn the house down if I'm out for five minutes. And not to tell tales to their mum about negligent dads.'

'Sure,' she said, draining the last of her scotch and heaving herself to her suddenly decrepit-feeling feet.

Dora rubbed the small of her back. Backache already, at her age? Well, forty-three was only a blink of an eye away from middle age. Soon she'd be middle-aged, then she'd be old, then she'd be dead.

That twinge was right where the epidural needle went in. Which called for some sort of profound thought. Or a rapid change of subject. 'Jo, guess who I met tonight.'

No answer.

Well, guessing games weren't really Jo's thing.

She propped up the panda at the foot of the cot. He was always falling over. Jo must be having a kick at him as soon as her back was turned.

That panda. Steve's first present to Jo. To make up for being called away to the Edinburgh office the day before she was born. Too bad, that, but it could have happened to any dad.

Miles away when Jo came into this world, miles away when she left it. Some dads get a rotten deal. The number of times he'd told her to blame him, if she must blame anybody.

The panda toppled slowly sideways again as she watched. He was the only terrestrial creature in this room. Rare things, pandas. Not many left now. Maybe only this one.

Christ, if she didn't go to bed right now she'd fall asleep on the space rocket rug. And if she did that once she'd do it again, and again, and then what would become of her? She hugged the tin, hugged it for a second or so longer than usual. She kissed the 'J' and the 'O', and put the tin back in the cot.

Only one more thing to do. Last but not least.

She pushed the button, and the sun and the moon and the stars and the planets started on their merry way as the music tinkled into the room.

Twinkle twinkle little star
How I wonder what you are
Up above the world so high
Like a diamond in the sky.

But I don't wonder, do I. I know. You're Capella, the nanny-goat star, also known as Amaltheia. You suckled baby Zeus when he was hidden on Mount Ida to stop his stupid jealous git of a father, Cronus, from eating him. When he grew up and became King of the Gods, grateful Zeus put you in the sky to shine down forever on people like me.

A wet-nurse. Why did you have spare milk, Capella, had one of your kids died? Did you have to watch it being carried off by an eagle, bleating? Did it help, having Zeus to nurse? Or did nothing help, ever again?

Three

Tom looked up at the grinning cow with the pendulum hanging from its udder that served Tommy for a kitchen clock. Twenty to eleven. Twenty minutes until his long Sunday morning chat with Mel. 'I wish you'd told me all that about Dora Clayton before I met her last night,' he said, taking a mouthful of coffee. 'What if I'd inadvertently said something that upset her?'

'I didn't want you to look as if you were thinking about it,' said Tommy. 'She dwells on it enough as it is.'

Hm. Didn't this sister of his know him well enough by now to realise that he was capable of keeping thoughts to himself?

Going to pick up your baby one morning and finding it dead in its cot: he just couldn't imagine it. The mind slid off that kind of thing, it wouldn't grip. At close quarters last night, Dora Clayton had looked older than he'd thought. Her face had a drawn look, and there were lines around her eyes. Still, was it any wonder?

'I like Dora but I wouldn't say I really *know* her,' Tommy went on, taking a swig of her coffee. 'You know those people who're full of chat but sort of hard to get at? Well, she's one of them.'

Hard to get at… So what would she have said if he'd asked her whether Capella was important to her? He'd been close to saying something of the kind in that hut last night. But if you have to ask, does it count?

'I'm hoping she'll open up a bit when we're in Wales next weekend,' said Tommy. 'It might be good for her, because Syd thinks this situation with Steve has gone on long enough.'

'When did he move out, exactly?'

'I think it was about two years ago, but I didn't know her or Syd then.'

'So you haven't met him.'

'Yes I have, quite a few times, actually. He's renting a flat in Summertown, nice place, but small… He and Dora see a lot of each other. It's one of those relationships where they can't live together and they can't live apart, you know what I mean? He's a great guy, Steve, he's put up with a lot, her blaming herself every hour of every day, but…'

'… there's only so much a guy can take,' Tom finished for her.

'Yes.' She took another mouthful of coffee, but she was frowning. 'Well, sort of yes. Syd's never been quite sure if Steve left or Dora threw him out.'

'Bit of both, maybe. And is it now a question of where they go from here?'

'Yes, pretty well,' she said, glancing at the clock. 'Talking of going, I've got to go or I'll be late meeting the Wild Bunch.' She upended her mug, swallowed the last of her coffee, and swung herself off her barstool.

Cows for clocks and barstools for chairs and supervising a Down's Syndrome children's swimming club on Sunday mornings: was it Tommy's whackiness or her good-heartedness which always made him feel washed up on the shores of cynical middle-age? She wasn't middle-aged, and it would be a long time before she was.

30

He drank the last of his coffee and looked again at the clock. Just past ten to eleven. Not time yet. He could make himself useful and clear away the breakfast things. There was still some coffee left in the pot, though. He refilled his mug and propped himself on his barstool again. It struck him that he and Dora Clayton might have something in common besides looking at stars: neither of them had much idea of where they were going from here. Although he, at least, didn't have bitten nails.

Hell, it wasn't as if he hadn't known what the law said about inappropriate relationships between teachers and pupils. If you find yourself looking with new eyes at a girl you've been teaching for years, you carry on looking if you must but only a fool would touch, especially if she hasn't had her eighteenth birthday yet.

The Sexual Offences Act 2003. How many tarts, perverts, dirty old men and women, lechers and rapists had it sucked out of schools by now? And how many fools? He must have been crazy to think Mel's parents wouldn't find out – they must both have been crazy. That cover story about her being at her best friend's was going to fall down, sooner or later. All it took was what had in fact happened: her father on his way to work noticing her coming out of a house that wasn't Debbie Priday's, not ten minutes after she'd phoned home to say that was where she was. Gary Baines was never going to swallow Mel's 'talking about books' line, and her not wanting to tell him where she really was because she knew he'd get the wrong idea. No: outraged father Baines had to get on to the Head straight away.

Ross, I've had some extraordinary allegations about you from a parent. I think we'd better have a word. Tomorrow morning at ten, please.

Tom took another sip of coffee. He'd been drinking coffee when he had that phone call from the Head. One of these days he might consider cutting down.

He had to hand it to Mel, getting to see David Dent the next morning ahead of him, insisting that they'd only been talking about books, insisting so hard that at ten o'clock he was told by the Head what had happened, not asked. *You've been having one-to-one teaching sessions in your house with a student, I gather.*

He'd had his mouth open ready to come clean. But that look in Dent's eye: he was as good as telling him to keep quiet.

Dent didn't believe Mel. But he was clever. If what he, Tom, had been up to was 'only' favouritism and a lamentable lapse of judgement, the Head could tell him to resign, rather have to sack him and turn him over to the police for breaking the law, as Mel's father was demanding. No hard evidence… *I'm sorry, Mr Baines.*

Yes, Dent was clever, a lighting-quick thinker. *Have a Damascus Road conversion, Ross. Decide you're going to write full-time, or some such thing. Take a trip away, get a fresh perspective.*

For how many others would Dent have done that? But Dent had his limits, and could Tom blame him? *If you go for another teaching job, I can't give you a reference. I'm sorry.* They both knew what that meant: don't go for another teaching job, ever. Without a reference from your previous Head, it'd be wasted effort.

Tom took another sip of coffee. Last term, with Mel, he'd found out what it meant to lose all track of time. But time rather speeded up after that session with the Head, didn't it. The damnedest thing about the whole business, really, was the amount of 'talking about books' that he and Mel had managed to fit in, from Shakespeare right down to the first books they'd read and would never get rid of. He'd never had such conversations with anybody.

Lying with a girl in your arms and reciting *The Owl Who was Afraid of the Dark* to her… Was it any wonder time was meaningless? The future, if he'd thought about it at all, was just going to be more of this. Until death us do part? A sane man would have considered that prospect; all sorts of questions would have entered his head, not least whether he was the type who could commit. But a sane man wouldn't have been there in the first place, not with a seventeen-year old schoolgirl.

He sighed, swirling the remains of his coffee around in the mug. There was one thing about the future, the immediate future, that was clear. He'd have to make some money again, and soon. It was no good carrying on like this, he'd have to register with a temping agency on Monday.

When the clock told him it was exactly eleven, he squared his shoulders, took a long breath, and picked up his mobile phone. As he dialled a number which was programmed into his brain as well as into the electronics he was holding, it occurred to him that he could ask Mel to come here next weekend, what with Tommy being away.

Mel's phone rang, and rang, and rang. Come on, she must know it was him.

As if Mel's stomach wasn't already feeling dodgy enough, the bleeping sound coming from her bag made it five times wobblier. Oh God, was she going to be sick? It'd be him, it must be. He was right on the dot, like he always was. Shit, let it ring.

No, no, that was stupid, she had to answer it, she had to get this over. She took a deep breath to steady her stomach. *Please don't let me be sick, not here.* She reached into her bag and took out her phone. 'Hi,' she said.

'Hi, Melly. Where are you? I can hear some sort of noise.' It was him. Normally her stomach would be lurching just at the sound of his voice, but now…

No. She *couldn't* be sick.

'I'm in Costa Coffee.'

'Oh, right. I thought I heard a shop door opening. Is it getting awkward to talk to me from home, then?'

'No, I – I fancied getting out for a bit, that's all.' Awkward? Well, it just might get awkward if Mum or Dad did happen to hear what she was going to tell him.

Say it. Say it now.

'So, what are you having? Double latte and a Danish?'

'No. Peppermint tea.'

'That's not the Mel I know.'

You bet. 'Isn't it? You know I don't like getting into a rut.'

He laughed, and asked her how the poetry essay had gone. The last thing she wanted to talk about was the bloody poetry essay, but she found herself telling him about her A, and how Mrs Thorpe gave everybody an A as usual because she was scared shitless of the A-level class and kept coming out with stuff like how hard Lowell was and how they shouldn't really be doing him at this stage, and what good was crap like that from a teacher when they were going to have questions on twentieth-century American writers in four months' time, like it or not?

She was wittering. She had to stop this, she had to tell him.

'It's as well we had that chat about Lowell last week, then,' he said. 'I know Liz Thorpe's a bit out of her depth, she should be sticking to *The Illustrated Mum* with Year Seven, but she's only standing in until they get a replacement for me, you know that. Just take the As and keep your head down. OK, so it's Restoration Drama next week, isn't it. What are you going to say about it?'

Oh God. 'I haven't thought. Tell me what to say.' *No, tell him! Now!*

He didn't answer right away. 'Are you all right, Mel?' he said eventually.

Nooo, she wasn't! Christ, did she sound like she was going to cry? She felt like it. But she couldn't cry, any more than she could be sick.

'I'm fine. Been working on a German essay, that's all. Can't seem to switch off.'

'All right, I'll give you a few points to go on.'

'Hang on, let me get a notebook out.'

How she managed to write stuff down about Wycherley and that lot as he was talking, she'd never know. But it was the only way she'd ever get a Restoration Drama essay done, the way she felt. As she scribbled, the sounds of Costa Coffee washed around her: mugs being put down on tables, bursts of laughter, a background buzz of people relaxing on a Sunday morning. Now she knew how an alien who'd landed on Planet Normal by mistake would feel.

'That should give you something to go on,' he said at last. 'E-mail me a draft – Mel? Are you still there?'

'Yeah. I'm still here.' It was all she could do to get the words out. *Tell him, tell him!*

'So, how's it been at school this week? Any more news from UCAS?'

Oh God, she didn't want to talk about school, she didn't even want to talk about UCAS. But she found herself wittering again, telling him Bristol must have turned her down because shouldn't she have heard from them by now?

'Don't worry, Mel, they'll be taking their time sifting through the Oxbridge rejects. Things'll be fine, you'll see.'

'Yeah, well,' she made herself say. Fine? Oh if he only knew… But he wouldn't unless she told him!

'Mel, come here next weekend. My sister's going to be away, we'll have the house to ourselves.'

Aah. *Tell him!* 'I, er, I can't. Gran's eightieth on the Sunday. Big party.'

'Oh. What about just the Saturday, then?'

'Um… I'll be helping to get the party ready. Look, I'll have

35

to go, there's some Year Eleven guys coming in. Bye.' She switched her phone off before he could say anything else, and sat there looking at it. Her hand was shaking. She'd chickened out. She hadn't told him. Why, why, why hadn't she had the guts to tell him? Oh *Christ*.

She shoved her phone back in her bag, pushed her peppermint tea aside, and rushed out. No Year Eleven guys stopped her and said Hi, because there weren't any.

Her phone rang again before she'd gone ten yards. God, if it was him again, she'd tell him, she really would.

It was Debbie, her best friend since before they were potty-trained. 'Did you tell him?'

'No,' she whispered.

'Oh, Mel!'

'I know. Don't go on at me, I just can't face it right now.'

'Are you coming back to my place?'

'No, better go home.'

'Look, stay chilled, OK?'

'I'll try. See you in school tomorrow.'

'See you, Babe. We're going to talk, though, about when you're going to the doctor's.'

All the rest of the way home, Mel had a plastic tube in front of her eyes, a plastic tube from Boots that she'd used at Debbie's earlier that morning. A tube whose contents had given her a message she didn't want to hear.

One pill she'd missed, one fucking pill. Only it would have to be the day before he left!

She's facing him across his kitchen table, the way she faced him three months ago when it all started, but it's all so different now. 'What are you going to do, though?' she says. 'For a living, I mean?'

'I don't know, to be honest.' He smiles. 'I'll find something. My typing speed's good, there's always temping.'

36

'Oh, Tom!'

'I'll be all right, Mel, don't worry.'

'Oh God, tell me you don't want to go on seeing me, go on, get it over.' She has to say it.

'Melly, don't talk nonsense. We'd better lie low for a bit, but we'll see each other again soon, don't you fret. In the meantime, nobody can stop us phoning one another, can they?'

'What, to talk about books? Like we've been doing?' She tries to smile, but it doesn't feel like it's coming out right.

'Just like we've been doing. When your father's calmed down enough not to shoot me on sight, I can think about coming back here.'

'Yeah… Hey, though, I could come to Oxford on the bus. It doesn't take much more than half an hour from the Hillingdon stop. My parents don't have to know.'

'I've been wondering about that myself… Let's leave it a couple of months, though. Best to be on the safe side.'

'A couple of *months?* God, it's going to be a fucking awful Christmas. I'm going to really celebrate the New Year, though. First I'm going to kill the Head, and then I'm going to kill my dad. Fuck the law, I'm old enough to decide what I want to do and who I want to do it with. I'm bloody eighteen on the sixth of January!'

She hasn't told her mother she's come here to see him, but Mum must have guessed. Any moment now, her mobile might start ringing.

'I don't want you to go,' she says, struggling not to let tears into her voice, but it's hard, it's bloody hard.

'I don't want to go,' he says, coming round the table to her.

He takes her in his arms, the way he's done at the end of their 'tutorials' over this last term. God, those sessions, both of them knowing what's coming, but somehow the discussions having an extra something because they're holding off for now… He tilts her face towards him and kisses her, and in

37

spite of herself her body relaxes into his. This was only going to be a quick goodbye, but to hell with quick goodbyes…

'Melly,' he whispers. Hand in hand, they go out of the kitchen and up the stairs.

The whole of last term, she'd been walking on air. Even though she'd had to keep pinching herself in case she was dreaming it all, she'd been happier than any girl could possibly be. Seeing him in the corridor, eyes meeting, sharing their secret… Now look at her.

The tears she'd held back in the coffee shop began to fall. They felt as if they'd never stop.

'Yes, there's goat's cheese in it,' said Dora.

'And garlic and thyme,' said Steve, 'if my taste buds are telling me right. It's fantastic. And to think we used to live on microwave chicken curries.'

'M&S ready meals, surely.' Chicken curries? They were fit only for flies.

Those flies that morning. Finding herself sprawled on the sofa, then turning over and seeing those two flies gorging themselves on the remains of the plate of cold curry. And sitting up too quickly, and having her head shriek in unison with her Caesarian scar. Hangovers were like that sometimes. It took moving to make you realise you'd got one.

Her stomach heaved. She put her fork down and pressed the back of her hand against her mouth. Steve looked up, his eyebrows raised.

'A hiccup coming on. I think I've stopped it,' she said.

'Do you want a thump on the back, Pet?'

'No thanks. A thump from you, and my back would be my front.'

A quick flicker of a smile from him, lasting no longer than her quip deserved.

'So that grouting's holding up, is it?' he said, forking up some more farfalle.

'It's fine. You can hardly see the tile was ever cracked.' As she'd told him three times since he arrived, or had it been four.

'Grand. I'll have a go at the washer on the cold tap in the kitchen later on.'

'There's the light on the landing, too.'

'That bulb's not gone again? It was a long-life one.'

'Well, it's not working. Maybe—' It's jinxed. Like me. *No, don't say it.*

This was bad. It wasn't as if talking with him since they'd been living this semi-detached life had ever been straightforward, but this conversation wasn't so much being made as constructed, brick by brick. And they hadn't yet mentioned The Subject.

'Maybe what?'

'Oh, nothing.'

She moved a few farfalle around her plate. He prodded his, then put his fork down and took a sip of wine. A large sip, more like the mouthful someone at a party takes when they're looking over your shoulder to find someone to move on to. But there was nobody here but her.

He reached for the chianti bottle. As he refilled his glass and hers, she speared three farfalle and lifted them to her mouth. He'd been two years now in that poky flat, with no sex from her. What man in his right mind would put up with that? He must have had women, surely. Just the occasional one to help him remember he was still a man?

Steve, I can't, I just can't. I'm locked up.

No point in actually saying the words, she must be imprinting them on the air in front of his eyes. Anyway, he knew them by heart.

'So, how's that new sidekick of yours slotting in?' she said.

He shrugged. 'Fine. Should be a great asset to the team.'

'You haven't told me his name. Details, details, I need details, man.' Yes, she had a thing about details. The day he stepped into her office was no exception. A couple of hours' hard interviewing, and he was singing out his details like a bird. And asking her for hers in the pub that evening.

That barmaid who tried to flirt with Steve. That lipstick of hers. A vicious dark gothic purple slash across her face.

'You and your details,' he said, taking a mouthful of wine. Was he thinking about that day too? He might be, by the way he was staring at his glass. 'OK, for a start, it's her, not him. Her name's Yvonne. Yvonne Bradley.'

'Yvonne. Nice. Is she blonde? Brunette? Tall? Short? Pretty? Cross-eyed—'

'She looks a lot like you, Pet.' He gave her a smile, but it was the kind of smile which fades so quickly that you wonder whether it was a smile at all.

She helped herself to some salad. The leaves fell out of the servers onto the table before she could get them onto her plate. 'Bugger,' she said, scooping up the leaves. She blotted the vinaigrette smears with her napkin.

Steve put his fork down, leaving two farfalle impaled on it. 'Dora, I'm not going to ask you if you love me. I know the score on that by now.'

'Dora.' He never called her Dora. Only Pet. 'For the millionth time, you don't know the score. I don't know the score. Remember that marriage vow we wrote?'

'"We"? You wrote that vow as I recall, I just held the pen. Yeah, I remember it. Something about love being too heavy to mention, and there was to be certainly no saying the three little words – I'll recite the exact line if you like. But.'

'But what?'

'Do you know what day it is?'

'It's our tenth wedding anniversary. I thought of getting you a present involving tin but all I could come up with was tintacks and you've already got a lifetime's supply.'

He was blinking. She'd surprised him. For once, she'd actually remembered what day it was. And she had some sentimental detail about its significance lodged in her brain, God knew why.

'Well, I didn't get you any tin but I did get you this,' he said, reaching into a trouser pocket. He put a box on the table. A small box. So small that it could contain only one thing.

The ring was stuck all over with diamonds and sapphires. Gaudy, Christmas-crackerish, looking far less expensive than it undoubtedly was. He'd never got the hang of her pared-down taste. But to give her this, after everything.

'Very pretty,' she said, resting the ring in the palm of her hand.

'It's an eternity ring.' He was looking at her. Looking at her hand. Waiting for her to put it on. 'Look. All right. You killed Jo,' he said urgently, leaning across the table. 'I don't know how you weren't locked up, the police must have been asleep.'

She drew a deep breath, turning the ring over in her fingers.

'Maybe you're right,' he went on, 'it wouldn't be a good idea to have another.'

She looked at him.

'Look, please, please let's get back to being the Clayton-Mitchell double act, guaranteed to make parties go with a swing. I should never have pressured you into having a kid in the first place, I admit that now.'

This ring. So easy just to slip it on. Never mind whether it was the style she would have chosen. Or whether he knew what he was saying.

'All I ask, all I ask, is one thing.' He leaned closer. 'Let me please redecorate that room.'

Ah yes. The room, the room. It always came back to the room.

Her shoulders began to shake. She shoved a fist against her mouth to try to stop up the laughter but it bubbled up anyway, like champagne around a loosened cork.

He looked at her until she'd finished. He didn't move.

'Sorry,' she managed to say at last.

He passed a hand over his eyes. 'Pet, why don't you give that shrink another chance?'

'And have another year and half of talking about my father? Can't these people talk about anything but fathers?' She put the ring down on the table. The light from the window caught one of the diamonds, and it flashed and twinkled. *Twinkle twinkle.*

'I'm just going out for a quick walk,' Tom called to Tommy.

'You sure? It's going to rain,' she called back from the sitting room, where she was wading through her Sunday-night marking.

'You know what I think about rain,' he said, putting on his jacket.

'Yeah, yeah, if we don't go out when it rains in this country we never go out.'

It wasn't that, or not only that, but he wasn't going to have a debate about it now. As he stepped outside, he drew a deep breath of the night air into him. There was nobody about, which was fine by him. This was walking the way he liked it. He flipped the collar of his jacket up, put his hands in his pockets, and moved off.

Night walking. Even through suburban streets like these, he couldn't do without it. In no other circumstances did his thoughts flow more easily, and in no other circumstances could he forget his thoughts. This walk, he knew, was going to be about thinking, not refraining from thinking, and what he'd be thinking about was Mel.

He looked up. Was Capella visible? No, the cloud cover was

too thick. Maybe Tommy was right, and it was going to rain. A fine mist of rain, caressing his face, blurring the light cast by the street lamps into hazy pools: he could cope with that.

That phone conversation this morning. So she couldn't come next weekend. If it had been anybody but Mel, he'd be wondering about Gran's party, not to mention those Year Eleven guys. He'd heard too many stories from teenagers. It was rare that an equivocal tone of voice got past him. Her tone of voice, though: it had been like that throughout the conversation. It was no use pretending to himself she'd sounded normal. Oh hell, couldn't it just have been that she was missing him particularly badly but trying to seem cheerful, trying not to make him feel down as well?

But she as good as cut him off at the end of the conversation. No mention of alternative dates to come to Oxford, or phoning again later: nothing. If it were anybody but Mel, he'd have to conclude that she didn't want to talk to him.

He walked on, the thought lodged indigestibly in his brain like lead. A solitary man passed with a small dog on a lead. In daylight Tom might have said hello, but he'd walked enough at night to know that others wanted to be left alone with their thoughts at this time, as much as he did.

This was what had finally turned all his relationships sour when it came down to it: walking at night. Needing no-one with him. Needing, in fact, not to have anyone with him. Cold, distant, self-centred: he'd had it all said to him, and more.

He'd never been able to make them understand. But he'd had to keep walking, even at the risk of coming back and finding an empty house or flat and a note propped against a coffee mug in the middle of the kitchen table.

No, he'd never been able to make them understand why he did it. Maybe because he himself didn't quite understand. But those are always the important things, the ones you don't fully understand. Like his obsession with Capella, of all the thousands of stars on offer in the sky, his need of her as a guiding beacon, a name to be invoked when no other name would do. The shrinks would say the walking went back to boyhood, as Capella did. Maybe they'd be right.

Could he make Mel understand? It hadn't been an issue with her as yet, probably because she was always back in her own house by the time he went out walking.

At the next junction of streets, he realised he'd reached the road where Tommy had said Dora Clayton lived. Just along there was the house she now occupied alone, but for noticeably frequent visits from her husband. He turned into the road; he might as well go this way as any other. What was the number? If Tommy'd said, it didn't seem to have stuck in his mind.

Most of the houses had several lights blazing, but there was one, about half way along, where only one room had a light on, an upstair room just above the front door. Perhaps that was her house? Still, he was hardly going to ring the doorbell and invite himself in.

He paused for a moment outside the house. It looked the same as the others in the road: a solid sort of place, suggesting neither undue wealth nor the reverse. There was something about it, though. It was a sad house.

He wriggled his shoulders. He didn't know if it was her house, and even if it were, would he be thinking it was sad if he hadn't been told what happened there? He took a final look up at the one lighted window and walked on.

As he neared the end of the road, he saw another walker coming his way. The light of a street lamp revealed the face of a young woman talking into a mobile. She was loud, shattering the silence. 'Look, just tell him,' he heard, from several yards away. 'Say you're seeing Des, get it over for fuck's sake.'

Tom was half way along the next street before a thought started taking shape. It was a thought so obvious that it was a wonder it hadn't hit him as soon as he switched off his mobile after the morning's conversation with Mel. She'd sounded so odd, as if she didn't want to talk. Maybe… God, maybe it was over, and she didn't know how to tell him. Maybe she'd been seeing that biologist with the Cambridge offer who'd been asking her out and didn't seem to have the word 'No' in his vocabulary. What was his name? Something Mills… Dan – no, Dean Mills. Yes, Dean Mills.

Ah. He stopped in his tracks, closed his eyes and blew out a long, slow breath. Well, would it be so surprising? Without him there, was she seeing how crazy the whole thing was? She was young, she had a life to get on with… Bloody hell. The more he thought about it, the more evident it was. He leaned against the nearest garden wall. He felt winded, as if he'd just stopped a punch in the solar plexus. Was it even possible that he'd only ever been a fling as far as she was concerned? Maybe she'd had a bet on with her friends about whether she could score a teacher… No, for God's sake, surely there'd been more than that?

He gave a long, weary sigh before he shoved himself upright and walked on. Maybe he ought to sell his Uxbridge house and move to a remote glen in the north of Scotland. He could spend the rest of his life going for night-time walks in a place where there was no other soul, and especially no women. Yes, walking was all he was fit for – and looking at Capella, provided there was no cloud.

He looked up. The clouds were as thick as ever. As he began to make his way back to Tommy's, the rain started.

Four

'Friday tomorrow, thank God,' sighed Dora's office-mate, Susie Cooper. 'Anything on this weekend, Dora?'

The voice yanked Dora away from Steve's email, sitting on the screen in front of her. 'I'm going to Llantwit Major with my friend Tommy,' she said. 'That's Tommy as in Thomasina, before you start.' Office banter. It was getting harder by the day, but if she let the mask slip here in the University Offices she'd be done for.

'Start what?' said Susie, grinning. 'Hey, Wales at this time of year – I'm impressed. I've been hang-gliding round Llantwit, but only in June. Where're you staying?'

'Oh, just a little bed-and-breakfast that Tommy knows.' Not a bad game this, seeing just how close to the truth you could come while saying no more than they'd expect. This Satori Centre, it was near Llantwit, it did have beds, it did serve breakfast, by all accounts. While she was speaking, her eyes drifted back to Steve's email:

'OK, keep the room, do what you like, but for God's sake let me come back.'

The room. He was as good as saying black was now white, up was now down.

Before she went home this evening she had to send him a reply. One which would be worth his while opening, even if he had that deputy of his, Yvonne whatsername who looked a lot like herself, in the room discussing the latest performance figures.

'We camped near a place called Llys-something,' said Susie, musingly. 'Or was it Tre-something... Oh, hey, that bloke's coming this way.'

'What bloke?'

'That new maintenance man, Larry Wise. You know, the one who hums. He's coming, listen.'

Dora listened, and there it was, a faint humming, growing louder: 'Nh, nh, nh-h-h-h-nh.' Susie was right, bugger it. It was Larry Wise, the one they were supposed to be nice to because he couldn't help the way he was, and they were getting plenty of practice seeing as he was up here every five minutes, or so it seemed. Was he bringing back that library book she'd let him borrow the other day just to get rid of him? Finding him in here when she came back from the ladies', leafing through it without a by-your-leave... She closed Steve's e-mail, hunched low over her keyboard, and gazed at the text she was supposed to be amending. Busy body language: was it too much to hope that Wise would get the message this time?

'Nh, nh—' A shuffle of heavy feet, coming to a halt in the doorway. 'Good afternoon, Miss Cooper. Good afternoon, Miss Clayton.' That voice. If ever voices resembled their owners, this one did: heavy and lumpish, like clods of earth falling into a bucket.

'Hi, Larry,' said Susie.

'Hello, Larry,' said Dora, moving her nose an inch nearer the screen. From the corner of her eye she could see her library book on Welsh landscape under his arm.

'Miss Clayton.' Footsteps, coming towards her. Plod plod plod.

'Yes?' she said, turning her head as little as she could.

'I am returning the book which you loaned me. It was very enjoyable.'

'Good. Fine.' She stretched out her hand for *Overground and Underground in South Wales*.

'Do allow me,' he said. He put the book down on her desk, on top of the stuff she was typing. 'Cave exploration is not to be attempted except under experienced leadership,' he went on, smiling, if what he was doing could be called smiling, as opposed to exercising his cheek muscles. That incredible laser-gaze of his, boring right between her eyebrows – if he were anybody else, she'd say a massive spot had popped up since she last looked in a mirror. She had to say something, and quick, before his stare vaporised her brain.

'I'm not planning to go caving when I'm in Wales this weekend,' she managed. 'My interest in Wales is strictly open air.' She could feel Susie hanging on every word. It was the way her typing speed had slowed right down that gave it away.

'I shall be working in this office tomorrow, Miss Clayton. I shall be attending to the leaking window,' said Larry Wise.

Christ, those eyes. Like a ventriloquist's dummy's. Too blue, too bright. Bright blue shiny glass marbles, under a haircut that looked like a fright wig that had been caught in a heavy shower.

'Oh, right, good,' she said, trying not to grit her teeth too obviously.

'Great,' added Susie. 'Last Friday, everything near that window got soaked.'

'Friday, Friday…' said Wise. 'F-Friday is a – an excellent day. The child born on a Friday is loving and giving. I was born on a Friday.'

'Oh, were you?' said Susie. 'I was born on a Monday.'

Whereas Wednesday's child was full of woe. The more so at having this individual breathing down her neck.

Her phone rang, and she snatched it up. Please let it be the Vice Chancellor's PA asking her to come around and collect the VC's comments on the draft Corporate Plan.

'It'll be nice to get that window fixed, Larry,' Susie was saying. 'It's like a fridge in here sometimes with the draught.'

'Siobhan Bailey's office,' said Dora, but beyond establishing that the woman at the end of the line was PA to Dora's boss's opposite number at Lancaster University, she didn't make much progress. It wasn't that Larry Wise's half-mutter, half-chant was particularly loud, rather that it seemed to be setting her ears vibrating as if she'd been plugged into the mains.

'Nice to get it fixed.' He was actually saying, 'Nice to get it fixed, nice to get it fixed,' as if it were some mantra.

An auburn head appeared around the door. 'If that's Lancaster, tell them I can't make it until Tuesday afternoon—Oh. Hello.'

If Wise had anything about him resembling his name, he'd push off sharpish. Siobhan wasn't as nice as she herself was. Dora Clayton, unquenchable ray-of-sunshine, at the service of all and sundry... Siobhan didn't actually mean 'Hello', she meant 'Not you again?'

'Hello,' he said. 'How do you do.' But he was, at last, moving away toward the door. 'It will be very nice to get it fixed, Miss Cooper, Miss Clayton,' he pronounced as he went out.

'I'm sorry, could you just say that again, please?' said Dora to the woman from Lancaster.

As she put the phone down, Susie gave a massive smirk and said, 'I think he likes you.'

'It was only a library book, Suze,' said Dora, going back to her screen.

'Susie's right,' said Siobhan, propping herself against Dora's desk. 'Otherwise there must be something they're not telling us about this end of the corridor, such as it's going to fall down. I mean, the amount of maintenance work we seem to be needing these days… Christ, where does he get his hair cut?'

'I bet his mother does it,' said Susie, 'round a pudding basin.'

Siobhan snorted.

'He does live with her, though,' said Susie. 'He must be fifty, at least. Poor guy, fancy going through life being like that… Hey, though, did you know there's a rumour going round he's got a PhD?'

Dora started typing again. If they wanted to chat about Larry Wise, that was up to them.

'Eh? If that weirdo's got a doctorate I'm the Regius Professor of Time Travel,' said Siobhan.

'Well, when you listen to the way he talks,' said Susie.

Siobhan snorted again, louder. 'I'm sure Dora's very impressed.'

'I always did like a well-spoken gent,' said Dora, typing steadily.

'No accounting for tastes,' said Siobhan. 'He gives me the creeps, with those immaculately pressed overalls. He ought to be scruffy, for God's sake.'

That was Larry Wise's trouble, in a nutshell. He gave people like Siobhan the creeps. People like Dora Clayton, on the other hand, at least felt vaguely guilty about wanting to see the back of him. Or they might, if they didn't have one or two other things to think about.

'Oh, come on,' said Susie, laughing, 'He's just a harmless old saddo. The maintenance guys treat him as a bit of a pet.'

'Why don't they just get a cat,' said Siobhan. 'Now, why did I come in here? My God, this memory, I'll have to start taking something… Oh, I know – Dora, when you've got a mo, could you pop in? I've had a go at revamping that discussion paper for the VC's half yearly review.'

On which note Siobhan propelled herself back into her own office, and peace descended again. Or if not peace, that

50

commodity rarer than diamonds, at least quietness, punctuated by the sounds of two sets of fingers tapping on two keyboards. But the e-mail from Steve in the guts of Dora's computer was doing its best to shatter the silence.

'Answer me,' it shouted, 'answer me.'

Dora leaned her head against the bus window, then sat up again as the bus jolted her ear against the glass. Outside, a siren was wailing. The noise built up to a shrieking crescendo, then fell off in pitch as the Doppler effect stretched the sound waves away down the Woodstock Road. People around her were wincing, but if they thought that had been loud, they should have tried listening to Steve's email yelling as she shut down her computer for the night.

As the bus drew to a stop near a college annexe, a crowd of young people hauled themselves to their feet. They filed along the aisle, their coloured backpacks inching past Dora's nose: grey ones, brown ones, green ones, a cherry red, an orange, a turquoise – and one which appeared to have leaping kangaroos all over it.

The students were slower than ever getting off tonight. Everyone seemed to be having to make doubly sure that everyone else was clear about where they were meeting up later. A tiny dark-haired girl seemed to have a tall blond boy in tow. If she, Dora, had had Jo when the medical pundits said she should, Jo could have been that girl.

Stupid bloody experts. Didn't they know that women of twenty-five would sooner pole-vault through a mine field than shackle themselves to a pile of nappies? Some twenty-five year old women, anyway. Like the one she'd been.

Impossible. It would always have been impossible. No point thinking about it.

But people did do impossible things, though. People climbed mountains and went deep-sea diving without oxygen.

She was still fertile, how many times had Steve reminded her of that? Yes, she could still reproduce, just. What if she said 'Come back, and we'll have another.' Never mind emailing, what if she phoned him tonight and said it?

As the bus moved off again, a woman sat down in front of her. A little head popped up over the woman's shoulder. Brown eyes began to study Dora, eyes bright with the clear, unselfconscious gaze of childhood. These eyes were nine or maybe ten months old at the most. *At three months she holds her head up. At six months she sits up unaided. At ten months she looks over her mother's shoulder on buses and coos at people with a bright, winsome, toothy smile.* But this one was a he, not a she: he had that 'let-me-through-I-can-fix-it' look already. Now he was gurgling and laughing, and putting his head on one side. He wanted to play Peep-Bo. Aah.

She turned her head. She looked out of the window, looked for all she were worth, as if North Oxford's academic villas had metamorphosed into a row of Taj Mahals. But when her stop came, it was inevitable. His eyes locked onto hers as she stood up.

Huh. Useless mother you'd have made.

Judging from the sounds downstairs, Tommy was back from school. Tom closed down his laptop. It was time, thank God, to stop pretending to himself that he was working on a manual for teachers of GCSE Drama and go down and ask Tommy about her day.

Downstairs, he found Tommy in the kitchen leaning against the table. She was staring at the kettle, which was coming to the boil. The hunched shoulders and folded arms said 'bad day.'

'Looks like somebody was a pest today,' he began. 'Was that boy you were telling me about the other day winding the others up again?'

'No, Jacko Leyton was as good as gold,' she said, sighing. 'It's the Head that's the trouble. She heard this morning that Ofsted are descending on the school on Tuesday, and she wants all heads of year groups in for a council of war over Sunday lunchtime.'

'Sunday? Why Sunday, for God's sake?'

'It's the only time she can talk to us all together. She's got a Heads' Away Day on Monday.'

'Couldn't she skip the Away Day?'

'She's had to miss the last two.' She sighed again. 'She's going to bring sandwiches in for the lot of us. Which is something, I suppose.'

The kettle boiled. Tommy dropped a tea bag into a mug and sloshed boiling water in after it. She waved the kettle at him, eyebrows raised.

'No thanks, I'm awash with the stuff, been drinking it all afternoon. So this truncates your weekend in Wales a bit, doesn't it.'

'It puts the lid on it totally. I'll have to get stuff ready for the meeting, and that could take most of Saturday.'

'Ah. What a bugger.'

'You could say that. Especially as I phoned the Satori Centre and they say you can't cancel at this short notice, so I'm wasting a hefty booking fee. And I'm letting Dora Clayton down. I had to twist her arm to come as it is.' She took a gulp of tea, frowning. Then, as she looked at him, her frown began to clear. 'I've just had a brilliant idea. Why don't you go instead, Tom?'

'Me?' he said, beginning to laugh. 'Me, go to a Buddhist retreat centre? For a whole weekend? You're the whacky one, not me.'

'Oh, Tom! Look, the Centre's in a lovely spot – wild coastal scenery, just your sort of thing. It'd take you out of yourself.'

'Do me a favour,' he said, still laughing. 'Anyway, Dora

53

Clayton thinks she's going with you. Won't she be a bit peeved if I turn up instead?'

'She might be a lot more peeved if she's stuck in a place where she doesn't know a single soul. Go on, Tom, give it a go.'

Tommy wouldn't give up. She never did. 'Ask me again in an hour,' he temporised. 'Go and do your marking while I start the supper.'

'OK,' she said, taking her tea and heading for the door. But there was a glint in her eye.

Tom began getting the ingredients assembled for their regular sling-it-in-the-oven Thursday night chicken stew. As he began to chop onions and carrots, it did occur to him to ask himself what in hell else he'd be doing this weekend, apart from wondering if he ought to phone Mel at their usual time or wait for her to phone him, and contemplating this temping job at the University Offices that he was starting on Monday.

Not a single text or email from Mel this week. Not even a reply to that email he'd sent on Tuesday hoping the Restoration Drama essay was going OK. She couldn't be thinking that silence was a good way to tell him he was dumped? Not Mel, surely?

Well. Maybe he ought to have a weekend in Wales. Maybe it would 'take him out of himself' as Tommy put it. It would be one way of discovering if he'd slipped so far down inside himself as to be beyond recall.

He put down the vegetable knife and went to the kitchen door. 'Hey, Tommy,' he called. 'You win. I'll go.'

'Well, bye. Have fun on Sunday,' said Dora, not being able to come up with anything punchier to say to Tommy. She put the phone down. So, an unforeseen development. Tom Ross was going to Wales instead of Tommy. She didn't like unforeseen developments, not these days. She liked to see things coming.

Did people ever see things coming, though? Or was that as

impossible as mountain-climbing and deep-sea diving without oxygen, and pole-vaulting through mine-fields. And deciding what to say to your husband. She wasn't getting very far with that. Only one thing to do: talk to Jo about it.

She tried not to blink as she went into the room, but Jo was gone as soon as she appeared. It was always the same. Did all dead babies do that, hide themselves just beyond the limit of visibility? Why not, Peep-Bo was a good game.

She rubbed the small of her back. That stabbing sensation, it *was* right there, wasn't it? Right on that spot where the epidural went in?

She propped up the panda and ran a finger along a furry tentacle of the green and grinning Thing From Outer Space hanging at the foot of the cot, and then told herself to stop putting off what she'd come in here for. The tin's stars seemed to twinkle at her particularly brightly as she lifted it out of the cot.

'Right, Jo, I need advice. You won't believe this, but your dad's trying to fool himself he wants to come back on our terms. That's not all you won't believe, though. I've actually been wondering if I can have a little sister or brother for you after all. Yes, I know we've been over and over it a thousand times, but… The thing is, Jo, I've got to say something to your dad. So, what's it going to be?' She stood, the tin at arm's length, gazing at it.

Nothing.

Well, what did she expect. This was crazy. This was not fair.

Over the door, the man-from-Mars clock ticked away. His ticking grew louder and louder and louder.

'Come on, Jo. Stop being a sulky little sod who won't talk to Mummy.'

Still nothing.

Oh God, this backache! She subsided onto the space rocket rug, holding the tin to her chest. The pile of jumpsuits was peeping out at her from behind the half-open cupboard door. All except the orange one. She should have asked the nurses for it back, never mind what state it was in. Interesting, how much she minded about that orange suit.

To bring another child in here. To lay it down in that cot, in Jo's space.

Her head was blank where the image should be trying itself out for size.

Blank. Drawing a blank. If you had to sketch a blank, what would it look like? It wouldn't have a face like the man-from-Mars clock. It wouldn't have faces like the sun and the moon and the stars and the planets, hanging there waiting to be put through their night-time paces.

Oh hell, why did Steve have to back down, why did he have to give her everything she wanted? Why didn't he threaten to leave and go off with another woman, like a normal man would? This Yvonne of his, wouldn't she do? As it was, the ball was entirely in her court. It wasn't fair!

The panda toppled slowly sideways. That panda, the look on Steve's face when he brought that in to the hospital. He'd have made a good dad. Still would. Given the chance.

Five

'Nh, nh, nh-h-h-h-nh,' hummed Larry Wise. He was ferreting through his tools by the sound of it, but Dora wasn't going to turn around and check.

She took a deep breath in, and let it out slowly. Yet again, there was only one thing to do with the line of type on the screen. She pressed 'delete'.

There wasn't a middle way. Maybe six months ago, three months, one month, there might have been, but not now. She couldn't say to Steve, 'Come back and we'll play it by ear.'

She took another deep breath, then found her stomach making sharp contact with her keyboard.

'Nh, nh, nh-h-h-h-nh.'

Wise had knocked into her chair. He didn't seem to have noticed, but why didn't he do it again? Why didn't he keep on doing it, and maybe by the time he'd finished here today he'd have knocked it out of her, made her miscarry this idea which seemed to have taken root in her overnight, this little embryo of an idea.

'The range of colours is vast, Miss Clayton.'

'Oh. Is it?' What was he on about?

57

'Some limestones are almost white, but one can find yellows, browns, reds…'

Ah. So he had geology on the brain this morning, he must have learned that library book of hers by heart. 'All the colours of the rainbow, then,' she said. How could she get on a train to Wales this evening in this state? Especially as it wasn't Tommy she was going with but Tommy's brother.

'Colours of the rainbow… No, I fear not, Miss Clayton. There are no limestones of such vibrant colours. There are many crystals of striking colour: purple chalcedony, blue-green labradorite felspar… But no rainbow colours in crystals either, alas. No, no rainbow colours.'

'Oh. What a pity.'

'There are some interesting limestone formations, however. The oolite and pisolite stones are granular, as their names suggest, and when lias limestone is layered with shale, a striped effect results, as at Lyme Regis, Whitby and of course Glamorgan… Nh, nh, nh-h-h-h-*nh.*'

He was drifting toward the leaky window again, and about time. Right: the position paper for Council had to be copied before lunch; it was going to be done now.

As she made for the door, she heard: 'Miss Clayton, I neglected to mention that carboniferous limestone is to be found in a number of areas, including Wales, Derbyshire, the Pennines, and the Scottish Lowlands.'

'A lot of it about, then,' she called back over her shoulder.

He said something else as she went out – she half-caught '…but our local Corallian…' – but this time she didn't reply. By the time she got back, please let Susie be back from helping the temp in the VC's office unjam the fax. How long could it possibly take to see to a window?

Photocopying. Watching blank sheets of paper go in one end and come out the other with print on them, *zip zip zip.* It was the one thing that could make her mind go blank. But maybe there were limits to what you could let drift out of centre field into a hypnotized limbo. Little embryos, for instance, ones which seemed to be sprouting extra cells in time with the photocopier. *Pop pop pop.*

A baby for Steve. In the arms of a woman who looked a lot like her. But who wasn't her. It was neat. It was brilliant.

On the way back from the photocopying room, rounding a corner, she walked into a rock – a rock in the shape of an immaculately pressed blue overall. Down onto the floor like a waterfall went fifty pages of photocopied position paper plus annexes, and fifty pages of top copy. '*Oh*—' She bit back the rest. Not right outside the VC's office. She'd lower the tone, and that would never do.

'Oh,' said Larry Wise. 'M-miss Clayton. Dear me.'

'Sorry,' she made herself say. What in hell had he been doing, standing right in the middle of the corridor?

'Th-that's quite all right, Miss Clayton.' He was smiling at that spot between her eyebrows again. His cheeks were flushed bright red. She took two steps back. This was too much proximity.

'Any problem?' she said.

'Problem…?'

'You were standing there. I wondered if there might be a problem.'

'No, there is no problem. I did not lose my train of thought, thank you.'

Oh, Christ. Right: pick up the papers, Clayton.

The Vice Chancellor's office door opened a foot or so. The VC's head emerged around it, like a tortoise's. 'Dora? Something wrong?'

'No, er, Bryan – just a small accident.'

The VC's head disappeared and the door closed again. 'Keep the noise down, a Man Like Me has to Work,' it seemed to declare. Dora took a long breath and knelt down.

'Do allow me to help,' said Wise, getting down beside her.

'It's all right, I can manage.'

'Not at all.' He began collecting sheets, placing them on top on one another so neatly that they could have come straight from the pack. 'There was no need to apologise for the accident, Miss Clayton. We all make mistakes.'

She took another long breath and let it out slowly. Then she made herself smile.

Back in the office, Susie was giving the spider plant and the African violet their Friday watering. Dora dumped the pile of paper on her desk and began to sort through it. 'Larry's finished, then?' she said.

'Finished? No way. He took a phone call just now, something about a loose light fixing on the other side of the building. He's coming back when he's sorted it.'

As he kept doing for the rest of the day. The Head of Maintenance must have been short of staff, such were the calls on Larry Wise's time and tool box from all four corners of the building, but he kept coming back to 'attend' to the window, that stubborn pane of glass which could not, would not, seem to fit its frame. Each time, that 'Nh, nh, nh-h-h-h-nh' came into the room about five seconds ahead of him. Each time, another of Dora's nerves frayed and snapped, and her fingers forgot which key was where. And each time, her embryo of an idea squirmed and kicked inside her, and the email to Steve, which now said 'Come on Sunday evening and we'll talk,' remained unsent.

By four o'clock, the Humanities funding summary, which Siobhan wanted typed up before Dora left for Wales, was nowhere near finished. The window was, but judging from the noises behind her, the tools were having to be particularly carefully placed in their box. When, when, would he go?

'Miss Clayton.'

Oh, what *now*. 'Yes?'

'Those pens must be annoying you.'

What? 'They're fine,' she said, continuing to type.

'But they are out of order. Rainbow order would look tidier.'

Christ, Christ! 'All right, sort them if you like.'

Wise leaned right over her to pick up her packet of felt-tipped marker pens, so that she had to duck to avoid hitting her head against his chest. 'Mother and I shall be entertaining a guest this evening,' he said. 'It's Mother's eighty-sixth birthday. The guest is Aunt Anna.'

'I hope you have a lovely time,' she said, typing faster.

'Thank you, Miss Clayton. However, I – I don't like Aunt Anna.'

'Oh, not very nice, is she?'

'She is not at all nice, Miss Clayton.'

'Bad luck. Don't let me distract you from those pens.'

'Oh, the pens…' He shook the marker pens onto the desk. The red one fell on her mouse mat. She brushed it aside.

Just type, Clayton. Just type.

'The red goes in first,' he said, picking it up, 'then the orange, then the yellow. Now, you have two shades of green… I shall cook lamb chops this evening, Miss Clayton. I hope Mother will enjoy them. And I hope she will enjoy her birthday cake.'

'I hope so too. Wish her many happy returns from me.' How long until the train to Bridgend left? Forty-nine minutes, according to the clock on the computer screen. At this rate she didn't have a hope of making it.

'I will, Miss Clayton, thank you, thank you!'

'Don't mention it.' Hang on, wasn't that what she wanted – not to make the train?

'Oh, but I must mention it, I must.'

'How are those pens coming?' Bugger Wales. Seeing Steve tonight had to be the priority. If she had to live with that idea inside her until Sunday –

'The pens? Ah yes, the pens… The lighter green next to the yellow, I think, and then the darker… How quickly you type, Miss Clayton.'

'Thank you. Do you think you could shift a bit? I need to get to the phone.'

'The phone… Oh, indeed. Yes.' He stepped back one pace. She managed to pick up the phone without brushing against his arm, but the nerves in her hand were screaming.

Steve's PA answered: a new one, not the one she'd spoken to in the past. 'Is Steve Mitchell there, please? This is his – this is Dora Clayton.'

'He's out of the office and I'm not expecting him back this afternoon. Can I take a message?'

'Oh. Well… Is Yvonne Bradley there, by any chance?' *No! Crazy, crazy.*

'Dr Bradley's at the same meeting, I'm afraid.'

Doctor Bradley. *Doctor* Bradley. 'OK. Thanks. There's no message, goodbye.' Between one breath and the next, her embryo had a massive growth spurt. After the meeting, Steve and Yvonne Bradley would go to the pub… There'd be a barmaid there, one with purple lipstick…

How long until that train? Forty-four minutes. OK. OK. Type, damn it.

She typed. She typed with fingers like daggers, stabbing at the keys, and in minutes she had the final row of boxes on the sixth page filled.

Right. Print out.

The printer began to whirr. Then it gave a cough, and stopped. She tried again. Silence. Then the 'paper jam' message came up on the screen. But there couldn't be any paper jammed, Susie had used the printer at lunchtime and it was fine! This was all she needed, *all* she needed.

OK. This man who taken up residence in her office fixed things, he could fix the printer. 'Look, can you get this printer going?'

'Oh, is it not working, Miss Clayton?'

No, it's tap dancing around the room. 'It's not working. Can you fix it?'

'Computer equipment is outside my domain. I would advise calling an engineer on Monday.'

'I can't wait till Monday, I want it working now. Look, I won't tell anyone.'

'Well…'

'Do it. Please.'

'I will do my best, Miss Clayton.' Oh God, he was looking at her as if she'd suddenly grown long golden plaits and was stuck in a tower surrounded by a thicket of thorns. She yanked her facial muscles into a smile, the umpteenth of the day.

The printer's problem turned out to be a trivial case of addled memory. After switching off and then restarting, the machine spewed out several pages of neat spreadsheet. She sorted this kind of thing out most days. But most days, she wasn't busy gestating ideas.

'All's well that ends well, Miss Clayton.'

'So it is. Thanks,' she said, grabbing the spreadsheets.

'I find reminder cards very useful. Shall I make you a card to attach to the printer?'

'A card?' Thirty minutes left now. Fifteen to finish here, and fifteen to get to the station. If she sprinted she *might* just make it. 'Yes, all right, do me one in all the colours of the rainbow. Could I get out, please? Siobhan's desperate for this stuff.'

The funding summary was pronounced to be 'almost there' but the footnotes were 'a bit thin, on second thoughts.' As Siobhan scribbled on the draft, Dora watched the minute hand on the wall clock tick around, and around. Superimposed on the clock face was one that looked a lot like Dora's, but wasn't. That face's owner wasn't in a rush. She didn't have a train to catch. She was happy to be right where she was.

Back in Dora's room, Larry Wise was sitting in her chair.

He had actually parked his great all-in-wrestler bulk in her chair, for God's sake! He didn't look up. If he was aware that she was back, he wasn't giving any sign of it whatsoever.

'Larry, could I have my chair back, please?'

'Oh? Oh…' He leapt to his feet, almost overbalancing the chair. 'I – I was admiring your coffee mugs, Miss Clayton. They are very psychedelic. That was a term used for a lively design when I was younger. You are far too young to have heard of it.'

'No I'm not, I have heard of it,' she said, lowering herself into the chair.

'Oh? Oh… Miss Clayton, your pens are now in the correct order. Red, orange, yellow, green, blue, indigo, violet are the colours of the rainbow. "Richard of York Gave Battle In Vain" is a useful mnemonic.'

'I know, actually. I've got a degree in physics.'

'Oh, how splendid. My degrees are in classics. I follow my parents.'

'Do you? Great.' She had to get rid of him, whatever it took. 'Look, I'd love to go on chatting but I've got to get this stuff finished before I leave, OK? And I've got to leave in' – she looked at her watch – 'exactly seven minutes.'

'You'd love to chat? I – I'm – '

'Have a good weekend,' she said, her fingers attacking the keys. 'Why don't you drop in on Monday? We can carry on with this conversation then.'

'Oh… Oh dear, I – I have commitments elsewhere in the building… but I will drop in for a few moments early on Monday. I *will.*'

'Great, fine, look forward to it.'

'Oh, I shall!' He picked up his toolbox and, thank God, went out. 'Nh, nh, nh-h-h-h-nh,' drifted away down the corridor, growing fainter and fainter.

Before Dora left, she deleted the email to Steve and typed

yet another. It wasn't a long message, but the ten seconds she took to send it meant that she arrived at the station to see the train going out. She watched the last carriage disappear down the line toward Didcot before going back inside the station foyer to find out when the next train left. For she'd have to go to Wales now, after what she'd said to Steve.

Not a long message, indeed. But long enough: 'No, Steve, I'm sorry. Why don't you stop wasting time on me and concentrate on Yvonne.'

'Happy birthday, Mother,' said Laurence. He kissed her forehead and handed her the Blackwell's bag. Such a relief to come home and be Laurence, not Larry. 'And I have been asked by – by someone at work to wish you many happy returns.'

'Ah, your superior, Mr Stewart? How agreeable of him.'

'No, no – Miss Clayton. Miss Dora Clayton. She has a very important job, her office is on the top floor of the building.' To speak Miss Clayton's name in this house, how strange that felt.

'Does she? Well, how agreeable of Miss Clayton, then.' Mother looked up at him for a moment, but said nothing more before returning her attention to the Blackwell's bag. She pulled out the parcel he had wrapped and decorated with coloured twists and twirls of ribbon from W H Smith before coming home. Such fun to wrap presents! Mother picked at the paper, then said, 'So sorry, dear, I'm all fingers and thumbs this evening. Could you, please?'

Laurence took the parcel from her, fetched a pair of scissors from the bureau and removed the paper. Always, always essential to cut paper, not tear it, so that it might be re-used. He smoothed the wrapping paper and folded it to add to his store. Then he handed the gift to Mother.

'Ah,' she said. 'The new commentary. Thank you so much, Laurence.'

Laurence smiled. It was never difficult to choose gifts for Mother. He had only to read her Times Literary Supplement and note the titles she had ringed. The new commentary on Tacitus was the obvious choice.

Laurence... He was two people: Laurence here, with Mother, and Larry everywhere else, with the world. Larry, the name other boys had called him at school: did people like him more for allowing them to use it? It was so hard to tell. Miss Clayton, though, she would have loved to continue chatting with him, *loved* to. Miss Clayton therefore must like him, what joy! But now, he must stop thinking of Miss Clayton and attend to Mother. 'Shall I pour your sherry now, Mother?'

'Thank you, dear, but I think we should wait for Anna.'

'Oh. Yes, of course.' His birthday card to Mother was slightly askew on the mantelpiece. He adjusted it a fraction. *Eighty Six Today, Hip Hip Hooray*, in a border of balloons in all the colours of the rainbow. It was such fun making cards. And now Miss Clayton wanted him to make one for her – in all the colours of the rainbow! Ah, it was so difficult to stop thinking of Miss Clayton. This strange feeling, a feeling he had not known for so long, that someone – a lady – might want to be his friend... But no, he must not think of time past, he must think of time present. Was Aunt Anna's card askew too? Possibly, but he was not going to give himself the trouble of adjusting that one. 'I shall see how the supper is progressing, Mother.'

In the kitchen, Prinz Eugen was asleep in his basket under the table. On Monday, if there were time after he and Miss Clayton had finished discussing their degree subjects, he could ask her if she had a cat. Cats were a valid topic of conversation. He must devote some time during the weekend to thinking of further topics, for other times next week when he might visit her office. He could tell her about his model collections, for example, or where he went for walks. 'Nh, nh, nh-h-h-h, nh,' he hummed as he inspected the lamb chops and the roast potatoes.

The doorbell rang. He began to count: one, two three… On ten, Mother would open the door. It always took Mother a count of ten to walk from her chair to the front door.

By the time he reached ten, there had been no sound from the hallway. He wiped his hands and returned to the sitting room. Mother had not moved from her chair. How very surprising.

'So sorry, Laurence, I seem to be a little tired this evening,' said Mother. 'Would you mind answering the door? It will be Anna, I'm sure.'

'Oh. Of course, Mother. Are you too tired to see Aunt Anna? Shall I tell her to go away?'

'No, no, let her come in, dear.'

Aunt Anna said, 'Ah, so you are at home, I was beginning to think I'd come on the wrong evening,' and pushed past him into the hall. She held out her arms and he helped her out of her coat. Without a word of thanks, she went into the sitting room.

How could she think this might be the wrong evening? It was Mother's birthday, of course it was the right evening.

'You may pour the sherry now, Laurence,' came the voice of Mother. It was puzzling that she was tired. She had never been tired on her birthday.

He did not stay in the room after pouring the sherry, he went to the kitchen again. It was preferable to spending a minute longer with Aunt Anna than was necessary. 'The boy's odd. Venetia won't hear of it, but he is.' The words he'd overheard her speak to some relative now long-dead when he was fifteen, would he ever be able to forget them? He had researched oddity thoroughly, so wanting her to be wrong. She must be wrong! He had usually understood what people said to him, and by fifteen he had trained himself to look at them when they were speaking, and to smile. He could empathise, predict behaviour – there was Prinz Eugen, stretching as he stepped out of his basket, and he knew well that the cat would go to his food bowl and look up expectantly. He was not aggressive, he had never played with his own excrement as a child, nor banged his head, nor experimented with fire, not in any way that was dangerous or untoward. No one, surely, could regard those funeral pyres for dead birds and mice brought in by a succession of cats as playing with fire.

Was he odd? If not to be liked was to be odd, then perhaps he was. How he had tried to be liked! Aunt Anna was not the only one to have spoken wounding words, there was every master he had ever encountered at school: 'Exceptionally able, but I do wish he would make more of an effort to contribute in lessons.' And all he was doing was giving other boys the chance to speak, refraining from answering each and every question so that they would like him more.

But Miss Clayton liked him. Miss Clayton would have loved to continue chatting. Perhaps Miss Clayton would be his friend? Perhaps he could give her a delightful surprise by calling at her house during the weekend! It was so serendipitous that a postcard addressed to her had been tucked inside the book she'd loaned him, so that he now knew where she lived. But, on second thoughts, it might be wiser to wait for an invitation. He must not say or do the wrong thing. He must be so, so careful.

Six

The substantial grinning woman in the sweater with sheep all over it led Dora down a flagstoned hallway panelled in dark wood. Where in hell had the taxi from Bridgend brought her? Could this be the Satori Centre, long and short courses on all aspects of Buddhism, complete novices especially welcome? It looked more like a cod-historical film set.

'There's only one house rule, really,' said the woman, whose name seemed to be Anthea, 'and that's no yakking on mobiles. Texting's just about OK but we don't encourage it. You won't believe the number of mobiles I've had to confiscate on weekends like this.' She laughed, which had the effect of sending the flock of sheep grazing across her front into a frenzied frolic. Off they scampered, over the hills and far away. A giggle escaped Dora, which she turned into a cough. Where did that come from? She hadn't laughed for days.

Anthea took her into a massive kitchen packed with people, but Dora registered little more than a vague background buzz of noise as a plate of food she didn't want was shoved into her right hand and a glass of wine she desperately wanted was shoved into her left.

69

She took a large glug of wine and looked around at the sea of faces. Two days of this. Was there ever a more appalling, insane waste of time? She should be with Jo, she should be spending every spare minute in Jo's room while she still could. Steve couldn't afford to give her his half of the house, and she couldn't afford to buy it from him. So it didn't take much brain to see what the way forward was going to be. They'd have to sell and split the proceeds. Funny that she hadn't seen it until she was sitting on the train in the Severn Tunnel with her ears popping. Darkness rushing past her, darkness breaking down the carriage window and roaring in. Shouting *Jo will lose her room, you silly cow.*

Anthea parked her with a foursome, none of whose names she caught. She was smiling her way through the 'Hi, have you come far?' stage when there was a tap on her shoulder. She turned, to see a man standing next to her – a man with an astonishing resemblance to the Angel Gabriel.

'Oh – hi, er, Tom,' she said. 'Hi, Dora,' he said, in the same moment.

'I did say "hi" just now, but not loudly enough, evidently,' he went on.

'Yes, the noise in here…'

Tom Ross. She'd all but forgotten he'd be here, thanks to that train journey.

Hm. People who came at you like this, throwing you off balance: annoying. Especially when it wasn't their fault. Wasn't he like the Angel Gabriel, though. Wasn't he just. That hair… He didn't look any happier than he had last Saturday. Less so, if anything. In fact anybody would think the Angel Gabriel was the one to be nailed to a cross.

'Well, you got here,' he said.

'Yes, I got here, on the next train. I missed the train you were on by about half a second. I actually saw it going out.'

'I looked out for you. I must just have gone to sit down when you arrived.'

'It's always the way, isn't it. Well, I didn't realise we'd be quite so much in the back of beyond. There's a ten-mile slab of solid darkness outside with Bridgend at the other end of it and the taxi driver told me to mind I didn't fall over the cliffs.'

'Cliffs?' said one of the men she'd been introduced to. 'You won't have time to fall over any cliffs. They work you like billy-oh on this course.'

'This house is a bit spooky, isn't it,' said one of the women.

'Somebody said it's haunted,' said the other woman. 'There's a grey lady who *floats* along the landing on moonlit nights.' She made undulating movements with her free hand. The man she was with said 'Woo-oo,' and she did a mock-shriek, then giggled.

Dora caught Tom's eye as she took a mouthful of wine. Or did his eye catch hers? Catching another's eye: what universal laws governed the swing of the gazes until they interlocked – the sure and certain knowledge that you were both wishing you were miles away?

Oh bloody hell, first thing tomorrow morning she'd just go. She'd say she'd had a message from her parents' nursing home saying that her mother was still wandering off and could she get there asap. She'd spend the rest of the weekend where she ought to be, in Jo's room.

Jo's room....

There was a sound of hands clapping: Anthea. A laddish looking man in a Grateful Dead T-shirt made a wisecrack – something about surely she could do it with one hand by now – and there were titters.

'I work up to that,' said Anthea, laughing. 'You'll be *amazed* what's going to happen here by Sunday afternoon. OK, people, I want two volunteers to load the dishwasher when you've all quite finished noshing. If you do it this evening, you won't have to do it for the rest of the weekend.'

It happened again: a meeting of eyes. Only this time, Tom's

had a question in them. Dora nodded. 'Dora and I will do it,' called Tom.

The room began to empty. In the bustle, Dora managed to lose her all-but untouched plate of food.

When they were alone, Dora grabbed two used glasses that still had some wine in them, and gave one to Tom. 'Cheers,' she said. 'I don't know who's been drinking from these, but alcohol's an antiseptic.'

'Cheers,' he said.

'Here's to Tommy's Head, but for whom you'd have been getting on with your life this weekend.' She raised her glass and took a mouthful.

'Well, I suppose I'm getting on with it here.'

'That sounds like a Buddhist sort of remark. Not that I know anything about Buddhism.'

'Which is why you're here.'

'I'm here because your sister said how about a weekend in Wales and I said yes before she told me where we were coming. Actually, I do know one thing – don't Buddhists say something like if you've finished your supper, don't just stand there chatting, put the plate in the dishwasher?'

For a moment his face relaxed into a ghost of a smile, then the smile faded. 'Tell me about the University Offices,' he said, beginning to stack plates on a tray. 'You work there, I gather. I'm going to be temping there from Monday.'

Temping? The Angel Gabriel must be cash-strapped, maybe that was what was eating him. He must have really hated teaching to get out of it before he'd lined up something resembling a proper source of income. Still, he'd have to brighten up a bit if he was going to survive in Wellington Square, even as a temp. 'My neck of the woods is hardly typical, I'm afraid. I'm PA to the woman who runs a sort of think-tank for the Vice Chancellor,' she said, reaching for the nearest empty glasses.

'I'll be in the Admissions Office, or so the agency told me yesterday.'

'I don't think they're any crazier down there than anywhere else, but I've got a good tip for stress should you need it. Photocopying. Piles and piles of photocopying.'

'Do you find yourself doing a lot?'

'Mountains of it.' And there'd be more from now on. Much more, until Jo's room… Jo's room ceased – to – be. But what then? What then? 'Watch out for one of the maintenance men, though.'

'Why, is he a photocopying freak?' he said, putting down his tray of plates on the work surface next to the dishwasher.

'No, just a…'

'Freak?'

She wrinkled her nose. 'He's just a bit strange, that's all. He's one of those types who gets on your nerves even when you're trying to be nice. Whether there's some sort of technical name for how he is, I don't know, but I suppose he's what you might call an equal opportunities employee. He's the reason I missed the train.'

'Over-friendly?'

'A bit. Just don't loan him any books.'

'How will I recognise him?' He took a mouthful of wine.

'By his haircut. It's beyond description, but you'll know it's him when you see him. Oh, and by his unbelievable—'

The door swung open as if attacked by a gale force wind. 'Chop chop,' called Anthea, 'the opening session starts in ten minutes. Mustn't be late, must we.' The door swung shut again.

'That would never do,' said Tom quietly to the door. 'His unbelievable what?'

'What? Oh, his accent. Pure Thirties-radio-announcer – you know, the sort who used to e-nun-ci-ate into the mike in a dinner jacket.'

As she reached for a plate to stack in the dishwasher, his gaze seemed to slide to her left wrist. He couldn't be seeing it more clearly if she'd shoved it under his nose, that white line of scar slashed across the skin. Not the moment to forget that sleeves ride up when you stretch.

It's the definition of an intimate friend, Tom: someone other than Steve or Syd whom I allow to see my scar. You seem to have wandered into that category by accident, and I'm not sure you ought to stay. Look around, you'll find there's no-one there but you.

The first session was about 'watching the breath.' It was led by a shaven-headed man called Jason who hadn't been among the crowd in the kitchen earlier. In his sharp suit he could have been any of the senior executives Dora had head-hunted in the past. She'd have said she was looking at a marketing director worth around a hundred grand a year plus car and bonuses.

Could she go back to Duckworth and Dunn, even now? How long would it take her to make enough to buy Steve out? Oh God, it would take years and years and years. She might manage it if she deferred retirement until she was eighty.

She turned her head very slightly to her left. Tom was looking at the back of the seat in front, but too fixedly, in the way people do when they were looking at you until a moment ago. Trying to catch another glimpse of her wrist?

She turned her head very slightly to her right. The man in the Grateful Dead T-shirt next to her seemed to be eyeing the legs of the woman on his other side.

Bloody hell, how much longer?

A flicker of movement on her left. She turned her head back in Tom's direction, and caught him unfolding and re-folding his arms. The candlelight was glinting off the face of his watch.

Quite a number of glances had come their way when they slipped into these seats, the last to arrive. Did people think they'd sneaked off for a quick one after the washing up, for God's sake?

All right, Clayton, *do* something. Find something to count – count the candles, there must be hundreds in here. One, two, three –

There was a noise as of a pebble being rattled in a bucket. The man in front of Tom jerked his head upright and gave a loud snort.

'Well, people, what happened?' said Jason. A few raised their hands, like kids at school. They'd tried to visualize things like streams and clouds and mountains, or so they said. 'What about the lady at the back there?' Jason went on.

Always her. They always picked on her, sooner or later, what was it about her? 'I tried singing *Twinkle Twinkle Little Star* to myself but I was out of tune.'

Laughter rippled around the room. Out of the corner of her eye, she saw Tom look at her. When Jason moved on and put somebody else on the spot, she turned toward Tom. 'Sorry. That just came out,' she whispered.

'No need to apologise,' he murmured.

Jason announced that it was getting-to-know-you-time. Everybody had to say who they were and what they wanted to get out of this weekend. Grateful Dead turned out to be called Fred Benson. He was here 'basically to get out of London for a couple of days, mate.' Preoccupations? Just a few. Pension provision hardly enough to keep him out of the gutter, contract finishing in four months' time, marriage finishing next week if the lawyers could shift their asses for once. He stopped abruptly, his voice wobbling. When Ms Legs next to him said she had problems with men – there weren't any on her part of the planet – Fred Benson's eyes stood out on stalks.

Too soon, it was Dora's turn. 'Hi, I'm Dora Clayton, I'm

here for the sea air and to see what stars look like without any atmospheric sludge in the way,' she said, giving the group the line she'd been cobbling together while others were speaking.

Then it was Tom's turn: 'Tom Ross. I'm here for the sea air and the stars too.'

'Copy cat,' she murmured. 'Sorry. That just –'

' – came out?' He managed something closer to a smile than anything he'd produced yet.

'There's enough sea and stars to go round,' she said. 'Be my guest.'

When the session ended and the milling about and chatting were starting, Tom said, 'Do you feel like popping outside for a minute to check what the stars do actually look like down here?'

'Good idea, but I'm knackered, frankly. It's been a long day.'

'Sure, sure,' he said, and his smile flickered for a moment. 'Well… Sleep well. See you in the morning.'

'Right. Night night sleep tight yourself.' *Sorry, that just came out*.

A narrow single bed. And almost within touching distance, another narrow single bed.

'It's dark here with the lights out, isn't it,' said a voice from the other bed.

'Yes, they ought to simulate a diffused streetlight glare and traffic noises for town types like us,' said Dora, yawning loudly again. Most people would have taken the hint by now. It was just her luck to be stuck with Nanette Farmer as a roommate, the one with the legs who'd been sitting next to Fred Benson.

Put a sock in it, Nanette, please. Leave me in peace, I have a great pile of thinking to get on with.

'That Fred Benson, God,' Nanette went on, 'do you know what he said just now? "Fancy swapping with Tom Ross?" he said. "I bet he snores. I'd rather have you in my room than him." Bloody cheek. I shouldn't for one moment think Tom snores.'

Which was a question, not a statement. She was fishing, the nosy bitch.

'No, I shouldn't think he does.'

'So are Tom and his sister identical?' said Nanette.

Oh, God. 'About as much as I and my twin brother are. Which isn't much.'

Evidently Nanette knew as much about genetics as she, Dora, did about Buddhism. Or about handling impromptu suggestions from men.

The way Tom had reacted just now. She wouldn't mind betting that he thought she'd taken him to be proposing something rather more than looking at stars. That could make things a touch embarrassing tomorrow. Shit.

Well. She could hardly announce to him at breakfast that he couldn't be more wrong. That she'd only said no because she couldn't face communing with Capella. It hadn't occurred to her that he might be propositioning her, because these days nobody ever did. And if anybody did try their luck, she'd have a very clear answer for them.

Mel sat down at her computer. She typed: 'Hi, sorry I've not got back to you, been a bit busy. Talk to you on Sunday. Bye.' She read the words, frowning. Pathetic. What in hell would he think? But she had to say something, otherwise she'd be a basket case by tomorrow. She clicked on 'send', then sat there staring at the screen for several seconds, biting her lip. She gave a long, shuddering sigh, and rested her head in her hands. All right, she'd sent him a message. She'd at least let him know she'd got his emails and texts over the last week.

What was the time? Half past midnight. She yawned. She ought to get started on that Civil War essay, there was going to be sod-all time over the weekend, what with Gran's party.

Oh God though, she could hardly see straight, let alone think about the role of the bloody Scots. She switched off the computer and got into bed. She reached for Bono, her old squashy teddy, and hugged him tight, something she hadn't done for years. She couldn't have another week like this one, handing in crap work, and Debbie on at her all the time about when she was going to the doctor's.

On Sunday she'd tell him. She really, really would.

Seven

A grey world. Grey cliffs behind Tom, grey pebbles under his feet, grey rocks at the water's edge, grey sea breaking on them. A distant grey line of English coast half-hidden in a bank of thick grey cloud. Was ever a view more beautiful, unless it was the view from that path running west along the Firth from St Monans. *His* view. But if he were Welsh, this would be his view.

He zipped up his jacket and started walking along the beach, insofar as picking footholds on these pebbles could be called walking. Jesus, it was cold. The walk down through the sheltered cwm hadn't been too bad, in terms of keeping the circulation going, but this wide, exposed beach was another matter. The Bristol Channel in February was every bit as stern as the Firth of Forth, bringing you the kind of air which cut you like a knife. He'd be frozen solid if he didn't keep moving.

He looked at his watch. Eight thirty. He had ten minutes at most here if he were going to get back in time for the first session of the day.

He made his way down the beach to where the pebbles gave way to blackish sand, and then to the rock stratum which the surf was wearing away, molecule by molecule. He stopped only at the point when to go an inch further would have meant having that sea inside his trainers, and then he turned and walked along the shoreline taking breaths of the icy air, as deep as he could bear.

That was an awkward moment with Dora Clayton last night. How on earth could she have got the wrong idea? He'd only been picking up on what she'd said in that session, damn it. OK, so there had been one or two moments when they'd seemed to connect, and there was undeniably something about her, such as eyes the colour of this sea. In any other circumstances... But the circumstances weren't other, they were as they were.

There were going to be no more women. Not until he'd digested some lessons.

Out to the west, a thicker grey agglomeration of cloud told him where wet weather was hitting the English coast. Dora Clayton was still married, of course – to whatever extent... He hadn't been a marriage-breaker yet. Not unless it was a marriage that was hanging by a thread, as good as broken.

He folded his arms and hugged his jacket closer around him. That sea, how long could a shipwrecked man survive in that? Not long enough to swim to shore. Hardly long enough to see the freezing waters close over his head.

A bird flashed past about twenty feet overhead, wheeled, and swooped down to settle on the water for a second or so before thinking better of it and taking off again. Herring gull, was it? Must be, with those wing tips.

What would Mel be doing right now? Still in bed? Phoning Debbie Priday? He took a deep breath and gave his head a shake. Mel was in the past. He needed to work a bit harder at accepting that fact, evidently. Mel was with Dean Mills, doing what any normal girl would be doing at this time on a Saturday: making toast to take back to bed.

Oh bugger it. With thoughts like this getting in the way of the view, he might as well turn around and go back now.

At the top of the beach, by the stream which was throwing itself over a rocky ledge on the way to losing itself in the sea, he turned. One last look, just one last look, at those waves. It was sacrilege to leave a beach with your back to the sea.

Half way up the cwm, he stopped to push aside a bramble, which was hanging across the path at eye-level. The stream was particularly lively here, cascading down a series of steps in its rocky bed. Having negotiated the bramble, he stood for a few moments gazing into the water. If Dora Clayton liked photocopying, maybe she'd like running water too. He wasn't going to suggest coming down here to look at it, though.

He walked on slowly. Dora Clayton had slashed her wrist, and he'd bet that she'd done it in the last three years. Tommy hadn't warned him about that. Which could only mean Tommy didn't know.

Uncharted territory, here be dragons. Why was that in his head, suddenly?

Well. On one level, maybe it was because he'd never been involved with a woman who'd cut her wrist. If the woman were amazing, though, would he let himself be put off by that one fact?

He chewed his lip as he rounded a bend in the path. Up ahead, the wood was thinning. What was the time?

His watch said five to nine. He'd been down here longer than he realized. He was going to be late. All right, he'd be late, then.

Dora propelled herself into the meeting room. She was almost but not quite last, judging from the few empty spaces. Anthea had on a different sweater today. A spouting whale had ousted the sheep. Its waterspout started just where the woman's right nipple must be.

Amazing how far milk can spurt out of nipples. You press

on the breast and out – phitt! – it comes. Then you sit in the bath and watch it drip uselessly into the water.

She'd wanted to donate expressed milk, but they smiled and said no, it would take longer to dry up if she did. Ah well. They were only trying to help, poor sods.

She clamped her lips together, trying to stifle a yawn. But, denied outward expression, the yawn opened up instead in the grey gunge which was filling her head.

She must have slept at some point last night, she supposed, otherwise she'd never have had that dream.

A quick glance around the room revealed that Tom wasn't here. Had he done a bunk already, found some pressing reason to go back to Oxford so as not to have to spend time with women who got the wrong end of the stick? She eased her aching body into a vacant chair next to Fred Benson. He turned away from his other neighbour, Nanette Farmer – dragged himself away, more like – and grinned at Dora.

'Morning. You didn't go down to the beach with Young Lochinvar, then?' He winked at her, the swine.

Don't, Fred. I'm not in the mood. 'Sea air disagrees with me this early in the morning,' she said. So, Tom had gone for a paddle.

Oh God, that dream, that dream. Walking slap-bang into a man outside a room and dropping something. The room wasn't the Vice Chancellor's office, it was Jo's room. The man wasn't Larry Wise, but who he was, she couldn't tell. The something she dropped wasn't a pile of papers, but an object swaddled in an old-fashioned shawl. Such a snowy white shawl, unfurling endlessly as it slipped from her arms, and she couldn't see what happened to whatever fell out of it; it rolled somewhere out of sight. She had the feeling she ought to look for it, but not until afterwards, not until she and the man had finished having sex. Right there on the space rocket rug in Jo's room.

Who was the man, who? Why didn't she know? Why didn't she know whether she wanted to know? Was he going to help her look for the thing she'd dropped? Or was he going to stop her from looking?

Ten minutes into the first session, as Jason was telling them that they were now going to break up into groups to 'do a little experiment in surfing your thoughts, folks,' Tom slipped into the only unoccupied chair in the room. It happened to be the one next to her, on the other side of her from Fred Benson.

Perhaps it was the breath of sea-air he seemed to bring in with him. Perhaps it was the slight dishevelment of his hair, lying this way and that on his forehead and clinging in strands to his cheeks. Perhaps it was simply that he took her by surprise, coming in by a side door out of her field of view, but something in the region of her heart seemed to jump as if a badly insulated electric cable had touched it. She counted *one, two, three,* smiled, and said 'Hi.' He said 'Hi,' but if he said anything else, it was lost in the general chat as people got up and started to mill about.

For Dora, breaking up into groups turned out to mean going into another room to sit for twenty minutes in silence at a round table with a ten-inch long mummified snake in the centre, a snake which on closer inspection turned out to be a piece of driftwood. Tom was at the next table. It had a lighted candle in the centre.

The snake didn't do much. He didn't rear, flash his tongue, or do a twirl on the point of his tail. It looked as if he was going to spend the whole twenty minutes just lying there asleep. Dora's gaze drifted past the snake to the edge of the table. It slipped between the woman in the leopard print T-shirt with the Medusa-head pendant and the man with the John Lennon specs, and moved on to the lighted candle on the next table. Past the candle it went, and on to the far side of the table, where solid flesh blocked the way: Tom's. He lifted a hand and scratched his nose.

She counted to nine before the itch began to tingle at the tip of her own nose, and to fifteen before she couldn't stand it any longer. As she scratched, she saw his lips flicker into what might have been a smile, but if she'd blinked she'd have missed it. A second later, he was gazing at the candle.

Back into focus came the snake, every dry brown millimetre of him, and she didn't take her eyes off him until Jason shook his pebble-in-bucket bell and moved them all back into the main room.

The post-'experiment' discussion hadn't been going for more than a minute when Anthea bounded into the room and began whispering to Jason. 'Yeah, OK,' he sighed, taking out his mobile. 'Chat among yourselves for a minute, people.'

Right. Chat, he'd said. If there was one thing she was good at, it was chatting. 'I thought we weren't supposed to use mobiles here,' she said, turning to Tom. 'I've been trying the sea air,' he said, in the same moment.

She laughed. He laughed, then gave a cough. 'One law for him and another for us, evidently,' he said, indicating Jason with a nod of his head.

'Evidently. And how was the beach?'

'Well, there was no funfair, nobody selling ice-creams or hotdogs, no sandcastles, and no surfers. Nothing but rocks, driftwood and the odd plastic bottle.'

'No old flip-flops?'

'There might have been one.'

'Colour?'

'Purple-ish blue. No, Blue-ish purple.'

'Sounds great. You need a bit of junk on a beach.'

'You're familiar with a wide range of beaches?'

'I wouldn't call it wide. I know beaches like Shanklin, Bournemouth, Torquay – places I went with Syd when we were at the burying-Dad stage. Places I've been with Syd since his divorce, now that his kids are at the burying-Dad stage. It's down to me to dig him up.'

'Who dug up your father?'

'I only said we were at that stage, I didn't say we did it. Our father never came within a mile of the beach, which was fine by Syd and me. All the more time for playing ducks and drakes. Actually, if my nephew were here now he wouldn't let me rest until I'd taken him down to the beach and played ducks and drakes.'

'So you still play ducks and drakes?'

'Oh, I've carried on throwing stones over the years.'

'OK, people, sorry about that,' called Jason.

Five minutes into the resumed discussion, a thought occurred to Dora. What if she suggested going down to the beach to play ducks and drakes – after lunch, say? Wouldn't that be the ideal way of setting things straight after last night?

Tom let the voices of others wash around him. He was beginning to feel that conversations with Dora Clayton were like fast games of ping pong: you were swept along by the momentum of the exchanges. The trouble was that you could be off the table or in the net before you knew it. Was that what happened last night? Maybe when this session finished he ought to turn to the woman on his right and start talking; he hadn't said much to her yet.

The moment the session finished, almost before Jason had stopped telling them where coffee was going to be served, Tom heard from his left: 'I'd like to tell Jim I'd beaten you at ducks and drakes. He'd say I was fibbing, mind.'

Oh? *Be careful.* 'A bit disrespectful to Aunt Dozza, surely?'

'Well, that's kids today for you.'

'What if I told him?'

'That would be fine. After lunch, then?'

Tom followed Dora out of the room in the direction of coffee. Maybe he'd got it all wrong about last night. Sometimes a woman who says she's tired is just tired, full stop.

*

Mel rolled over on Debbie's bed and propped herself on one elbow. 'I mean it, Debs. Next week I'm going to the doctor's. And I've changed my mind, I'm not going to tell him.'

'What, just because you haven't got an email back from him yet? You only sent him one last thing,' said Debbie, tucking a foot underneath her in the armchair.

'No, it's not that. Well, not only that. It sort of hit me at four a.m.: what if he doesn't want to know? What do I do if he tells me to get lost?'

'Telling him would be a way of finding out if he really cares,' said Debbie. 'If he does, he'll go to the doctor's with you. Anyway, what did you tell me last term when Dave dumped me? I'd cope. And I did. So would you.'

Mel bit her lip. Would she? Dave wasn't Tom. None of the boys were. 'I'm a hypocrite, Debs. Next time I tell you what to do, just tell me to fuck off, right?'

'But you were right! Dave's only interested in himself. Lisa's going through hell now.'

'OK, you tell Lisa. And she can tell Dave's next girl.'

Debbie sighed. 'All right, all right. Look, do you want me to go to the doctor's with you? We could do it Monday afternoon.'

Monday afternoon. It had to be the time. Yes, what with frees all afternoon, it had to be the time. She'd do it. Christ, if she didn't go to the doctor's on Monday she'd be completely off her head by Tuesday. 'Yeah, OK. Thanks.'

'Debbie, Mel, I'm just off,' came a shout from downstairs. 'Don't forget, when Pete gets back, make sure he leaves his football boots in the porch this time.'

Football boots. A picture flashed into Mel's mind, a picture of a tiny little midget boy with miniature football boots. Did *it*, the thing inside her, have feet yet? Oh God, she couldn't let herself think about stuff like that. It wasn't a human, it was just a collection of cells.

A collection of cells that was on track to grow into a girl, not a boy. Why was she so certain of that?

'OK, Mum,' Debbie called. 'That's the third bloody time today she's nagged me about Pete's football boots,' she went on, tucking her other foot under her. 'Mel, why don't you tell Tom after you've been to the doctor's?'

'What would be the point in that, for fuck's sake?'

'You've been going through shit. I think he ought to know. If he tells you it's over, sod him.'

'Let's talk about it after I've been to the doctor's.'

'OK,' said Debbie, sighing again. 'Look, I could do with another coffee. More water all right for you?'

'No, I'd better be going, I'm supposed to be helping to get Gran's party ready for tomorrow. Fingers crossed I can stick being in a house full of cooking smells without throwing up.'

'Oh Mel,' said Debbie, jumping up and putting her arms around her. 'Hey, when Monday's over and you're feeling OK again, let's really celebrate. Let's go to Costa and have two massive lattes.'

Latte. A big steaming mug... Mel fought down the nausea as she shoved herself to her feet. The thought of ever wanting a latte again, it was just impossible.

As she walked home, Mel didn't so much breathe as gulp down air. London air it might be, but any air was good right now if it stopped her feeling sick. How in hell was she going to get through this big lunch for Gran tomorrow? Could she lose her champagne somewhere without Dad noticing? If he once got the idea she was pregnant... Christ, he mustn't, he just mustn't.

Oh God, Debs was right, she had to tell Tom sometime. Why didn't she just get on an Oxford bus now and go and see him, like he'd asked her to? Mum and Carla and Gemma could manage without her, she could phone home and make an excuse. But she'd better phone him first. She could tell him Gran had a cold and the party'd been put off.

She got as far as pulling out her mobile. It lay there in her hand, and it was as if it was saying, 'Come on then, what are you waiting for?' It rang, and she almost dropped it. Was it him? Please let it be!

It was Mum. 'Mel? Are you on your way? I'm relying on you to get the lounge and dining room hoovered and the table laid, don't forget.'

Mel's lip quivered. God, she couldn't cry in the street, it was worse than being sick. Especially as there were two guys from Year Twelve coming this way.

'Mel? Are you there?' said her mum.

'Yes, Mum. I've left Debbie's, see you in about five minutes.' She snapped the phone shut and walked on quickly, before the two guys from school could catch up with her.

'Until I looked up the old grange in the guidebook, I thought dovecotes were just aviaries for dove-fanciers,' said Dora. 'Still, the Cistercians didn't use their fishponds to keep expensive ornamental carp in, so I suppose eating what roosted in the dovecote needn't have been any different.'

There might be more point to these guidebook details she was giving Tom if they could actually see the nearby ruined grange she was talking about, but the main thing was to keep chatting, to be friendly, to signal to him that she didn't think he was a creep who was going to pounce on her.

The man in that dream. Maybe it was one of the spacemen, come down from Jo's wallpaper… Oh, for God's sake, she couldn't think about Jo's room, not now. She had to get this 'friendly' walk over, and then she could go back to thinking about Jo's room all she wanted.

What was she going to talk about now, though? There wasn't much to say about those banks on either side of the lane. If you've seen one grassy bank you've seen 'em all. And fields like the ones ahead, and bits of sea like the grey strip in the distance. Particularly telegraph poles like that one on the left. And these double yellow lines on either side of the lane, they weren't exactly talking points.

One pair of lines for him to walk along, and one for her. They were walking as far apart as this lane would let them, which wasn't very far. Christ, it was cold out here with this breeze off the sea clawing at your clothes.

'A local farmer grazes cows on the site of the grange now, from what somebody was saying over lunch,' said Tom.

'I'm glad we've come this way, then, cows make me nervous. How much longer to the beach?'

'Fifteen minutes or thereabouts. Round the next corner there's a small wood with a path through it which leads directly to the beach.'

Sure enough, the lane dropped down to the edge of a wood, which seemed to be some sort of nature reserve. On the stile they had to climb over to get into the wood was a notice telling them not to pick the flowers.

So, a change of scene. Trees, a stream babbling away down in a gulley – babbling so hard it was making a caricature of itself – and a narrow path alongside the gulley. With no yellow lines.

She pulled a pace or two ahead, shoving her hands further down into her pockets. 'Warmer in here,' she said.

'Yes… There's some sort of a wall down there. Any idea what that was?'

'The guidebook mentioned a mill that might have belonged to the Cistercian grange. That's probably what's left of it. The daffodils by that bend in the stream over there look very yellow, don't they. I mean, against all this brown and greyness. I can't see a daff without thinking of the poem.'

'Recite it if you like.'

'No thanks. I don't know it by heart any more and I never much liked it when I did.'

89

'But you like daffodils themselves?'

'If I had my way they'd be in flower all year round. I prefer the rare orange and purple paisley-patterned sort, mind you.'

'I don't see any of those, I'm afraid. The one by that tree down there looks particularly yellow, though.'

'The one right by the water? Not bad, I grant you. If I were a better mountaineer than I am, I might just nip down and pick it.'

'I've done a bit of climbing,' he said, and before she could tell him she was only joking he was swinging himself quickly down the steep bank, hanging on to overhanging branches. He picked the daffodil, tucked it into his jacket, and came back with as little fuss as he'd gone down. When he presented the flower to her he wasn't even panting. As she took it, the tips of her fingers touched his for a second.

'We could be arrested for this,' she said, looking at the daff.

'It was worth the risk.'

'I didn't pack the jam jar I put flowers in but there's always the tooth mug,' she said, feeling the need to keep words in the air, light bantering words. Steve never gave her anything he'd picked himself, only big showy bouquets from a florist. You knew where you were with one of those.

That email she'd sent him yesterday. Was there a reply sitting waiting for her?

There was a scuffling sound in the branches overhead. Something plopped into the undergrowth about a yard from her feet. She looked up into a bright eye.

'Your best nut from the winter store, was it? Well, come down and get it then, I'm not picking it up for you,' she said. But the squirrel shrugged, or seemed to, and scuttled out of sight in a flash of bushy tail.

What would Steve's reply say? Would he have understood?

That stream down there. So loud, babbling and bubbling like that, getting inside your head....

'I never got that far with Jo, though I dare say she'd have been good at the toys-out-of-the-pram bit if I'd let her live long enough.' Odd things, words. Not there one moment, very there the next, gushing out like the stream, and leading to things you could never have predicted. Like him taking hold of her left wrist and cradling it in his hand. Like him running a finger lightly along her scar.

'Be careful, you'll get onion on you,' she said. 'I'd been chopping one. In the hospital all I could smell was onion. I tell a lie, it was a shallot. Damn, I pride myself on my grasp of detail.' Laughter exploded out of her, laughter loud enough to send a flock of birds cawing into the sky. 'I'm sorry,' she said at last, between gasps. 'I don't cry, but I laugh quite a bit. Shall we go on? Those ducks and drakes'll be getting impatient.'

She took a step, not looking where she was putting her foot, and caught it on something. An arm went around her before she fell.

'Tree roots. They catch you out,' he said.

Another arm went around her, and then lips sought and met hers, and for the rest of her life she would have the sound of that babbling brook in her ears.

And then, and then, came another sound, nothing to do with water: the murmur of a man's and a woman's voices. And giggles. Giggles, coming from a little way along this path. Tom sprang away from her as if she'd turned red-hot. But not fast enough, it seemed.

'Weh-hell!' said the man, who turned out to be Fred Benson.

'Shh!' said the woman, who turned out to be Nanette Farmer.

'Hello Fred, hello Nanette,' said Tom.

Dora had a huge urge to put a hand up to cover her mouth, but she didn't.

'Nice walk?' she said.

'Up to a point,' said Fred, grinning. 'The bloody beach is crowded, everybody's down there. There's some even going for a paddle, would you believe.'

'You had a better idea, staying here,' Nanette chipped in, still giggling. Even the primrose in the top buttonhole of her jacket had a smirk on its face. 'Anyway, we're going back now. You coming?'

'Hey, don't rush them, girl,' said Fred, his grin broadening.

'It's OK, we were just thinking of going back,' said Tom.

Yes, they might as well go back. There wasn't any real point in going on. Not now.

She'd just let herself be kissed in a Welsh wood in the middle of nowhere by a man she hardly knew. Which must be why, on the way back, she wasn't hearing a word Fred and Nanette were saying. Still, a bit of laughter from time to time seemed to be enough of a response. She was good at laughing.

As they got to the top of the hill, they fell in with some others coming back from an encounter with the cows. That started Fred and Nanette off again, and Tom turned to Dora. 'Sorry,' he whispered. 'I had absolutely no intention of doing that, believe me.'

'It just came out?' she murmured.

He nodded, looking at her feet, not her face.

Back at the Satori Centre, as they were going through the gates, a flock of large black birds dropped down to perch on the roof. Four and twenty blackbirds baked in a pie. No, these were too big to be blackbirds. Too macho-looking.

Sing a song of sixpence, a pocket full of rye? It made about as much sense as saying little boys were made of puppy-dogs' tails, or little girls of sugar and spice. Or that this daffodil Tom had given her was golden, when it was yellow. Just plain yellow.

'I'll go and put this in that tooth mug,' she said when they were inside. Tom gazed at the daffodil as she spoke. Anyone would think he'd never seen a daffodil before, let alone gone to some lengths to collect this one.

Golden daffodils. Yes, that made about as much sense as eggs falling off walls or cows jumping over the moon.

Was there a rhyme about kissing a man in a wood? Must be. Must be.

The afternoon session had something to do with herding oxen, but why Tom should be interested in oxen, he had no idea, and he wasn't paying enough attention to find out. Snatches of sentences drifted past him: 'It's hard to control so powerful a beast,' Jason was saying. 'One false move and an animal like that'll trip you up and have you flat on the ground.'

He'd tripped. In that wood, he'd made a move that put him on the ground as effectively as if he'd been the one to catch his foot on the tree root. Beside him, Dora seemed to be hanging on Jason's every word. Was she? Or was she deciding that that kiss didn't just 'come out', there was a reason. Intended or not, there was always a reason. Was it the look on her face as he gave her the daffodil: surprise mixed with a sort of wistfulness? And then she'd begun talking about her baby... There was so much vulnerability there. Was it pity, then, no more and no less? He bit his lip; he ought to know. He'd had enough practice in the past at working out what the crucial trigger had been. Still, it wasn't because of a wasp.

What the hell did he do now, though? Pretend it never happened?

As they were breaking up into groups, apparently to think about their own oxen, Fred and Nanette materialised on either side of him and Dora, like a pair of brackets. They had a proposition to make. If Tom and Dora got their drift.

Fred and Nanette had it all worked out. Nanette would

swap with Tom because the boys' room was closer to the outside security light, and she – giggle – always slept better with a bit of light around.

Before Tom's brain could convey any words to his mouth, Dora said, 'Fine, we don't mind the dark, do we, Tom.'

For the next half hour, oxen lumbered all around him: brown ones, grey ones, blue ones with pink stripes, green and yellow checked ones. When pressed, he told his group that his was see-through.

As everyone filtered back into the main meeting room, a man in front of Tom said to his neighbour, 'Do you play Scrabble? I noticed a set in the dining room.' The other man said, 'Do I play Scrabble? When I was at university I used to play Scrabble all night. I'll never forget the night I got zygotoblast, it's still the high point of my existence.'

'Zygotoblast.' Zy-go-to-blast. Tom would remember that. He'd have it on his lips on his death bed.

That afternoon, Mel managed not to throw up until her mother started frying onions. It would have to happen that her dad and her brother Scott arrived home with a mountain of booze just as she was running for the toilet. They started joshing about would there be enough for anybody besides Mel and they'd have to send her out to the supermarket if the stuff ran out, and all she could do was push past them, head down, and sprint up the stairs.

In the toilet, everything she'd managed to force down since the last time she was sick three hours ago came back up to meet her. One thing she could be thankful for, if she was capable of being thankful for anything right now, was that Dad had sound-proofed all the facilities in the house, so nobody could hear her puke.

Before she went downstairs again she checked her emails for the tenth or was it the eleventh time since she'd got back from Debbie's. Still nothing in from Tom. Oh Christ, was he pissed off because she'd left it so late to get back to him?

Downstairs, her dad was stacking the drink in the kitchen. He gave her a funny look. 'What's up with you, girl?'

'Nothing. It's not a crime to go to the toilet, is it?' She ducked into the dining room before he could make any more remarks and switched on the hoover, but later, as she was sorting out cutlery and serviettes, she heard him ask Mum if she'd noticed Mel was looking peaky. Mum said, 'She's fine, it'll be time of the month, that's all,' but that evening when they were eating she caught Mum glancing at her once or twice, with a sort of look in her eye. Mel kept her head down and tried to seem as if she was eating something. She made sure it was her who cleared the plates, and she scraped her leftovers – like, most of what she'd had on her plate – into the bin before Mum came out into the kitchen.

But last thing, as they were checking everything was ready for tomorrow, her Mum cornered her. 'Mel,' she whispered, 'you all right?'

Her mum's whispers always seemed louder than shouts. Maybe it came from being Italian. 'Yeah, course I am,' she said. 'Just a bit of diarrhoea earlier, that's all. Dodgy burger or something.' Her sister Carla came in then saying something about wine glasses, and Mel made herself scarce.

That night she lay in bed hugging Bono to her chest. If she didn't manage to put on some kind of show tomorrow, Mum was going to be on at her again. It wouldn't take much for her to ask point blank was she in trouble. A tear trickled down her cheek and onto Bono. She couldn't hold out against Mum. Not a hope.

But there was another thing. Why in hell hadn't she thought of it before? If Dad found out, he'd be on about going to the police again. He'd have all the evidence he needed to get Tom sent to jail, they'd have no chance of stopping him this time. She *had* to be OK tomorrow. She had to fool them all until she got to the doctor's on Monday if it was the last thing she did.

Eight

'I really am sorry about this,' Tom said, following Dora into the room.

'Never mind, worse things happen at sea. Right then, what I think I'll do now is go and grab a quick shower.'

'As a matter of fact, I was thinking of doing the same. You take the one outside, I'll go to the one at the far end of the corridor.'

'OK. And you'll be in Scotland before me. Or whatever.'

He laughed. She laughed.

She began bustling about the room. 'Towel, bathrobe, pyjamas… where's my sponge bag… ah, right where I left it. See you later.' She was gone.

For several seconds he stood gazing at the door she'd closed behind her. Then he went to the window and threw it open. The cloud bank which had hung overhead all day had moved off while they were having supper. There was Capella, shining straight at him. He took a slow breath. *Capella, Capella, how many more things am I going to get wrong?*

He took another breath. Clear, cold air with a hint of salt in it filled him down to his toes and fingertips. He closed his eyes for a moment, then retreated into the room and shut the window. He collected his shower things, not forgetting the clean T-shirt and shorts in which he was going to be spending the night, in the bed on the left-hand side of the room. The bed that didn't have her things lying on it.

A few minutes later he was standing under a jet of steaming water. Maybe he ought just to stay here all night.

When he got back to the room, Dora was sitting up in bed with a book resting against her knees. She was in striped schoolboy pyjamas buttoned to the chin, and spectacles were perched on her nose. If she'd looked vulnerable in the woods, she looked ten times more vulnerable now, somehow. He turned aside quickly.

'I just thought I'd check a few more details,' she said. 'There's a wrecker's tower a little way along the coast that I didn't tell you about.'

'That was slack of you,' he said, giving his hair another rub with the towel.

'Ah well, nobody's perfect. Especially me.'

'I reckon I could give you a run for your money,' he said, draping his towel over the radiator alongside hers. He switched off the overhead light and slipped into what had been Nanette Farmer's bed the previous night. He wrinkled his nose: the sheets smelled of that rather strong perfume Nanette wore.

'You know, for an area that feels like the back of beyond, there've been quite a few people here,' she said, nose still in her guidebook. 'Imagine a night like this twenty five thousand years ago. If the fire went out in your cave, you were buggered.'

'You wouldn't let it go out,' he said, switching off his bedside lamp and easing himself down in the bed. 'You'd throw your best deerskin cloak on it if you had to.' A night like this? Palaeolithics didn't have nights like this. It had taken millions more nights for evolution to bring humanity to a night like this.

'Mm. And then your granny,' she said. 'Right, I think that's enough about Wales.' She closed the book and put it and her glasses on her night table. Then she switched off her bedside lamp. 'Night, Tom,' she said, out of a darkness so total it was as if he'd been blindfolded.

'Good night, Dora,' he said.

The silence was as thick as the darkness. Her old-fashioned alarm clock was tick-tocking away to itself, but the sound only served to emphasise the surrounding hush.

Between one tick and the next, he sensed her stiffen. 'What was that?' she said.

'What?'

'That. Outside. Listen.'

He held his breath. She was right, there was something out there, some creature scuffling and scratching.

'Probably that cat that hangs around this place out hunting,' he said. On cue, a screech and a yowl tore through the night, and through him, sending his heart racing.

As the racket died away, Dora gave a long sigh. 'Some cat was in our garden that night,' she said, in a low, by-the-way tone. 'Steve had just rushed back from Manchester, poor bloke, and he threw a bucket of water over it. Totally out of character, Steve's soppy about animals – he grew up with a menagerie of them. He was always on at me to get a dog.'

That night? She must mean the night after her baby died. 'Do you like dogs?'

'As a concept, yes. As great lollopy smelly things that lick you, no. Tom, what's Tommy told you about me?'

He had to be careful. 'That you're the way you are because of Jo.'

'She's got it the wrong way round. Jo's the way she is because of me. I break things.'

'You broke Jo?'

'Yes. I broke Jo.'

He had to be so, so careful. 'How did you come to break her, Dora?'

No reply.

He'd got it wrong. Any moment now she'd tell him to leave, go outside and join the cat, and she'd throw a bucket of water over both of them.

'Thank you,' she said at last. 'Thank you, it makes a change from being told it can't have been my fault. You've no idea…' Her voice sounded shaky. 'Well, I suppose it all started with the Wendy House.'

'Tell me about the Wendy House.'

'All right. It was a very nice Wendy House as Wendy Houses go, with checked curtains and cute little chairs and a table, and a doll's tea set to go on the table. My parents gave it to me for Christmas when I was five. The trouble was, I didn't want it. I wanted a pedal car like the one they'd given Syd. So I got up early on Boxing Day morning and found the kitchen scissors and cut the house to ribbons – it was only a glorified tent – and stamped with all my tiny might on the furniture and the tea set. When the family came down for breakfast I was trundling up and down the hallway in the pedal car. Well, there was a lot of huffing and puffing and growling and roaring and subjecting of an ungrateful, wicked girl to a lengthy interview, but I didn't cry. Little Dora Madeleine Agnes was damned if she'd let her big bad father have any advantage over her. Professor Robert Clayton FRS was the last man in Oxford to have had mutton-chop side-whiskers, by the way. You might like to know that. According to a shrink I once knew, it is rather relevant.'

'"Dora Madeleine Agnes." My God, those heroines Dickens used to dream up… Do your names tell me all I need to know about Professor Robert Clayton FRS?'

'They do. And about my mother, Mrs Professor Robert Clayton FRS. Straight from Dickens, both of them. Syd is Sydney David

Oliver, for what it's worth. I should have hated Syd, shouldn't I, for being a boy. I think I probably tried to, but I didn't get very far. You can't hate Syd. Anyway, it wasn't a complete write-off, that Boxing Day. Syd stuck by me, he understood. He let me have a go in the pedal car when our father was asleep after lunch.'

'I'm glad. But later on, you cut your wrist.'

'Later on… Yes, later on I cut my wrist. But I wasn't going to waste my wrist on a Wendy House alone, you understand, there had to be a much more spectacular trail of destruction than that. So I kicked down every sandcastle I built, then, in the fullness of time, there were a certain number of plates and what-have-you thrown at Steve in, shall we say, my volatile moments. Not that throwing things at him ever did any good, he always caught them. He used to play rugby and cricket for Durham University. But three years ago I finally made it worth my while picking up that kitchen knife. I fell asleep one night on the sofa.' Her voice trailed away, as if there were no breath to shape any more words.

'Glass of wine too many?'

'Bottle too many, more like. When I woke up, do you know what the first thing I heard was? "Will be very warm again throughout the south and the midlands." It was the sodding breakfast TV weather forecast. It was nine o'clock in the bloody morning, would you believe.'

Silence again. The clock tick-tick-ticking.

'That was the year of the Indian summer, wasn't it?'

'Yes, that was that year. What were you doing the first week in September that year, Tom, where were you?'

'Gearing up for the new term, I imagine.' Looking forward to talking to sparky, bright-eyed little Melanie Baines about her GCSE choices? Oh God.

'Did they have wasps at your school, Tom?'

'I don't think so, but I've had one or two in my house.' Why was she talking about wasps?

'So have I. That first week in September, every time I opened a window a squadron of them zoomed in. I'd been meaning to get the pest people in for days, but what with the washing machine on the blink, and one thing and another... Then Jo went down with a cold. I thought of taking her to the doctor, but with Steve away I couldn't raise the energy, I just couldn't. Getting her into the car, driving her there, finding a parking space, getting her out of the car... Hell, it was only a sniffle. Babies get them all the time. Christ, the time it took me that night to get her to settle. I don't know who was sweating more, her or me.'

'And you couldn't leave the window open to let any air in because of the wasps, and when Jo had cried herself into an exhausted sleep in a stifling room you went downstairs and opened that wine.'

Silence yet again. The clock tick-tick-tick-tocking.

So, but for wasps. But for fucking *wasps.*

'They found the nest a week later, just above the bedroom window,' she said at last. 'The guy from the pest control firm said it was the biggest he'd ever seen, and I should have got him in weeks ago. He said it was just as well the baby was out, what with a lot of angry displaced wasps about. I'd told him she was at her grandparents'. Well, I had to tell him something, there was baby stuff still around all over the house. There was no need to tell him the truth, though. That she'd have taken one look at her grandfather and screamed the house down.' She began a high-pitched keening, the 'hih-hih-hih' of all mothers crying for their children, the sound made by the faces you saw on TV news, night after night after night.

She'd said she didn't cry, but all dams would break, given enough pressure. Should he do something? Hell, he had to. He got out of bed and felt his way toward her. Kneeling down beside her, he slid an arm around her. 'It's all right, it's all right,' he murmured. But it wasn't all right, was it. It was bloody well not all right, and no amount of there-there-ing would make it so.

'Sorry,' she gasped at last. 'I wasn't crying, I told you I didn't. I was laughing. It's the only thing worse than laughing at bad jokes, isn't it, laughing at your own bad jokes.'

Sweet Jesus. She'd been *laughing?*

Now what. Did he withdraw his arm, or not? She didn't seem to be minding it. Or even noticing?

'I haven't told you the worst thing,' she said. 'Not the really awful thing. I haven't told anybody, not even Steve or Syd. The day before, I'd shouted at her. She wouldn't stop crying, and I shouted at her.'

'Her cold must have been making her miserable.'

'Miserable? She was whining and grizzling, hour after bloody hour, she just wouldn't stop. Eventually I said, "Oh fucking shut up, will you? Shut up!" That's what I said. And – and she – looked at me. Just lay there in her kick'n'play bouncer and looked at me. The look in her eyes – I've never quite been able to put a name to it. Surprise comes somewhere near, but not near enough. The world wasn't what she'd thought it was, I suppose. It wasn't a nice place, it was a very nasty place.'

'Nasty enough that some people cut their wrists.'

'Yes… When I did that I'd been back at Duckworth and Dunn three weeks. I'd always intended to go back when Jo was three months old, you understand. We were joining a nanny-share with another couple down the road, I'd have gone crazy looking after a baby all day. Funny thing is, when I was sitting waiting in the hospital while they were working on Jo, I was saying things to myself like "Make her well and I'll cancel the nanny-share and tell the office I'm not coming back, ever." But I digress. The night of the shallot episode, Steve was in the living room watching TV. It was a football match. Why is there so much football on TV? Poor old Steve, he never did find out if United or Arsenal won. It's bound to have been United versus Arsenal, isn't it.'

'Bound to. I dare say it was a draw.'

'Steve told me to blame him. The air conditioner we'd bought the week before was still in the box in the garage because he hadn't got around to setting it up at the weekend, and then on the Monday he had to go to Manchester at no notice. He's got the sort of job where you have to keep an overnight bag packed and ready in the office.'

'But you didn't blame him.'

'Of course not, Steve doesn't break things, he mends them. He's a genius at DIY.' A proprietorial tone there. Protective, almost. He felt her take a long breath in, and let it out slowly. Then she laughed, but not with the manic laugh of just now, rather the laugh of a non-swimmer on Dover beach who'd had the French coast pointed out to her and been told to get on with it. 'Have you ever had a Plan B, Tom?'

'I'm afraid Plan A's as much as I've ever been able to manage.'

'Hm. Well, Plan B's only taken shape since Friday, but it's a humdinger. Steve wants more children. He's saying he doesn't, but he does. My childbearing days are, shall we say, over, but Plan B will give Steve a bus-load of children so that he can buy them all dogs. Plan B is so good that it'll put every other wrecking job I've done in the shade, Jo excepted.' She laughed, and this time her laugh did have that edge to it. 'Steve's got a bright new sidekick,' she went on. 'Her name's Yvonne. Pretty name, isn't it. Apparently she looks a lot like me.'

'So Steve wants more children, and under Plan B it's Yvonne who's going to be the mum? I don't see why that makes you the wrecker in this case.'

'Steve needs a little push… And he's getting one.'

'What – you're telling him to go?'

'I am.'

'But wait a minute, I think you still care for Steve. Does he care for you?'

Silence, for maybe three seconds. Then: 'If we did still care for one another, it would make it even more of a wrecking job, wouldn't it. You might say it was the ultimate train crash.'

By the tone of her voice, here was an avenue he'd better not go down any further, such as by speculating about this Yvonne's views on office affairs and potential motherhood. But if Dora was prepared to destroy her marriage to give her husband what she thought he wanted... Christ. 'What happens to you under Plan B?'

'I can't afford to buy Steve out. So we sell up, and I look for a little shoebox somewhere in east Oxford with my share of the proceeds.' Her voice was tight, small, as if it were trying to roll itself into a ball. 'Of course, I could always buy myself a bank-robber's outfit next week, couldn't I...'

'Debenham's must have one in your size.'

'I'm not so sure, we petites are hard to fit, you know.' She began to laugh, but almost as soon as she started, she stopped, like a tap being turned off. 'Right. That's enough talking after lights out. Good night again, Tom.'

'Good night again, Dora.'

'Oh, hang on a minute.'

He felt her turn towards him, and then lips were touched to his cheek.

'That's for letting me witter on,' she said.

'Don't mention it.' He did, at last, withdraw his arm. He wondered whether he might risk kissing her cheek, then thought better of it.

As he got back into bed, she said, 'Oh, one more thing. Jo never smiled. They're supposed to at six weeks, but she hadn't.'

'Maybe she would have if she hadn't had that cold.'

'Yeah. Maybe.'

Silence again, settling like the sediment in a pond after a

storm has stirred up the water. Then, unbelievably, steady breathing from the one in the other bed. She'd fallen asleep. She'd talked herself out. And then, even more unbelievably, a huge wave of protectiveness passing through him, at the vision of her lost in an outsize comedy robber's outfit with a striped top and a mask. She'd unsettled him more than once just now, to be sure, but he had an almighty urge to get out of this bed and into hers, to hold her fast and not let go, an urge strong enough to make him catch his breath.

But for those wasps.

But for wasps, his wasps, he wouldn't be here.

As he lay there, a plan began to take shape. Plan C.

Nine

M el made it to the bathroom just in time. When the retching had stopped she tiptoed back to her room, shivering, and got back under the duvet. Thank Christ nobody else was up yet. What was the time? Not even half past six. It was going to be an hour at least before anybody in the house got moving. Well, she couldn't lie here a whole hour thinking about that dream and wondering if she'd be OK today. She wouldn't be OK, that was bloody clear already. Oh God, what was she going to *do?*

Before the hands on her Donald Duck alarm clock had moved through another minute, she knew what she was going to do. She was taking the bus to Oxford. She was going to disappear out of her family's sight for the day, and she was going to see Tom. She slipped out of bed, heart thumping, and wriggled out of the outsize T-shirt with Scooby-Doo on the front that did her as a night dress. She looked down at her stomach. Totally flat, as usual. How *could* there be anything in there? But there was, there fucking was. She threw on some clothes and grabbed her bag.

As she was tiptoeing out of her room, she stopped. She had

to leave them a note, for God's sake, otherwise they start thinking she'd been abducted by aliens in the night. She went to her desk and grabbed a sheet of paper and a pen:

'Gone to Oxford,' she scribbled. 'Have to see Tom. Sorry.'

She sucked the pen for a moment, staring at what she'd written. Dad would go ballistic. Well, fuck him. He could always have believed her story, he could always have not phoned the Head. Then none of all this would have happened, not Tom going, not her forgetting a sodding Pill.

Going downstairs, she held her breath. This would be just the moment when somebody woke up and decided they needed a pee. But nobody did. She put the note on the kitchen table and tiptoed along the hallway to the front door. She was biting her lip as she undid the various noisy locks her dad had installed. Why did he have to be so paranoid about security? She shut the door after her as quietly as she could, but the sound still seemed loud enough to wake the street, never mind the house. She froze for a few moments in the porch, but she didn't hear anybody charging down the stairs to find out if there'd been a break-in.

She took a deep breath of chilly February air. The sun was coming up, and there was enough light in the sky to show her the empty park, covered in frost. Even Uxbridge could look beautiful at times. Pity she wasn't in any mood to appreciate it. Oh God, it would be so good to be a kid again and play on the grass, crunching the frost under her boots, not a care in the world.

She started walking in the direction of Long Lane, her footsteps ringing on the pavement. There wasn't a single other person about. She was alone in the universe. It was just her here, everybody else had been taken away by those aliens. Just her – and Faith.

Oh God, what in hell was she doing, giving it a name? And why Faith, of all the names? Did she dream it? She must have.

After all, she'd dreamed about football boots: sugar-pink football boots with fluffy pink and white laces which started dancing and sort of morphed into those pink Cinderella slippers she'd had when she was five…

Her nose started to run. The cold air must be getting to it. She fished a Kleenex out of her bag. Right sight she was going to look today: red nose, white face, no make-up. Tom'd take one look at her and wish he'd never got involved. Oh hell, he'd wish that anyway when she told him what she was now, finally, going to tell him. Hang on though, maybe he already did wish it? What was in it for him, really, being with a schoolgirl? Oxford was full of women clever enough for him, he'd be bumping into them on every street corner. Interesting women, older than her, women who'd been around a few blocks. Maybe he'd met somebody already. Maybe he invited her to Oxford this weekend to tell her it was over? Oh, but it was so good while it lasted!

Oh shit. She was going to be sick again.

She bent her head over the nearest garden wall. Where was it coming from when she hadn't had any breakfast? When it was over, she fished a wet wipe out of her bag and wiped her face. She looked at the closed curtains of the house whose garden she'd just added a feature to. Sorry, whoever you are in there. Put it down to some drunk late last night.

Christ, if only the bus would stop jolting like this.

Mel braced herself against the sides of the toilet and let the stuff pour out of her into the bowl. She ought to be glad it was only liquid now. Not that it smelt any better. How *could* she be this sick?

OK, was that it? Seemed to be. She pulled the flush. Nothing happened. She pressed the tap pedal. Nothing. Not a dribble. She couldn't even rinse her hands. Bugger.

She got herself out of the cubicle and back to her seat. Just as well there was only one other passenger on this bus, and he was fast asleep. But if he did wake up and want the toilet, he'd find he'd have to bottle it.

The bus pulled out of a sort of ravine with cliffs on either side, and a whole expanse of country opened up. Where was Oxford? Should she be able to see it by now? She fished out the piece of paper with Tom's sister's address on which he'd given her when he left. Did she have enough money for a taxi? She looked in her purse: a fifty p and three tens. That wasn't going to get her very far. She'd have to borrow the money from him when she got there. Fuck, what a way to have to start. As if it wasn't going to be bad enough.

She ought to phone him. Bit early, though, wasn't it? For a Sunday? Come to that, what actually was the time?

It was ten to eight. She'd be there well before half past. Maybe she ought to walk around the centre a bit first, if she could face it. She might find some café open that was selling peppermint tea.

She looked out of the window, stared hard, and kept her lips firmly together. She wasn't going to cry, even if the only other person on the bus apart from the driver was that guy who was asleep. This was practice for not crying in front of Tom when he told her it was over. She wasn't going to look like a bloody victim. Hell, she could say she'd been seeing Dean Mills, she could say she wasn't sure whose baby this was… Bit hard on Dean, though, even if he was a bit of a geek… OK, some other bloke's, then – somebody that nobody knew, because he didn't even exist.

A tiny girl in a ballet tutu and pink football boots appeared in her mind's eye, a tiny girl with a thumb in her mouth and a tear running down her cheek. Mel screwed up her eyes and put a hand to her mouth. No, she wasn't going to cry. She wasn't!

Dora drew back the curtains and looked out. 'Great view out

here,' she said. 'Fields, a few trees – short ones, mainly, growing sideways. The cat's sitting in the middle of the Zen garden scratching itself.' Was this what it felt like to have slept? She must do it more often. What was the secret – having a roommate sprung on you at practically no notice? It hadn't worked the previous night. Maybe it depended on the roommate.

'Oh, there's Anthea, coming through the gate. Today's sweater's covered with Adelie penguins. Come and look.'

'She'll see me,' said Tom, his duvet still up to his nose.

'No she won't, she's not looking in this direction.'

'Oh, all right,' he said, giving her an embarrassed-sounding laugh. He came up behind her and looked over her shoulder. 'Aren't those penguins Emperors? They're big enough,' he went on. He was close enough that she could feel the warmth of him.

'No, they're Adelies. They haven't got orange patches at the neck. Jim's into penguins. Auntie Dozza's been helping him find out about every type of penguin in Antarctica. He could give a lesson on them and let Tommy have an extra half hour with the staff room coffee machine.' She should be hoarse from last night, and yet here she was, talking again.

'I'll let her know,' he said. She felt him stiffen slightly and take a breath. Was he going to tell her he wasn't up to any more talking?

'Dora, I've got a house,' he said, speaking fast and low. 'It's in West London, and I don't think I'm going to be living there again. If you and Steve really are splitting up, I could sell my house and buy him out, and then you wouldn't have to move. I don't need much space, only some bookshelves. You wouldn't know I was there if you didn't want to.'

What? *What* was he saying? 'Are you putting yourself forward as a housemate? If so, thanks for trying to make me feel twenty-two again, but—'

111

'It may take a little while before the sale goes through. How much do you want by way of rent in the interim? I've presumed on Tommy long enough.'

'Tom,' she said, half-laughing and shaking her head, 'the phrase "a bit sudden" comes to mind. I mean, I don't even know if you're the sort who steals other people's milk.'

'Do I know if you are?'

'You don't know how morose I can get. And milk-thieving apart, for all I know you might be a secret axe-murderer. They're often quiet types.'

'Are you have-a-drink-with-me morose or piss-off-and-leave-me-alone morose? Either way, I can cope. As for the axe-murdering, it's a risk you could decide to take.'

She looked at him. Was he actually serious? It looked as if he might just be.

'Dora, if you're wondering if you'd end up having to buy me out because I'd met somebody and was moving out to have a bus-load of children with her, forget it.'

'So you're not a having-children person?'

He shook his head. 'I like them, but coping with them in school hours was enough for me.'

'And you're not a meeting-somebody person?' There was a caricature-rustic horse and cart coming up the road. She couldn't make out what sort of load it was carrying. While she watched it, the silence in the room seemed to thicken.

'Dora, I've met all the women I ever want to meet,' he said at last.

She kept her gaze fixed on the horse and cart. Any moment now it would be out of sight, around the bend in the road. This idea of his was crazy, crazy. He'd surely run a mile when he saw the room. The room, *Jo's* room.

'I think we could manage to get on, couldn't we?' he went on. 'Enough to share a house, anyway?' The look in his eyes. He really was serious. Any minute now, would he go down on his knees and beg her to let him move in? Did she want that, a man around the place who wasn't Steve? Especially one who did things on country walks that he'd had absolutely no intention of doing?

'Tom, I think you ought to look at the house first.'

'I don't think I need to.'

'Maybe I haven't cleaned up for ten years.'

'All right then, how about when we get back tonight? We could get a take-away and eat it in your filthy kitchen. Afterwards, we could chuck the foil dishes on the floor.'

'Whoah, I only said maybe I haven't cleaned up. All right, we'll get a take-away.' She'd show him around after they'd eaten it, not before. Otherwise she'd have half a dozen untouched foil dishes to throw out after he'd run a mile, and the way she'd be feeling, she might just throw them on the floor.

'Good. Let's shake hands on that, at least.' He extended a hand towards her. Close together as they were, his hand didn't have far to come to meet hers, but it would have been churlish to let it have a wasted journey, and doubly churlish not to let her eyes meet and hold his.

Which may well have been why, in the space of ten seconds or so, the world seemed to shift sideways. 'Tom, I'm going back to bed. My feet are freezing.'

'So are mine,' he said, his eyes not leaving her face and his hand still holding hers. Who was pulling the world? Maybe it was moving of its own accord.

'Talking of sudden, this is a bit, isn't it?' he murmured as he climbed in under her duvet after her.

'Is it?' she murmured in her turn.

He smiled. 'You may a have a point,' he said, taking her in his arms.

'Would you cut the grass?' she said into his chest. 'Would you take out the bin bags?'

'I'm good at cutting grass,' he said into her hair. 'And taking out bin bags. And going to Sainsbury's on a Friday night, and –'

'And doing the washing up.'

'And doing the washing up.'

He kissed the tip of her nose with a touch so light, it was as if a moth had brushed it with a wing. She kissed his nose, then his forehead, then each cheek, then his chin, and then his lips.

'The thing is, Tom,' she began.

'It really doesn't matter, it's fine, lying here, fine, just fine.'

'There you go, interrupting, just like a bloke. What I was going to say was, have you got anything. I, er, I'm not – equipped.'

She had to give him his due. He didn't pull away, and all he said was, 'I'll have a look.'

He got out of bed and picked up his sponge bag. 'I never get around to clearing this out,' he said, rooting through it. 'There's three almost-used tubes of toothpaste, two shower gels… ah.'

He took out a foil packet and held it up.

'It's not past its use-by date, is it?' she said. 'Sorry, but attention to detail's always been one of my strong points.'

He examined the packet. 'Fifteen months to go. Do you want to see?'

'I'll take your word for it.' Was she going to do it, then, unlock herself? Judging by the way her heart was beating, it seemed like it. Please, please God let it work. He turned his back to her and began to pull off his T-shirt. She turned away and wriggled out of her pyjamas under the duvet. When he got in beside her, he was still, she noticed, wearing his shorts.

'From my point of view, we won't need many preliminaries,' she said. 'Just thought I'd mention it. In case you were wondering.' This was either going to work, and work now, or…

'Good,' he said. 'My point of view's pretty close to yours, I think.' He was taking off his shorts as he spoke.

When he put himself inside her, her first thought was,

114

Christ, the works do still function, I *can* still do it. Her second thought was, so this is what it was like. Actually, though, no: it was different. Because there was no such thing as 'it', there was only the one you were with. That was one of the first things she'd learned as a student, surely she hadn't forgotten it?

He was a good fit, this one. Very good. *Sorry, Steve. Sorry, sorry, sorry—*

'Dora?' He was slowing down. Why, for goodness sake?

'What?'

'Is it OK? You were, er, making faces.'

'It's OK, it's OK. Don't stop, for Capella's sake don't stop.' Too much thinking. There was a time and a place for thinking, and this wasn't it.

Tom didn't stop, he speeded up. She sped up with him, so that they were one movement, and the air became filled with murmured names, his and hers. When she began to feel the moment coming, a laugh started up in her – a gentle laugh, nothing manic. He began to laugh too. Well, laughter was infectious.

'Oh Dora,' he said between laughs, 'Dora, Dora.'

Her moment came and seized him mid-laugh, and in a next breath, which seemed to belong to both of them, his moment came too.

He was still laughing when he removed himself from her. They lay there for perhaps half a minute, not speaking. God, she'd done it. She'd done it.

'You know, this is a weird room,' he said at last. 'By rights it should have daylight in it, but as far as I'm concerned it's full of starlight. Jesus, that was cheesy, wasn't it.

'Oh, I don't know. Lots would say it was quite poetic.'

'Would you?'

'Don't press me.' With her finger tips she stroked the side of his face, very slowly, from temple to chin. 'Hello,' she said.

'Hello,' he said. His own fingers travelled down her face,

down her neck, and on down, down, until they reached a place she'd rather they hadn't found, but it was inevitable that they would. It was a central part of her.

'What you've found there is Jo's exit route,' she said. 'She had to be cut out of me.'

He ran a finger along the indentation in her flesh. 'I hope that didn't hurt?'

'It was fine. Just don't tickle my nose with a feather right now, it feels as if I'm being pulled apart like one of those polythene envelopes if I sneeze when I'm lying flat.' *Does it disgust you?*

He must have read her mind. He rolled back the duvet, slid down in the bed and kissed the gash through which they'd pulled her baby, touching his lips to it all along its length. Then he sat back on his haunches and studied her.

'Jo got stuck. I wasn't built to give birth to anything bigger than a Barbie doll but you can't tell from the outside,' she said, looking not at him but at the ceiling. 'Thank God for modern high-tech obstetrics, that's all I can say. All that aromatherapy and soft music and birthing pools – a load of bollocks if you ask me.'

He didn't say anything. All right, in for a penny: 'I'm older than you, you know,' she went on, still looking at the ceiling. 'I trashed that Wendy House before you were born.' Now all she had to do was tell him about the room.

'You must be making some sort of point, but I'm damned if I can see what it is,' he said. He lay down beside her again and took her in his arms, cradling her head against his shoulder.

She moulded herself to the line of his body, but still she looked at the ceiling. Oh God, he'd find out about the room soon enough.

It struck her: something she'd said to him just now. 'For Capella's sake don't stop'. Strange. Of all the things to say.

*

116

'No, Fred, holding the sword as if not holding it isn't some sort of gag,' Jason was saying. 'Get it right, and it could save your life.'

Tom stifled a yawn. Oh for an hour somewhere quiet, not to think about anything, just to catch his breath. It was amazing. People usually said things were amazing when they weren't even special, but this – it – Dora – himself – was all utterly amazing.

'OK folks, I want you to break up into your groups and think of three instances in the coming week when you're going to be needing a sword,' said Jason.

Tom was the focus of grins and stares as he drifted out behind Dora into the side room: *Late down this morning, eh? Well, always nice to have a lie-in on a Sunday.* He didn't want to think about swords, not this morning. The last sword he'd held was only a piece of plywood painted silver, but he'd been killed by one equally spurious. *Oh Harry, thou hast robbed me of my youth.*

He shivered. It had been twenty years ago, but he could be speaking the line right now, that seventeen year-old Hotspur who lay dying on a school stage with all the girls in the front row sniffing into their handkerchiefs.

Well, he, Tom Ross, wasn't dying now. He was alive, alive, alive, and he had a woman in front of him who was amazing. Disquieting and vulnerable, brittle and soft: she was a mix he couldn't begin to describe, and there was no point in bothering. Maybe now he could let Mel slip into the past – into the future, rather, with Dean Mills and whoever might succeed Mills, until she found somebody who was right.

He was taking his seat when Anthea came in. She scanned the room quickly, and stopped when she got to him. 'Phone for you, Tom.'

As she spoke, there was a stirring in his guts. He took an

involuntary look at his watch, knowing as he did so that not only was it nowhere near eleven, but the caller couldn't be Mel. How could it be, she didn't know he was here. And she was with Dean Mills, for God's sake. She'd dumped him.

All the way to the door, he felt himself being tracked by a pair of eyes. Dora's.

Anthea let him into the adjoining room, which seemed to be some sort of office, and made herself scarce. He inhaled, exhaled, and picked up the phone.

'*Tom?*' His sister shot his name down the line at him like a bullet.

What in hell? What in all the hells ever created—

'Yes, it's me. Any problem?'

'She's here.'

'What?'

'She's *here*. Melanie Baines.'

'*Mel?*'

'Tom, she's in a state. She says she's pregnant.'

'No.'

'Yes!'

'Oh Christ. Oh Jesus, Jesus.'

'Can you get to Bridgend by ten fifteen? There's a through train to Didcot with a connection to Oxford which gets in just before one.'

'Er, ah…Yes, yes, I'll— Oh, bloody *hell*. When did she get there?'

'Not ten minutes ago. She went straight to the loo and she's still in there, throwing up. Look, we can talk later. If you miss that train I won't make the pre-Ofsted meeting, I can't leave Melanie on her own.' She rang off. The phone slipped out of his hand as he put it down and fell with a clatter onto the desk.

No. No, no, *no*. Shit, *shit*.

'Everything OK?' said Anthea, putting her head around the door. 'Oh lumme, it's not, is it?'

118

'Anthea, can I get a taxi quickly? I've got to be on the ten-fifteen train.'

She looked at her watch. 'Twenty-five to now... You won't get a taxi in the time, not a hope. Get your stuff, love, I'll run you to Bridgend. I'll see you in front of the house in five minutes.'

In the room, Dora's pyjamas were still lying on the floor. His shorts of last night were on top of them. As he shoved the shorts, the T-shirt, and his sponge bag into his overnight bag, that alarm clock of hers ticked the seconds away. But not so fast that he didn't have time to seize the pyjamas to his nose and take a deep, long draught of the smell of her. He should leave her a note, but he'd left all he had to write with in the meeting room. Could he search her stuff? Oh God, no time! He'd have to contact her later.

He glanced around the room as he let himself out. He would remember it. He would remember every last inch of this room.

He ran downstairs and out of the house and threw himself into the massive, dusty-looking Volvo estate, which already had its engine running. The car began to jolt up the narrow country road as he fastened his seatbelt and tried to catch his breath. For ten minutes or so he sat looking at his knees, aware out of the corner of his eye of fields and hedgerows slipping past, the occasional stunted tree blown sideways by the wind, and grey stone houses and farmsteads with slate roofs. No need to gaze out like a child on an outing, he would remember all this.

'Tom, there's generally a bloke or a girl on these workshops who I have to run to the station on the Sunday morning,' said Anthea as they turned onto the main Bridgend road. 'I'm going to the wedding of one guy next month. Funny old life, isn't it.'

'It is,' he whispered. He carried on staring at his knees for the rest of the journey. How in God's name could it have

119

happened, Mel had been on the Pill! Did her parents know? Christ, had her father thrown her out? No, he might be a prize bigot, but surely, surely, not even Gary Baines would do that.

He caught the train with three minutes to spare. As it pulled out of Bridgend station, the realisation hit him. The odd way Mel had sounded on the phone last Sunday: she must have known. There was no Dean Mills in the picture. She was sitting there in Costa Coffee with an egg he'd fertilised embedded inside her.

Oh Capella, Capella.

All the way back, he could see Dora's eyes, her great grey eyes, gazing at him.

Ten

When Tom let himself in, Tommy was hovering in the hallway. She dragged him into the kitchen and closed the door behind them.

'Where is she?' he said.

'Upstairs in your bed,' she whispered, fast and low. 'The poor kid was practically on her knees when she got here.'

'Look, is she sure she's pregnant? I mean, really sure?'

'A Boots test kit told her so last Sunday morning. Is that sure enough for you? Apparently she did the classic thing and missed a Pill. Too much on her mind after things re you and her blew up at school.'

Last Sunday morning. And then she went to Costa Coffee. Tom closed his eyes for a second. 'So she just… turned up?'

'The doorbell rang, and there she was. Hey, she's awake.' Tommy raised her eyes to the ceiling.

The flush was going upstairs. Had Mel heard him coming in? 'I'll go up to her,' he said. But before he'd reached the door, there was the sound of feet on stairs. Mel was coming down.

When Mel came in, it was Tommy who got to her first.

'Sick again, Melanie?' she said, putting an arm around the girl who seemed to fill the room, little scrap though she was.

Mel nodded. 'Yeah,' she murmured. 'You making me that toast was a waste of time. Sorry.' She wasn't looking at Tom. She was looking anywhere but at him.

'God, you poor thing,' said Tommy, hugging her.

It was time to start making a contribution. 'Hi Mel,' he said, trying not to croak.

'Hi Tom.' At last she looked at him, with eyes which seemed bigger than ever and blacker than black. But maybe that was because of the dark circles under them, like bruises. The T-shirt she was wearing – one of his – reached to her knees. Her hair, ruffled with lying on a pillow, stuck up here and there, as a child's would. Under that cap of black hair, her face looked chalk-white. A white mask with two black fires burning in it. Burning into him.

He had to hold that gaze. He couldn't let his own drop, not for a second, and especially not to her abdomen, but that didn't stop his field of view from being large enough to take in her bare feet with their bright red toenails.

Dora hadn't had red toenails. Dora's had been painted only by Nature, in Nature's gentle pink. Counter-intuitive, that. Hell, this wasn't the time to think of Dora.

'Right, I'll leave you to it, then,' said Tommy, giving him a look that said *Sort this out.* 'I hope this meeting at school doesn't go on too long, but don't expect me back before you see me.' She picked up her car keys from a dish with a grinning china toad perched on it and then she was gone, leaving – silence. And there he was, in the silence, with this girl and the thing she carried inside her.

Mel didn't move, she just stood there looking at him. Then she folded her arms as if hugging herself for warmth. 'I decided to give Gran's party a miss and come after all.'

'Good,' was all he could think of in reply.

'You didn't tell me your sister was a teacher too,' she went on.

'Didn't I? She's a good one. Six-year olds queue up to be taught about dinosaurs and dragonflies by her,' he said. 'Oh, Mel.' As he pulled her to him, for a second or so she seemed to resist. Then she let him take her in his arms and hold her, but it was like embracing a statue, rigid and unyielding.

He hadn't held fear in his arms before, not fear like this, but that's what this must be. She was frightened, just a very frightened little girl. Oh bloody, bloody hell. 'It'll be all right, Mel,' he murmured, 'it'll be all right.' It occurred to him that that was the second time in less than twelve hours he'd said something like that.

She looked up at him. There was something in her eyes, something hard to define. Challenge? No, not that, exactly. Appraisal?

'Do your parents know?' he said.

'God, no,' she said with a quick, bitter laugh.

'Do they know you're here?'

'I left them a note. I just said I wanted to see you. Poor old Gran, I've really fucked up her party. Right now they'll all be there, everybody talking over everybody else, wondering what the hell I think I'm up to. The noise in our house must be quite something. But that's what you get with Italian relatives.' Her voice dwindled down to a whispered squeak.

'Sit down, Mel,' he said, leading her to a chair. 'Can you face anything by way of lunch? Let me get you some soup or something.'

She shook her head, but she did allow him to sit her down. He sat down opposite her. Once again, he felt the force of those extraordinary eyes you only had to glance at to know half of Italy was in her genes. If she'd had ordinary eyes, ordinary bored and boring eyes, like any other teenager in the countless classes he'd taken, maybe neither of them would be

123

in this situation. And there wouldn't be a grey-eyed woman in Wales wondering where the hell he'd gone. Oh Jesus.

'I tried to tell you,' she said, beginning to play with the marmalade jar, twisting it this way and that. Tommy, understandably, hadn't had time to clear away the breakfast things. 'I tried to tell you last Sunday. I went to Costa because I didn't want anybody in the house hearing, but I sort of didn't want to be on my own. Then when I was in Costa I just couldn't get it out.' Again, her voice dwindled away.

She must be about two months gone. How big would it be by now? Her belly was still board-flat, but there was only one way to make things all right for her: get her to a doctor. And there wasn't all the time in the world to do it.

'So you were at a Buddhist workshop thing,' she went on.

'Because Tommy had to back out, that's all.'

'Sorry I got you away early.'

'Don't worry, you got me out of a session that was going to be unmitigated purgatory.' He tried to laugh, but the laugh wouldn't have been worth a C minus if he'd heard in it a Drama lesson.

'What about the friend you went with, though, weren't they a bit pissed off?'

'Friend'? What had Tommy said? That look was in Mel's eyes again. Was it challenge or appraisal, or both or neither? A faint jingle-jangling began to sound from the hallway: a mobile phone.

'Shit,' she said, putting a hand to her mouth. 'I thought I switched it off. Fuck, I'll leave it.'

'Mel, I think you'd better answer it. It might be your parents.'

She looked at him. 'Oh Christ,' she whispered.

He followed her out to the hallway. As she fished the phone out of the bag she'd left on the hall table, its bleep grew loud and peremptory. 'Yeah?' she said into it. Then, silently, *Oh shit*, as she listened to the voice at the other end.

124

'Look, will you stop shouting,' she said. 'I just wanted to see him, OK?' Then she screwed up her eyes and mouthed again, *Shit shit shit.* 'No, I'm not bloody pregnant!'

Then she held out the phone to him. 'He doesn't believe me and he wants to talk to you,' she said faintly.

Tom had Gary Baines' anger spearing into his eardrum almost before he'd put the phone to his ear. 'You're supposed to be fucking staying away from her!' yelled Baines. 'OK, you bloody get her back here now, because I want a word with you.'

Behind him, Mel began to groan. She flopped down on the stairs and put her head in her hands.

'She throwing up over you?' snarled Baines. ''cause she practically did over me yesterday. She's pregnant, isn't she.'

'Oh God,' moaned Mel, getting up quickly. 'I'm going to be sick.'

As she rushed upstairs, Tom said, 'Yes, she's pregnant. I'll bring her back, but not now. I'll bring her later, when she's in a fit state to travel.'

'You do that. We've got some sorting out to do, Sunshine.' He rang off, leaving Tom gazing at the scarlet fascia of Mel's mobile.

The first thing Dora saw was the silver-grey BMW parked next to the gate. She'd seen that slight dent above the rear bumper before. Steve was here.

Before she could put her key into the lock, the front door swung open, and there he was. 'You're back, then,' he said.

'Yes, I'm back.' She should have foreseen this, instead of spending the whole time on the train wondering why a man who'd been happy to miss breakfast for her had rushed off without a word.

'How was it?' he said.

'How was what?'

'The weekend, of course. This Buddhist seminar thing you've just come back from.'

'The Satori Centre? Oh, it had its moments. I'd better unpack. If I don't do it right now, my stuff'll fester for days.' She strove to keep her voice level as she made for the stairs.

'I'm collecting the overcoat,' he said, following her upstairs. 'I've got to pop over to Moscow on Tuesday to sort out a contract.'

'Oh? I thought Joe Drake did the Russian stuff these days.'

'Joe broke a leg skiing last week. Third bloody accident in five years.'

'Showing off to another girlfriend, was he? So how long will you be stuck in Moscow?'

'How long's a Russian piece of string, Pet?'

He wasn't here to talk about string, he was here to talk about her email, he must be. Christ, he had *got* the email? Surely the bloody server hadn't chosen Friday evening to play up again?

Steve held the bedroom door open for her. For a moment it looked as if he were going to pick her up and carry her across the threshold, but he didn't.

As she began pulling things out of her overnight bag, he moved across to the bed and sat down.

'I thought you took that overcoat with you,' she said.

'And have to rent the next door flat to accommodate it?' said Steve. 'It's in the loft – was in the loft. It's now in the back of my car in one of your spare tote bags. You seem to have a daffodil there.'

'Yes, so I do. They have a lot of them in Wales.' The daff had survived the journey well in one of the spare plastic bags she always carried, and with its stem wrapped in damp Kleenex. Why, *why* had Tom just vanished?

'You've haven't cracked that plastic bag thing yet, have you. There's a bloody great mountain of them in the cupboard under the stairs.'

126

'OK, I'll look out for a weekend course on giving up bag hoarding.'

Silence. One second, two, three. This was ridiculous, she had to say something. 'Steve—'

The phone on the landing began to ring.

'I'll get it,' said Steve, getting up.

'No, don't bother, I'll get it,' she said, trying not to gasp. Trying not to run as she went out of the room, trying not to snatch the phone out of the rest.

'*Yes?*'

'Hello Dozzaaa!'

'Hello, Jim,' she said, holding the receiver a little away from her ear. Her heart dropped out of her chest onto the floor. It lay there at her feet, shrivelling to the size of a walnut.

Down the phone came a muffled-sounding, 'All right, all right, haven't you got some reading practice to do before tomorrow?' and then Syd said, with a sigh, 'His latest thing, you'll be ecstatic to hear, is getting the number for me. Anyway, you're back. Good time?'

'So-so.'

'That bad?'

'Oh, it was all right. How was your weekend?'

His weekend hadn't been bad, it seemed. He'd had Tommy over for supper last night, to make up for having her weekend ruined, together with his new teaching-practice student and her boyfriend. What he was really phoning about turned out to be their mother's birthday next weekend. What were they going to do this year?

Bugger Mum's sodding birthday. She managed to cut the conversation short by offering to phone the manager of the care home to see if they could set up a lunch. Their mother was too far gone to take to a restaurant this year, not if they didn't want a repetition of last year's soup-throwing episode.

She put the receiver down. The answering machine

indicator was showing one message. She ran a finger around the keypad and looked at it. Dust.

There was a noise of throat being cleared. She looked up. Steve was hovering in the bedroom doorway with his arms folded. 'I spent quite a bit of time this weekend trying to get hold of you,' he said, gazing at the phone, not at her. 'When I got that email of yours, I decided, after a bit of cogitation, that I'd like a word. So I phoned here at eleven on Friday night, but you weren't answering. Then I remembered about this Welsh trip. I tried your mobile but you weren't answering that either. I bet you haven't charged it up again, have you.'

So he got the email. And that phone message was from him.

'So yesterday morning I phoned Syd, on the off chance he'd know the number, or at least the name, of the place you were staying at,' he went on, 'and you know what? I couldn't get through. I phoned Syd I don't know how many times yesterday and I couldn't fucking get through, one of the kids must have left the phone off the hook or something. I finally got through at ten o'clock this morning. By the way, I surfed the Internet on Saturday for – oh, just an hour or two – trying to track down likely looking Buddhist centres in Wales. Have you any idea how many Buddhist centres there are in Wales, Pet?' He took a step towards her. And another.

'Anyway,' he said, 'at ten this morning I got Jenny. We had a little chat – I am still her uncle – and then I said could I speak to Dad, because I wanted to find out where Auntie Dozza and Miss Ross were. And she said I'd got it wrong, it was Miss Ross's brother you'd gone with. It was Tom, not Tommy. Tommy was round at Dad's house last night. She did a bit of a giggle at that point, the scamp. There isn't anything going on with your brother and Tommy Ross, is there?'

'She is Jim's teacher, don't forget.'

'So? Anyway, Jenny said she'd fetch Dad in from the garden,

and I said don't bother him, on second thoughts it would wait till I saw you. So here I am, seeing you. You're not looking too well, Pet. What's the matter, getting a bug or something?'

She shook her head, held out her hands, then let them drop to her sides. 'I hope you found time over the weekend to ask Yvonne out.'

He was close enough by now to grab her arm. 'Would you like to tell me just what you think you're on about?'

'I'm sorry you spent all that time on me. I was hoping you were having a dirty weekend with Yvonne. Just as I was with Tommy's brother.'

He let her arm drop. 'Well,' he said, sounding winded. 'Well. Did you, er, enjoy it?'

'Yes, actually.'

'Yes, *actually*. Hm. Right, I suppose I'd better bugger off, then. I mean, he'll probably be coming round soon, won't he.'

He was down the stairs before she could think of a reply. After the front door slammed she stood for a moment watching the turbulent air he'd left behind him. It wouldn't settle.

She sat down on the top stair, shaking. She hugged herself, but the shaking wouldn't stop.

Tom shifted a few inches nearer the French windows he'd probably have been pushed through when he and Mel arrived just now, but for the fact that Baines the Builder had not long put them in. This was like a scene from a soap opera. Only he himself didn't seem to have any lines to speak, he was an actor reduced to the status of a spectator. But he had to find a role, and quickly, before the Baines family had the neighbours coming around to complain about the noise.

There were daffodils out there in the garden. A crowd of them, if not a host.

'She's not having it, she's getting rid of it, you fool,' said Jackie Baines to her husband.

'If she gets rid of it she's out of this house,' said Gary Baines, jabbing a thick finger at Mel.

'If she goes, I bloody go,' said Jackie, stepping between father and daughter.

'Oh yeah?' said Baines. 'Back to Mama Battaglia? After this one wrecked her party?'

'The only one who wrecked it was you!'

'You can't tell me what to do,' Mel spat at her father. 'Stop trying to run my fucking life.'

'I can tell somebody what to do, young lady,' said Baines, 'Just watch me.'

Baines turned. His jabbing finger turned with him, like a weathervane, until it was pointing at Tom. At his heart. 'She's having it and you're marrying her. I'm not having any grandchild of mine born outside wedlock. Oh, and if you don't marry her, I go to the police. It's not too late to get an investigation going, and boy oh boy is there hard evidence now.'

Wedlock. Did anyone still use that word? This man was telling him to marry Mel. To *marry* her...

'Oh God, you never give up, Gary, do you,' sighed Jackie. 'Look, that law can't touch him now she's eighteen.'

Those daffodils out there. Too dark to see how yellow they were... *Christ, man, concentrate!*

'Oh yes it can,' said Baines. 'She wasn't eighteen when she started telling us she was at Debbie Priday's when she wasn't.'

He was right. The Sexual Offences Act was like any other Act on the statute book: a crime once committed remains a crime.

'Shut up, shut up, both of you!' Mel screamed. 'It's not his!'

What?

'*Not* his?' said Baines. 'Then who bloody well is the father, then?'

'Oh, some guy.' She shrugged.

'Mel, love,' Jackie Baines began, sounding winded.

130

'Mel—' Tom tried, before Mel cut in.

'Look, I pulled a bloke from Brunel at New Year, OK? That party I went to with Debbie and her sister, I met him there.'

Gary Baines folded his arms and looked down at the floor. 'OK Mel,' he said, 'you bring this bloke from Brunel round here tomorrow night. And you' – he turned to Tom – 'can bugger off out of it. Looks like you're off the hook.'

'Right, Gary, that's enough,' said Jackie.

'Just as well it's not yours, isn't it,' said Baines, ignoring Jackie. There was a smirk playing about his lips.

There wasn't a word Tom could find to say. Mel was protecting him. She was so transparent he could cry.

'OK, Melly,' Baines went on, 'what's this Brunel guy's name, then?'

'I can't remember. He was just a bloke, for God's sake!'

'Come on, Mel, what do I say when he comes in the door, Hi Mick? Hi Joe? Hi—'

'Oh fuck it, I'm not listening to this,' said Mel. She was through the door before Tom had registered what she'd said. Seconds later the front door slammed.

Well. The next step was obvious. 'You'll have to excuse me,' he said, making for the door. 'I'm going after Mel.'

'Leave her,' said Jackie, planting herself in his way. 'She'll only be going round to Debbie's. Just leave her, OK? And Gary, get out of here.'

'Gladly, Jacks, I've got accounts waiting for me. I'll go and do them when he says he's the father and he's going to marry her.'

'Gary, go, will you? For Christ's sake just go and do your bloody accounts!'

Baines still didn't seem to think much of this suggestion, judging by the sneering smile he gave Jackie by way of response. Then he leaned a hand on the back of the huge new-looking cream leather sofa, and the smile faded. 'OK, I'll go.

You talk to him. Only by the time you've finished with him I want you to've planned the wedding, right down to the decorations on the cake. A registry office do, mind, I don't want her standing up in front of Father Finnegan in her state.' He brushed past Tom, knocking against his arm, and slammed out of the room.

The silence filling the room seemed hesitant, wary of taking over the space which Baines had vacated.

'Well, sit down then,' said Jackie at last, indicating with a jerk of her head one of the Brobdingnagian arm chairs that matched the sofa. 'I didn't get rid of Gary just so we could stand here staring at each other.'

As Tom lowered himself into the chair, it seemed to open a giant maw and engulf him. 'I'm sorry your mother's party was spoiled.'

'Huh, nothing fazes my mum, she's seen it all,' said Jackie, flopping onto the sofa. She grinned, but there was no mirth in her smile. 'Christ, I'm knackered. Mum's all right but I could've killed all the others. I've had Jackie-you-gotta-do-this and Jackie you-gotta-do-that, all bloody day. If I don't have a cigarette right now I'm done for. Still, I could hardly light up in front of my pregnant daughter, could I.' She reached for a pack of Lucky Strikes lying on a coffee table and shoved one in her mouth. 'I know you don't, so no point offering you one,' she said, flicking her lighter. She drew deeply on the cigarette, then leaned back and closed her eyes. '"Bloke from Brunel,"' she said, shaking her head. Then she looked straight at Tom. 'She's a good girl, my Mel, she sticks up for people she cares about.'

'I know she does.'

Her face didn't change. 'You know, you must be wondering,' she went on. 'I mean, why Mel didn't just see the doctor as soon as she knew.'

His stomach seemed to drop an inch or so. She'd seen inside his head and found a thought he'd been trying not to think since he and Mel left Oxford. 'She was frightened,' he began, 'she was confused—'

But Jackie didn't seem to be listening. 'I got rid of one Gary doesn't know about,' she said, her voice dropping low. 'It was when Mel was two. She'd have had a little brother or sister and I'd have had six kids, the oldest of them only eight, and I think I'd have killed myself. I had a coil put in after that. Gary doesn't know that, either. As far as he was concerned I'd had a bout of gastritis. You can fool Catholic men, but you've got to do it right. A clever girl like Mel would know not to pick a day like today to go rushing off to you.'

A clever girl like Mel. Yes, if girls like Mel have to deal with things, they deal with them cleverly. He shifted his weight from buttock to buttock, or tried to. Chairs like this weren't helpful. He should have stayed on his feet.

'How the hell I didn't guess she was pregnant I'll never know,' Jackie went on, blowing smoke at the ceiling. 'It must be like they say, you don't see what you don't want to see.' She took another drag on her cigarette.

Smoke drifted past Tom's nose. He couldn't, wouldn't, cough. He couldn't so much as let a nostril twitch.

'You know what I think?' said Jackie. 'I think there's a little bit of her that wants this baby. And I think she ran out just now because she couldn't face hearing you say you wouldn't marry her.'

He opened his mouth to say – what? Jackie didn't give him time to decide.

'She's been mooching around the place like death warmed up since you left,' she went on, 'I know she's been phoning you. I've been telling her it's no good, there's no future in it, but she won't bloody listen. I mean, it was a fling, wasn't it. You'd have been on to the next girl as soon as she was away at uni. I reckon a guy like you does a hell of a lot of "talking about books" with schoolgirls.' The irony she packed into those last words made his toes stab into the soles of his shoes.

133

'You're wrong, Jackie. I cared about Mel. I do care.' A vision of a grey-eyed woman floated into his mind. He suppressed it with all the force he could muster.

Jackie's eyebrows lifted. 'Do you? Really? OK, if you care about her, Mr Teacher, do her a big favour. Leave her.' She got up from the sofa and began to pace the room. 'Do like Gary said and bugger off back to Oxford. Go now, before she comes back. Get a new phone number, change your email address. Debbie and me, we'll get her over this. Gary won't push her out after I've marched her round to the doctor, not his little princess. And if he makes any more stupid noises about calling the police, I'll tell him I really will go back to Mum, that'll shut him up. We'll get by until Mel goes to uni, and maybe by next year, or the year after that, or the year after that, she'll have met somebody who's right for her, somebody her own age, and you'll just be – well, you can fill in the rest, you're the one who's good with words.'

As she finished, she came to a halt in the centre of the room, feet slightly apart, one arm across her middle like a barrier, the back of the hand serving as a prop for her other elbow. She held her cigarette up like a beacon. He gazed at its smoke spiralling lazily into the air, then turned away. There was something mesmerising about smoke, and he couldn't afford to be mesmerised.

Jackie was a good mother, the salt of the earth. There was nothing a good mother wouldn't do for her daughter, even cause pain if she had to.

He stood up, detaching himself from the chair's grasp. 'Debbie Priday's is first left and second right, isn't it,' he said, 'the house with the wishing well in the garden.'

'For Christ's sake, you're not going to talk to Mel yourself? Can't you see it'll be easier for me to handle her if you look like you're a bastard?'

'Bye, Jackie. I'll let myself out.'

'If you talk to her you're a bloody criminal, like Gary says,' she cried after him.

A criminal: so be it. But he was going to talk to Mel. And he knew, now, what he was going to say.

Debbie Priday, Mel's best friend, greeted Tom with an 'Oh my God.' But Mel wasn't there, nor did Debbie have any idea of where she might be.

'The park?' he said, looking over his shoulder at the dark expanse.

'What, at this time of night? No way,' she said, frowning.

'Sorry, I'm not thinking straight. I'll try her phone.'

He got a robotic voice telling him that the phone he was calling was switched off.

'Oh God,' said Debbie, her hand going up to her mouth.

'I'll find her, don't worry.'

'When you do, tell her to phone me,' Debbie called after him as he retreated down the garden path. 'I want to know she's all right.'

All right? She'd be all right. He'd make sure she was if it took all night.

It took half an hour of fast walking, half an hour of a street-by-street search which wouldn't have disgraced the Met, breath rasping in his throat, before he thought of it: his house, around the corner from hers. It was a million-to-one against. But that meant it wasn't impossible.

He redoubled his pace. By the time he reached his street he was sweating, and it was a chilly night. He saw her straight away. She was sitting on his doorstep blowing into her hands.

Oh. There he was. He'd taken his bloody time while she was parked here on his doorstep, her bum freezing to the concrete.

Right. The moment he says no wedding bells, say OK, you don't much want to either. Act cool. Act like somebody who pulls blokes from Brunel.

She didn't move as Tom came up the path towards her. She didn't even move when he stopped, a foot from her.

'Hi Mel,' he said. 'Did you come out without your jacket? You must be chilled to the bone.'

'Hi,' she said, trying to stop her teeth chattering. Cool was one thing, ice-cold was something else.

'Come inside,' he said. He held out a hand, but she shoved herself to her feet without taking it.

He unlocked the door and she followed him in. The house felt sad. There was a sort of dank, shut-up smell around the place and it was colder, if anything, in here than outside. If he was planning to tell her it was over, there couldn't be a better place or time. Funny: right now, she didn't feel remotely sick.

Envelopes were littering the doormat. He bent down and picked them up and started to flick through them. 'Looks like junk, mostly,' he said. 'Ah, here's one you'd think they might have remembered to re-direct: the phone bill.'

What was he doing, playing for time? He didn't really want to talk about his mail. Sure as hell she didn't.

He turned towards her. He dropped the post and put his hands on her arms. 'Mel, have the baby and marry me.'

What did he just say? For a moment she couldn't speak. She couldn't even breathe. Her heart was beating so fast she felt as if she might fall down. 'Yeah, OK,' she said. Somebody said it, anyway: somebody who sounded like a lot like her.

'"OK"?' he said. ' "OK" as in yes, you want to?'

Yes, I want to… No, don't say it, stay cool! "OK" as in sure, fine, it's a deal,' she said. She switched on a smile, left it in place for two seconds, then switched it off again. 'I've got to go, Mum'll be wondering where I am.'

'Wait a minute, Mel, we've got to make plans.'

136

'What, now? Can't we make plans next weekend or something? I've got double History first thing tomorrow and I haven't finished the essay yet. Mrs Burgess is going to kill me as it is.'

'Well…all right. Shall I come here, on Saturday, say?'

'No, I'll come there again. I don't mind the ride.'

She tried to stop him walking her back to her house – it was only round the corner, for goodness sake – but not only did he not listen, he insisted that she put his jacket on to walk back in. Somehow, she kept a flow of chat going about what a cow Mrs Burgess was, giving them all these history essays, and she wished now she'd done French as her third subject like Debs, it was a real doss by all accounts. Having a bloke's jacket round you, though, the smell of him next to you, it made it hard to stay cool. It was weird, it was sort of more like sleeping with him than sleeping with him was. Maybe it was like being married already?

She didn't let him walk her to the door, she handed him back his jacket at the gate. When he moved towards her to kiss her, she made sure it was her cheek his lips came into contact with. 'Cheers then, see you Saturday,' she said. She made herself walk up the path without looking back. He was watching her, though. She could feel his eyes on her back.

As she reached the door, it opened. Her parents were both standing there. She pushed past them saying, 'Don't start, I'm not in the mood, I'll talk to you tomorrow.' Before they could say anything, she ran up the stairs and into her room and shut the door behind her.

Her heart was still racing. Leaning against the door and taking a long, deep shaky breath didn't slow it down one bit. She took another breath, then she gave herself a shake, sat down at the desk, and switched on her computer. She had this bloody essay to do and she was going to do it if it took her all night. Well, she'd acted cool. She'd done brilliantly, if she said so herself.

She gazed at the screen as the computer powered itself up. Christ, she was having a baby. And she was getting married. To him. She shook her head again, but she couldn't take it in, she just couldn't. But whether she could or she couldn't, she had to get on with this sodding essay. She had to stop thinking about Tom and type something, anything.

Her fingers started attacking the keys. At two in the morning she switched off the computer and collapsed into bed with Bono. She was knackered enough that she should have fallen asleep straight away. She didn't, though. She lay there, wide awake, and her own words of earlier that evening were in her ears again: 'It's a deal.'

Well it was, wasn't it? Her dad couldn't contact the police now. She was keeping Tom out of jail. And she was getting… Hm. What was she getting, exactly?

She'd stayed cool, even after he'd asked her to marry him. Wasn't it funny that some little voice inside her told her to do that? A lot of girls would have caved in at that point. A lot of girls would have decided to stop wondering about who else he might have met and what was really going on inside his head.

That friend his sister'd said he'd gone to Wales with. It'd be nice to know if it was a man or a woman.

She sighed. She'd bet anything Tom wasn't lying in bed now wondering about the bloke from Brunel. He hadn't believed her for one minute. It was funny, though, she almost knew what this bloke looked like. What was his name? Not Mick, and not Joe. Sean, maybe. Yeah, Sean…

Well. If Tom did have somebody else, somebody he might be thinking of keeping going on the side, like Charles and Camilla, maybe she really did have that fling with Sean.

Eleven

Dora let her bag drop onto the floor. Another week in front of her. All over this building, there were people dropping bags on floors and thinking, *Another week*. It was a wonder the structure could stand the weight. She'd done it last night, she'd broken the thing that was herself and Steve. Why wasn't this floor collapsing in celebration? Why wasn't she lying in the basement in a heap of rubble?

What in hell was *that*.

She pulled off the postcard-sized card Sellotaped to the printer:

IN CASE OF FAILURE TO PRINT
SWITCH OFF AND THEN RESTART

Each letter of each word was formed in gold. Each gold letter had a multicoloured border: red followed by orange followed by yellow – the full rainbow, in fact. A marvel of precision, if you wanted to look at it from an artistic point of view. How in the name of God did it get here?

'That you, Dora?' came a call from the next office. Siobhan.

'Yes, it's me,' Dora called back.

'That bloke Larry Wise,' Siobhan began, as she appeared in the doorway. 'He was in here when I arrived just now. Have you seen your desk? And in particular, your keyboard?'

'No – oh, bloody hell!'

Days-old coffee. Smearing the keys, dripping down between them. Coffee over the desk, coffee all over the Post-It note pad. Her own coffee from Friday, which, thanks to Larry Wise, she hadn't had time either to finish or to throw out. There, in the middle of the mess, was the half-empty mug.

'He was standing right where you are,' Siobhan went on, 'and he was holding up your coffee mug like Indiana Jones checking over the treasure or something. Then he saw me. I suppose I must have given him a fright, because the next thing I knew was he'd spilled the damn thing. As you see. Before I could tell him to push off, he was out of the door like a frightened rabbit. I wiped the coffee up with some Kleenex – well, sort of wiped it. Dora, I know we're supposed to be nice to that man, but he's getting to be a bit of a nuisance, don't you think?'

'I'm not exactly encouraging him, Siobhan.'

'Well, OK, but I think we're going to have to do a bit of discouraging. I mean, frankly, he's starting to get on my tits. But my tits pale into insignificance beside the VC's. When Wise was buggering off he walked straight into Bryan, and you won't believe what Wise came out with. "I'm so sorry, did I hurt you?" ' She had his radio-announcer voice off to a T. 'Then he said – God – he said, "Is there a problem?" Dora, I couldn't look at Bryan's face, I just couldn't.'

'OK,' said Dora, dumping the stained Post-It note pad and the multi-coloured card in the bin, 'I'll go down and find him.' Of course, now she came to think of it, Larry Wise had offered to bring some card or other to remind her what to do if the printer played up again. She must have said yes when she was trying to get rid of him.

Well, he didn't pick the right morning.

It wasn't only the maintenance staff who had their headquarters in the basement. The Admissions Office was down there too. Tom was due to start temping for them today. It was all Dora could do not to push open doors as she passed and look in.

Not a sight nor a sound from him yet. Wales was broken too. Must be. She walked quickly on.

When she got to where she might have expected to see maintenance men hanging about, there was no-one. Not a single overall in sight. Damn. Still, here was a door marked 'Head of Maintenance'. It was ajar. She knocked, while at the same time pushing the door further open. No-one there. Bugger.

'Excuse me Miss, you looking for me?' came a voice from behind her.

She turned. A short, thickset balding man with a bushy grizzled beard was coming towards her, holding a mug in each hand.

'I was actually looking for Larry Wise,' she said.

'He'll be down in a minute to drink this,' he said, indicating the mug in his left hand with a jerk of his head. 'Is it about a job?'

'No, it's not about a job – well, in a way it is,' she backtracked. No need for him to know this visit was purely social.

'Oh?' he said, beginning to frown.

'Hang on, there he is.' She edged quickly around the man and made off the way she'd come, toward the figure who'd just lumbered into sight at the end of the corridor.

Before she'd covered half the distance between herself and Wise, he stopped dead. Evidently the sight of her was enough to root him to the spot, as well it might be. God, this was going to be embarrassing.

'M-miss Clayton,' he said when she was up with him. 'Good morning. I did visit your office but you were not there, I fear.'

'I overslept a bit. I've never liked Mondays.'

'Oh. Ah, I must, ah, apologise for a – a small accident.'

'I noticed. Don't bother apologizing, though. Accidents happen.'

'I – I would have mopped up the coffee,' he went on, 'but –'

'Never mind the coffee. Look, I, er, I don't think it's a good idea for you to hang around in my office when I'm not there, you know.'

He stared at her, frowning, but making no move to speak. Hadn't he understood? How much simpler could she make it, for God's sake?

'Larry, would you mind not coming up, at least for a while. We're busy at the moment.' Please get the message, please!

'Would I mind?' he said, at last, still staring at her. 'I – I… b-but on Friday y-you asked me to drop in.'

Did she? Shit. 'I shouldn't have. I wasn't thinking, I – I'd forgotten we had a lot on this week. So, as I said – ' Wait a minute. What was that sticking out of his chest pocket, her monkey pencil? It couldn't be, surely.

'What's that you've got in your pocket?' She strove to keep her voice level, but an edge must have crept into it, judging by how he was blenching.

'It's, it's…' he faltered.

'It's my pencil, isn't it. Give it to me. Please.'

'Oh, yes, I – I… ' His hand went into the pocket and brought out the pencil, and still his eyes didn't leave her face.

He held out the pencil. It was all she could do not to snatch it, which was probably why the pipe-cleaner monkey clinging to it fell off as she took it from him. She bent down to pick it up, and then she saw the state the monkey was in. Crushed

142

spider might come somewhere near it. A crushed spider in a red felt jacket and blue hat. 'Oh God, my nephew gave me that as a Christmas present!' she cried, before she could stop herself.

'It, er, fell off as I was moving the pen tub—'

'You were moving the pen tub?'

'I – I was moving it to a more convenient position. I tried to reattach the monkey, but… Please, Miss Clayton, I was not stealing the pencil, I took it away to mend. I have a special tool at home—'

'No, no. I'll mend it myself.'

'I – I'm so very sorry, Miss—'

'I'm going now, Larry. Please don't come to my office any more.'

At the end of the corridor, she tried not to look back as she turned the corner. But it was impossible to avoid seeing Larry Wise out of the corner of her eye. He was still standing where she'd left him. He was still looking at her.

Back at her desk, she stroked the battered monkey, which looked pretty well unmendable. She had a thick, clogged feeling in her throat. If she didn't know herself better, she'd say she was within an ace of crying. Everything was broken, everything.

Lunchtime. She could either sit here, staring at the space on her desk where a keyboard would be when the computer guys got around to supplying her with a replacement, or she could drag herself out. Oh God, she had to get out, maybe fresh air would help this throat of hers. Clogged it might have been earlier, now it was feeling as if a litre of quick-setting concrete had been poured down it.

On the way out of the building, Dora found herself keeping well in the outside lane as she turned corners. Better to see Larry Wise coming than run into him. Still, if she did see him coming, what then? This wasn't an environment where you

143

typically had much choice of route between points A and B. Oh, damn it, she was bound to see him haunting the place, she'd just have to ignore him. She'd handled him as well as anybody humanly could, surely?

The mouthful of cold air she took as she went out into the square rasped her throat and made her head ache. Now she was out, what was she going to do, just walk, put one foot in front of the other? She might as well do something constructive, like getting her mother's birthday present. It wouldn't jump at her out of a shop of its own accord.

She made her way into Little Clarendon Street. So, what was it going to be this year, the usual brightly coloured knickknack? Something which her mother could stare at bemusedly for a minute, then turn aside from?

Bright colours. Rainbow colours... *Do me one in all the colours of the rainbow. That* was what she'd said to Larry Wise on Friday. God, she'd been an idiot.

If she hadn't had Larry Wise in her head, if she hadn't been looking at the pavement for want of anything more enticing to look at, she might have noticed Tom before she did. As it was, she didn't register him until she heard, 'Dora.'

She jerked her head up, to see him practically within touching distance. He was with two women. 'Did you get my email this morning?' he said. He sounded, if not exactly breathless, then the next best thing.

'No,' she said, taking a step toward him – only one. 'But my keyboard's out of action.' *Damn Larry Wise!*

'Oh.' He was biting his lip. Then he blinked, and cleared his throat. 'Do you know Christine and Jodie?' he said, indicating the women. 'We're just going to have lunch in the Duke of Cambridge.'

'Hi,' said Dora.

'We've got to tell Tom who to look out for,' said the younger, blonder woman, giggling.

'Yeah,' said the other one. 'The boss, for a start.'

'Now now, Rose Jenkins is *lovely*,' said the blonde, rolling her eyes.

'Glad to hear it,' said Dora. 'Right, fine, enjoy. Well, must dash, shopping to do. I'll give those computer guys an earful when I get back, Tom. How they expect people to function beats me.'

'Bye, Dora,' he said as she moved away. She had her back to him by the time he was saying, 'I'll catch up with you later, OK?'

'OK,' she called over her shoulder, without turning her head more than she could help.

She walked down Little Clarendon Street towards Walton Street. This was the way she'd already come, not the way she'd intended to go, but bugger the way she'd intended.

Tom didn't look very happy, even by his standards. It didn't look as if he'd had to rush away yesterday just because there was a spider in his sister's bath. Anyway, Tommy liked spiders. You had to if you were going to be a successful primary school teacher. Actually, it looked rather as if the Angel Gabriel was back up on that cross. Wales must be very broken indeed.

She turned into Walton Street and kept walking, then realised she was still wearing her social smile. A giggle bubbled its way out of her. A man who was passing gave her a startled glance. She walked on, faster.

She'd said 'enjoy' just now. She never said 'enjoy'.

Outside the newsagent near Worcester College there was a pram, a black pram of the old coach-built type that used to be pushed by nannies in parks with fountains and herbaceous borders. A line of blue and pink plastic ducks was strung across the hood opening.

A few yards further on, she stopped.

Go on. Have a look.

But it'll be empty. Little Johnny will be in the shop with his mother. All right, look at the imprint of the head on the mattress. Go on, make a bad thing worse. You know you want to.

So much was broken, all she could do now was make a bad thing worse.

The pram wasn't empty. A clenched fist was resting on the quilt.

So Mummy took a chance. Only going into the shop for a minute, couldn't face waking you. You and she have been up all night, and she's at screaming point. Still, not even I would ever have left you. Not even I.

The pram looked shabby at close quarters and smelled a bit of ancient baby sick.

A woman came out of the shop. No, not a woman, a girl, but a girl with a grey, opaque complexion and badly cut bleached hair. She had a cigarette in her mouth. She stared at Dora. There was not a flicker of expression in her eyes. She took hold of the handle of the pram, kicked the brake to release it, and trudged off up the street.

The girl hadn't got any sort of bag with her except a tiny pink plastic shoulder bag, hardly larger than a purse. She must have gone in for something small: a packet of cigarettes, maybe. Did she risk her baby for a smoke? Or was she gambling her last few pence on a lottery ticket because that was the only way she could give her baby a decent start in life?

The sun came out from behind a cloud. It took aim at Dora's eyes, drilling her headache an inch further into her skull. By the time she was half way along Beaumont Street, the pavement seemed to be rising up to meet her. She'd have to take the quick way back along St John Street, otherwise at this rate she'd be crawling into the office on her hands and knees.

Fifteen minutes later she was slumped in front of the screen; the computer guys had brought a new keyboard while she was out. Which meant she now had Tom's email in front of her, drifting in and out of focus.

'God, you look awful,' said Susie, coming in brandishing yet another Primark bag. 'Go home.'

'Siobhan wants these revisions done by five.'

'I'll do them. I'm not particularly pushed this afternoon.'

Dora swallowed. Her throat now felt as if it was being scoured with heavy-duty sandpaper. 'OK, thanks, I'll go, then.' But not before dealing with Tom's email.

'Dora, can I see you? Are you free for lunch?' it said. It had come in at 9.29. Tom must have sent it as soon as they'd shown him to a desk. If his boss was as bad as his two office chums were making her out to be, that would have taken guts.

She typed: 'Bit late to say yes now. Actually, I'm feeling like shit and I'm going home. Must have caught a bug. Hope you don't go down with it.'

She was on the verge of pressing 'send', and then she went back to the text and deleted the last sentence. Too much something or other... Intimacy? Yes, more intimacy than the current situation required, she wouldn't mind betting.

On the bus, she slipped into a doze and almost missed her stop. When she got home, it was all she could do not to go straight to her bedroom and collapse on the bed. But she never went to bed without looking in on Jo.

She pushed open the door on a room that was smaller, distinctly smaller, than it had been last night. Why was it shrinking? If it carried on like this she could put it in a shoebox, the shoebox she'd mentioned to Tom. It looked as if she'd have to find that shoebox.

Oh Christ, wasn't she jumping to conclusions? There might have been any number of reasons why he had to leave yesterday morning – his favourite great aunt might have keeled over, or something. He couldn't have guessed this room existed. He'd have left it until she showed him in before withdrawing the offer.

That's all it would have taken for him to back off, though. Just one glimpse of this room.

'Well, Josey,' she said, taking the tin out of the cot. 'Here's a nice kettle of fish. Hang on, I think kettles of fish are pretty rather than nice, aren't they.'

No answer. She wasn't getting much feedback from Jo these days.

What happened in Wales? Was it just a classic case of one thing leading to another? It had worked, she'd enjoyed it. Enough to want more of it. At the risk of complicating the issue. And of coming out with weird stuff about Capella. Why on earth did she say 'for Capella's sake don't stop?' Maybe she should have asked him.

She cradled the tin in her arms and pressed her back against the wall, but the action did nothing to numb the sudden grinding ache around the spot where the epidural went in. Aching throat, aching head, aching back. Aching self: heart and body. Her soul would be aching if she had one.

Steve wouldn't have left for Moscow yet. What if she phoned him...

No. She'd done well, breaking all that. She mustn't spoil things by trying to mend it.

Her gaze began to travel around the room. The spacemen wallpaper, the glow stars on the ceiling, the paintwork in the colour of a summer sky at twilight: this would all have to go. Strangers would redecorate this room. Strangers would kill it.

No, no, what was she thinking of? There was only one person who should kill this room. She'd killed the one it had been for; it stood to reason she must be the one to kill the room. Only she could paint these walls, this ceiling, and she'd have to do so before any prospective buyer set foot in this house. What colour would she paint them? Black, of course, what else.

She kissed the tin and put it back in the cot. Only one thing to do now. She pushed the start button of the mobile, and the sun and the moon and the stars and the planets began their revolutions.

'How I wonder what you are,' they sang. Particularly inquisitive-sounding today.

Do you wonder? Think harder, then. I'm not that difficult to read, surely.

She tiptoed out, and just made it to her bed before her legs gave way.

After Laurence had finished the washing up, he went into the dining room. So rarely used these days; only on Mother's birthday and at Christmas. Now, the table could revert to what it customarily was: a display surface for the battle of Trafalgar. One by one, he took the ships out of the cupboard he'd built for the purpose of storing them, and arranged them in the battle formation that their namesakes had taken up on the morning of October the twenty-first, 1805 – all but the *Principe de Asturias*, still in pieces on his work table upstairs. When the ships were all in place, two British divisions bearing down on a Franco-Spanish fleet, which in a few hours would cease to exist, Laurence stood back and surveyed the scene. There was the *Redoubtable*, waiting to lay about the *Victory*, there the *Victory* herself…

Laurence picked up the French commander-in-chief's flagship, the *Bucentaure*, and brought her to his near point of vision. Such clean elegant lines; the most beautiful ship in the French navy. He had modelled her perfectly, if he said so himself. But so fragile, in the thinnest plywood… With one squeeze of his fingers he could reduce this model to the shattered, dismasted state to which hours of fighting had brought the real *Bucentaure* two hundred years ago. With two squeezes, and a hurl onto the floor for good measure, he could replicate quite faithfully the total destruction of the ship in the storm that followed the battle. Why not do so? In fact why not render each and every ship as she was four days after the battle, when the gale had finally abated? That would be as

149

authentic a depiction of an iconic engagement as the proud display on the table before him. Why not do so now?

Laurence's hand shook. His breath came hot and fast. He murmured, 'No, no,' and with fingers that still trembled, replaced the *Bucentaure* at the midpoint of the Combined Fleet's line. Still breathing hard, he left the dining room and shut the door firmly behind him. He stood, eyes tight shut, in the hallway, and counted *one, two, three, four…*

On seven, he heard, 'Laurence?'

He opened his eyes and went into the sitting room. Mother was putting down her book. 'Yes, Mother? Is there something I can get for you?'

'No, Laurence, I just wanted to say I rather think I will have an early night, I'm feeling a little weary… You seem at a loss this evening, dear. No modelling?'

Laurence's attention was taken for a moment by the fire, the steadily flickering but ever-changing flames. How could people immolate themselves? It would be such a painful death. Drowning would be infinitely preferable.

'No, no modelling this evening, Mother, I – I find I'm not inclined. I think I will take a short walk, the fresh air might clear my head.'

'Oh? The wind is getting up.'

'Not much, surely. Good night, Mother.' He left the room quickly, before she could see that he was weeping.

Twelve

The doorbell made Dora jump. It would be Syd with the shopping. Syd: just now, the one person on earth she'd get out of this chair for and drag herself to the door.

But it wasn't. And her first, unutterably silly, thought was how horrible she must look, with her red nose, red eyes, wan face and mouth open with the shock of seeing who actually was standing on the doorstep.

'Hello,' said Tom, putting the bulging carrier bags down at her feet. 'I think it's all here, except that Sainsbury's didn't have Original Extra Strong Fisherman's Friends, so I got Honey and Lemon Lockets instead. They always hit the spot for me.'

'Do they,' she managed to say. 'Well, I'll give them a try. You don't seem to be Syd, by the way. Has he been waylaid by a gang of pushy parents since he phoned me this lunchtime?'

'No, by the police. Drugs in the boys' changing room this afternoon, and his star pupil caught red-handed. So Syd phoned Tommy—'

'And helpful Tom, who knows his way around Sainsbury's, offered to go instead and let Tommy get on with preparing tomorrow's lessons.'

151

Staring at one another, while lips moved. And somehow the lips were even speaking sensible words.

'Well, come in, come in, but don't stand too close or you'll be sniffling by tomorrow.'

He came in. He put down the Sainsbury's bags and closed the door. For a moment, he looked as though the one thing he wanted was to be sniffling by tomorrow, but before she had a chance to ask herself how far she was going to sidestep him, he picked up the bags again. 'Where do you want these put?'

'In here,' she said, leading the way to the kitchen.

'How are you?'

'How am I? Well, after a day of what you might call pampering myself I suppose I should say, not so bad. That's what people say, isn't it. "Not so bad, considering."' She pushed open the kitchen door. 'Considering what, I always wonder.'

She put the kitchen table between her and him before she turned to face him. 'You've got something you want to say to Auntie Dozza, haven't you.'

He dumped the bags on the table, took a large bunch of green grapes out of one of them, and pushed it towards her. She pulled off one of the grapes and put it in her mouth. She swallowed the grape quickly, in case what he was going to say made her choke.

She was wise.

'Dora, I'm afraid I can't move in after all. I'm getting married.'

'Oh. Are you? Right, well, what people normally say now is congratulations, when's the big day,' she said, groping for a chair. 'I, on the other hand—'

'Would like to tell me to get lost,' he said, taking another chair and sitting down as slowly as if he'd aged fifty years. From the way he was looking, that was how he felt. But how much worse must she be looking than she was a minute ago?

'Hold your horses, don't you know yet who you're dealing

152

with here? What I was going to say was, I want details. Times, places, names, what he said to her, what she said to him, that sort of thing. So get going.'

He took a deep breath. 'All right, I'll start at the beginning.'

While he talked, Dora's hand moved grapes to her mouth. What she learned was that a bright girl called Melanie Baines, daughter of a pugnacious father and a fiercely protective mother, had had an interesting autumn term, but she now had rather more in her timetable for the coming months than getting through her A-levels. She also learned that the head of Tom's old school was a very fast thinker.

'I care about Mel,' he said finally, 'but the idea of actually *marrying* her, and of being a father… Oh God, I wouldn't have been ready for all that even if I'd never met you.' He spread his hands wide, and shook his head. Then he rested his elbows on the table and leaned towards her. 'But I have met you, and I care about you, too, enough to have made you an offer. And now I can't follow through on it.'

The way he looked at her then, like a man on the rack, it was all she could do not to reach across the table and take his hand. But Auntie Dozza couldn't kiss this pain better. If she tried, she'd make it a whole lot worse. For both of them.

'Well, I'm relieved you thought Melanie'd dumped you,' she said. 'I've got strict moral standards, you know. It's all right for me to go behind a husband's back, but not for you to cheat on a young girl.'

'I know it isn't,' he said. 'I've got standards too.' He carried on looking at her, pulling off a grape and putting it in his mouth. 'I missed out one detail, which might interest you. The night David Dent phoned me, he'd not long come back from checking whether his mother's new carer had got her ready for the night. He'd found his mother sitting on the stairs and the carer vanished. He wasn't pleased.'

'Poor old thing. The mother, I mean.'

'Quite.'

'What sort of leaving present did they give you?'

'Leaving present?' He blinked, then gave her a sad sort of smile that emphasised lines of weariness etched in around his eyes that hadn't been there on Sunday morning. The Angel Gabriel could do with a sabbatical in Eden.

Hm. Come to think of it, Eden might have a lot going for it just now. How many Air Miles did she have saved up?

'It was Shakespeare, the complete works,' he said. 'I have three complete works already, with annotations by me in the margins. I offered it to Mel. She said she couldn't face having it in the house, so I took it to Oxfam.'

As he was speaking, a sneeze gathered itself together in her nose. She pulled the Kleenex out of her dressing gown pocket just in time. Soon, very soon, she was going to have to find a flat surface and lie down on it. 'You know, I'm sitting here thinking Melanie Baines is a good name for someone who might get a decent degree and go into broadcasting, say. "And now we go over to Washington to join Melanie Baines for an update on how the voting stands in the Presidential election." Sounds good, doesn't it.'

'She'll be staying on track for university,' he said, 'make no mistake.'

'And if you have to be a hands-on parent who does a bit of temping in odd moments, so be it?'

He didn't reply straight away. 'If that's what it takes,' he said at last.

Brave words, but he had no idea what he was in for, who ever does… Wait a minute. There couldn't be a better time than now to let him see the room. 'Come upstairs for a minute, Tom,' she said, pushing herself slowly to her feet.

His eyes widened.

'Don't worry, I'm not going back on what I said just now about morality. I want to show you something, and I guarantee it's relevant to the matter in hand.'

She led him up the stairs in silence. When she opened the door of Jo's room he began to go in, then stopped in his tracks. She watched as he swung his gaze over the space rocket rug, the little-green-man-from-Mars clock, all the furry creatures, the bright-painted furniture, the spacemen wallpaper, the glow stars on the ceiling, and the sun and the moon and the stars and the planets dangling over the cot.

He came to the tin last. He looked down at it without blinking. His face was wiped clean of all expression.

She pushed the start button of the mobile. As it began to revolve to its tinkly, twinkly tune, Tom's face didn't change. It still hadn't changed by the time the music finished and the mobile had come to a stop.

'Have a go?' she offered.

He looked at her. 'I can't, sorry,' he whispered, shaking his head.

Ah well. She pushed the button again.

'Only Syd and Steve know about this room,' she said, as the sun and the moon and the stars and the planets smiled and twinkled on their way. 'When anybody like Tommy drops in, or Jim and Jenny – especially Jim and Jenny – I lock the door and hang Steve's old notice on it. It says "Steve's den, trespassers will be persecuted" – that's what the room once was, you see. Have you ever heard anything so naff?'

'Never.' He sounded hoarse. Well, he'd been doing a lot of talking.

'So, Melanie Baines,' she said. 'She's a bright girl, you say. She evidently cares about you, judging by that bloke-from-Brunel story. Is she pretty? Sorry, I'm going to have to do something about this insatiable need for particulars one of these days.'

'She's a lovely girl in every way,' he said, sounding even more hoarse. He seemed to be addressing not her but the green and grinning Thing from Outer Space that was hanging at the foot of the cot. 'Actually, she looks a bit like you.'

155

You don't say. 'Fine, I'm glad to know that. Well, now you know why I thought you should see the house first. Just as well Plan C's off, you'd have been terrified. Just how crazy must I be, for God's sake.'

He lifted his hands a few inches, in what might have been a gesture of incomprehension and despair if he'd gone so far as to raise them to a respectable height, but he dropped them again. Maybe he was too tired to lift them any higher.

Go on, tell me Plan C wouldn't have been off. Tell me.

'I don't know about "terrified",' he said. 'Once I'd got over the shock, I... Oh, for God's sake, Dora, I'd have tried, I really think I would.'

The mobile seemed to be moving again. The sun and moon and co weren't revolving though, they were swaying. She grabbed the side of the cot. 'Tom, I think I'm going to have to lie down now.' The cot didn't seem to be helping. In fact it seemed to be swaying too.

He put an arm around her and helped her into her bedroom. Without letting go of her, he pulled back the duvet and shovelled her into bed. He kissed her – on the cheek: the sort of kiss a friend gives a friend when they're saying goodbye. 'Sleep, Dora,' he said. Then he went out of the room.

She dropped into a doze, deep enough for her head to fill with suspended figures she half-recognised but couldn't put names to, twisting and turning like corpses on gibbets in time to some music she couldn't place. But the doze wasn't deep enough to blot out the noise of a car starting somewhere down the street. She woke suddenly, with the irrevocably wide-awake feeling that meant she had several hours in front of her of staring at the ceiling. Getting up had to be better, even if she had to crawl around on her hands and knees.

She staggered downstairs. The kitchen clock told her she'd actually slept for a couple of hours. The table was covered with unpacked shopping and there was a note propped up next to a

156

can of chicken soup: 'I wasn't sure where to put the non-perishables, but everything else is in the fridge. I've thrown out the yoghurts at the back of the top shelf, by the way. They were five weeks past their use-by date.' He'd written the note on one of her hoard of junk-mail envelopes.

You see, Steve? They do have a use.

He'd be in Moscow by now. Let the hotel be not too awful this time.

The can of chicken soup was standing next to another can of chicken soup. Behind them, like children in a school crocodile, were more cans standing next to cans: lentil, mushroom, minestrone.

No tomato. Had he guessed she couldn't have faced tomato?

Next to the soups were three boxes of Kleenex, and next to the Kleenex were two packs of the Honey and Lemon Lockets that always hit the spot for him, a large box of maximum strength Lemsip, a bottle of Olbas oil, and a Vick's nasal spray. Next to the cold cures were four large bottles of fizzy water and two still.

Next to the water was a large bottle of Lucozade. And another note: 'You didn't put this on the list but I wondered if you might like it.'

She reached into the dishwasher for a clean tumbler and poured a couple of inches of Lucozade into it. She took a sip of the sweet-tart liquid, letting the bubbles tickle her nose. When did she last drink this? It must have been when she was eight years old and catching things like chicken pox and German measles.

Eight years old. What if she could go back there and start again? No, no, by eight the damage had been well and truly done. She was already on track to here.

She took another mouthful. Eight: wasn't it then when it first began to dawn on her that it was Syd that her father expected to like science at school, not her?

157

She poured the rest of the Lucozade into the sink. No thanks, Tom. She stood for a moment, looking at the drink draining down the plughole. Tom hadn't said he was sorry about Wales. And he hadn't put 'See you around' on either of his notes. She'd never have spoken to him again if he had. But what now for her, though?

The empty plughole stared up at her.

'Look, Tommy, for God's sake let's have a truce,' said Tom.

Tommy looked up from her marking. 'All right, if I promise to stop asking you how long you honestly think it's going to last, will you promise to talk to Melanie?'

'You know I'm going to. I'm seeing her on Saturday.' He tried to keep his voice level, but a sharper edge than might be helpful came cutting through. To give Tommy her due, though, she didn't respond with anything more combative than a sigh.

'I mean really talk to her,' she said. 'Make the poor girl believe you're not marrying her just because of the baby.'

But he was, wasn't he. The baby was what it was about, Mel's wanting the baby. But from Mel's point of view he hadn't exactly rushed to propose last Sunday. No wonder she'd reacted the way she had, he couldn't fool himself otherwise. He had to try to repair the situation on Saturday, but how?

'I'm going out for a walk,' he said.

'One of your long ones? If so, don't forget your key this time.'

'I'll be back well before you lock up. I just want some air, that's all.'

He let himself out of the house, into the welcoming darkness. At the gate, he paused. Which way? Left, toward the river, the way he'd gone last night? Or right, toward Woodstock Road – toward Dora's? What about that old boyhood trick of his, letting Capella decide? If Capella were visible, he'd turn right. If Capella were not visible, he'd turn left.

He looked up. The sky had been half-covered with cloud when he came in from work, and there were still a few dense pockets of blackness here and there, but Capella wasn't obscured. She shone clear and bright. He took a long breath, pulled his jacket collar up, and started walking. Toward Dora's. But not *to* Dora's. He couldn't allow himself, not even on the pretext of seeing how she was.

'Almost over it,' according to Dora's office-mate this morning when he phoned, not knowing if he'd find Dora there, not knowing what he'd say if he did, just wanting to make some slight amount of contact.

When he reached the end of Dora's street, he stopped. From here her house was visible, the house he'd intuitively known was hers when he walked this way ten days ago. All the windows were dark, except for one upstairs directly over the front door. It was the window of the room she'd taken him into. That room which was still – *still* – her daughter's… How would he have coped with that if he'd moved in? Would he have been able to let it – and her – be? Or better, would he have helped her at last to deal with what had happened? He'd never know now. The thoughts were heavy in him, like lead.

As it was, what would happen if she really did have to sell up? Would it be a question of how fast she disintegrated, rather than whether?

Wait a minute. There was a man right outside her house, a man who seemed to be looking up at that window. A prowler? Or her husband, perhaps, tired of being cooped up in a small flat in Summertown? In which case why wasn't he going in? Or had he just been in, or tried to get in and she hadn't heard him? If she were in that room, she wouldn't hear a bomb going off.

He couldn't walk on, not while the man was there, whoever

he was. If he were careful, and stayed on the opposite side of the street and kept to the dark patches between the lamp posts, he could get a better look at this man. Not that the man showed any sign of noticing him, or anyone or anything, for that matter. He was just standing there, not moving, shoulders bowed.

After two or maybe three minutes the man's shoulders lifted, then sank down again, as if he'd heaved a sigh. Then he turned, and moved off up the street in the direction from which Tom had just come. Tom took a step or two back into the shadows, until he was brushing what felt like a thick hedge, and waited until the man had gone past.

There was something about the way the man was walking. He was going slowly, almost dragging his feet, as if every step he took was painful. In fact there was something about the man himself. He seemed sad, the embodiment of sadness.

Tom began walking the way the man was going. It suddenly seemed important to keep the man in view. If that were her husband, one thing was clear. He wasn't needing a little push to leave her, as she'd said on Saturday night, he was needing a mighty big shove.

The man walked toward the bridge over the railway line. Tom let the man get to the middle of the bridge before he stepped onto it himself, but then he hung back. The man had stopped and was looking down. Judging from the faint noise to the south, a train had not long left Oxford station.

The man continued looking down until the train had shot away up the line. He must have a good head. Up there on that narrow footbridge it was difficult not to feel a little dizzy as you looked down onto the line of rushing carriages under your feet.

Or maybe he was too sad to care. What if he'd tried to throw himself off in front of that train? Tom would never have got to him in time. Anyway, the man was much taller and broader than he was. He'd have had him over the railing and onto the line as well if he'd tried to restrain him.

The man walked on. Tom kept pace, twenty or so yards behind.

Outside each of the pubs in the middle of Wolvercote, the man stopped. For a moment or so it looked as if he might be going in, and then he moved off again.

And then there wasn't anything much ahead except the Trout, and the river.

Christ. The weir.

Tom walked faster, shortening the distance between himself and the man. Not once did the man look back. Tom might well have been dogging his heels and not been noticed, the man was sunk so deep inside himself.

The man shuffled up to the door of the Trout just as it opened from inside. Two young women came out, talking and laughing. The man bumped against one of the women. Tom couldn't see whose fault it was, but it wasn't hard to detect from the woman's body language that she thought she'd run up against some sort of dirty old man, in the literal as well as the figurative sense.

'I'm so sorry, did I hurt you?' said the man in a cultured, academic-sounding voice. But the women were already moving off, not responding.

The man didn't go into the pub; he plodded away again, head down. He brushed against Tom in passing but showed no awareness that he'd done so. He was wearing a rough and rather battered donkey-style jacket, but it didn't have that neglected, stale smell you associated with sad men. His hair, though: the style was bizarre, as if a blindfolded barber had hacked around a bowl with a pair of kitchen scissors.

Tom watched the man walk back toward the road. If the man turned left, toward the river, he was going straight into the pub to raise the alarm.

161

But the man didn't turn toward the river, he began to trudge back the way he'd come. Tom followed him. He followed him back over the railway line, on to Woodstock Road, and down the road into the depths of the academic ghetto. He followed him along one of the roads linking with Banbury Road, across Banbury Road, and into a road where surely every house was occupied by a professor.

The man turned in at a gate about half way along the road. As he went up the path, he fumbled in a pocket of his jacket. He let himself in and closed the door behind him without looking back, as if the one thing he needed now was to shut the world out.

And this man had been outside Dora's house. Well, he wasn't her husband. She'd said Steve Mitchell had played various sports for Durham University, but the man who'd gone into that mansion had surely never played team games in his life.

Tom stood looking at the massive house with its pinnacles and gables until it occurred to him that anybody seeing him might take him for a prowler. Did he have enough change in his pockets for a bus? A ride was going to be essential if he stood any chance of getting back before Tommy's usual locking-and-bolting time.

As he found a seat near the back of the bus, something started to shift in his brain, some memory struggling to take shape. Before the bus reached the next stop, he'd got it. Terrible hair, cut-glass accent: the man he'd trailed wasn't an Oxford University professor, he was surely the maintenance man from work whom Dora had mentioned over the washing-up last Friday. 'Strange,' she'd said. She'd have said a bit more if she'd known he was watching her house after dark. But unless he himself had lost all ability to judge character, that man wouldn't harm a fly. He was the one who was harmed.

Was he a fellow walker-by-night, this man? He could certainly put the miles in. If Tom saw the man again, maybe he ought to break his long-standing rule and say hello.

As Tom lay waiting for sleep that night, the question of what a husband was, exactly, seemed as unanswerable as ever. He knew what a friend was, he knew what a lover was, but a husband? Was there something extra, some elusive magic ingredient?

As regards the baby, it was pretty clear what the extra ingredient was: genes. Being a teacher was one thing, being a friendly older presence was something similar, but giving your own flesh a separate existence was another thing altogether. It made him feel vertiginous, as if he were looking down from that railway bridge earlier. It might actually be easier if this baby were some other man's.

Mel was as close in age to the baby as to him. She had a lot of growing up to do. Tommy thought it wouldn't last. In five years or so, an older Mel – a Mel who wanted to go into broadcasting, say – might be the one to prove her right.

He gave a long, weary sigh and flicked on the bedside light. Right now, falling asleep seemed as likely as flying out of the window and off into the night, like Peter Pan. Oh shit, maybe he *was* Peter Pan, the boy who couldn't and wouldn't grow up. What would Dora say if he asked her?

Dora, Dora... What now? He couldn't just leave things as they were. He couldn't just leave *her*. Could she and he be friends, could they manage that? The test might be whether he could introduce Mel to her without either her or him batting an eyelid. Oh hell, what a thought! He had to get up, he couldn't lie here with that image in his mind.

He swung himself out of bed, went to the window, and drew back the curtains. Capella, very bright, shone directly in at him. She shed not light but the blackest, deepest darkness.

163

Thirteen

Dora pressed the start button of the lavatory drier again and gave herself another blast of warm air. This hadn't been a clever idea, coming to the pub after the first day back at work. Even though it was Friday. Better to have stayed home. A minute out of that room was a minute wasted.

It would have to happen soon, the death of that room. What if she just put the house on the market before Steve got back?

No email from him. Not even a message saying he'd got to Moscow. That was surprising. Even considering. But it was all the more reason, wasn't it? To get on with selling the house?

As she threaded her way back through the long riverside lounge, she saw him standing by the bar: Larry Wise. Please, *no*.

She kept her head down as she went back to the table. At least her seat had its back to the bar, so with any luck he wouldn't spot her.

But she hadn't been the only one to spot Larry Wise. She'd only just sat down when Tommy said, 'That guy's never going to get served. He's just standing there letting everybody barge past him.'

'What guy?' said Syd.

'The one over there with the hair. He came in a few minutes ago, when Dora was in the loo.'

'Maybe he's not as rude as the people shoving past him,' said Tom, taking a sip of his beer.

She'd only dragged herself out tonight because Tom was going to be here. To prove to herself she could say 'Hi' and just chat, as if he were anybody.

Pity he hadn't been able to bring himself to have a go with the sun and the moon and the stars and the planets the other night, though. It might have helped. Then again, would it?

He was looking over her shoulder. He must be looking straight at Larry Wise. 'He's a maintenance man at the office, isn't he, Dora?' he said.

'I think so.' She gave him a look, which she hoped said *change the subject.*

'Oh, really?' said Tommy.

'Well, you wouldn't have taken him for an investment banker, would you?' murmured Syd. 'So, any ideas yet on what you're going to be doing in the longer term, Tom?' he went on.

'*Not* temping, I hope,' said Tommy, looking at her brother. 'If only, if only, Tom could go back to teaching.'

'Please, Tommy, not again,' muttered Tom.

'Well, I can't help thinking of that maternity leave fill-in job Syd was talking about the other day, it would be tailor-made for you.'

"What fill-in job?' said Dora.

'Linda Mason, our Head of English, is going on maternity leave at the end of term,' said Syd. The way he looked at her spoke volumes: *sorry about all this baby talk.*

It's all right, Syd. I can cope. I love babies, bring them on in their squillions.

'Might I ask what you recommend?' came a thirties radio-announcer voice, cutting through the burr of all the other voices in here. Larry Wise must have caught a barman's eye, and from the sound of him he couldn't be more than a couple of yards away. She hunched down lower over her glass of orange juice. The barman said something, but she couldn't make out the words.

'Thank you. I shall take your advice and have a single whisky,' said Wise.

'Ice in it?' said the barman, evidently feeling the need to speak up, slowly and clearly.

She leaned forward, closer to the others, who were now talking about where Tom and his Melanie plus baby were going to live. She hadn't thought to extract any information from him on that subject the other night. She was slipping.

Bristol, it seemed, was where they'd be, provided the girl got the right A-level grades.

Tommy was wondering if being pregnant might impact on her work:

'But she'll have you coaching her, Tom,' said Dora.

Bristol. Not that far, but far enough.

'I *prefer* not to have ice,' Larry Wise was saying. The ice question was clearly taking some thinking about. 'But tell me, should I?'

'Up to you,' said the barman.

Had Wise ever been in a pub before? Why, of all the drinking places around Oxford, had he chosen this one, tonight?

'This is a rather small quantity,' he said. 'How much does it cost?'

The price the man quoted didn't seem to be what Wise wanted to hear:

'Good gracious! That is very expensive.'

'It's the going rate for a single, sir.' The barman's voice had that flat, patient tone of a man who had a queue of people to serve. Straightforward, uncomplicated people.

166

The others were onto what was happening tomorrow. Melanie was coming to Oxford, it appeared. 'So I don't suppose you'll be going skating,' Dora said to Tom. 'Jim will be disappointed.'

'Apologise to him for me,' he said.

'Astronomical Society meets tomorrow night, why not bring Melanie?' said Syd.

But Melanie would have gone back to London by then, according to Tom. Just as well. A girl in her condition might be a bit much for Capella's peace of mind. Come to that, did she herself actually want to meet Melanie? Maybe. Out of idle curiosity. She'd always been good at that.

'Hey, why don't you give Dora and the children a lift to the rink tomorrow when you go in to collect Melanie?' said Tommy, looking at Tom.

'The bus'll be fine, we don't need to take Tom out of his way,' said Dora.

'No problem,' he said. 'Half past ten at Syd's suit you?'

'Oh. All right,' she said.

He raised his eyebrows very slightly and let them fall, as if to say, *it's only a ride in a car.* He wasn't being over-voluble tonight. Maybe he only came out to prove he could sit next to her in a pub without choking on his drink.

'You're letting him borrow Gertie?' said Syd to Tommy.

'In the circs, yes I am,' said Tommy, but she wasn't looking at Syd, she was looking over Dora's shoulder. 'What *is* that man doing?' she whispered.

'Hey, hey, watch it!' came a sharp male voice from just behind Dora.

Funny how things which happen faster than you can think seem to have a sort of slow-motion quality about them. Dora saw the cascading arc of liquid and heard Tommy's 'Oh!' and Wise's 'Oh… Oh,' for what seemed like several seconds before the liquid hit the leg of her jeans and a heavy body crashed against the back of her chair.

'Oh, I'm so terribly, terribly sorry— Oh. Miss Clayton.'

Dora's scotch-soaked jeans were cold against her leg. That was what seemed to register most, even more than the jolt to her ribs when they came in contact with the table. Before she'd found a Kleenex to soak up the scotch there was a second voice behind her saying, 'I think you'd better leave, sir.'

'But I – I…'

'Come on, sir.' A third voice. Another barman, by the sound of him.

Dora waited a second or two to give them time to start leading him away, then looked. It was a mistake. He was looking back at her.

She turned away.

'Hm,' said Syd. 'Bit high-handed, throwing him out like that, isn't it? I mean, it was an accident.'

'Well, it isn't the first drink I've had tipped over me,' she said, blotting her jeans with the Kleenex, 'and I dare say it won't be the last.'

The look in Larry Wise's eyes. It was how a drowning man would look.

'He looked so sad,' said Tommy. 'A lost soul, sort of.'

'It was pretty spectacular, though,' said Syd to Dora. 'He sort of bounced off the guy standing next to him as he was turning away from the bar, and then he ricocheted into you – like a scene from a *Carry On* film.'

'The barmen should have given him a round of applause, then. Tom, which course did you say Melanie was going to do at Bristol?'

There was no more talk of Larry Wise. That is, until they were all getting up to go:

'Hey, what's that,' said Tommy. 'Those, rather.' She was looking down at the floor behind Dora's chair.

'They're lids,' said Syd, picking them up. 'They're from those little tins of paint model makers use. That bloke who knocked into Dozza must have dropped them. Look, they're strung together into a sort of bracelet. Not something you see every day.'

'It can't be a bracelet,' said Tommy, taking it from Syd. 'The loop's too small. It wouldn't even fit Jim's wrist.'

The lids each had a tiny hole punched in the rim. A length of fine string was threaded though the holes and tied in a knot. It was a doll's bracelet in bright colours. Rainbow colours.

That orange one. Jo's jumpsuit was exactly that colour.

'Do you suppose they're some kind of lucky charm?' Tommy was saying. 'Poor bloke, I wonder why he came here? I mean, he looked so totally not the type.'

'Maybe he wanted to get drunk,' said Tom. 'I'll take the lids, I can get them back to him on Monday.'

'No, give them here,' said Dora, holding out her hand for the lids. 'It was me he tripped over.'

Dora looked out of the window, then at her watch. Twenty five to eleven. It was time Tom was here.

'Dozz, you *sure* Tom isn't coming skating?' said Jim.

'Jim, how many times have I told you?' said Dora. 'His girlfriend's here today.'

'She's not his girlfriend,' said Jenny with a giggle, 'she's his fion*say*.'

'Girlfriend,' Jim said, not paying any attention to his sister. 'Huh. Why'd he have to have a *girlfriend.*'

Jenny giggled again.

Jim, your aunt's been spending untold hours asking herself that self-same question, and getting nowhere. But failure is more character-building than success, or so they say. We'll compare notes on that when you're older.

Tom turned up just after twenty-to in Gertie, Tommy's orange Volkswagen. 'Sorry,' he said. 'The car was practically out of petrol, and I ended up having to go to Kidlington to fill up.' He seemed a bit breathless – flustered, even. Well, he was a man who was about to meet his 'fion*say*'.

There was a lot of traffic clogging the roads into the centre. Tom kept looking at his watch.

'You don't have to take us all the way to the rink,' said Dora, 'not if Melanie's going to be stuck waiting.'

Tom looked again at his watch, pursing his lips. 'I think I'm going to have to take you up on that. I'll drop you by the entrance to the bus station car park, OK?'

The quickest way to the ice rink from where they got out of the car was through the bus station, past the London bus stop. As they drew near, Dora scanned the people standing by the stop. There were no girls who looked a bit like her. In fact there were no girls at all. That at least was something. She'd have felt weird, just walking by.

'I want the toilet,' said Jim, tugging at her hand.

'Oh, Jim. Didn't you go before we came out?'

'Yeah. Course I did.'

'Can't you wait until we get to the rink?'

'No. I wanna go *now*.'

Jenny gave a loud, theatrical sigh. 'We'll have to take him in the toilets over there, Dozz.'

Yes, they would, no two ways about it. As they went towards the public lavatories, Dora found herself wondering how many times the course of history had been changed by a child who wanted the toilet. Delaying like this would give Melanie time to turn up – and Tom time to emerge from the car park. Please God let there be nobody by the London bus stop when they came out of the lavatories.

God must have been busy elsewhere that morning. 'Look, it's them,' cried Jenny. 'Let's go and say Hi.'

'Jenny, for goodness' sake, we can't just butt in,' said Dora.

'Oh come on, I've never met a real live bride before, except Mum when she married Nick, and that doesn't count.'

'Tom!' called Jim, sprinting forward, 'Hey, Tom!'

Oh Christ, no!

Tom was quick at adjusting his face, Dora had to give him that. If she'd blinked she'd have missed it, that split second before he put a smile in place. But in that split second, he'd registered the full-on shock of a man caught on the hop. A man who knew too many women.

As they went towards Tom and Melanie, Dora etched a smile so firmly into the contours of her face that she'd probably die before it had faded. 'Hello again, Tom, and you must be Melanie,' she said. 'I'm Dora Clayton, I'm a friend of Tom's sister. This pair of reprobates are my niece Jenny and my nephew Jim.'

'Hi,' said Melanie.

'Hello again,' said Tom, sounding maybe a touch more winded than was ideal.

Tom's girl was certainly a head-turner, Dora had to admit. At close quarters, Melanie didn't look remotely like herself. For a start, she didn't have eyes like that. 'Arresting' would be putting it mildly. A couple of passing blokes eyed up Melanie, as well they might. Yes, Tom had taste. But the girl was pale, so desperately pale. And those dark luminous pools that were her eyes were almost too big for her face. She was too young for what she was having to cope with, far too young. She'd dressed up, though. That coat must be straight out of this week's Topshop window, and ditto those boots.

Had Melanie blinked just now? She wasn't giving much away behind that casual half-smile. 'Tom gave us a lift in,' Dora said, addressing Melanie and pumping up her own smile.

'I just went to the toilet,' Jim announced with a big grin. 'Hey, d'you wanna go skating with us?'

'Jim, they've got other things to do,' said Dora.

'Yes, Jim, I'm afraid we're a bit busy today,' said Tom.

But Melanie was smiling at Jim. 'You a good skater?' she said.

'I'm *briw-yant*,' he declared.

Jenny sighed and said, 'Mnyerr.'

Melanie turned to her. 'What about you?'

'Mm*well*... I'm OK. Not as good as *him*, of course,' said Jenny, and stuck out her tongue at her brother.

'Watch it, you two,' said Dora. 'Well, we'd better be getting on.'

Melanie's gaze slid in Dora's direction for a second, then she looked at Tom. 'Actually, why don't we?' she said. 'Just for a little while?'

What? Was this 'be nice to six-year olds' week?

'Yeah!' said Jim.

'Oh – well, fine, let's go skating, then,' said Tom. He did a halfway decent job of sounding enthusiastic, but Dora couldn't have looked at his face just then to save her life. Or his.

They all trooped down to the underground car park and got into Gertie.

So much orange around these days. This car; the lid hanging from that 'bracelet' of Larry Wise's that she still had in her bag.

Melanie sat in front beside Tom, and Dora and the children squeezed into the back. 'Jim, mind where you're putting your feet,' she muttered as Tom started the car.

'Sorree!' he piped. Full of himself. The morning was turning out just the way he wanted.

When they got to the ice rink, the car park was pretty full. Tom had to park some way from the rink entrance. Dora tried to muster a few conversational gambits to get them across the tarmac, but what with two full-of-beans children, she was reduced to not much more than, 'Jim, stop that.' Tom wasn't saying much, either.

When they were half way there, Jim began to prance ahead, singing some pop tune, but Jenny stayed with the grown-ups. She'd been taking looks at Melanie ever since they got out of the car, raking her from fake fur coat collar to heels of shiny boots, her eyes as big as saucers.

'Are you, like, having bridesmaids?' she said.

The girl smiled at Jenny. 'I'd never get my sisters to agree on dresses.'

'Really?' said Jenny.

'She'd volunteer like a shot,' said Dora. 'She'd even supply her own dress.'

'Dozza, that one's way too small,' sighed Jenny. 'I mean, it was two *years* ago Mum married Nick. D'you know, there was a wedding on ice here once.'

'Aren't you thinking of that Sleeping Beauty ice show I brought you to?' said Dora.

'No, it was a real wedding, my friend Katie went. They had a vicar in skates and everything.'

Weird-sounding wedding. Still, what did she herself know about weddings, she could count the ones she'd been to on half a hand.

'I'd be afraid I'd fall over,' said Melanie.

'Hey, yeah! Katie said she was, like, *terrified* the whole time waiting for it to happen. I mean, can you just *see* it. "Do you take this woman" – oh whoops, the bride's gone splat, nnngh!' She swung the bag with her skates in it from one hand to the other. 'I've got new skates, they're white. There's only black skates for hire here. What size are you?'

'Actually, I think I'll sit and watch, thanks,' said Melanie. 'I had an early start for a Saturday.'

Ah.

'Are you sure?' said Tom.

'Yeah. I've got *Mill on the Floss* to finish for next week's essay.'

'Stick with Dozza, she knows the best place to watch from,' Jim piped up, twisting around.

'Oh, you don't…' began Melanie.

'No, I don't,' said Dora. 'Reading's more my thing, too.'

For the rest of the way to the rink, Dora kept her attention on Jim. Nobody would have expected anything else, as first he tried walking backwards, then galloping crabwise, then hopping with both feet together.

Mel turned aside and pretended to check that her bag zip was closed. She didn't particularly want to catch anybody's eye, not right now when Tom was taking the two kids onto the ice and she was being left with this Dora Clayton.

'See you both later,' said Tom.

'See you later, alligator,' sang the little boy, Jim Clayton.

'He's into retro,' said his sister Jenny, rolling her eyes.

The three of them skated away.

God, what had she got herself into? Trying to be cool, trying to let Tom know that she really wasn't that bothered about spending every minute alone with him…

Dora Clayton, this 'friend of Tom's sister', was she the friend he'd gone to Wales with? She'd bet anything she was. The way he'd looked when he saw her and her niece and nephew. Like they'd just pulled a knife on him. Hm. Hm.

'They're cute, the kids,' she made herself say, 'especially Jim.'

'Don't for goodness sake tell him that,' said Dora Clayton, 'he's enough of a handful already. The other side of the rink's best for watching, by the way.'

'OK,' said Melanie.

'"Lead on Macduff", eh? Hang on, is that right?'

'It's "lay on", actually.'

'Oh, right. Maybe I should have paid more attention in English lessons.'

Mel smiled. There didn't seem like much she could say to that.

'This is my spot,' said Dora Clayton when they'd got half way along the other side of the rink. 'I'm sort of attached to it.'

'Looks good,' said Mel, and sat down.

'Where are they? I can never – oh, there's Jim,' said Dora Clayton, sitting down next to Mel. 'He looks so like a cherub from this distance... Ah, there's his friend Simon, we're always running into him here. Oh, and there's Jenny. My God, those trousers. Still, that lime green makes her easier to keep track of... Oh, there's some girls from her class, I don't know their names. Tom's going to have his hands full.'

'He'll cope,' said Mel. She glanced at Dora Clayton's hands as the woman took off her gloves. No wedding ring, but a mark where a ring might have been. Hm.

'I fancy a coffee, would you like one?' said Dora Clayton. 'It's only machine stuff but it is hot and brown.'

'No thanks.'

'Tea, then?'

'OK.'

'Milk, sugar?'

'Milk no sugar, thanks.'

Mel watched Dora Clayton move off in the direction of the vending machines. A bit chatty, wasn't she? Wasn't that one of the signs of guilt? Hm... Oh, sod it! She pulled *The Mill on the Floss* out of her shoulder bag. She had to finish it, so she'd better get on with it.

There was Jim Clayton and another boy, skating past the barrier, and Tom was right behind them. He was looking straight at her, and he had a hand raised in a wave. She put on a cool-but-big smile – or was it big-but-cool? – and waved back.

When she saw Dora Clayton coming back, she bent lower over her book. 'Thanks,' she said, turning a page as she reached for her tea. Dora Clayton took a paperback out of her bag. Mel couldn't make out the title, but it seemed to have some sort of

175

sci-fi scene on the cover. Would Tom go for a woman who read sci-fi?

Where was Tom now? She raised her eyes from her book, trying not to move her head as she did so. Ah, he was close again, on this side of the rink, still keeping Jim and his friend in front of him. She watched them make their way along the rink, Tom grabbing a shoulder or an arm when either of the boys looked as if they were drifting too close to other skaters. She took a sip of tea. Machine tea: yuk. Still, she'd asked for it, she'd have to look as if she was drinking it.

Did Dora Clayton go to Wales with Tom? Was she his friend as well as his sister's? Hell, she couldn't just ask point blank *are you having an affair with him?*

'I want a lolly,' whined a child's voice from close by, making Mel jump. She glanced up to see a woman a few seats away with a little boy on her knee dressed in a blue all-in-one, and a slightly older girl next to her in pink. But no football boots…

'Luke, sweetheart, if you have one now you can't have one when we go home,' said the woman.

'I-want-a-lolly!' cried the boy, louder. The girl began to grizzle.

'Oh, come on then,' said the woman, sighing. Mel watched them go. There was a funny feeling in her insides – not as if she was going to be sick, but a sort of clamming-up feeling.

'The terrible twos,' said Dora Clayton. 'They say if you can cope with that stage, the rest is a breeze.'

Oh, God. What was it going to be like? 'My mum says the worst time is fourteen,' she said. 'She should know, she's had five.'

'Ah well, there must be some who are angels from birth until the day they're finding you a nursing home. Maybe yours will be.'

Melanie bit her lip. This woman was seeing inside her head.

She'd better be careful, she might see something she didn't like. 'Mm,' she said.

'Still, what do I know,' said Dora Clayton. 'I'm just an auntie, not a mum. That suits me fine. It doesn't suit my husband, though, he's going to be hooking up with somebody else just as soon as he gets back from a business trip.'

'Oh,' was all Mel could think of to say. Too much information, for God's sake. Another sign of guilt?

'Still, "As one door closes another opens," so they say,' Dora Clayton chuntered on. 'There's a man who's driving me crazy; someone from work. I spent last weekend in Wales boring Tom out of his mind, did he tell you? Tommy was supposed to be going but she had a meeting. What I think is she didn't have a meeting at all she just couldn't face a weekend of me rabbiting on. Well I think he was regretting it by the Sunday. Tom I mean. The thing is every time I run into this guy I feel about fourteen, not that I've got a mother I can be a pain to.'

Christ. What? 'Tom's sister might've mentioned something about him being in Wales with a friend, I can't really remember,' said Mel. 'You in the same office as this guy, then?'

'No, no… he's just – around. Sorry, you'll be wanting to get on with whatever you're getting on with.'

'Mm. Yeah.' Mel went back to *Mill on the Floss*. Her heart was beating fast, as if she'd been physically running to keep up with Dora Clayton's outburst. She didn't look at the rink, not even when she could sense Tom skating past.

Where did all that get her?

Somewhere behind, toward the back of the bus, the baby which had been whimpering since Dora and the children got on began to cry, then to howl, then to yell.

'I wish we'd got the next bus,' said Jenny, sighing.

'Huh,' said Jim, 'there's always babies on buses.'

You bet, Jim.

She'd as good as denied Jo's existence this morning. Never, ever had she done that. Sorry, Jo, sorry, sorry! But how could she have told a pregnant eighteen year-old that she'd had a baby who died?

And then she had to go and say all that stuff about Larry Wise, of all people. What on earth came over her? Well, unless she was grossly mistaken, Mel had been doing some thinking about her – her and Tom. Mel had had her eyes open in the bus station, she wouldn't mind betting. So, maybe it was just as well that she'd come out with a load of rubbish about Larry Wise. Maybe.

The baby at the back of the bus pumped out more decibels, and yet more. People were turning around to look. 'You can stop that right now, do you hear?' said a woman's voice. A ratty, bored snap.

No wonder motherhood wasn't rated as an occupation. Any fool could do it, anybody who kept her brain between her legs.

The baby's screams rose to nerve-severing pitch. 'Fucking shut up!' yelled the mother.

Somewhere inside Dora, a fuse blew. *Right. That's it.*

She got up, ignoring Jenny's wide-eyed: 'What're you doing, Dozz?' She marched down the bus until she got to the only woman who had a baby with her.

'Excuse me, but I think you ought to know that isn't going to work. In fact it's going to make her cry harder. It is a her, isn't it.'

The woman stared at her, open mouthed, showing discoloured teeth. 'Who the bloody hell do you think you are? Fucking nosy cunt.'

The baby began to wail as if its life were ebbing away. The man sitting next to the woman burrowed down further into the newspaper he was pretending to read. He didn't look as if he were anything to do with the woman, but you couldn't always tell from the way men held a newspaper.

'I'm somebody who knows from experience,' Dora heard a voice say. It sounded as if it were in control, the voice of a wise, reasonable older woman. It was her own, how could that possibly be?

'Yeah? Right, you have this one,' said the woman, thrusting the howling mass at her. 'Go on. *If* you know so much about them.'

Go on, go on. The woman's voice seemed to echo in Dora's head. She gazed at the baby's red, tortured face. About six weeks old. Poor scrap. Poor, pathetic little fragment of humanity.

Go on, take it. Take it before she kills it.

For a moment, Dora's hands wavered towards the baby. Then she turned quickly and ran the gauntlet of gazes, half-curious, half-embarrassed, back to her seat.

'God, Dozz,' whispered Jenny, as red-faced as the baby, as Dora sat down.

Grown-ups. Why do they have to make exhibitions of themselves? Dora took a deep breath, in and out, to try to slow her heart before it burst.

The woman with the baby got off at the next stop. She pushed past Dora, not troubling to stop her heavy bag from swinging into Dora's shoulder.

You should have taken it.

Dora shivered. Something seemed to have shifted inside her. By the time she and the children got off the bus, she had the feeling that somewhere within her world, tectonic plates had slid apart, revealing a void so deep, so black, that if you fell into it you'd carry on falling until the end of time. Stand anywhere near the edge of it, and the vertigo would drive you mad. So she'd better stand back, hadn't she. Well back.

Fourteen

Mel's pen was running out. 'Stop a minute,' she said. It took her two seconds to find out that she didn't have another pen on her. Bugger. But Tom was holding one out to her: 'Thanks,' she said. 'Right, what was that last thing you said?'

He was off again, and so was she, writing fast. Since they left the ice rink all they'd talked about was how school was going. And since they'd got to this pub, she'd taken enough notes for next week's essay that she could have done it on the bus back this afternoon if she'd had her laptop with her. Maybe she ought to count herself lucky, nobody else she knew had a tutor on tap. Hell, at this rate they'd be doing more work together than when he'd actually been her teacher. Bit rich, seeing the excuse the Head came up with for getting shot of him was giving her advantages he wasn't giving to the others. Still, what engaged people talked about was their business.

When were they going to get on to what she'd come here for: wedding arrangements? Well, she wasn't going to be the one to bring up the subject. He was the one who proposed last Sunday, let him get the ball rolling.

'Proposed...' God, thinking of it like that made it seem like he'd gone down on one knee. Girls used to faint when blokes proposed, didn't they? Maybe it was the corsets. These days girls just threw up.

Still, it hadn't been so bad this week. Junior'd probably guessed she wasn't going to be turfed out. It was going to be a 'she', definitely.

'Got that, Mel?' He was looking at her.

'Yeah, sure.' She nibbled another piece of pizza, bent her head lower over her notebook, and scribbled faster.

That Dora Clayton this morning. She'd gabbed on about the bloke from work just like she'd learned the words beforehand. Yeah, she could just have been saying all that... Saying it to make her think there was nothing going on with Tom when there bloody well was.

'...the kind of school we think Maggie Tulliver must have been sent to,' he was saying. She scribbled on.

A minute or so later, he said, 'Right, that should do, but mind you give me a ring if anything doesn't make sense when you come to write it up.'

Yes, Mr Ross. 'Thanks,' she said, handing him his pen back.

'Keep it,' he said.

'OK.' She dropped the pen into her bag. One of these days maybe she ought to give him back that other pen of his, the one she had in her desk at home, to be looked at, not used. The pen he'd left behind after a lesson this time last year, the one she'd picked up and put quickly in her bag. It was something of his, wasn't it, it had his DNA on it. Only a year ago? A hundred years ago, more like.

She took a swig of her orange juice. Now what? By the expression on his face, he was gearing up to something. Was he going to tell her he'd had second thoughts and it was Dora Clayton he was actually going to marry?

'I dropped into the Register Office yesterday lunchtime to see what information I could pick up,' he said.

181

'Oh. Right.'

As he took a handful of what looked like official leaflets out of his inside pocket, some bloke going past with a tray of beers jogged his elbow and the stuff went on the floor. A woman at the next table picked the leaflets up and handed them back to him with a smile, which got bigger as she saw what the leaflets were about. She turned the smile towards Mel. A cool girl would smile right back. Mel smiled.

Tom spread the leaflets out on the table. Mel flicked through one or two, but without really taking anything in.

'It seems straightforward enough,' he said, breaking off a bit of baguette. 'You have to give notice at the Register Office in Uxbridge, and I have to go to the one here. All we really have to do for now is pick a date for the wedding, and then the bureaucratic machinery will start running.'

He was looking at her, waiting for her to say something. Did he want her to decide the day, then? 'Mum wants me to put it off but Dad says get it over with as soon as possible,' she said. 'Of course, Mum'll be praying I lose the baby, she must be. I'm still in the danger period, you know.' God, what a funny feeling it gave her, right around her heart, to hear herself saying that.

'I didn't know, but don't fret about it, Mel,' he said, grabbing her hand. 'Think positive, right?' The look he was giving her, it seemed like he actually cared. But she had to stay cool, stay cool. He'd been a Drama teacher as well as an English teacher, he knew how to act.

'Yeah, but don't you want to, um, wait and see?'

'What?' He evidently wasn't expecting her to say that, he looked thrown. But only for a second. 'No, I don't,' he went on. 'Your dad wants us to get on with it, let's make his day, shall we?' He really looked as though he meant it. And he wasn't letting go of her hand. Oh God, any minute now she'd forget to be cool if she wasn't very careful.

'OK,' she said, looking at her drink, 'Let's go for Monday week, if you can get the day off. I'll have a sickie.'

'We can't do it quite that quickly, I'm afraid. According to these leaflets there have to be at least three weeks between giving notice and the day itself.'

'Oh. All right,' she said, feeling a little bit silly. Shit, there she was, talking as if she was fitting him into a spare moment, and she'd bloody well managed to come within an ace of looking too up for it.

'Look, go along to the Register Office on Monday afternoon during your free,' he said. 'Go for the first day you can, and never mind me, I'll work around it. As for guests and so forth—'

'Oh, just family. And Debs, but that's all. Only people who, um, know…'

'Probably just as well,' he said, looking at his beer. 'I'll ask Tommy, but she might not be able to get the day off school. I won't ask anybody else.'

'OK.' *Not even Dora Clayton?*

Right, a cool girl would change the subject now. And she knew just the subject to move on to: 'Your friend Dora's a bit steamed up about this bloke, isn't she.'

'Bloke? Which bloke?'

'The guy at work.'

'Guy at work… Oh. Yes, I suppose she is, a bit. Did she mention him this morning, then?'

'Yeah, she did.'

'Well, he gets to her, poor bloke. That's the thing about working in offices, you can't avoid people.'

'"Poor bloke"? He sounded quite something. What was his name again…?' Dora Clayton hadn't said this morning. But Tom ought to know. If the guy existed.

He gave her a puzzled smile. 'I don't know his name, but the man's only 'something' in the sense that he's awkward and a bit inept. He's the sort who get labels like Asperger's pinned on them, not always rightly.'

'Oh. Maybe I got the wrong end of the stick.' And maybe I didn't.

'Maybe. Anyway, shall we have a quick look at Oxford before you go back?'

'All right. From what I've seen of it so far it could be anywhere, though.'

'Well, there are parts that are a bit different, as you'll see.'

For the next hour or so, he walked her around streets that could have been from a million tourist postcards, and probably were. He took her into Blackwell's Bookshop and showed her miles of books, all saying, 'Buy me' – if she'd had a mind to hear – and then they went and had a coffee and a peppermint tea in the café on the first floor and watched people going by. He seemed like he wanted to be with her. Bit by bit, she got to a stage where one half of her was bursting to ask him what was going on with Dora Clayton, and the other half of her was saying *Relax, you've got it out of all proportion*.

The two halves of Mel were still fighting it out when Tom saw her on to the London bus just after five. OK, she might be haring off down a wildly wrong track. On the other hand, if Tom and Dora Clayton were making a fool of her, she was going to be totally bloody fucking annoyed.

Tom was left to stand grinning up in the vague direction of where Mel was sitting, as the bus was too full for her to find a window seat. At last, the bus reversed away from the stop and pulled out into George Street. Then, and only then, did Tom allow himself to start thinking.

What did today amount to? Had he just waved goodbye to a girl who was happy at the prospect of marrying him, or hadn't he? There'd been odd moments in the pub…and yet, there was a constraint about her. As if she knew everything was going to end in tears, and the only question was when.

Dora and the children appearing like that this morning – Jesus, he could have done without that. To have both of them, Mel and Dora, Dora and Mel, in his field of view at the same time... The other night, he'd thought of it in prospect as a test. He shook his head. It was a test he hadn't passed. And Dora, how had she felt, sitting with Mel for an hour at the rink?

He turned up the passage leading to the square where the open market was held. He couldn't go straight back to the car, he had to carry on walking for a bit, to let his mind settle, if it were capable of settling.

The square turned out to be swimming with jetsam. Burger cartons, plastic coffee cups, food wrappers of any and every sort: they were all waiting to be trodden on as he threaded his way among the people, the knots and clusters of humanity who were seeing fit to spend the dregs of a Saturday afternoon just hanging about. The air smelt stale, from having passed through hundreds of lungs. Ah, if he were only on that cliff path in Fife, that path beside a cold sea, where the air was so clean, so clear, it could scour every last befuddled thought out of your head until only the empty skull was left. So narrow in places, that path, that you had to watch your step so as not to pitch yourself onto the rocks below. But the risk was infinitely worth the being there, with no-one around and no sound but the Firth of Forth caressing those rocks.

However, he was here. Here, where the sea was made of polystyrene garbage – oh fuck, he'd just stepped on a dog turd.

He looked down. No, it wasn't dog shit. It was a toy, a child's cuddly toy.

He picked up the three-inch high bear, holding it by the broken loop by which it must have hung from a pram hood. It had a tartan bow tie and tartan feet and paws. Paw, rather: the creature had lost one arm. It had a bedraggled, chewed look.

185

The tartan, wasn't that Ross tartan? Its owner would be missing it, but there was nowhere around here he could safely leave it in case they came back. The bear's eyes glinted dolefully at him. He shoved the creature into a pocket and walked on.

He turned into Beaumont Street and made his way past the theatre. *Hamlet* was on. 'Hey, let's see if we can get tickets for tonight,' a student-ish type was saying to the girl he was with.

Tom hadn't been inside a theatre for a while now. If a Feydeau farce had been on, he might have followed those young people in to the box office and bought a night of distraction. He wasn't going to *Hamlet*, though. Not tonight.

When he turned into St Giles, he noticed a few yards ahead a tall man who seemed to be lost in thought, judging from the slow, hunched-shouldered way he was walking, a plastic Sainsbury's bag dangling from each hand. One or two faster walkers bumped into him and gave him a look, but he seemed oblivious.

It couldn't be him again, the maintenance man? Christ, it was. Tom found himself falling into step behind the man. Dora must have been seriously stuck for topics of conversation with Mel this morning if she'd needed to mention this unfortunate man's supposed nuisance qualities. With no warning, the man stepped out into the road. Tom gasped as a car swerved to avoid him, but still he seemed utterly unaware of what was happening around him.

Tom stepped out into the road too. He had no choice, when this man might otherwise not reach the other side in one piece.

The man did survive the crossing, God only knew how, but he didn't deviate from a straight line by as much as a centimetre. Outside the Lamb and Flag, he stopped and looked in through the big bay window. Then he turned away and plodded on up the road, his shoulders sagging even more, if that were possible.

The slowness of the man's pace made following him less than straightforward. More than once, Tom had to make himself slow down. Should he just leave the guy? That house he'd gone into the other night wasn't far away, after all. On the other hand, about thirty yards ahead there was a road junction.

The man plunged into the road, again without looking, just as a car was about to turn into Banbury Road. 'Look out!' shouted Tom. The car and the man stopped in the same moment, inches from one another, and the driver wound down his window.

Tom took the man's arm as the swearing started. 'Come on,' he said.

The man looked down at him, a look of utter bewilderment on his face.

'It's all right, just keep walking,' said Tom. The driver of the car was still saying things like 'stupid fucking cunt,' and for a moment Tom was on the verge of letting rip with some appropriate Scots expressions in return, but common sense prevailed before he opened his mouth. He kept hold of the man's arm and all-but hustled him the rest of the way across the road. Big though he was, he was less resistant than Tom might have expected. Perhaps he was past caring what happened to him.

'Th – thank you,' said the man, slowly, when they got to the other pavement.

'That's all right,' said Tom. He resisted the urge to tell the man to be careful how he went in future, saying instead, 'Good night.'

'Good night,' said the man. He adjusted his Sainsbury's bags and walked on up the road, keeping the same slow, weary pace. Tom let him get twenty yards ahead, then followed. There were more road junctions between here and the man's house.

There were no more incidents, but Tom stayed with the man until he was safely behind the heavy, imposing North Oxford door he'd seen him unlock on Thursday night.

Half way back to town, it occurred to him that he should have told the man Dora was planning to give back those miniature paint tin lids on Monday. He could perhaps have lifted some of that cloud of gloom. If the man had given any sign of recognising him from the pub last night, maybe he would have. It had rather looked, though, as if the man only had eyes for Dora.

He might drop in on her tomorrow. Just in passing, as it were, to say he was sorry about this morning. He didn't have to stay long.

Tom detoured down Dora's road on his way back from buying the Sunday papers. As he waited for her to answer the doorbell, he cast a look around the garden. It was tidy, in an uninspiring way. Steve Mitchell's work, he supposed: the result of a quick trim and weed undertaken at odd weekends. Somehow, he didn't see Dora as a gardener. If the break-up was really going to happen, the garden could start going to rack and ruin and put off potential buyers. Perhaps he himself ought to volunteer to help keep it under control? That would be another test of whether he could be a friend, an easier one to pass. On the other hand, gardening was what he'd have been doing if he'd moved in…

She was taking her time in coming. He pressed the bell again, then looked through the letterbox. Maybe she was in the dead baby's room? Or maybe she was out.

He left it another minute, then retraced his steps down the garden path. Here and there, daffodils were showing tight yellow buds. They were a bit late opening, but by this time next week there'd be flowers.

It halted him in his tracks, the sudden vision of a daffodil.

That daffodil, the one he gave her a week ago yesterday. It'd be dead by now. Daffodils didn't last long.

He shook his head, took a long breath, rearranged the newspapers under his arm, and walked on. Perhaps it was best that she was out.

Fifteen

When Dora got to the office, the first thing she did was take the bracelet of paint tin lids out of her bag. That story she'd given Tom's Melanie on Saturday: why, why?

Larry Wise. The very *idea* of it.

Right. She had two possible courses of action. She could either put these lids in an envelope with 'Larry Wise, Maintenance Dept,' on the front and drop them in the out tray, or she could walk them down to the basement and put them in his great hot hand.

She paused in the act of reaching for an envelope. Was it as much of a no-brainer as all that? What if Larry Wise was so overwhelmed with joy at getting his lids back that he came up here and thanked her?

She put down the envelope and headed out of the office.

Down in the basement, it occurred to her that finding Larry Wise wasn't going to be any more straightforward than it had been a week ago. There was nothing for it but to ask the Head of Maintenance again.

Jock Stewart looked at her with narrowed eyes when he

opened his door to her. *Yes, it's me again*, she felt like saying, but didn't.

It turned out that Larry Wise wasn't in today. His mother was ill, apparently, and he'd taken the day off to look after her. She handed the lids to Jock Stewart – 'Just something he dropped,' – and made herself scarce in double quick time, before Stewart could ask her any whats, whys and wherefores.

Well. She'd tried.

As she made her way past the Admissions Office, she caught a glimpse of Tom through the window in the door. His desk was just inside the door: the rubbish position that temps always got. She could slip in for a moment. People did say hi to people they knew around the office, after all.

'Morning, Tom,' she said. His head jerked up, and for a second or so he looked rather the way he'd looked in the bus station on Saturday. 'I thought I'd look in and say Happy Monday,' she went on. 'I just popped down to leave those paint-tin lids for Larry Wise.'

'Oh, that's his name, is it? Mel mentioned you'd been talking about him.'

'Oh God, she didn't tell you, did she?'

'She said you were, um, steamed up about him – I think those are the words she used,' he said. Dora was glad he kept his voice down.

'Ah. Look, walk up to the cafeteria with me, will you?' she said.

He took a quick glance around. 'All right. I dare say I won't be missed for a few minutes.'

As they walked along the corridor, she told him what she'd said to Mel. 'God knows why I said all that,' she finished, seeing his puzzled frown. 'Some gremlin must have got hold of my tongue. But I thought afterwards, maybe it was just as well.'

He frowned harder. He frowned harder still as they walked

up the stairs, as she told him why she thought what she'd said to Melanie was just as well.

'Oh, God,' he said, closing his eyes for a moment. 'She saw me see you?'

'Yup, I'm pretty sure she did.'

'Right. Well, let me tell you what I said about you and Larry Wise.'

When he finished, they looked at one another for a moment. 'Shit,' they said, in unison.

'So, she smelled a rat,' he went on. 'Which could explain a few things.'

'I'm sorry.'

'How could it be your fault?'

'Well, if I hadn't… Oh bloody hell, I reckon I'll just slink off and kick myself for the rest of the day.'

What with more people about, there wasn't much opportunity to talk from then on. As they drew near the swinging double doors of the cafeteria, he said, 'I told Mel I'd be going to the Register Office to give notice, and I'm damned well going to go. This lunchtime.'

"Good idea. I'd probably better not offer to come with you, though.'

He smiled, then the smile faded. 'Perhaps not,' he said quietly. Dora went into the cafeteria with him, bought a muesli bar, and made herself scarce.

At various moments during that day, as Dora waded through the mountains of paperwork which Siobhan's forthcoming trip to the Far East with the Vice Chancellor was generating, her conversation with Tom repeated on her, like raw garlic. He was wrong: of course it was her fault. What else could it be, mistress of wrecking as she was? It was her fault, for having a leaky nephew. Oh, why couldn't Jim have waited until he got to the rink!

*

By Wednesday evening, Tom knew when he'd be getting married. A text message arrived from Mel saying she'd been to the Register Office in Uxbridge and booked the wedding for the Wednesday in four weeks' time. That was all the message said. There was nothing about when or where they might next meet. As Tom looked at the words, the few words, on his phone screen, something became very clear. On Saturday he was going to Uxbridge to see Mel. He wasn't going to warn her, he was just going to turn up, and if she were out, he was going to wait until she got back. He had to clear the air between them if there was going to be any hope of this marriage of theirs lasting longer than a week.

The Baines house seemed to glower at Tom as he walked up the drive, but it was built to intimidate. Only Baines would be putting up extensions to the extensions, so that you could hardly make out the lines of the original modest three-bedroom structure. What was going on in the roof space? Could even the Baineses possibly need another room up there? Maybe Jackie was getting Baines to put up battlements so that she could dash up there with jugs of boiling oil whenever he himself dared to approach this close.

He rang the doorbell. He'd hardly taken his finger off it when the door opened to reveal Jackie standing there, cigarette in hand. She said nothing. She merely raised the cigarette to her lips, took a drag, and blew out enough smoke to make his eyes smart. He forced himself not to blink. 'I'm back to forty a day,' she said at last. 'You'll be the death of me, Tom Ross. Well, you better come in.' As he followed her in, she shouted up the stairs: 'Mel, guess who's here.'

No answer.

Jackie climbed a couple of stairs. 'Mel! It's your intended,' she shouted louder, packing all the bitter irony in the world into 'intended'. She drew on her cigarette again, and blew out another pall of smoke. This time it went up the stairs, not in his direction. 'I'll send him up, shall I?' she called up after it.

'No! I'll come down,' came the answering shout. Tom heard faint banging sounds: feet, kicking something?

Jackie turned back to Tom, beckoning him furiously into the sitting room. 'Something you ought to know,' she hissed. 'I've told her till I'm blue in the face she doesn't have to go through with this, but she won't say a sodding thing, other than "Everything's fine, Mum." That's all she bloody says. I've twisted Debbie's arm but she says that's all Mel's saying to her, too. But you know what? You'd think this girl was going to her funeral in three weeks four days, not her fucking wedding.' She took another drag of cigarette and gave a deep, hacking cough.

'Jackie, I know she's not happy. That's why I'm here.'

'Yeah? Well, do something about it, right?'

As she was speaking, there was a noise of someone coming downstairs. As Mel came into the room, Jackie gave Tom a basilisk look and disappeared.

'Hi, Mel,' he said.

'Hi,' she said, flashing him the sort of quick smile she might have given the postman or the man who read the gas meter. She parked herself on one of the arms of the huge sofa, some yards away from him.

One thing was already evident. Inside this house, he was going to get nowhere. All right, he'd use the ploy he'd worked out on the bus. It was even true: 'I need to collect some books, and I thought you might like to come along and see if there's anything you fancy borrowing. Provided you're not in the middle of something, that is.'

'I'm doing my German essay, but it'll wait.' She put up her hand to cover a yawn. 'Sorry. Late night last night.'

He waited for her to elaborate, but she didn't. 'Let's go, then,' he said.

She was at the door and putting her jacket on before he had a chance to touch her hand, let alone kiss her. As they began to walk down the street, a passer-by gave them a glance. Word would get around soon. People were going to start thinking: *Hey, it's that teacher who left all of a sudden and that girl who's pregnant.*

'Mel, we're going to have to think about how we handle school,' he said.

'Why?' she said, glancing at him. 'Gran says I'm going to be like Mum, nobody could tell she was having a baby till practically the day it was due. I'll only be five months or so by the time I'm doing A-levels, and I'll hardly be in school much after that. If I wear loose tops, why does anybody have to know?'

'A bit risky, isn't it?'

'Not really. Not now I've stopped throwing up.'

'Oh, have you? Good.'

'Yeah. So, it'll be OK. As long as you're not round here too much, mind.'

'Well, I wasn't planning to move back in, Mel.' No, he wasn't, he supposed. But until now, no thought either way had crossed his mind. He felt – nettled? Snubbed?

'How's work been this week?' she said.

In other words, subject closed. But that didn't stop her strategy from being dangerous. Still, he could hardly press the issue out here in the street.

There wasn't much he could tell her about typing spreadsheets and clearing filing backlogs which could possibly interest a living soul, but he made it last until they were at the door of his house.

Except for photocopying. He didn't tell her about photocopying.

He led her into the unwelcoming house, picking up another pile of mail from the doormat before passing through to the

195

kitchen. 'I should have brought some milk,' he said, dropping the mail on the table, 'but there's probably some long-life stuff somewhere. Are you back on coffee yet?'

'No. The thought of it still turns me green,' she said. 'Hey, there's a squirrel.' She was right; there was one, scrabbling about in the back garden. It was getting to be a mess out there, now things were starting to grow.

He took a deep breath. 'Mel, why don't I tell the Head next week? I'll phone him and make it absolutely clear I'm behind you a hundred per cent. UCAS'll need to be informed, of course, as it's I who'll be supporting you, not your parents, but—'

'No,' she said.

'What?'

'I said no.' She turned away from the window to face him, folding her arms, one foot forward. *Girl at bay.*

'I know you said no. No what? Why no?'

'I'm not taking any money from you to go to uni.'

'*What?* Look, Mel—'

'I've pulled out of UCAS. I'll do A-levels, then that's it.'

'What in hell are you talking about?'

For several heartbeats, she didn't reply. 'I went online first thing and cancelled my UCAS application,' she said at last, speaking fast and low. 'As soon as the baby's old enough to go to nursery, I'll get a job, and when it starts school we'll get a divorce. I'll say I've had an affair. Nobody'll be surprised. I mean, if I'm enough of a slapper to pull blokes on New Year's Eve—'

'Mel, stop this!' It took him less time to cover the distance between himself and her and to grab her by the shoulders than to say the words. She didn't move, nor flinch, nor lower her gaze. 'If you don't want to marry me, don't. But I'm paying for you to go to university and I'm supporting this baby, OK?'

'No. I'll go to uni later, as a mature student, and I'll pay for myself.'

'So, you've got it all worked out.' He strove to keep his voice level.

She nodded. 'What I want is no strings. Not for me, not for you.' She sniffed. 'I might even give Sean a ring tonight.'

'Sean? Who's Sean?'

'The guy from Brunel, of course.'

'Mel, there is no guy from Brunel! He's about as real as the Man in the Moon. Admit it, will you?'

'I think I'd better go,' she said, turning her head aside. She shook off his hands and made for the hallway.

'Mel, for God's sake don't run off, we've got to sort this out!' he cried, following her. 'Do you think *I'm* having an affair, is that what's worrying you?'

'Oh, it's OK,' she said. 'Have one if you want, I don't care.'

'Mel!' He grabbed her arm again. 'This baby. It *is* mine, isn't it. Please, I've got a right to know.'

'I've told you, it's not yours!' she cried, shaking him off again. She was out of his house as if the hounds of hell were after her, leaving him standing in the doorway.

Mel's mum came out of the kitchen as Mel let herself into the house. 'So?' she said.

'So what?' said Mel.

'So what did he say? What did you say?'

Mel shrugged. 'We had a chat about stuff, then I told him I had to get on with this essay and I came back. So I'm going to get on with the essay, right?' She put her foot on the bottom stair.

'Oh *Mel*,' said Mum.

'Look, it's all right, OK?' She took the stairs two at a time; she wasn't waiting to hear any more. Besides, she had something to do she couldn't do in front of Mum.

As soon as she was in her room, she did the thing she could only do in private. She threw herself on her bed, buried her face in the pillow, and burst into tears.

She'd overdone it. She'd let herself get carried away, thinking about him and Dora Clayton, thinking about them so hard she could practically see them in bed together, and pulling out of UCAS to spite him. He'd hate that, it was the one thing she could be sure of. Yes, she'd screwed things up well and good. Next time she heard from him, he'd be calling it off. Oh shit, shit, *shit*.

Sixteen

Laurence spread a tray cloth on Mother's ebony tray and stood Mother's pot of Darjeeling, a full one in case she were feeling well enough to drink her customary two cups, in the middle of the tray. He placed a Rich Tea biscuit and a Digestive on her favourite Royal Worcester plate, and put the plate on the tray to the left of the pot of tea. He placed the milk jug, cup, saucer and spoon to the right of the pot of tea, and stood back and surveyed the tray. All was as it should be; may Mother please be as she should. She had said yesterday evening that she felt better, that she expected to be able to get up today and he really ought to go to work. Oh, please may she be better! Then perhaps he would be able to summon the energy to tidy the house, and in particular this kitchen. Such chaos and disarray, used dishes everywhere; he had never allowed it to become like this, ever. But then, Mother had never been ill, never.

As Laurence carried the tray upstairs, the thought came again, the thought that had assailed him all this last week since Mother had not been feeling well:

Mother was his one true friend. Without Mother, he would be quite alone. Oh, please, please, let Mother be better!

He knocked at Mother's door. There was no answer. He looked at his watch: he hadn't been wrong, this was the correct time, Mother's usual time for early morning tea. He knocked again. Again, there was no answer. But Mother always answered. Even during the time she had not been well, she answered, 'Come in, Laurence.' Could she still be asleep? What should he do? Should he leave the tray outside her room, or should he go in?

Oh. Oh dear. If only Mother could advise. But Mother could not advise…

Slowly, tentatively, he turned the door handle. He pushed the door open just enough to allow him to slip in with the tray.

Mother was propped up on the pillows as usual, in the position that kept her heartburn at bay most effectively. Ah, she wasn't asleep, her eyes were open. 'Good morning, Mother. I did knock, but perhaps you didn't hear me.' He put the tray down on the night table and went to open the curtains.

Mother didn't reply. 'I said, good morning, Mother,' he said, louder, but again, Mother said nothing. He bit his lip. Was she annoyed with him for coming in uninvited? 'I'll leave the tea for you to pour when you are ready, Mother.'

There seemed nothing else for him to do. Perhaps Mother was meditating. If so, he had better leave. 'I shall go to work today as you suggested, Mother,' he said. 'I shall see you this evening. Have a good day.'

Mother did not move as he left. She was in the habit of thinking, often very ruminatively. This must be such a time, but he would have been so grateful had she greeted him.

Downstairs, he filled Prinz Eugen's bowl, then put on his jacket and left the house for his customary walk to work. As he turned into Banbury Road, he remembered the helpful man who had come to his assistance on Saturday, and the jolt it had given him to have been so nearly the victim of an accident. Mother would have been so sad. But who else would have minded? No-one at all. No, not one.

He took a long, shaky breath. He must take greater care in future. He must not make Mother sad.

When Dora arrived at the bus stop, the Monday-morning assembly of silent, hunched, work-going people included Tom. He hadn't noticed her, he was several places ahead.

Some would queue-jump and go and join him but she was in a law-abiding mood this morning, maybe because there were one or two thoughts in her head that she hadn't been able to leave behind at the kitchen table with the dirty mug and muesli bowl.

Still no email from Steve. He'd been in Moscow two weeks now. Assuming he was still there, of course. He could always have come back with a done deal and be getting on with his life. But there was the divorce and house sale to think about.

Divorce. Sale. Oh God, it was like having two pigeons weighing a ton each coming to land on your shoulders. Well, she could always do what she'd thought of doing over a week ago and put the house on the market, couldn't she? She could do it as soon as she got into the office, before she took her coat off, before she made coffee, She could pick an estate agent at random out of the book and phone them, why wait for Steve? And there was nothing to stop her making a start on killing that room.

Killing that room… Not a pigeon-sized concept, that. More albatross-sized.

When the bus came and Tom turned to get on, he caught sight of Dora and moved back in the queue. 'I thought you were running to work to stay fit,' she said as they got on.

'I never was much good at resolutions,' he said.

They managed to find two seats together. 'Actually, I couldn't face the run today,' he said as the bus moved off. Close up, he looked tired to the point of being haggard.

201

'Seen Melanie?' she said.

'Yes.'

'Got things sorted?' Stupid question. It was pretty obvious what the answer was going to be:

'No. Anything but.'

'OK. Tell Auntie Dozza all about it.'

As he filled her in on what had happened in his kitchen in Uxbridge on Saturday morning, Dora found herself trying to visualise this room where his life had changed last autumn, and where it seemed to be going down the pan now. She'd bet it was just an ordinary boring kitchen with a cooker and a sink and a fridge, like her own: the sort of place where you could lead a life that had nothing going on in it at all. People did, after all. Maybe the woman in front of her on this bus did, the one who was hanging on every word Tom uttered, judging by the rigid set of her head.

'Pulled out of UCAS?' said Dora. 'Melanie would do that because she's got it into her head that we're having an affair?'

'Mel's always been a determined sort of girl, Dora. Actually, I've just made a decision. I'm going to Mel's school today, and I'm going to see the Head and tell him to phone UCAS and say there's been a mistake.'

The woman in front seemed to give a quick nod, or maybe it was the movement of the bus.

'So what will you tell Rose Whatsername?' said Dora. "Sorry Rose, it's a lovely day and I feel like a trip to London"?'

'Maybe. Or maybe I'll tell her the truth. It'd be good for her, I don't think she gets much exposure to life.'

'She wouldn't normally get this level of service from a temp. I hope she appreciates it.'

'If she doesn't, she can sack me. There's plenty more like me at the agency to choose from.'

Dora wasn't sure about that, but this wasn't the place to say so, and so she gazed ahead of her and said nothing. There was a baby three seats ahead. It was wearing a cute red hoodie. She took a long breath, and let it out slowly. He must have noticed, because he turned to her, a questioning look on his face.

'You're blaming yourself again, aren't you,' he murmured.

'Not yet, but I'll get around to it… Have you noticed there's a baby up ahead?'

'No, but I have now. You can't stand them, can you,' he said, his voice dropping even lower.

She took a long breath. 'It's not that. It's more that the little buggers are like ants, they're taking over the world. I'm seeing them everywhere I go.'

'I'll make sure you never have to see Mel's.'

'Well, I didn't think you'd be asking me to be her godmother.'

'"Her"?'

'It's a girl. Trust me, I've looked in my crystal ball.'

The bus was just moving off after picking up several passengers at one of the Woodstock Road stops, more passengers than there were empty seats. A woman materialised beside Tom, a woman who looked about as pregnant as it was possible to get without exploding. He stood up for her. A man like Tom couldn't have done anything else.

The woman flumped down next to Dora. 'That's very chivalrous of you, thanks so much,' she said to Tom.

Tom might have said 'That's OK,' or something, but by then Dora wasn't listening. She was looking out of the window, bottling a huge urge to laugh. She made herself as small as she could, but the woman was spilling onto her seat to such an extent that the bump was pressing hard against her. Please let the baby not move. Let her not have to feel it kicking and squirming in there.

Not long to go until she and Tom got off. She held her breath.

When the stop came in sight, she made herself turn, smile,

and say, 'Excuse me.' As the woman got up to let her out, she felt something convulse against her. She told herself it was just the bump itself shifting as the woman moved. But she was still holding her breath when she and Tom began to merge with the flow of bodies heading towards the University offices, so much so that when Tom put a hand on her arm, she jumped.

'There's Larry Wise,' he said, nodding in the direction of the charity shop.

She followed his gaze. There indeed was Larry Wise, a couple of yards away, staring into the charity shop window. 'Let's keep walking,' she murmured. She moved around Tom as she was speaking, so that he was between her and Larry Wise, but almost lost her balance as Tom darted away from her, saying, 'Hey, stop that!' She almost lost her balance a second time as a boy in a grey hoodie brushed past her and sprinted away in the direction of Walton Street.

'Another second and he'd have had his hand in your pocket,' said Tom. But he wasn't speaking to her.

'Oh… Thank you, thank you,' said Larry Wise. 'I – I fear I was distracted. I was looking for a gift for Mother. She has not been well, you see.'

He was talking to Tom but looking at her. God, those eyes. After over a week of not seeing them, they were bluer and more staring than ever.

'I'm sorry to hear that,' said Tom. 'We ought to report that boy to the police, I'll do it, I'd recognise him again. You work in the University Offices, don't you?'

'Ah… Yes, yes… I was on the point of going into the building.' Wise was still looking at Dora, and looking terrified. Because he'd almost been mugged? Or because he was expecting a telling-off about the incident in the pub? What on earth went on in a mind like his? What a sight he looked. He couldn't have shaved for days. And that hair, when did he last comb it?

As they moved on down the street, Dora kept Tom between Larry Wise and herself. Wise's mind might be a mystery, but her own was pretty clear to her at that moment. It was full of hideously embarrassing images, which was a bit much after days of trying to blot out her outburst to Melanie at the ice rink. Some Monday this was turning out to be, and it wasn't even nine o'clock yet.

Larry Wise was going slowly. He was going so slowly that at this rate they wouldn't get inside the building before lunchtime. 'M-mother. Mother...' he said. His voice was quavery, like a very old man's.

'Is your mother still not well?' said Tom.

No answer. Tom glanced at Dora, his eyebrows raised.

She shook her head. Did he think she knew how to get through to Wise any more than he did? But now Tom was frowning and making sideways motions with his eyes. It didn't take much intuitive nous to work out that he wanted her to try.

Right. Nothing for it. She took a deep breath and changed places with Tom. 'What's wrong with your mother?' she said to Wise. No response. 'Larry, what's wrong?' she said, louder.

Slowly, his head swivelled and he looked down at her. 'Miss Clayton, oh Miss Clayton,' he quavered at last. 'Mother won't get up.' He was biting his lip. And was that a tear on his cheek? Christ. 'She won't get up,' he said again.

'Maybe she's tired. Maybe she just wants a lie-in.'

'Maybe she's tired,' said Wise, sounding as if this were a philosophical proposition worthy of deep thought. 'Maybe she's tired, maybe she's tired...'

'Why don't you phone her as soon as you get in? She might have got up after you left.' Then again, she might not. And by the frown that was still hovering over Tom's face, he was allowing for that possibility too. Yes, there were a number of reasons why a woman old enough to be Wise's mother might not be getting up very early.

It was impossible to tell whether Wise was thinking along similar lines, but he speeded up – so much so that by the time they were going through the main door, Dora was breathing fast. Still, they'd got him indoors. Just over there were the stairs to the basement, ready and waiting for him to go down them. 'Right, well, we'll leave you to –' she began, when there came from behind, 'Morning Larry, is your mum better now?' It was Wise's boss, Jock Stewart: good. Wise could go down to the basement with him. As far as she and Tom were concerned, this was job done.

Wise's mouth opened and closed, and opened. But he wasn't looking at his boss. 'Miss Clayton,' he said. So, so quavery.

Did he want her to ask permission for him to phone home, for God's sake? 'Can Larry make a phone call?' she said. 'He's a bit worried about his mother and he wants to check she's OK.'

'Sure, sure,' said Jock Stewart, looking at her in an appraising way which she decided not to notice, but which might have something to do with her trips down to the basement recently. 'He can phone from my office.'

But Wise didn't follow Stewart towards the stairs. 'M-miss Clayton?' he said.

He wanted her to go down with him? 'Um, well,' she began. How in hell did she get out of this?

'Come on, Dora,' murmured Tom.

OK, OK. She wasn't getting out of this. On the way down to the basement, Jock Stewart told them in a confidential whisper that Mrs Wise was 'a bit poorly' last week, and that Wise had been off work the whole week looking after her. 'He's a good lad,' Stewart concluded.

A smile might as well do for a response, so Dora smiled.

Down in the basement, Tom didn't turn at his office door, he stayed with the rest of them.

'You've got to see Rose,' she whispered.

'Rose can wait ten minutes. I'd like to see if Larry's mother's OK,' he whispered back.

So. Larry Wise wasn't the only good lad around here. But she already knew that, didn't she.

Wise was all fingers and thumbs with the phone, and eventually Jock Stewart said, 'Here, let me get the number.'

Stewart did more than that; he sat holding the receiver to his ear, the fingers of his other hand drumming on the desk. Mrs Wise didn't seem to be rushing to answer the phone. Wise stood there looking at the phone. He reminded Dora of somebody. No, of something: that old wooden soldier Syd used to have. It was how he was standing there, arms stiff at his sides as if they didn't belong to him.

'Come on, come on, Mrs Wise, stop petting the cat and talk to me,' muttered Stewart. Wise carried on just standing there.

Stewart put the phone down, shaking his head.

'Larry, can you tell us exactly what happened this morning?' said Tom.

Wise opened his mouth, and closed it again. Then, slowly, hesitantly, words emerged, some story about teapots and biscuits and Royal Worcester. Dora could almost hear the cogs in his brain clicking slowly around, like an antique clock's. Had she ever seen a man this scared? He wasn't looking like a wooden soldier now, he was looking like a boy, a small boy who didn't know where his mother was.

'Did she have her eyes open?' said Tom.

'Oh yes, she was awake. It was so odd that she should be awake and not speaking. So unlike her,' said Wise, in a half-whimper, half-whisper. 'So unlike her.' He began to fiddle with his hair, tugging the central tuft until it stuck up, little-boy fashion.

Dora saw Stewart catch Tom's eye. Was he turning to Tom because Tom was a man? Or because he was a fellow Scot? Or because he wasn't the one who'd been down here two weeks

207

ago losing her rag about a pencil? 'We call an ambulance now, right?' said Stewart. Tom nodded.

'An ambulance?' said Wise, 'an ambulance…?'

'Just a precaution, Larry,' said Tom, putting a hand on Larry's arm.

Jock Stewart was already picking up the phone again. And Wise was staring at her.

'My father had something which sounds similar,' she said. 'He was better after a spell in hospital.' Well, it was the truth. Professor Robert Clayton FRS was better after four months in hospital than he'd been when they found him dribbling, speechless and incontinent on the floor. Eventually, he could get a word out. Whether she'd wanted to hear it was beside the point.

Jock Stewart put the phone down and said, 'Right, Larry, I'm running you home.'

'Home…? But the carpet fixing on the second floor… I should have repaired it last week…'

'The carpet can wait another week if need be,' said Stewart. 'I've got to talk about recruitment with Mrs Thatcher in half an hour, that can wait too.'

Mrs Thatcher? Must be some in-joke. Dora rose to her feet and began inching toward the door. Neither she nor Tom had anything to do with this any more.

'Miss Clayton,' quavered Wise, 'M-miss Clayton…'

Oh, God.

'Jock, we'll go with you,' said Tom. 'Just drop us there. We'll stay with Larry until the ambulance comes. Could you let our offices know what's happened when you get back?'

'But you've got to see Rose,' she whispered to him.

'Never mind Rose!' It wasn't much louder than a whisper but it had the force of a shout.

'You're a star, lad,' said Stewart. 'It wouldn't be a bad idea if I got to this particular meeting.'

They were all looking at her. 'Well, I haven't got anything urgent on this morning,' she said.

Larry Wise lived *here?* Oh God, how many more pockets was he going to need to search through to find his keys?

Ah. The ambulance was coming. That wail of the siren, that blood-racing wail, getting louder and louder as it came closer and closer and closer… But there was no need for her heart to beat like this, no need at all. It was an old woman in there, not a baby. Not a baby.

At last the house keys appeared – at the precise moment when the siren's scream jumped up several decibels in volume. Wise dropped the keys and stood looking at them. Dora bent down and picked them up.

Back at the gate, Tom was waiting to signal to the ambulance driver that this was the place. She saw him raise an arm and wave.

It hadn't quite been the sound of the vehicle, and it wasn't quite the sight of it. It wasn't even quite the sight of the two men in green overalls getting out of it. It was the way those men hurried to the door with their bags of equipment which, for a second or so, stopped the clock and sent time spinning into reverse.

The looks on those faces. Grave, purposeful, prepared for anything.

It was not, *not*, a baby in there. She had to block babies out. She had to focus with all her might on Wise's hand finally succeeding in putting the key in the lock.

When they got in, it was almost comical. While the paramedics were rushing for the stairs, Wise was stopping in his tracks and cocking his ear in the direction of a closed door at the end of the ballroom-sized hallway.

'Which room is Mrs Wise in?' a voice called from upstairs.

Wise didn't seem to be listening. 'Prinz Eugen,' he said. 'Oh my goodness, I haven't fed him.'

So that's what that faint noise was: a cat mewing.

'Er, hello?' called the voice upstairs.

'I'll deal with Prinz Eugen,' said Tom. 'Larry, you go up to your mother. Dora will go with you.'

'Come on, Larry,' she said, avoiding a hall table on which was a display of model vintage cars. This hallway was eccentric, even by North Oxford standards. Tables, dressers, shelves of every description, all in deepest, darkest mahogany, and on all these flat surfaces, models. Ships, cars, tanks, buses: modern and historic. In the air above the surfaces, other models: planes, squadrons of them, hanging from the ceiling. There had to be every plastic kit in existence here. What was she seeing – fifty years of deathly quiet evenings?

Somehow she succeeded in manoeuvring him up the stairs. This staircase: wood as dark as the hallway, and the sort of banister you might see in a museum. And the carpet under her feet was actually anchored by stair rods. When had she last seen a stair rod?

On the landing, more planes were flying overhead, enough to fight the Battle of Britain. Door after door stretched away in front of her, all with great heavy-looking brass door handles. When had she last seen a brass door handle?

One door had been flung open; there's only so much standing on ceremony paramedics have time for. For a moment it looked as if Wise was going to hover outside the door and not go in. Didn't he know the rules: there needs to be a watcher, praying to a god they don't believe in? Then he seemed to come to. 'After you, Miss Clayton,' he said.

'Larry, I'm not sure I should be going in,' she whispered.

'Please,' he whimpered.

She went in.

Dominating the enormous dim L-shaped room was a vast dark wood bedstead. In the bed lay a woman, her head with its straggly white hair lolling sideways on the pillow, her right eyelid drooping, almost closed, and her left eye staring straight

210

ahead. The tea tray on the bedside table was exactly as Wise had described, down to the two untouched biscuits.

This smell. Faint, but not hard to place: pee. Everything in here added up to one diagnosis, a diagnosis that couldn't be clearer if there were a placard nailed to the bed head saying BRAIN ATTACK. On that pillow, brain cells were failing, maybe dying.

The paramedics were hovering over Mrs Wise like bluebottles over meat. No, greenbottles, in those overalls. Why were flies called bluebottles? Who but the colour-blind ever saw a bright blue house-fly?

So green, those overalls. Even greener for this dimness.

Two men in green overalls bending over a heap in a bed, muttering words that no-one but they could understand… but the urgency in their voices telling the listener much. Too much. She swallowed, shifted from foot to foot.

Larry Wise was staring at the paramedics, wide-eyed, open-mouthed. Was that how she herself had looked? If she counted – counted to fifty, say – something would surely have happened, something would have changed.

On thirty nine the slightly taller paramedic said, 'OK Mike, let's go.'

It was when he lifted his head to speak that she saw it. How could she have missed it until now, the mole above his lip that bobbed up and down as he spoke? Maybe she'd missed it because he looked older, greyer. Must be all the pain he'd seen in the last three years. Should she greet him, say hello?

No. What could she say after hello – ask him if he had any idea what might have happened to that orange jumpsuit?

There was that mewing sound again. Tom must have let the cat come up – no, he hadn't: the mewing was coming from the man she was standing next to as he watched them lift his mother into a canvas contraption midway between a chair and a stretcher.

211

'Mother?' he mewed as they followed the paramedics out of the room with their blanket-covered load. How short she looked in that thing. In the bed she'd looked tall, for a woman of her age. Tall enough to have given birth to a son this size, at any rate.

'Mother?' he said again, the little boy lost.

Look on the bright side, Larry Wise. It's not your child. It's not your child!

So. The same paramedic. All she needed now was that dog, the one that trotted past as she was climbing into the ambulance. He'd had a brown patch on one ear. But which ear was it? What was his name, that dog? There'd been a man with him, a man who'd called to him to keep up, or something.

Out in the street, there was no dog in sight. Maybe Mrs Wise would pull through.

'Miss Clayton?' said Wise, who was hovering beside her. 'Please, will you come?'

Not again... 'Can I?' she said to 'her' paramedic, who was busy loading Mrs Wise into the ambulance. 'I don't think he can manage on his own,' she went on, as quietly as she could.

'Hop in,' the man said, not even looking at her. He still didn't waste words, then.

'Dora, will you be all right?' said Tom, quietly. 'Why don't I come too?'

'This is an ambulance, not a bus,' she murmured back. 'I'll be all right. I've seen hospitals before.'

'That's what I meant.'

She tried to smile. 'I know. If you've got a moment, can you phone Siobhan and tell her what I'm doing? Better let Jock Stewart know what's happening too. Anyway, good luck with the UCAS business.' She stepped up into the ambulance. 'Come on, Larry.'

The paramedics were hooking Mrs Wise up to various bits of apparatus along one side of the ambulance. Dora sat down on the opposite side, and Wise sat right next to her, almost squashing her. Mike, the shorter paramedic, disappeared into the driver's compartment, and they moved off. Mike was new since last time, but this ambulance was the same one, oh yes. Sane, sensible people would tell her ambulances were all alike, but sane, sensible people were wrong about so many things in life. This row of plastic-covered seats which she and Larry Wise were sitting on, the trolley Mrs Wise was lying on, the screen and dials and wires, she'd seen them all before, just as she'd seen the expression on this paramedic's face. *Should* she say 'Hi'? This was on a par with cutting your best friend in the street.

The screen was showing regular blips. The woman wasn't dead. Yet.

NO SMOKING said the notice over the archway to the driver's cab. At some point in the last three years someone had underlined the words in red.

'Miss Clayton,' said Wise.

If he said that *once* more. 'Call me Dora. Please.'

'Oh. Oh, yes. D-Dora, what is happening to Mother?'

'They're trying to make her well. Don't worry.'

It was pushing his mother's luck a bit to be saying that. This wasn't the sort of stroke where the patient walks into the hospital on her own two feet complaining of slight wooziness.

Christ, it was what that nurse said. The one who sat with her.

Seventeen

In a situation like this you don't have time to think, they say. From the moment the double doors slide back and they rush the patient in, all you're supposed to have time to do is run behind while alarm bells ring and whistles blow.

But it isn't like that, of course. It's about sitting and waiting on a plastic chair which turns your bottom numb. It's about watching brown liquid pouring into paper cups from a machine and looking at the carpet between your feet and finding yourself wondering what colour it is, grey or blue. It's about staring so hard at the floor that after a while you can see the earthworms tunnelling under the foundations of the building.

There were some differences from three years ago, though. No nice nurse holding her hand this time. And no stain like the map of Australia on the floor in front of the coffee machine. The NHS must have robbed a bank and had it cleaned off.

It wasn't a particularly hilarious thought, but a laugh seemed to be trying to force its way out of her, a laugh she put a firm lid on as two harassed-looking nurses scurried past. She glanced at her watch. It had been an hour now since Mrs Wise had been trundled away, and her panic-eyed son with her.

The way Wise looked back at her as he went. But they'd never have let people who weren't next of kin beyond where she was sitting. He was lucky they'd let even him into the treatment room.

Three years ago, she wasn't given the option. Should she have asked to watch? Would it have made any difference? Bloody, bloody—

She looked at her watch. It was all of two minutes later than when she last looked. If she were less nice than she was, she might just push off now. Fat lot of good she was doing sitting here. Still, what if Larry Wise came out to go to the gents or something and found her not here? Hell, she was stuck. Stuck, stuck, stuck...

She picked up a dog-eared gardening magazine, the only one she hadn't already looked at, from the table next to the row of seats and began leafing through it. She'd have been more use going with Tom to see Melanie's headmaster. She could have told this David Dent it was her fault, and if he knew his job he'd put her in detention.

How long would somebody like her deserve to get? More time than you'd take to write a hundred lines, for certain. *I must not make bad things worse, I must not make bad things worse, I must not...*

Dora must have drifted into some sort of trance-like doze. She woke up with a start when she felt a hand on her shoulder. She looked up. It was Jock Stewart.

'Hello, lassie. Well done for staying, but I'll take over from you now,' he said.

Thank God. At last, she could go.

But Jock thought that before she left they ought to let Wise know what was happening. He flagged down a nurse:

'Mrs Wise? Oh yes, the lady with the son,' said the nurse, and by her expression it looked as if she'd personally had some dealings with the son over the last couple of hours. 'I think they've stabilised her for the moment,' she went on. 'You're friends of Mr Wise, are you?'

'We are,' said Jock Stewart straight away, '*close* friends. We'd just like to tell Larry we're swapping over, so he knows who to look for afterwards.'

'Yes…' said the nurse, looking from one to the other of them. Then she seemed to make up her mind: 'Second door on the right. Tell them Sister Edmunds said you could, but don't stay too long, will you.'

Larry Wise was sitting by the bed, gazing at his mother. There were three other people in the room, moving purposefully about: a middle-aged man who looked like the doctor in charge, a girl so young-looking she could only be a junior doctor, and an older woman, a nurse. The nurse looked toward her and Jock Stewart, raising her eyebrows. 'Erica Tate' said the name badge on the woman's chest. What name had been on that other badge, the one she'd had in her face three years ago – Maureen-something, wasn't it? Maureen Knight? Maureen Wright?

All the time Jock Stewart was doing the explaining, Larry Wise gave no sign of knowing they were there. To get his attention, Dora had to stand over him and put her hand on his arm.

Wise looked at her hand. Then he looked up at her face. He blinked, then the surface of his face seemed to convulse, and finally it melted. After several seconds it began to reform, and eventually the features ended up in approximately their original states and positions. Except for those eyes. They were bluer, if that were possible. 'Oh, Miss Cl— Dora,' he said, half-rising.

'Don't get up. Larry. We just wanted to tell you Jock's here now and he'll give you a lift afterwards. I have to get back to the office now, all right?'

Wise didn't say anything. All he did was gaze at her, his mouth opening and closing. But he wasn't the only one gazing at her. His mother was, too – out of her left eye. The right eye was shut, its eyelid drooped over it like a saggy curtain.

Mrs Wise had her head propped up. She was visibly a woman, not an indeterminately gendered heap, but she was a woman surrounded by equipment, besieged and hemmed in by monitor screens, dials, switches, lights, wires and tubes, and she was wearing an oxygen mask. The doctors were bent over the bed, fiddling with the dials and switches. A bit too much of this and not enough of that, and by the end of the day this woman would become another mortality statistic. The grey face would drain down to off-white, and the staring eye and the drooping eye would each glaze over.

That staring eye. Blue, like her son's. Why should it be so hard to look at an open eye?

The little girl doctor made another adjustment to a dial, while the nurse checked the drip.

Time to make themselves scarce, but Dora could hardly leave without making sure Wise knew she was going. He was gazing at his mother again. 'Larry,' she tried. No response. 'Larry,' she repeated, louder, putting her hand on his arm again.

When he turned towards her, she had to will herself not to look aside. God, the blueness of those eyes looking up at hers. And that eye of his mother's, it was still watching her. How could that be? She herself had changed position, and that eye had no power to follow her. But what was it people said about eyes in paintings following you around a room?

'I have to go, Larry,' she said. 'But Jock's here now.'

'Aye, here I am, lad,' said Stewart, gruffly.

Lines deepened in the forehead of Wise's open-mouthed face and around his bright blue eyes. What else could she do now but pat his arm and turn to go? But somewhere between

217

her decision to do so and her body acting on it, he turned slightly, moving his arm at the same time. Which meant that she made contact with his hand instead.

His gaze dropped to her hand, resting on his. And then his other hand was over hers, and he was hunching forward over the sandwich of hands as if it would vanish unless he watched it like a hawk.

If it hadn't been for Nurse Tate saying to Wise that she was sorry but his friends ought to go now, Dora might have been standing there until the eye scrutinising her from the bed had taken a full inventory of all the cells in her body. Provided, of course, the eye-brain link was still working. If it was, that eye had already had time to collect a fair bit of information, enough to feed the brain behind it with plenty to chew over. It might be bleeding, but the cogs in that brain could be whizzing and whirring as well as anybody's.

'I'll see you later, Larry,' she said slowly and, she hoped, clearly.

For a second there was that look in his eyes that she'd seen in the pub ten days ago, that drowning look. Then he took his hands slowly away and clasped them together in his lap. It was all she could do not to look at her hand to see how much he'd flattened it. It was even harder not to flex it until she and Jock Stewart were outside the room. But she couldn't let so much as her little finger twitch, with that left eye of his mother's watching her all the way to the door.

The way Wise's two hands had come together just then. As if they had to hang on to something, even if all there was, was one another.

Nurse Tate came out with them. 'How is Mrs Wise?' said Jock Stewart.

'A bit poorly,' was the answer. What this stacked up to was total right-side paralysis and speech completely gone. It was going to take a day or two to find out exactly what 'the full extent of the situation' was. Mrs Wise was booked for a CT scan first thing the next day, which should give the doctors a good lead.

'Touch and go, I reckon,' said Stewart when Nurse Tate had headed off down the corridor. 'Poor old Larry, he could be needing a lot of TLC.'

'Yes,' said Dora, keeping her eyes on Nurse Tate's retreating back. 'Right, I'll be off. What did my boss say, by the way, am I in for a roasting?'

'As of when I left, your boss was still stuck on the M40. Massive pile-up at eight o'clock this morning and she's some way behind it.'

Phew. Bit rough on the ones in the pile-up, though, she supposed. There was a bus for central Oxford already waiting at the hospital bus stop. Nobody was on it apart from an elderly woman near the front and a man of indeterminate age in a shabby-looking anorak two seats behind the woman. Dora took the seat across the aisle from the woman. As the bus pulled away from the stop, one thing became clear in her mind: avoiding Larry Wise around the office wasn't going to be an option from now on. And if Mrs Wise died? If that happened, she could see herself having to let Wise come up and spill more coffee over her desk whenever he liked, and whatever Siobhan might think.

TLC. People like Jock Stewart and Tom were good at it. Bit of a bugger that she'd been at the back of the class when aptitude for it had been dished out. She was a bit old to be learning new things now. Looked as if she was going to have to try, though. If there was going to be any 'TLC' on the agenda, sure as anything the one Larry Wise would want supplying most of it was 'Miss Clayton.'

The almost-empty bus rattled down the hill. It was a funny time to be on a bus, the middle of a working day. Just her and those two others on board, two lonely people without anywhere much to go, by the look of them. Everybody she knew was somewhere else doing things, constructive things. On this bus, she was as alone as she'd ever been.

At the bottom of the hill, the bus passed a row of shops. The signboard on one of them, a computer repairers, said 'E-Zee PC.'

Why it should make her want to laugh, God only knew, but it did. She managed to keep the laugh contained until she got off the bus, and for most of the way to the office. But on the way down Little Clarendon Street, her shoulders began to shake. In the short distance to the office entrance, she had a number of the honest citizens of Oxford turning around to stare at her.

Eighteen

Tom arrived at Blackstone School just as break was finishing. Debbie Priday, Mel's friend, was walking down the main drive, doing her prefect's duty of herding some younger children back inside the school building. She stopped dead when she caught sight of him.

'Hello, Debbie,' he said as he drew level with her.

'Hi – er, hello,' she said.

About a dozen young faces were gazing up at Tom. He recognized a fair number of his Year Seven group, the ones he'd been doing theatre-in-the-round with on his last day in this place, and gave them what he hoped was a relaxed smile. 'I'm just popping in to see the Head,' he said to Debbie, making it sound as if it were something he did most days of the week.

'Oh. Right,' said Debbie, looking mystified.

'Hi, Mr Ross,' said one of the children, a boy. 'You OK?'

The kid meant it. *Jesus.*

'Hello, Luke. Yes, I'm OK, thanks.'

'You coming back, Mr Ross?' a bright-eyed girl piped up.

'I'm afraid not, Shareena,' he said. *Keep smiling.*

'Oh,' they all said. The chorus's sagging cadence made it hard to hold his smile in place, but hold it he did, before telling Debbie he had to dash, he wanted to catch the Head before he started his Monday morning walkabout.

As soon as Tom pushed open the main door, the smell began to wind itself around him, the smell of paper and books and biros and hundreds of trainers and young bodies barely able to contain the swirling tides of hormones. A school smell, nothing like it in the wide world. How could he have forgotten it so soon?

The door to David Dent's outer office was open. He put his head around it.

'*Tom?*' said Betsy Drew, the Head's secretary, jumping out of her chair.

'Yes, it's me, Betsy,' said Tom, going in and shutting the door behind him. 'I'd like a word with DD about Melanie Baines.'

'About Melanie?' she repeated, frowning.

'There's a problem with UCAS. I think it can be sorted, but DD's got to be the one to sort it, and he's got to do it now.'

'Tom, he's up to here with the budget. He was supposed to be finalising it over the weekend for this afternoon's management meeting but his mother's boiler broke down and it took hours and hours to get one of these emergency people to come and fix it. He's even abandoning the walkabout this morning. See that door?' She jerked her head towards the inner office, its door firmly shut. 'He said on no account let anybody through it before lunchtime. So, what sort of problem with UCAS?'

'Mel's withdrawn her application. She's got it into her head she wants to put off going to university for a while,' he said, picking his words carefully. 'She wants to get a job and save enough to finance herself through uni. I don't think it's one of her better ideas.'

'Oh, sugar. One of our cleverest pupils. Are her parents pressuring her?'

'Not that I know of,' he said, again picking his words. 'Anyway, if you don't mind, I'll knock on DD's door now, please.'

'All right. Be it on your own head, though.'

'I'll say I forced my way past you.'

'Hm. On second thoughts, let me go in first,' she said, coming out from behind her desk. 'You're still in contact with Melanie, then?'

'Yes. We chat.'

She was looking at him, steadily, her eyebrows raised. She was no fool, she must have guessed what had gone on. She'd been a good friend to him in the past; she deserved the full story if anybody did. For a moment he was on the verge of telling her about the impending wedding, but that would mean going behind Mel's back. On the other hand, wasn't that what he was already doing? 'I'm keeping in touch with her school work,' he said.

As Tom finished speaking, the inner door opened. 'Betsy, could you,' began David Dent. Then he stopped, and his jaw hit the floor. In any other circumstance it would have been comic. '*Ross?* What in hell are you doing here?'

'Hello, DD,' said Tom. As he repeated what he'd said to Betsy, the Head's jaw dropped again. He shook his head, as if in a daze.

'Withdrawn from UCAS… Are you sure?'

'She told me on Saturday.'

'I have to sit down,' he said retreating into the inner office. 'Betsy, get Melanie Baines out of whatever lesson she's in.'

Well. This wouldn't be happening behind Mel's back for much longer. 'It's double German,' said Tom to Betsy as he followed Dent into his office.

'Don't let on Ross is here, tell her it's about the prefects' lunchtime supervision rota or some such thing,' called Dent. 'Shut the door and sit down,' he went on, motioning Tom to a

223

chair. Dent eased himself into the chair behind the desk and pushed aside a mountain of papers. The Head looked greyer than when Tom had last seen him. His face was as grey as his hair, and his hair was as grey as his suit, his London-comprehensive-headmaster-suit. Was there any grey so grey.

He himself would never have gone for a headship. Never in a million years.

'So, Ross, you're still talking to Melanie,' said Dent, passing a hand over his face. Unless Tom's imagination was working overtime in the stress of the moment, there'd been the very slightest emphasis on the word 'talking.'

'Yes. We talk about her schoolwork. I hope that doesn't count as favouritism any longer, given my change of circumstances.'

Dent looked at him, frowning, but there was concern in the eyes, or at least it looked as if there was. 'What are you doing with yourself, exactly?' he said.

'I've started a bit of writing, as you suggested. And I'm temping.'

Dent carried on looking at him for a couple of seconds. Then he lowered his gaze toward the desk. 'Temping?' he said. 'What, filing and that sort of thing?'

'Yes, typing memos and so forth. You meet some interesting people in offices, I've found. And who knows, maybe the agency'll send me to a school next time.' He forced a smile.

A second or so passed, then Dent gave a quiet sigh.

Tom shifted in his seat. He wasn't here to talk about himself. They were drifting off the only subject that mattered today. 'Mel's regretting pulling out of UCAS, I'm sure of it,' he said. 'I think you ought to get on the phone and tell them there's been a mistake. Do it right now, before Betsy gets back here with her.'

'Hang on, hold your horses,' said Dent, putting his elbows on the desk, 'I'm going to hear her side of the story first.'

Her side? And what side was that going to be? Oh Jesus, he had to tell Dent everything, he had to. 'Look,' he began, leaning forward in his chair. Then there was a knock at the door.

'It's me, Headmaster,' came Betsy's voice.

So Betsy was back, and her use of 'Headmaster' said all too clearly that there was a pupil with her. Tom's stomach felt suddenly queasy, and he swallowed. Whatever happened in the next ten minutes, please God let him stay calm.

The door opened. Betsy came in. 'Melanie Baines to see you, Headmaster,' she said. As she stood aside to let Mel pass, Tom's heart rate doubled.

At first, Mel didn't see him. He was sitting to one side of the desk, away from her line of sight. 'Sit down, Melanie,' said Dent.

Mel turned, and saw Tom. Her face went white. Then it flushed scarlet. 'Oh!' she cried. 'Oh shit.'

'Hello, Mel,' he said.

'This isn't about lunchtime duty rotas, is it,' she said to Dent.

'No, Melanie, it isn't,' said Dent. 'Now sit down, please, we're going to have a talk.'

Mel looked from the Head to Tom and back. For a moment, her lips quivered and her eyes looked stricken. Then she took a long breath and sat down.

Dent picked up a pen and began twiddling it in his fingers. 'Melanie, I gather from Tom here that you've withdrawn from UCAS,' he said. 'Is that right?'

Tom? The Head had never called him by his given name. Only ever Ross.

'Yes,' said Mel. 'I – I've been thinking about the money,' she went on haltingly, 'and if I worked for a bit, then…'

Enough of this. He'd been interrupted a minute or so ago by Mel's arrival, and now he was going to interrupt right back.

'Melanie doesn't want to be dependent on her future husband,' he said. 'Me.'

'No, no, shut up!' cried Mel, flapping her hands at him.

Dent now looked twice as shell-shocked as he had when he set eyes on Tom in the outer office. His mouth opened, and then closed.

'Mel's a very moral girl,' Tom went on, before Dent could say anything. 'She doesn't like the idea of taking money to go to university from a man who has less of it than he used to.'

Mel was now hiding her face in her hands.

'You're getting *married*?' said Dent at last.

'Three weeks on Wednesday. I would say pop into the Register Office at 11.30 if you're free, but we're keeping it strictly family and close friends.'

'Three *weeks*,' began Dent. Then: 'Oh. Ah. I do believe the penny's dropping. Oh my God.'

'Mel is ten weeks pregnant,' said Tom, saving Dent the trouble of asking his next question.

'It's not his!' cried Mel, jumping out of her chair. 'It's – it's somebody else's.'

Poor Dent. He wasn't going to forget this day in a hurry, the day the budget wasn't finalised on time.

'Mel,' said Tom, but Mel waved at him to be quiet.

And so did Dent. 'Let's all get our breath back, before my brain goes into meltdown,' he said, looking hard at Tom. 'Just tell me one thing, Melanie. Is this baby's father connected with the school? In any capacity whatever?'

'No,' declared Mel, and gave him the story about the fling with the 'guy from Brunel'. 'He was at school in the Midlands,' she finished. If she was trying to disguise the flush spreading across her cheeks, she was failing.

Dent blinked once or twice, and pursed his lips. 'The Midlands, eh,' he repeated. 'The Midlands… So, Tom,' he went on, slowly, 'you're going to be father to the baby of some chap who, I take it, is off the scene.' He was twiddling his pen again as he spoke.

'Yes,' said Mel, before Tom had a chance to answer.

'And you're planning to be the one funding the million and one things the student loan won't stretch to,' Dent went on, still addressing Tom. 'Or, for that matter, stopping Melanie from getting herself any more in hock than strictly necessary?'

'Yes,' said Tom. 'No!' said Mel, in unison.

'Well,' said Dent, 'not many men would do that. No, not many.' He put his pen down and leaned back in his chair. 'He's a serious-minded bloke, Melanie. I'd let him support you if I were you. I wouldn't be surprised if he's planning to get his hands dirty when the baby arrives, too. There's nothing stopping you from carrying on with your university plans, you know.'

'With a baby?' Mel shot back.

'The Head's right, Mel, I'm intending to be very involved,' said Tom.

She looked at him, only for a second, but he had the impression of a cornered wild creature. Such creatures submit to circumstances in the end. Please let it be soon.

'Melanie,' said Dent, 'the last admissions officer I met said they were doing everything to help students with young children, short of getting the teaching staff to bottle-feed while they're lecturing.'

'What if I want to look after this baby?' said Mel.

'I know. I'm being an interfering old git,' said Dent. 'You get like that in this job, I'm afraid. Look, if you nail the university place now, any worthwhile institution will give you a gap year to get the baby established. I'll have a word with them if that's what it takes.' He picked up the pen again and started turning it end over end. Tom made himself look away. The effect was more hypnotic than he needed.

'But what's the point of all this?' said Mel. 'I've pulled out of UCAS. That's it, surely.'

'As Tom knows, UCAS withdrawals can be un-withdrawn in exceptional cases,' Dent said, still playing with his pen, 'And here's why this case is exceptional.' He paused, and gave a wide smile, turning first to Tom and then back to Mel. 'It's exceptional because of what I'm going to do to him.' He jerked his head toward Tom.

What? Was the Head going to turn him over to the police after all? But he could hardly take care of Mel and a baby if he were in jail! It was Mel's face, though, rather than the Head's words which made Tom's heart stop: the pain in her eyes beyond anything he'd seen, even on the day he left Uxbridge for Oxford.

'You can't do a thing to him!' she cried, jumping up and putting her hands on the desk. 'I told you, it's not his!'

'I heard what you said, Melanie,' said Dent, his voice as mild as milk. 'But can't I even write him a reference?'

A reference. A reference? What was the man saying?

But it was Mel who spoke the question aloud: 'A *reference?*'

'Yes, Melanie a reference. For a job. Something along the lines of: "Tom Ross is one of the very few teachers I have met in my career whom I would recommend to any school, anywhere, at any time, but preferably one in the town where his wife's got a university place" – that sort of thing.'

'Oh,' she said, subsiding into her chair.

Tom could think of nothing to say. So he said nothing.

'Of course, it means Tom putting the writing on the back burner and going back to teaching, but he's the kind of man who knows how to sort out his priorities,' said Dent. 'So, what I'm actually saying is,' he went on, turning to Tom, 'you're going to have to find a decent steady job again to support this young girl in the proper manner. That understood?'

'Er, yes,' said Tom. Croaked, rather.

Mel had both hands up to her face. Unless Tom's eyes were playing tricks, she was shaking.

'Melanie,' said Dent, sounding almost fatherly, 'once Tom gets stuck into a new teaching job, you'll be fine, both of you. A teacher's pay isn't sky-high, as we all know, but you'll manage on it. So, do I phone UCAS?' His hand hovered over the phone.

After what felt to Tom like an eternity but couldn't have been more than a few seconds, Mel nodded.

In a matter of minutes, Dent had everything sorted out. A misunderstanding, now clarified, was the gist of what he told UCAS. When he put the phone down, he told them that UCAS had been 'particularly grateful' for his call because Bristol were in the process of offering the candidate a place, and there'd been some confusion.

'Right, so clear off and celebrate, both of you,' he finished. 'Oh, and on your way out tell Betsy to be a love and put some more coffee on, will you? I've got a million sums still to do before this afternoon.'

In the outer office, Betsy was at the computer. She looked from one to the other of them, eyebrows raised. 'DD would like some coffee,' said Tom. 'I wouldn't mind some myself, actually, after I've said goodbye to Mel.'

Outside, the corridor was deserted. 'Well, Melly,' he said, 'a place at Bristol. Fantastic.'

'Yeah,' she said, without meeting his eye.

He reached for her hand. She didn't resist, but her hand felt tentative. A wild creature who'd submitted, but to a set of circumstances that had set her head reeling? That made two of them. Somewhere close by, a door opened and shut, but Tom didn't let Mel's hand go until she wriggled it free, saying that she had to get back, she didn't want to miss any more of the German lesson.

He set off down the corridor with her. 'What about next weekend?' he ventured.

'Maybe,' she said, still not looking at him.

At the bottom of the stairs leading to the Senior School Centre she said, 'You don't have to come up.'

'Not even to see where I used to teach? To remind myself what a school looks like?'

She looked down at the floor, chewing her lip. Then she said, 'OK. If you like.'

He was on the point of putting his foot on the bottom step when an internal voice said *Don't push it*. 'On second thoughts, I'd better get back to Oxford. My boss isn't in the best of moods today. I'm overdue with some spreadsheets.'

'Well, now you can tell her where to stick her spreadsheets, can't you.'

'Yes, I suppose I can.' *Thanks to you.*

'Bye, then.' She turned away and began to run up the stairs.

'Bye,' he called after her. Half way up, she looked back for a second, but without stopping – not a thing to do on those stairs if you didn't want to trip and fall. After she'd disappeared from view, he found that he was standing with his arms held out to catch her.

There were noises a little way away, as of a lesson finishing: a classful of what sounded like younger children must be spilling out into the corridor. He made his way smartly back to Betsy Drew's office, before he was spotted. He'd have that coffee before he headed back to Oxford. He needed it.

Should he have thanked Mel? He was going back to teaching. But for this UCAS episode, that wouldn't be happening.

Jesus, what was he thinking? This whole business must be addling his brains. No, of course he shouldn't have bloody well thanked her!

Try as she might, for all Mel was taking in of the German lesson, she might just as well have gone for a walk with Tom in the school grounds. But if she hadn't got away from him

230

when she did, she might have said something she didn't want to say, something neither of them had said up to now. Like, 'I love you.' *Oh, fuck, fuck, fuck!*

He was going back to teaching. She'd got into Bristol. She should be over the moon. Instead, she was completely up in the air. She was blowing about like a kid's kite on a windy day, and any moment now she'd come crashing down.

No, no, that wasn't right. She was feeling more than just blown about.

It took her another ten minutes of listening to Frau Mezger firing questions – and making sure she didn't catch the teacher's eye and be put on the spot – before she got it. She felt like a little girl. She was nine again, and the grown-ups had caught her doing something incredibly stupid. She was standing there looking at her shoes with her lower lip stuck out feeling like she wanted to disappear, and hating everybody, herself most of all. Except she couldn't make herself hate Tom, fuck it.

In the Head's eyes Tom was a hero, looking after her, the naughty little girl. Oh God, he'd be a hero in anybody's eyes, even hers. If she let him.

If only she knew for certain he didn't have anybody else, like that Dora Clayton. No way was she going to ask him, though. No bloody way.

Nineteen

Dora was flicking through *Yellow Pages* when the phone rang. It was Tom, wondering if she'd seen Larry Wise yet today to ask after his mother. 'I was just popping down,' she said. Well, it was true. It was going to be true, anyway. When she'd geared herself to actually phone an estate agent and get the house put on the market.

Tom suggested she pick him up from his office in two minutes and they could see Larry together.

'OK,' she said, letting *Yellow Pages* fall shut. 'I'll want a full breakdown of what happened at school, mind.'

It took her less than a minute to extract the salient facts from him.

'Ah. You're going back to teaching?' By the look on his face, he couldn't quite believe it.

'Looks like it. I'm applying for that fill-in job at Syd's school. I have to, to shut Tommy up.'

'Not Bristol?'

'I can't tempt Providence, Mel still has to get the A's. I'll be here until the summer.'

'Will you? Well, if you're still here in September, you can help me swat wasps.' *Sorry, that just came out.*

He didn't reply straight away. 'Where will you be living in September, Dora?' he said after a few seconds.

'Christ knows,' she said, and closed a shutter on the thought.

One detail Tom hadn't given her was what Mel now thought about any affair between the two of them. Maybe the subject hadn't come up. There's only so much you can discuss while a clever headmaster like this David Dent is busy trying to sort you out so he can get on with his budget.

They found Larry Wise in the basement kitchen area, drying up a trayful of mugs.

'Hello, Larry,' said Dora. No response. She cleared her throat and said, louder, 'Morning, Larry.'

He jumped, and dropped the drying-up cloth. He turned, blinking at them. 'Oh…er, hello Miss Clayton,' he said, 'and…'

'Tom,' said Tom. 'Tom Ross.'

'Oh, ah, yes… We have met, I'm so sorry. You very kindly came to the house yesterday with me and Miss—'

'Do call me Dora,' said Dora, suppressing the flicker of irritation. He wasn't looking great. The hair was still uncombed, the chin was still unshaven, and he couldn't have slept last night. He looked a good ten years older since yesterday. 'We came down to see how your mother is,' she went on.

He looked at her, frowning. No, he was looking slightly to one side of her. 'To see how Mother is,' he repeated. 'Mother is… Mother is as well as can be expected.' It was as if he was reciting a line he'd been taught.

'So no change for the worse?' said Tom.

'No change for the worse,' came the answer, if it was an answer.

'Is there anything we can do – come with you to the hospital this evening, for instance?' Tom went on.

Eh? He might have given her notice that he was going to say that.

'Oh, er…' said Larry Wise.

'We could give you a lift there,' said Tom, 'I'm sure my sister would be happy to lend me her car.'

'A lift…that would be most kind,' said Larry Wise, blinking again, 'most kind.'

'Shall we pick you up at seven tonight, say, at your house?'

'Oh, yes, yes. Thank you, thank you so much.'

When they were on their way back to Tom's office, he said, 'I didn't get a chance to tell you yesterday, but Larry's kitchen is a spectacular tip. Dishes in the sink isn't the half of it, it has to be seen to be believed. It may be like that as a general rule, of course.'

'Oh? Was it so much of a tip that you couldn't find the cat?'

'Prinz Eugen? Oh, I found him. I could hardly not have, given what he'd left all over the floor. Animals get stressed. He'll have sensed something was wrong.'

'What sort of cat is he? Big? Small? Black? White? Tangerine with green stripes?'

'He's massive. I've never seen a cat so black, and so muscular. He wears a red collar with a medallion hanging from it. I noticed his name and address on the medallion.'

'Only his name and address? No phone number, fax, email?'

'There might have been. I didn't have time to check.'

'Tut tut. What would you call a cat if you had one?' What would she herself call a cat? Not Snowy or Fluffy, definitely not anything like that. When she moved to Christ knew where, maybe she could get a cat. She could turn into one of those batty women who took cats for walks in shabby old prams, muttering to themselves.

'The naming of cats is a difficult matter, it isn't just one of your holiday games,' he said.

'Funny thing to do on holiday,' she said. *Not a patch on ducks and drakes…*

'It's TS Eliot. From his poem, "The naming of Cats". It's in *Old Possum's Book of Practical Cats*. When I was eight, I read and re-read that book until it was falling apart.'

'Oh. Myself, I was more of a train-set person than a poetry person.'

'There's nothing wrong with train sets. I had one too.'

'I always did like a broad-minded man. Right, we seem to have reached your office.'

'So we have. I'll collect you tonight at ten to seven, if that's OK.'

'All right. See you then, then.'

She sensed him looking after her as she walked away. Exchanges like this with him, they did have a certain…energy. Maybe people who weren't having an affair should be rationing them? Then again, these conversations might be all that was keeping her sane. Her shoulders began to shake, and she clamped a hand against her mouth. Not here in the corridor, for God's sake.

Laurence stood in his kitchen and surveyed the scene. What a dreadful, dreadful mess. How could he have allowed this to happen while Mother was ill? What would she say when she came home? The bathroom and lavatories were just as bad, possibly even worse. It was not only since Mother had been ill that he had been so slapdash, if he were honest. It was since the morning when Miss Clayton asked him not to come to her office. His chest constricted at the memory of the pain. He picked up an overflowing bin, from which egg shells and burnt toast fell to the floor as he lifted it, and put it down again. There was no time to deal with this now. That kind young man – Tom Ross, he *must* remember – would be here very soon with Miss Clayton. No, not 'Miss Clayton' – Dora. Dora, Dora. He must remember that, too. She was so helpful yesterday, staying with him in the hospital. Might she, after all,

235

wish to be his friend? Might she let him visit her in her office again?

The thought dazzled him, so much so that he had to sit down, first moving a pile of damp drying-up cloths from the one unencumbered chair. The thought was so compelling that he dropped the drying-up cloths on the floor, rather than distract himself by taking them to the laundry bin. He was still sitting contemplating the thought when the doorbell rang. The sound in the empty house made him start, and for a few seconds he wondered who it might be and what they might want.

The clock in the hall struck the hour. Seven o'clock... Ah, it must be Tom Ross and Miss— Dora! He jumped up and hurried to the door.

Laurence looked out of the passenger seat window as they drove. How intriguing, to see the world from a car. From a bus it looked very different. He must tell Mother. Would Mother be able to speak to him today? Oh, she must, she must! She must come home soon, she did not belong in that hospital.

'M— Dora, are you sure you are comfortable in the rear?' he said, turning his head as far as he could.

'Really, I'm fine, Larry. As I said just now, it's far roomier than it looks.'

'Oh. I – I am glad.' He made an effort to smile. One could never be too solicitous for a friend's comfort.

In a very few minutes, Tom Ross was bringing the car to a halt. Laurence gazed at the huge building across the car park. 'Is this the place?' he asked Tom – he must accustom himself to thinking of the young man as Tom. Perhaps Tom would be his friend too? 'It looks so different from yesterday,' he added for clarification, not wishing to seem to be questioning Tom's ability to find the hospital.

'You're seeing it in the evening,' said Tom. 'With the natural

236

light almost gone and all the lights on, places like this do look rather different. I've found that myself on a number of occasions.'

'Oh, have you, indeed?'

'Right, shall we go in?' said Dora.

The interior of the hospital was a maze of corridors. 'Where are we going?' he asked his new friends after they'd been walking for approximately two minutes. 'Are we lost?'

'No, it's all right, this is the way to the stroke unit,' said Dora.

'Oh.' He looked at her. 'How clever you are, how brave. Without your help and Tom's, I fear I would be quite unable to find Mother.'

'That's OK, think nothing of it,' said Tom.

They took him to a room in which they said Mother was. 'Go in, Larry,' said Dora. 'We'll be just outside.'

'Oh, ah, yes… Oh. Should I not have brought flowers and grapes? Are those not the things one brings to sick people?'

'She won't mind, she just wants to see you,' said Dora. 'Trust me.'

'Trust… Yes, I shall. Thank you, Miss— Dora.'

He pushed open the door. Mother was half sitting, half reclining, in much the same position as yesterday. 'Good evening, Mother,' he said.

Mother did not reply. He took a step towards the bed, and another. Mother still did not reply. He sat down on the chair next to the bed. Mother's face was as it was yesterday, with one eye closed and the other open. 'Are you comfortable, Mother?' he said. She did not reply, but the hand nearer to him twitched. He took it, and held it for the rest of the silent hour he spent with her.

Dora lost count of the number of times she looked at her watch. And of the number of times she told herself to regard this as lesson one in that knottiest of subjects, TLC. In the end, it took a nurse going in to get Larry Wise out of his mother's room. Between Dora and Tom, they shepherded him out of the hospital and back to the car. All he would say was 'Mother is as well as can be expected,' and he carried on saying this at intervals as they drove back to his house. 'Thank you so much for accompanying me,' he said when they arrived. 'Would you like to come inside and take some refreshment?'

'Great. Thanks,' said Tom – not looking at Dora first.

Dora wanted 'refreshment' about as much as she'd wanted the coffee she was now awash with, thanks to the trips she and Tom had made to the hospital coffee machine. 'Yes, thanks very much,' she said.

Tom's remarks that morning about the kitchen primed her to look about her as Larry Wise led them in. There was something tired and forlorn about the place that she hadn't really noticed yesterday: an untidy heap of old newspapers under one of the hall tables, for instance. They followed Wise into an enormous sitting room. It felt cold, and smelt of something. Cat pee?

'Oh dear,' he said, rubbing his chin. 'The house is somewhat dishevelled, I fear.'

'That's all right, Larry,' said Tom, 'you've had a lot more to worry about than housework. Look' – and now he did give Dora a glance – 'could you do with some helping hands to clean up? When I fed the cat yesterday, I couldn't help noticing that the kitchen was a bit, well…'

'The kitchen is very dirty,' Wise pronounced. 'The house is very dirty.'

Tom was still looking at her.

Oh God, say the words, Clayton: 'We could come on Saturday and give you a hand,' she said. 'We could get the house in a fit state for when your mother comes home.' The instant she said that, she knew she shouldn't have. He was looking at her with a great beam on his face, all set to have his mother home by next Monday at the latest.

It was soon settled. She and Tom would turn up on Saturday morning at nine. 'Refreshment' was duly brought. It turned out to be sweet sherry from tiny crystal glasses that seemed clean, but she decided not to look too hard.

As she swallowed the sticky liquid, she found herself grappling with an equation, but perplexing as it was, the answer was obvious: any hour spent here would be an hour less in Jo's room. She could hardly bring Jo here. Even Wise might wonder why she had a tea caddy strapped to her front in a baby sling.

She'd had a lot of practice by now at turning bursts of laughter into coughs. 'Sorry,' she said. 'A drop went down the wrong way. It's lovely stuff, though, Larry.'

She shouldn't have said that, either. She had her glass refilled to the brim.

At last, Dora and Tom got away, having arranged a repeat trip to the hospital the next night. 'I did ask Mel to think about coming here next weekend,' said Tom as he pulled out into Banbury Road. 'Still, I dare say we'll have finished the cleaning by the end of Saturday.'

'Hm. It's a big house,' said Dora.

Before they'd gone another fifty yards, she was hit by an idea so amazing, so outrageous, so unlike any idea her mind had ever come up with, that for five seconds or so, all she could do was try to unthink it. But the harder she tried, the brighter the idea became. 'Get Melanie to come and help,' she said.

'*What?*' he said, staring at her, seemingly forgetting he was driving.

'Hey, keep your eyes on the road. Look, if Melanie sees me being as nice as pie to Larry Wise and him hanging on my every word, it might help get that affair notion out of her head.'

He glanced at her again, then back at the road. 'It's risky,' he said.

'You think I can't be as nice as pie?' *Go on, Tom. It's a bit more likely than me turning cartwheels in the nude down Oxford High Street while playing Twinkle Twinkle Little Star on a mouth organ.*

'No, I think you can,' he said. He blew out a long breath from puffed cheeks. 'It's risky not because of you but because of me. I'd have to watch myself like a hawk for a whole day.'

'I could guarantee not to appear in doorways unannounced.'

She saw him half-smile, half-frown. 'It's not just me. What about Larry? Mightn't he get the wrong idea?'

'Don't worry, I'm not planning to full-frontal snog him.'

He pursed his lips. Then he seemed to come to a decision. 'All right, I'll try it. I'll ask Mel.'

Last thing, Dora felt particularly in need of a session with Jo. 'Well, Jo,' she said as she went into the room, 'I've actually committed myself to doing something for another human being who could do with some help. Shall we place bets on whether I can keep it up for a whole day?' She picked up the tin and held it this way and that. The stars twinkled in the light, but they told her nothing. What were things coming to, when Jo wouldn't give her an answer to even a simple question like that? It wasn't as if she'd asked something really difficult, such as how should she sort out her reactions to what Tom had said in the car. He'd have to watch himself like a hawk. *Good*, had been her instant thought.

It wasn't good. Not for her, not for him, not for Melanie.

It had been a weekend fling, that was all. In six months they might have been sick to death of one another. Still, on Saturday he wouldn't be the only one watching himself like a hawk.

240

Twenty

On Saturday morning Tom was at Dora's house at ten to nine. He found her ready and waiting.

'New apron and rubber gloves,' she said, brandishing a tote bag at him.

'I'm impressed.'

'Good. Though "astonished" might be nearer the mark,' she replied. 'Jim's a bit disappointed there's not going to be any skating today,' she went on as they got into Tommy's car. 'House-cleaning doesn't really feature in his scheme of things.'

They made their way through a neighbourhood that still looked mostly asleep, and out into the Woodstock Road, Dora still chatting about her nephew and Syd's attempts at house-training him. She seemed bright and breezy – almost too bright and breezy, filling the air as if she didn't want him to get a word in. What did she think he might be in danger of saying?

He'd spent days preparing for this. He had himself as much under control as a man could. So he had to find something to say: 'How much hope do you hold out of getting to Astronomical Society tonight?' he said, when she was drawing breath. The instant he heard himself saying the words, he knew he couldn't have said anything more stupid.

She looked at him for a moment, her eyes wide. Then she laughed, a bright, breezy laugh. 'On a scale of nought to ten,' she said, 'where ten is dead cert and nought is you must be joking, I reckon the chances are minus three.'

Tom stayed at Larry's long enough to tackle some of the pile of washing-up, while Larry and Dora started on the bathroom and lavatories. At ten o'clock he left for the bus station. This might, of course, be a wasted journey. He hadn't been able to get through to Mel's phone, and all she'd said in reply to the email he'd sent on Tuesday night asking her to help out was: 'Sorry, phone's on blink. Might make it Saturday but got a lot of stuff to do. If I'm not in the bus station by 11, don't wait.'

Maybe she was wondering if he'd been spinning a line. In which case, wouldn't anger − curiosity, even − impel her onto a bus today? She'd probably been chewing it over with Debbie Priday all week. At any rate, let her not have been brooding on her own.

He parked in the underground car park, positioned himself by the London bus stop, and settled down to wait.

He'd been there perhaps five minutes when an Oxford Tube pulled in. He walked the length of the vehicle, dodging puddles of engine oil, while he squinted up at the queue of passengers waiting to get off. Ah, was that her, in the middle of the line? He ran back to the bus entrance and watched each passenger get off − until a woman of around thirty, short and dark, jumped down. She wasn't Mel. His heart rate halved.

Well. There'd be another bus in soon.

There was. And another, and another. Mel was on none of them. He took to walking up and down the dismal stretch of pavement by the bus stops, to the Italian restaurant at the end and back.

He hadn't mentioned anything in his email to Mel about the interview in David Dent's office, not wanting to seem to rub her nose in it. But should he have? Maybe he'd come across as casual… God, had he ever walked such a tightrope as this? He looked at his watch: two minutes to eleven. How long should he give her? Ten past eleven? A quarter past? Suppose there'd been heavy traffic on the M40 – an accident, even?

As he was turning away from the Italian restaurant for maybe the fifteenth time, another London bus arrived. He raced to the stop, and there Mel was, first in line to get off. She was scanning the crowd, if you could call this straggly bunch of bystanders a crowd. She was frowning. Then she saw him, and her eyes widened for a second. And then she turned aside – she seemed to be adjusting her shoulder bag.

'Hi, Mel,' he said. His voice sounded wrong. Too tight, and at the same time too cheerful. How a voice sounds if it's trying to seem relaxed, but isn't.

This time, she actually had an overnight bag with her. He made to kiss her as he put out a hand to take the bag, but in the same moment she stepped up onto the pavement, looking down as she did so, and he caught her ear instead of her lips.

Great start. But she was here. At least she was here. 'Good trip?' What an idiotic thing to say, she'd only come forty miles. But his voice sounded more normal, more under control, or what passed for it.

'Could have been better,' she said. 'I got on a bus ages before ten but there was a load of traffic at the M25 intersection. I tried to phone but the bloody thing's still not working properly.' She was taking darting glances at him, then looking away. But she was here, she was here.

'Well, that's the way of it,' he said. Was it? Way of what, exactly? Christ, was everything he said to her today going to be utterly fatuous?

'Yeah,' she said, still not looking at him.

'Right, let's go.'

'OK.'

They began walking, she a couple of feet away from him, still doing something with her shoulder bag.

'How are you feeling, are you ready for some exercise?' he said. 'Larry got way behind with the cleaning when his mother was taken ill, the kitchen's in a real state.'

'I'm OK. I've brought rubber gloves like you said.'

'And an apron?'

'Yeah. One of Carla's joke ones.'

'Not a rude one, I hope?' he said as he led the way down the steps into the car park. 'I dare say your sister's sense of humour hasn't changed from when I taught her.'

'It's got a cartoon cow's head on it. No udders or anything. That OK?'

'It sounds fine.'

While trying to unlock the car, he did something he'd never done in his life. He dropped the keys in a patch of oil. *Shit*. He began ferreting in his pockets. Fruitlessly. Whoever has Kleenex when they need it?

'Give me that,' she said, indicating the overnight bag he still had in his other hand. He gave her the bag, and she took a Boots bag out of it. In the Boots bag was a packet of wipes and a small box of Kleenex. She pulled out a handful of Kleenex, picked up the keys in it, handed the lot to him, and opened the packet of wipes.

'Thanks,' he said, when the keys were clean again. And now, where was he going to put the filthy wipes and Kleenex? 'Can you see a bin?'

'No I can't. Hang on a moment.' She put the remains of the packet of wipes and the Kleenex into her overnight bag and held out the empty Boots bag, open. He dropped the dirty stuff in, she tied the handles together, and he dumped the bag in the boot.

'We work so well together,' he said.

'Mm,' she said.

When they were out of the car park and turning into the street, she said, 'So this guy Larry Wise's mother's pretty bad, is she?'

'She's very seriously ill. The hospital's being a bit cagey on what the outcome might be.'

A moment of silence. Then: 'He's upset, is he?'

'Upset? He's shell-shocked. He can't take it in, he keeps saying she's never been ill in her life. They seem to be very close – she lives with him, you see.' Strictly, that was true: the huge house was Larry's. His mother had taken care of the inheritance tax angle after his father died, it seemed. The house was his, along with a portfolio of solid, recession-proof investments, and she was his guest. But Mel didn't need to know everything Larry had told him and Dora in the Lamb and Flag last night, his gaze never leaving Dora's face except to pick up his lemonade, talking as if they were the first audience he'd had in decades.

Dora. He took a long breath. He was going to manage it today. He was going to have to manage it.

'Never been ill?' repeated Mel. 'That's what Mum said when my grandad had his stroke. He just dropped dead, mind. In front of Gran.'

'And what did she say, your Gran?'

'She said, *"È così che capita."* Which means, "Well, there you go," sort of thing. He was ninety-two.'

The words which came into his head then were hard to hold back, but he suceeded: *And if I drop dead at ninety-two in front of you, what will you say?*

The streets of Oxford seemed to be catching Mel's attention. At any rate she stayed silent, looking out of the window, until they pulled up outside Larry's house.

'Is this it?' she said as she got out. 'Christ. I wasn't expecting a mansion.'

'There's something else you won't be expecting. Larry's a maintenance man.'

'A *what*? You mean he unblocks toilets and changes lightbulbs for a living?'

He nodded. 'But he's not like any maintenance man you've ever met.'

'I haven't met any,' she said as they went up the path. 'Well, I suppose there's Baz the Boilerman at school. He lives over a chip shop in Hayes.' She gave him a sideways glance. 'I wouldn't have thought your friend would be connected with a maintenance man who's got his mum living with him.'

Your friend. Not the first time she'd referred to Dora in that jarring way. 'First impressions can be deceptive,' he said. 'As I said in my email, I'd evidently misinterpreted how Dora was feeling about Larry.' A twinge of unease gripped him. Was Dora going to strike the right balance? To set Mel's mind at rest while not overdoing it with Larry... Not straightforward.

'Mm,' said Mel. Which, as just now in the bus station, could mean yes, no, or I'll think about it and let you know.

Tom pressed the doorbell. Any second now, Mel and Dora would be sharing his field of view. Not straightforward, either. But he was going to manage it, he must.

Mel was looking up at the gabling around the roof of the porch. 'Nice woodwork,' she murmured, almost to herself.

Ah. That must be them. Dora went to the door, working on her smile. She left her rubber gloves on. They just might help, she didn't know why.

She opened the door, and there they were. Tom was smiling, and Melanie was smiling too, but with just a hint of caution in the eyes. All set to play it by ear, then, girlie? Right, let's begin.

'Hi, come in,' she said. 'You couldn't have picked a better moment to arrive, Larry and I were just wondering when to go up to the hospital. I've sent him upstairs to shave and change.'

It had only taken her ten minutes to convince him it would be fine to leave her scrubbing the downstairs lavatory, but they didn't need to know that.

'Hi,' said Melanie. 'I'm sorry to hear about Larry's mother. Do you know how she is today?'

Good start. Take a gold star, Melanie. 'I spoke to the hospital just now,' said Dora, 'but they don't tell you much over the phone. Apparently she spent a "passable" night.' A slight touch of proprietorship in the voice, the way a middle-aged girlfriend of the sick woman's son would sound? Maybe. Better hope so.

'Look out, Mel,' Tom murmured, but Dora was already snatching up the model vintage car that Melanie's bag was within an ace of knocking off its display table.

'Oh, Christ. Sorry,' said Melanie, clamping her bag to her side.

'Don't worry,' said Dora, putting the car back. 'They have a habit of getting interested in callers, especially this Bugatti.' Good line, on the spur of the moment. Maybe she was going to manage this.

'Did Larry make all these?' Melanie's eyes were all about her.

'He did. A little hobby of his. They're all over the house: cars, ships, planes... Larry arranges them in themes.' As he'd told her five times already this morning, or was it six. 'Have a look at this.' She threw open the door to the dining room. Or what would be the dining room, but for the fact that on the huge table a couple of squadrons of three-masted ships wearing the Union Jack were heading purposefully for a straggling line of counterparts under French and Spanish colours.

'God. What is it – the Battle of Trafalgar?' said Melanie.

'Almost,' said Dora. 'He's still got the *Principe de Asturias* to finish. That'll go in over there.' She pointed towards the rear

247

of the opposition line. What a mine of information she was going to become if she spent time with Larry Wise. Wikipedia had nothing on him. She'd have facts coming out of her fingertips, details beyond her wildest dreams.

'They're amazing,' said Tom.

'Aren't they just… That one's the *Victory*, and there's the *Royal Sovereign*… Larry only moves them off the table when guests come. Which isn't often. The only room where there aren't any models is the kitchen. Talking of which, Mel, come and see what you're in for.'

When she saw the kitchen, Melanie's reaction was direct: 'Wow.' Well, it was pretty spectacular, not a square inch of clear work surface in sight.

'I made a start in here earlier,' said Tom, 'but as you see, there's still a fair amount to do.'

Was he coping? Seemed to be, but Dora wasn't going to inspect him to make sure. 'Things have slipped a bit recently,' she said. 'Larry's had a lot on his mind.'

'Does he do everything around here himself, then?' said Melanie.

'Absolutely everything in the house and the garden, from the chimney pots to the gateposts. Larry's mother is eighty-six, and domesticity's never been her thing. They tried having a cleaner a few years ago but she broke one of the models when she was dusting, and that was that.'

'Oh. Right, well, what do you want me to do?'

It was the cat who answered. The loud miaowing sound from under the table had Melanie bending down for a better look.

'For starters you could see if Prinz Eugen's food bowl needs topping up. Larry doesn't normally give him seconds but present circumstances are exceptional.'

'Hi, Prinz Eugen,' said Melanie, under the table. 'Are you called after that old rent-a-guy, then?'

'I'm sorry?' said Dora.

'Prince Eugene,' said Melanie. 'I did him for History GCSE. He was French, actually, but he worked for the Austrians. He cleared the Turks out of Hungary in 1697. He was pretty effective, for a short bloke.'

Dora laughed. So, the girl just might have a sense of humour. Lucky Tom.

'Princie looks like he's got enough in his bowl to be going on with,' Melanie went on. 'Haven't you, big boy, eh?' Just as she was speaking, the kitchen door swung open and Larry Wise came in.

Right, Clayton, nice-as-pie time.

Wise had shaved, right enough. His chin and cheeks were pink, almost raw. And he'd changed, evidently. But those clothes, the polyester slacks, checked shirt and windcheater: they were what you saw on certain sorts of eighty-year-old men. He looked painfully clean and tidy in comparison with how he'd been in recent days. The hair, though: combed down all around his head, it looked even odder than when it was standing up in a mop.

This tight feeling in her throat. Was it pity? Pity at the sight of this man, at his nervous yet eager smile, directed at Melanie? How could it be, when she'd never pitied anybody? The people she knew either didn't need pity, or didn't deserve it.

'Larry,' said Tom, 'this is – '

'Melanie Baines,' said Mel, scrambling to her feet. 'Most people just call me Mel,' she went on, offering him her hand.

'Welcome, Miss— Mel,' said Wise, engulfing Mel's hand in both of his. 'May I differ from most people and call you Melanie? It's such a pretty name.'

'I wish you would, it'll make a nice change. I'm sorry about your mother.'

Hm, this girl was doing well. Not the slightest hint of *My*

God what's this? in her face, only a smile, open and genuine-looking.

'Thank you, thank you,' said Wise. 'You are Tom's fiancée, I understand.'

Maybe a fraction of a second passed before Melanie said, 'That's right.'

'May you be very happy, very, very happy.'

'Thanks,' said Melanie. If she were wondering when he was going to let go of her hand, she was doing an amazing job of concealing it.

Hey, you're here to watch me being nice, not to upstage me, girl.

Dora leaned against the table and pumped up her smile. 'The big day's coming up fast now, isn't it?'

Another fraction of a second, and then Melanie said, 'Two and a bit weeks.'

'It's so very good of you to come here, Melanie, at a time when you must be so busy,' said Wise, finally letting go Melanie's hand. 'I am so sorry that the house is rather…'

'It's OK, it's fine,' said Melanie. 'Actually this kitchen's fantastic. It's right out of my dad's period style brochures that he hands out to customers – he's a builder. Except I bet this is all original, right? God, these floor tiles.'

'Oh yes, the fittings are, as you say, original,' said Wise.

The twin-tub washing machine certainly looked original. As did the dishwashing arrangements: human hands, a dishmop, a sink the size of a bath, and a draining board the size of the Oxford ice rink.

OK, time to move matters along: 'Larry, how about if Tom and Mel run us to the hospital, then they come back here and get on with the kitchen?'

'Oh, ah, yes… That is, if it would not be too much of an imposition…'

'It's what they're here for. There's nothing they like more than cleaning kitchens. Right, Mel?'

Melanie didn't disagree. Why should she? She had hours ahead of her of washing up with Tom, hours and hours.

As they went out to the car, Dora noticed Tom looking anywhere but at her.

Wise took a few minutes to pick a handful of daffodils from the garden to take to his mother. Daffodils, why were there so many daffodils in the world? Before they were out into the Banbury Road, the scent of daffodils was filling the car.

OK, time to chat. Dora turned to Melanie, cosily tucked in the back with her. 'You've got that coat on again. Jenny was raving about it all last Saturday.'

'Thanks,' said Melanie, half laughing. 'Just a fluke I found it, really. You can't get much in the Uxbridge shops, you've got to go up to Oxford Street.'

Dora kept it going, asking Melanie about Uxbridge, which she'd only ever seen from the bus, until they arrived at the hospital. As she got out of the car, she tapped Larry Wise's shoulder. 'They'll need the house keys, Larry.'

'Oh?'

'Tom and Melanie. They'll need the keys.'

'Oh… Yes… The keys.' Wise ferreted in his trouser pocket, and the keys fell out onto the floor of the car. The bracelet of paint tin lids fell out with them. He shoved the lids quickly back into his pocket and got out of the car, leaving the keys where they were. For a second, she felt that pitying tightness in the throat of earlier.

Right, now for hours of sitting on a chair and drinking machine coffee, relieved only by getting lunchtime sandwiches from the hospital cafeteria. At least she had Terry Pratchett with her this time. But first she had to get Wise inside: 'Come on, Larry. This way.'

'Oh. Yes, Dora.'

Tom picked up the keys and handed them to Mel.

251

'Poor bloke,' she said softly, as Tom started the car. 'So they've got a whole separate hospital for children over there,' she went on, as they began to make their way down the hill.

'It's relatively new. Tommy says it looks like a gigantic nursery school inside, cartoon characters over the walls and boxes of Lego and what-have-you in every corner. She says they've done everything to make the kids feel happy, short of getting the staff to wear Mickey Mouse outfits.' That sounded too much like David Dent's quip about lecturers and bottle-feeding. But the moment seemed to pass. At any rate, Mel seemed more interested in looking out at the big, bright building where the sick children of Oxfordshire went to have fun.

Would he tell Mel about Dora's baby? No, no, no. Ridiculous thought!

Not now, anyway. Later, maybe. When could you be confident that a child was safe from cot death?

What *was* it like? On a morning which you'd thought was going to be nothing in particular, to look into a cot, and—

Jesus. He gave his head a shake.

Well, Dora had done the business this morning. She'd struck the balance, better than he'd ever have thought: caring but in a tactful way, the way a 'girlfriend' of a man like Larry would appear to behave... But there'd been a point on the way up to the hospital, as he was turning right, when he caught her eye in the driving mirror. It was as if he were looking into a glacial pool, a pool high in some remote highland fastness that was deep in shadow. This bright capable persona of hers today, it was about as substantial as the thin sunlight which occasionally penetrates such mountain glens.

They drove back via Marks and Spencer in Summertown to buy the wherewithal for a picnic lunch. It would be a late lunch, by the time they'd cleared enough of the table to eat it off. 'You should eat something before we start,' he said.

'OK,' she said, and began crunching her way through an apple.

Work talk got them through the afternoon, as they washed and scrubbed and dusted: her latest essay for Liz Thorpe, what his take on Toni Morrison was.

Was it better? They were co-existing, they were speaking. But Mel seemed like the conversational equivalent of a person with backache. As long as such people held themselves carefully, they could get about; as long as they avoided sudden spontaneous jumps and jerks. She'd been chattier with Larry – with Dora, even. She seemed rather pleased when it was time to go and pick them up from the hospital. Tonight he'd be driving them all to Tommy's for a supper cooked by Tommy and Syd, who'd phoned to say they were ducking out of Astronomical Society tonight to do what they could to help.

At least he could tell himself he'd managed things – so far. But that was by saying next to nothing to Dora.

Mel took a look along the table. Was anything going on with Tom's sister and Dora Clayton's brother? Hard to tell. Still, they were pretty good friends, that was clear.

It was all right with Tom, wasn't it? He'd spent more time tonight talking to Syd Clayton than to Dora. And she was looking at Larry all the time, not Tom. Oh Christ, it *must* be all right, surely? She'd got it wrong that time in the bus station, it was just that Tom wasn't expecting to see anybody he knew?

Poor old Larry, though, sitting there beside Dora saying, 'Mother is as well as can be expected,' over and over to himself. It was just about all he'd said since they'd come back from the hospital.

'Well, I'm glad to see you're all hungry,' said Tommy.

'Starving,' said Mel. 'But we got it all done, didn't we, Larry.'

No response. Dora leaned nearer to him and said, 'Larry, Mel was just saying we managed to finish the housework.'

He seemed to come to. Maybe it was Dora's tone of voice or something. 'Oh indeed, the house is now spick and span, thank you, thank you so much. Tomorrow, we shall polish the silver, however, Dora and I. Mother cannot come home to tarnished silver.'

Real silver. Still, it wasn't surprising, considering what he had in that house.

The food was great, almost on a par with her mum's cooking: carrot soup, risotto, salads. And she actually did feel hungry, which was a change. While they were eating, Tommy and Syd, who both seemed really nice, got Larry talking, and all sorts of stuff came out, like how he'd lived in that big mansion all his life. In fact he'd practically never slept a night out of it, apart from a week every summer in the Lake District – and of course the time at the fantastically posh private school for boys that he went to, and his Oxford college. The way he talked was so old-fashioned it was almost cool, she'd never heard anything like it except on TV. School was 'acceptable, after the initial years of rough-and-tumble, which were not altogether enjoyable.' At Oxford, 'the education on offer was up to par, but college life was rather exhausting, in its social aspects.' Which was why, in his final year, he'd moved back home 'in order to have a quieter atmosphere in which to work.'

Just why was a person with a degree in Greek and Latin and a PhD on somebody called Prudentius working as a maintenance man? She couldn't ask him, not point blank. But she could ask him something: 'How did you learn to fix things, Larry?' she said. 'Did you take a course?'

'Take a course… Oh, no, no… When younger, I merely observed how the workmen called to the house went about making repairs.'

'Oh, great.' What went wrong? He should be a professor, so why wasn't he? He might be old fashioned and a bit absent-

254

minded, but he wasn't weird, not like *freaky*-weird. Anyway, didn't you have to be a bit peculiar to get on at Oxford University? He wouldn't even be bad-looking – for an older guy – if he ever got a proper haircut and some decent clothes... She could sort-of see what Dora saw in him, she supposed.

Then something happened. A bulb blew in a Tiffany table lamp as Syd was bringing in the coffee, and Larry offered to change the bulb. Whether it was the lamp that wasn't positioned right or whether it was Larry's elbow giving it a jog, she couldn't see, but either way the lamp fell on the floor, making everybody jump about a foot in the air and – oh God – the fantastically expensive glass shade smashed.

'Oh,' said Larry, picking up a piece of red glass. 'Oh.'

Talk about *embarrassing*. Poor guy!

'It's all right, Larry, I never liked that lamp,' said Tommy. 'It was a present from a grandmother and I can't think why I didn't take it to Oxfam ages ago.'

Dora was so sweet. She got up, went over to Larry, knelt down beside him and put an arm around him. 'She means it, Larry. She's been hoping something like that would happen, you've done her a big favour.'

Larry looked at her. 'Have I?' he said. 'Have I? Oh.'

God, there must be something she herself could do. 'I'll get a dustpan,' she said.

'No, I don't want you cutting yourself, I'll get it,' said Tom.

'I've swept up glass before,' she said. But she left it to him. If he really cared that she didn't cut herself, that was OK by her, she supposed.

It *must* be all right. Mustn't it?

When everything was cleared up and the others had drunk their coffee, Syd said, 'It's a clear night, folks. It would be criminal not to pop outside and look at the sky for ten minutes.'

'I've never really seen a star before now,' she said when they were out in the garden standing in a circle, 'not properly, I mean. What's that bright one over there?'

'That's Capella, in the constellation Auriga,' said Dora.

'She's classed as a winter star but actually she never quite sets,' said Syd. 'You'll spot her just above the horizon in summer if you're lucky.'

'Why "she"?' said Mel.

'She's the nanny goat star,' said Dora.

'Oh, Dora, do you know the myth?' said Larry.

'Vaguely… You tell it to Mel.'

Larry came out with a story about the Greek God Zeus and his father on Crete and this little goat called Capella whose name was really Amaltheia, or maybe she was a princess who kept a goat – there were two versions, apparently – and what happened was really cute but a bit gut-wrenching at the same time.

'You know, if I had to choose I'd pick the version where the goat feeds the baby Zeus herself,' said Mel.

'Spot on, Mel,' said Dora.

'In both versions, Zeus honoured Amaltheia by placing her in the sky,' Larry said. 'I should say that other sources suggest that Amaltheia is the constellation Capricorn, but there is possibly a confusion with the goat-god Pan, who was Zeus' foster-brother and his ally against the Titans, and would quite rightly also have been honoured by being placed in the sky.'

'Larry, you've just given me an idea for a school project,' said Tommy.

'Have I? Splendid, splendid. If you wish to read more…' He started giving Tommy a list of books.

'I'm going to check out those books Larry's talking about,' Mel said to Dora. 'I bet there are some pretty good star stories.'

'There are. And a few of them would make your grandmother's hair stand on end.'

'Not my gran's,' said Mel with a laugh.

Dora smiled, then yawned. 'Excuse me,' she said. 'Long day.'

Mel herself could feel yawns coming on. Was she going to be sleeping with Tom tonight? She wanted to, and at the same time she didn't. It sort of felt a bit soon, considering…

He was standing there just looking up at the sky. Maybe he was wondering about the sleeping arrangements too.

It must *be all right. Mustn't it?*

Twenty-One

Dora cradled the tin more firmly in the crook of her left arm, and lowered herself until she was half-sitting, half-kneeling on the space rocket rug with her back against the wall. She looked down at the tin, at its swirl of coloured stars. Funny how she hadn't lost that instinct people say mothers have, to carry a baby on the left so that your heartbeat soothes it.

'Well, Jo,' she said, flexing her back – what *was* it with that epidural entry point whenever she was in here? – 'I've had quite a day. I actually went in with Larry to see Mother, who I have to say looks in worse shape than you do, and I've spent all evening with a lovely girl who's going to have a baby in thirty weeks, give or take. Character building, or what? The girl seems to like me, now, by the way. And do you know what? I think I like her.'

No response. Maybe Jo was in a huff, knowing what was to happen to this room. If so it was a touch premature, with the house not actually on the market yet.

On Monday she'd do it. She really would. First thing.

Oh God, go to bed, go to bed.

258

She hauled herself to her feet, stood up, and put the tin back in the cot. She ran a hand over the cot blanket, not that any amount of attention could make it smoother than it already was. She put her finger on the mobile's start button and pushed it.

Twinkle Twinkle Little Star,
Of course I know just what you are,
Up above the world so high
Your little hooves trotting across the sky.

Well, maybe the original was better. But her version was more... individual. Her breasts began to tingle. Must be time of the month again. Again, again. She shoved an arm underneath them to stop them being ripped from her chest wall by their own weight. They always felt like ... like bursting udders.

Oh Capella. You poor thing. You and me both.

'First thing' didn't happen on Monday, not in the usual sense of a few quiet minutes before Siobhan turned up. Dora's boss was already in when she arrived, faffing about the write-up of the Far East tour the VC had just come back from. The first moment Dora could draw breath, the phone rang. It was Tom, wondering if there was any chance of seeing her down in the cafeteria for a few minutes.

'Just about,' she said. 'Anything up?'

'No, I just wanted to have a word, that's all.'

Tom was already there when Dora got down to the cafeteria. He was sitting over a coffee. 'No time,' she said, when he offered to get her one, 'Siobhan's having one of her days.' What Tom wanted to see her about turned out to be tonight's hospital visit: Tommy needed the car, so would it be all right if they took Larry to the hospital on the bus? 'Well, I suppose we'll have to let Tommy drive her own car occasionally,' she said.. 'But you don't need to come.' She had to say it. After all, she was racing ahead with this TLC thing. She was almost getting the hang of it, even.

'Oh, but—'

'Oh but what? I'll cope. I was on my own with him most of yesterday, wasn't I? By God, I'm an ace silver-polisher and I never knew it.' And pretty good at pity. Those tight feelings in the throat on Saturday hadn't been flashes in the pan. That look on Larry Wise's face as he'd attacked the spoons yesterday. The helpful boy, doing chores for Mummy...

'Can you, really? Cope, I mean?'

'Yes, yes, yes. You'd get bored stiff sitting in the corridor now that I'm allowed in to sit with Mother. So, how did it go with Mel?'

He looked down at his coffee for a moment. 'We made progress,' he said.

Did you? Did you sleep with her? No, not even she could ask that.

'I think how you dealt with Larry made all the difference,' he went on. 'You couldn't have handled him better when he broke that lamp.'

'Thank you,' she said, and for a moment the arm that had gone around Larry Wise gave a sort of twitch. Still, that was the sort of thing a nice-as-pie person did. And Mel had seen, which couldn't be bad... 'Tommy was pretty good too.'

'Yes... It's odd, though, that clumsy streak of his. He seems too precise, too careful. Think of all those amazing models.'

'With those, he's on home territory. Maybe apparently inanimate objects fall over and break just to thwart people like Larry when they're outside their comfort zones. Right, I have to go now, I'm afraid.'

'Just a moment,' he said, putting a hand on her arm.

What was coming now? 'Yes?'

'Capella, on Saturday night… Did that story bother you?'

'No more than it has the dozen or so other times I've heard it.' But that wasn't true, was it. It had bothered her a lot. Quite a lot.

A searching look came into his eyes. Then he leaned toward her. 'Dora, there are other stars as bright or brighter, and there are plenty of stars much farther away. But what makes Capella special isn't the nanny goat story, it's that in the depths of winter when you've all but lost hope of spring ever coming, you look up and there she is.'

Well. This was something different. He must have some sort of soul tucked into that body of his. 'Have you just told me about your religion, Tom?'

He took a sip of coffee. Thinking what to say? 'I reckon I have, Dora,' he said at last. 'And I reckon yours isn't so different,' he went on, looking at her hard.

'What? I haven't got a religion,' she said as she got up. Was he thinking of what she'd said in Wales: 'for Capella's sake'? She'd said it on a Sunday morning, which was all it had in common with anything religious. 'I just get by from day to day. Bye, Tom.' As she left the cafeteria, she could feel him looking at her. She could feel him looking into every corner of her. It was as if she were totally transparent. Half way back up the stairs to her office, it struck her that Tom could have told her about the car over the phone, there was no need to tell her in the cafeteria. Anybody would think he couldn't survive the day without a look at her Monday-morning face.

The remarks about Capella, though. Those mightn't have come across so well on the phone. As it was, they'd come over a bit too well. All that about religions, it was too much. Especially as she didn't get by, of course she bloody didn't.

An evening of manoeuvring Larry Wise on and off the bus and into and out of the hospital led to Dora exhaustedly cuddling a wine glass when she eventually got home. It was just the one glass. After she'd poured it, she recorked the bottle firmly.

They were on the bus the next evening too, as Tommy's car was at the garage having its MOT, and, inevitably, some post-MOT tinkering done to it. But the bus journeys had their upsides, if you liked in-depth expositions of the Battle of Britain. Larry could have given a lecture course on the subject, just as he could on geology, or practically anything, she wouldn't mind betting. She had to admit it: she'd finally met a person who was as riveted by detail as she was. Yes: thank God she was blessed with the kind of relentlessly enquiring mind that could always ask 'And what happened then?' Because for now this had all the signs of being her life: going from the office to a hospital bed evening after evening, and being stared at by a motionless woman in that bed. Not knowing if she was actually being seen, thought about, chewed over, digested, or if that eye looking at her was just whiling away the time until the brain it was attached to closed down and switched off for good. It could get to her, that eye, if she let it.

Still, the woman might not be communicating much, but Dora was getting the gist of her, thanks to her informative son. Somerville Classics, year of graduation 1946, was lying in that bed. Finest quality bluestocking, as anybody looking at the grainy black-and-white portrait photo in the Wise sitting room of a severe young woman with a bun could see straight away. If Venetia Wise was up to any cogitating, what did she do when she didn't have Dora Clayton to stare at – recite the whole of Aristotle from memory? Was it possible to die of boredom? In Mother's place she'd be wishing the hospital roof would fall in on her. What would Mother think if she knew that this woman who appeared every evening had spent part of Saturday afternoon stripping the big bed in the enormous upstair room and swabbing the stinking patch on the mattress with soda solution? If she'd guessed, she wasn't in much of a position to complain.

This son of Mother's did realise, didn't he, what the weekend's CT scan result stacked up to? Had he grasped what intracerebral haemorrhage meant, other than the bare etymology of the words – that it wasn't the sort of bleeding you could put a sticking plaster over?

Nine thirty. Time to go. Time for the goodnight ritual.

Laurence leaned forward, kissed his mother's forehead, then kissed her hand. 'Good night, Mother. Sleep well,' he said. He rose from his chair, and Dora rose from hers. Were those flowers he'd brought *quite* symmetrically arranged in their vase on the window sill? Perhaps they needed a little adjusting. Ah yes. That was better.

The lift was slow in coming. 'Dora, do you think Mother might recover her powers of speech by tomorrow?' he said.

'These things take time, Larry. It took my father quite a while. Don't worry, when your mother shows the slightest sign of responding, they'll have an army of speech therapists in to her.'

'Oh,' he said, gazing at her. She was so wise in these matters, so understanding.

When the lift arrived, it was too full for them to get in. There were many people in overalls, and an unfortunate person lying on a trolley. Eventually, however, a lift with free places in it arrived. As they stepped in, a wonderful thought occurred to him. 'We will have a tea party for Mother!' he exclaimed. A man on crutches and two women in overalls who were already in the lift turned, and – oh dear – on their faces was that look, the look he'd seen so often, of irritation and annoyance, and, worse, unease. He really must learn to remember to be less obtrusive.

As the lift began to move – such a strange, unsteadying

sensation – he said again, 'When Mother comes home, we will have a tea party,' this time leaning toward Dora and speaking so very quietly that surely only she could hear. 'Tom and Melanie – such an attractive couple – will come, don't you think?'

'Of course they will,' she said.

The lift stopped and a man in overalls stepped in. '*Do* you think Mother can see that tube going into her nose?' said Laurence. They had discussed the matter earlier, but he so much needed to be sure.

'I really don't think so,' she said as the lift resumed its descent. She was stepping backwards, why… Oh, to make room for the man in overalls. He should do likewise—

'Aah!' came a sound from behind him. 'Mind where you're putting your feet, will you?'

He turned. It was the man on crutches. 'Oh, I am *terribly* sorry, I had forgotten you were there.'

The man laughed. Had he, Laurence, said something that could be construed as amusing? How odd.

Dora was saying something to the man, but too quietly for Laurence to hear, as the two women had begun to converse rather loudly. The man was grimacing, and looking at Dora with raised eyebrows.

The lift stopped again, and the doors slid open. 'Larry, this is where we get out,' said Dora, 'but we'll just let this gentleman go first.'

The man on crutches looked at Laurence as he passed, his eyebrows still raised. *Had* he amused the man? Perhaps he could ask Dora, but not now. There were more pressing matters to consider.

As they made their way toward the hospital exit, he tried an experiment. He opened and closed each eye in turn, while squinting down his nose. 'Mother is very near-sighted,' he said to Dora. 'If she were to look down, I very much fear that she would see it.'

264

'"It", Larry?'

'Oh, that tube, that highly unpleasant tube.'

'We've never seen her looking down her nose. I wouldn't worry about it.'

Was she right? But she must be, she was always right. He would not worry about the tube.

They left the hospital, stepping out into the night air that was so infinitely more agreeable to breathe than the air in the building behind them. Poor Mother, having nothing but that air to breathe. As they walked towards the bus stop he had another wonderful idea. 'We could engage Mother in conversation,' he said, 'even before her power of speech returns. We could put simple questions, to which she could answer "yes" with one blink, or "no" with two blinks.'

'Well, that's an idea. Why don't you think up a few by tomorrow?'

'Oh, you too, Dora, you too! Mother will so much like to converse with you.'

A bus was waiting. It set off just after they boarded. It felt very convivial sitting side by side with Dora once again as the bus conveyed them back to central Oxford. To have these journeys to which to look forward, evening after evening... He could almost— No, no, how could he be glad about any aspect of Mother's misfortune? It was horrible to think of, horrible!

'Anything the matter, Larry?' said Dora.

'A thought, a – an agitating thought,' he said. He could not tell her the full truth, it was too terrible. What could he tell her? 'Mother was never beautiful.'

Why should he have thought that, at this moment? It was true, however.

'Not many people are,' she said. 'I'd say she was better looking than most.'

'Oh, would you, would you? Father was distinguished, very distinguished looking.'

'Yes, he was, I could see that from the photo in your sitting room.'

Father. There was something he had to tell her about Father, that it was imperative he should tell her. 'I was a disappointment to Father.' To hear himself saying those words, words he had never before spoken to a living soul: his heart was beating fast. He put his hand into his pocket and began fingering the paint-tin lids.

'That makes two of us,' she said.

'*You* were a disappointment?'

'To my father, yes. What did you do that was so wrong?'

'The Fellowship,' he said. 'I failed to be elected. I failed.' He pulled out the paint-tin lids and began clinking them against one another.

'Or was it that they failed to elect you?'

He looked at her. What was she saying? He didn't understand.

'They could have got it wrong,' she said. 'It wouldn't have been the first time, and it won't be the last.'

He clinked the lids, faster and faster. 'Bruce Langton,' he said. 'Bruce Langton, Bruce Langton.'

'Bruce Langton? Haven't I heard of him, isn't he on TV?'

TV? Oh, Dora was talking about television. 'We don't have a television, Dora,' he said. 'We would not have time to watch it, I fear.'

'Yes, I know you don't. Sorry. Did Bruce Langton get the Fellowship?'

'They preferred Langton,' he said. '*Preferred* Langton.'

'If he's the chap I think he is, he's ghastly. Grandiloquent brown-nosing name-dropper isn't in it. Look, if they liked Bruce Langton rather than you, they had very bad taste. I bet they were all like Langton, you know. People prefer people who're the same as themselves. Even fellows of Oxford colleges.'

He turned in his seat, bending towards her, seizing her hands. 'Dora, I have so much wished that I were like everyone else, oh how I have wished it! As a small boy, when I read stories about fairies who could grant three wishes, I wished too, in case there were a fairy listening. Oh, to be exactly like everyone else. How easy life would be.'

'Hm, those fairies. A lot of lazy shysters if you ask me.'

'Shyster… what is a shyster?'

'A crook. A person you shouldn't trust.'

A new concept. It needed to be carefully considered. How many of the people he had encountered in the past might be shysters? 'Is Bruce Langton a shyster?'

'You bet. He's almost as big a shyster as the people who preferred him to you.'

'Oh.' He continued to clink the paint-tin lids. Dora was teaching him so much, it was almost overwhelming.

After they got off the bus, he walked with her to the stop for the Wolvercote bus. It was reassuring to be back in the centre of Oxford; he could regain his bearings here. At her stop there were some young people behaving rather noisily, and she said she would prefer to walk on to the stop near Somerville College.

Memories of past encounters stirred in him as they waited at the Somerville bus stop. This had been Mother's college. But not only Mother's:

'Ianthe Hurst, Ianthe Hurst… Is Ianthe Hurst a shyster?'

'Who's Ianthe Hurst?' said Dora.

Ah. Had he spoken his thoughts aloud?

He opened his mouth and closed it again, and opened it again, and closed it. Oh, oh, could he tell her, could he?

'Oh, here's my bus,' she said. 'Look, Larry, I think she must be.' She looked back at him as she stepped onto the bus. 'I think she must be the worst shyster of the lot. Bye, see you tomorrow.'

He watched the bus carry Dora up Woodstock Road and away from him. Now that she was gone, how alone he felt. He pulled his jacket collar up and crossed the road in the direction of home. He had come so close to telling her about Ianthe Hurst. Would he ever again feel brave enough to do so?

'But Dora is not like Ianthe Hurst, she is not in the slightest like Ianthe Hurst,' he said to himself. He said it again and again as he walked the short distance home.

Dora sat on the bus and tried to picture Ianthe Hurst. Tall, probably, with one of those closed-in, preoccupied faces you sometimes saw on female academics. It wasn't hard to write that particular story. Where was she now, this Ianthe Hurst – still in Oxford, a Fellow of some college? Somerville, even? *Hey, Ianthe, wherever you are, you could be doing what I'm doing.* Maybe Ianthe had considered the prospect and said no.

What set him off on all that just now? Still, it made a change from talking about Mother's naso-gastric tube. She began to squint down her nose, first with one eye, then the other, the way Larry had before she steered him out of the way of that nurse who was within a whisker of being knocked flat on the floor by him. Before long, she felt a giggle brewing. She put a stop to it by turning her mind to what tomorrow had in store. Like putting the house on the market.

She almost made it today. She'd got as far as picking up the phone. Maybe tomorrow she'd get as far as dialling the number. And the next day… The next day was way too far in the future to think about. By then there might have been a terrorist attack, or a meteorite might have wiped out civilisation.

Dora got to the office next morning to find two emails waiting for her. Tom's told her two things: that on Friday morning he had an interview at Syd's school, and that Tommy's car needed a bit of adjustment to the gearbox, or so the garage was claiming, and wouldn't be ready until Friday afternoon.

Well done, Tom. For not getting her down to the cafeteria to tell her that.

It had been a few days now, since she'd seen him and he'd seen her. Maybe he was managing to survive. Was she?

The second email made that question doubly hard to answer. It was from Steve. 'I wouldn't mind seeing you some time,' it said. 'How about tonight?'

So he was back. She began to massage the back of her neck. *I've dealt with you, Steve. Please don't make me have to deal with you again.*

She took a deep breath. She typed: 'I'll come to the flat some time after nine. Can't come earlier, got to do a hospital visit.' She clicked on 'send.'

Ten minutes later, back came: 'Anybody I know?'

She took another long breath. 'The mother of a guy I work with,' she typed.

Nothing came back.

All through that evening's visit, Mother was seeing her, as ever, but she, for once, wasn't seeing Mother.

When it was time to go, she had to kick her heels in the corridor for a few minutes while Larry disappeared into the gents. A nurse was hovering, and she pounced as soon as Larry was out of earshot. 'I'm glad I caught you on your own,' said the woman, in a low voice.

It seemed that Mother had been 'not too well today, I'm afraid.' The nurse went on speaking quickly and quietly until Larry came in sight, when she broke off and rearranged her face into a smile. She might as well have stopped before she started, for all Dora had registered of what she was saying.

You've picked the wrong night, Nurse Whoever-you-are. Sorry.

*

The door of the flat was open. Steve was standing there, waiting for her. His hands made a slight movement towards her, then fell back to his sides.

"Hi,' she said, stepping into the tiny hallway. 'You shouldn't have just opened the security door when I buzzed, you know. I could have been anybody.'

'But you weren't, you were you,' he said.

His flat smelled musty. Still, it would, locked up for over three weeks as it had been.

'Did you get the contract signed?' she said, going into the sitting-cum-dining room. There was a half-eaten freezer meal on the table with a beer beside it. Wouldn't she just know it? Whenever her back was turned, there he was, drinking straight out of the can.

'Yes, we got it signed,' he said. 'And then we went and had a few vodkas. That was three days ago. Thank God I wasn't flying the morning after.' He sat down again and picked up his fork, and she perched herself on the arm of one of the two easy chairs. He looked pale. Maybe the dregs of the vodka hangover were still with him. Or maybe there wasn't much sun in Moscow at this time of year.

'Get yourself something, if you like,' he said. 'No shortage of stuff in the freezer.'

'No thanks, I'm not all that hungry.'

'You OK? You're not looking well.'

'Oh, I'm all right. I had a bit of a cold the first week you were away. I suppose it's still hanging around a bit.'

'So you did pick up a bug on that Welsh weekend,' he said, swigging his beer.

'Yeah. I did.'

He prodded the heap of pasta on his plate. 'So, how's life?'

Before she could muster an answer, the doorbell rang. 'Bugger,' he said. 'I'll leave it. They'll go away in a minute.'

'Answer it, Steve. It might be somebody calling to say you've won the Lottery.'

He looked at her. He looked at her hard. 'My lucky night, eh?' he said. But he did get up and go into the hall.

She got up too, and picked up the *Evening Standard*, which he'd been reading as he ate. She cast an eye around the room. It didn't take long. Small, but a nice modern place: graduate students would give their eye teeth for it. Who needs room to swing a mouse? For years, Steve had been coming back here night after night. Because she made him.

'Oh, you are back, Steve,' came a voice from the hallway. A woman's voice: pleasant, lively-sounding. 'We weren't quite sure… So, how did it go?'

She couldn't hear what Steve replied, in his lower-pitched voice.

'So you got to St Basil's, did you?' said the woman. 'Great. I told you you'd like it, didn't I.'

St Basil's? Dora had vaguely heard of it, she supposed: some famous church or other. But Steve, visit a church? He'd never been inside one in his life.

'Hey, some of us are popping along to the pub in a minute,' the woman went on. 'Fancy coming, or are you too knackered?'

Steve said something, which again Dora couldn't hear.

'Yes, right, I'm not surprised,' said the woman. 'Well, there's always tomorrow. See you, Steve.'

As Steve came back into the room, Dora said, 'There's never anything in this, is there.' She tossed the *Evening Standard* back onto the table. 'The number of times I picked it up on the way through Paddington,' she went on, sitting down on the arm of the chair again, 'I could never work out why I was bothering. Who was that at the door?'

'Somebody who's sleeping on her sister's floor while her house is being done up. Her name's Jane. She moved in a week or so before I went to Moscow.'

'Sounds friendly.'

'Yeah. She's one of those people who makes other people gell. The block's getting to be one big happy family all of a sudden.' He picked up the newspaper, then put it down again. He didn't seem to be wanting to go back to the table. Maybe the freezer meal had lost its appeal by now. Or maybe he was working up to telling her why he wanted to see her so soon after stepping off the plane.

As if that wasn't obvious. Oh, Christ.

It was on the tip of Dora's tongue to ask Jane's full name, what she did, where this house was that she was having done up: was it a picturesque dump in Jericho, a bijou leaky cottage in Iffley? But this wasn't a moment for pandering to her unquenchable curiosity.

'Careful, Steve, Yvonne'll get jealous.'

He was looking as if she'd hit him. But it had to be said, *it had to.*

He sat down slowly at the table. 'Pet,' he said, sounding beyond weary, 'let me give you a detail about Yvonne that I should maybe have told you before. She's very happily shacked up with an anaesthetist from Bart's. The anaesthetist's name is Cathy.'

'Oh.'

'"Oh", indeed. I'm not bothered, by the way. I have never at any time had designs on Yvonne, and I've no plans to.'

Her chin dropped onto her chest.

'Look, can we be sane for a moment?' he went on, sounding even wearier. 'If it makes you happy sleeping with Tom Ross, you can, I don't care. But don't try and kid yourself I've got something going on the side, because I haven't. OK?'

All she had to do was get up from this chair and put her arms around him. So easy! And yet. And yet. 'Tom Ross is a good mate, that's all,' she said, not looking at him. 'He was just a fling, the real bloke's the one I went to the hospital with this evening, I've been seeing him for a few weeks.' Speaking fast, getting the words out before her will failed her, because any moment it surely would. 'It's over Steve, honestly.'

'Dora!'

He was coming towards her. She had to get out. Now.

'Bye Steve,' she said, getting up. 'There's still time for you to go and join Jane and her friends in the pub. I wish you would.'

She made for the door and ran down the stairs. She got herself home, she had no idea how.

Twenty-Two

Dora blinked, then screwed up her eyes. There was a lot of sun coming through the window, she didn't seem to have closed the curtains last night. It was warm outside, by the look of it. Funny weather these days. Cold one day, hot the next. Still, what could you expect from spring.

Soon be summer. Bugger summer.

Oh God, what was the bloody time?

She turned over and eased her body – if this thing, which was all one joined-up ache, was her body – into a sitting position. She looked up at the clock. Four, it said. The little green man from Mars was having her on, surely. It certainly wasn't four in the morning, and the sun was never in that position in the afternoon. The batteries must have run down. She looked at her watch: half past ten. It was half way through Friday morning. At last, she'd done it. She'd fallen asleep on the space rocket rug.

'Well, Jo,' she said, looking at the tin lying beside her on the rug, 'how are you this bright morning?'

No answer. But the air in here was flat and lifeless, it wouldn't support even the faintest flicker of a vibration. She'd poisoned it with hours of foul outbreathings.

She rolled over onto her hands and knees and sat back on her heels, pressing her thumbs into the small of her back. Then, one hand gripping the side of the cot, she pulled herself to her feet. Her eyes were gritty, with the contact lenses still in. Her face felt as if a layer of slow-drying slime had been painted onto it, and under her clothes her body itched as much as it ached. But all of that was nothing, nothing at all, compared with the state of her head. And – Christ – her stomach.

She made it to the lavatory two seconds before the contents of her stomach arrived in her mouth. When she couldn't retch up any more, she stayed hanging over the bowl, looking at the stuff floating in it. Three years ago there'd been semi-digested cubes of curried chicken: islands of them in a pool of pinkish-yellowish goo. What she'd produced this time wasn't as interesting, but she'd only had canned lentil soup to soak up last night's wine.

She pulled the flush, then rinsed her mouth, letting the strong peppermint mouthwash sink as far down her throat as she could. It was a pity she couldn't pump it into the space behind her forehead.

What now? Phone in sick? But if she did that she'd have an uninterrupted day of going over and over what happened last night.

The phone rang. Steve? Please, please, no! Oh, let the answering machine deal with him this time, she just couldn't.

'Hi, it's Susie, ringing at ten thirty-five,' said the voice. Dora picked up the phone. 'Oh, hi,' said Susie again. 'Are you in or out today? Your diary doesn't say.'

'I'm in,' she said. 'Dodgy curry last night, I was up half the night.' Christ, she shouldn't have mentioned curry. 'Look, I'll be there as soon as I've had a shower, OK?' She ran to the lavatory so fast, she almost twisted her ankle.

On the way out of the house, she took the empty wine

bottle from the coffee table in front of the TV and dumped it in the bin.

That evening, Tommy's car was on the road again, which was just as well, because the way Dora still felt, she'd never have made it to the hospital and back on the bus. In the past, she'd have shrugged off a hangover by lunchtime. She was getting old.

That one three years ago, though, she got rid of that pretty damn quick. Or was it that she didn't get around to noticing it much?

As the three of them, herself, Tom and Larry, drove through Oxford, it seemed as if she was seeing Tom – the back of his head, rather – down the wrong end of a telescope. It had been days and days since she last saw him, and a lot had happened to her, pretty well all of it last night. As he'd let her into the car, he'd looked drawn. Well, a lot had happened to him, too. Like being offered the temporary teaching job on the spot this morning.

Starting next Wednesday. After Wednesday, days and days and days would go past… Oh hell, stop it, Clayton.

Tom ought to be just a little exhilarated, though. He was going back to teaching. Still, why shouldn't exhilaration look the way he was looking? After all, pain and joy could seem remarkably alike.

As could life and death, if Mother was any example. They got to the hospital to find her looking two shades greyer than yesterday. Her skin was more wrinkled, as if she were slowly deflating, like a tired balloon. From what the nurse on duty was saying, they'd apparently put some sort of filter into a leg to try to stop blood clots getting to the heart. The nurse might as well be talking in Martian, the way Larry was frowning, sitting there with his mouth open.

The 'real bloke', she'd told Steve, using Larry as a

smokescreen for the second time in not many weeks. Was she going to make a habit of this? Steve's face would be a picture if he ever met Larry. But Larry was real, all right. He was a great big lump of reality sitting right in the middle of her life.

'It might be helping, but we can't tell yet,' the nurse went on. 'Anyway, I'll leave you with her now, but don't make it too long, will you. We don't want her to get tired.'

The nurse seemed to look meaningfully at her, Dora, as she left the room. Was she herself supposed to be breaking it to Larry, then, was she supposed to be telling him that a minute or two of looking through *Yellow Pages* for undertakers might not be time wasted? Was that what she was being told yesterday evening when her mind was pressing Steve's security buzzer?

Mother's eye looked glazed. And she hadn't got the excuse of having hit the bottle last night. Hang on Mother, hang on for God's sake. There's a man I wrecked totally last night, and a man who'll be working miles away from me next Wednesday, and I still haven't phoned a sodding estate agent. Just hang on for a couple of weeks – one week, even. Please.

Larry was muttering, something that sounded like 'Country air, country air.'

Which was exactly what it was: 'Mother needs a holiday!' he announced, sounding as if he'd been puzzling over a complicated issue for weeks and had finally cracked it. 'Country air, that's the thing for Mother, country air. She's fond of Grasmere – aren't you, Mother? I shall take Mother to Grasmere, her birthplace, when the hospital releases her. Will you accompany us, Dora?'

'Well, Larry, I...I think your Mother might not – she'll need a lot of nursing care. In the foreseeable – the immediate future.' Oh God. 'I mean, perhaps you should be thinking in terms of a nursing home. Rather than a hotel, I mean.' *Liar.*

'A nursing home...a nursing home?'

'There must be plenty around Grasmere. A nursing home with a hotel close by would be the thing. You – I – you and I could stay in the hotel, and…visit your mother every day.' Lies upon lies. Oh please, let me out of here!

'Oh, yes! Yes, that's a very good idea, a very, very good idea. Don't you think so, Mother? A nursing home close by the lake, so convenient for walks as your health improves.'

But Mother looked as if she couldn't care less about lakeside walks. Grasmere would be about as feasible as Lake Winnipeg before very long. Before they came back here tomorrow she had to say something to him.

Tom could have done without this drink at Larry's house to celebrate his new job. After striving for days to think of Mel and only Mel, of how he was going to build on last weekend, he could certainly have done without having Dora beside him as he waited for Mel's bus to arrive.

When they got to Larry's house, Mel topped up Prinz Eugen's water bowl so that he could join in the toast too, while Larry got out his antique sherry glasses, arranged them in a ruler-straight line on the kitchen table, and started to fill them with sherry the colour of treacle. What a far cry this kitchen was from how it had been last weekend. It was so clean you could do medical experiments in it. Larry's washed-up breakfast things were placed just-so in the dish drainer: a bowl, mug, plate, knife, dessert spoon and tea spoon. One man's few things, all alone. And his own breakfast things, before coming to Tommy's? They'd known what it was to be alone. But not alone in the way that those in front of him now were going to be alone quite soon, if he'd read Dora's face correctly as she and Larry came out of Mrs Wise's room.

'A very little one for me, please,' said Mel.

Dora looked as if she'd like an even smaller one, or preferably none at all. But she took a full one, smiling. She was standing with the overhead light directly on her face, and he could see how tired she was looking. More than tired: hollowed-out.

Right, that was enough looking at Dora.

Larry cleared his throat. 'To Tom's success, and may this new position be all he wishes it to be.' Glasses were raised. Tom said a few words of thanks and forced down a sip.

'Hey, I should put the flowers in water,' said Mel.

Tulips to be taken to Mother tomorrow, a large bunch brought from Uxbridge on the bus, in all the colours known to tulip breeders. If he hadn't already known it, that would have proved to him that Mel was a nice girl. But he did already know it.

Dora had taken a sip of sherry along with everybody else, but now she was just looking down into her glass. Something was wrong, something was different about her since he saw her a few days ago. Something he couldn't put his finger on.

'Don't ever change anything in here, will you,' Mel said to Larry as she filled a vase at the sink.

'Oh? But I should repaint from time to time,' said Larry, scratching his chin.

'Oh sure, but keep the colours as they are now, this sort of light apple green really goes with the floor tiles. Do you really do all the plumbing and the electrics and so forth?'

'Oh indeed, one is never at the beck and call of tradesmen…'

They were off, chatting away about household maintenance, Mel with all the expertise a builder's daughter could bring to the topic. Tom glanced at Dora. Perhaps he could risk moving a step or two closer to her.

'This was my first ever drink,' she murmured to him, taking a sip. 'Three quarters of a bottle of oloroso, knocked back when I'd just turned thirteen. My parents were out at some college do.'

'Three quarters of a bottle? No wonder you remember it.'

'Yes… The row with my father was spectacular, one of our best. Good old Syd, though, saying he'd drunk some too when he hadn't.' She took another sip, turning her head away from Larry, presumably so that he wouldn't see the grimace she wasn't quite suppressing. 'It was all a total waste, though,' she went on, her voice dropping lower. 'I spent the night in the loo puking it all up again. Oh, what was that?' She looked down. 'Ah, the cat, having a go at my ankles.' She bent down to stroke Prinz Eugen, but he moved on to Tom's ankles.

'That's the thing about cats,' she said. 'Smarming round you one minute, sucking up to somebody else the next. But you know about cats, of course.'

This was showing signs of turning into one of those conversations. *Careful, Ross.*

He didn't reply, but to cover the moment he bent down and tickled the cat's neck – and then Larry suggested going into the sitting room 'where we can be more comfortable.'

It may have been a change of scene, but Mel and Larry looked set to carry on their conversation about furnishings for a while yet. Tom had to get himself and Dora into that conversation. Resuming their tête-à-tête would not be a good idea. 'Sorry, you must be thinking I'm a total idiot,' Mel was saying, 'I'm going on like some hick who's never seen a proper piece of wood in her life, and I have, my Gran's got a couple of chairs like those.'

'Not at all,' said Larry. 'I'm delighted that you like the room.' From there, it was a short step to him saying she must come and see the house often – Mother would be delighted to meet her – and another short step to regretting that she and Tom wouldn't be staying in Oxford.

'Tom tried to get me to apply to Oxford,' said Mel.

Tom caught a flicker of reaction on Dora's face, a sort of silent, 'Oh, really?'

'I did suggest it,' he said, 'but Mel didn't like the idea, and that was that.' Oxford and Mel – and Dora. *Jesus*.

'Come on, you did a bit more than "suggest",' said Mel, laughing. 'He told me I was being narrow-minded and prejudiced, and not everybody who came to Oxford was the Honourable Lord Posh, or whatever. Anybody'd think he'd been here himself, not Bristol.'

'Oh. Ah. The Honourable... Yes, in my day...' said Larry. 'But I understand things have changed now. Have they not, Dora?'

'Oh, sure. You can be married, you can be old enough to remember non-decimal currency, you can have been to a school so under-resourced and overstretched that it didn't teach you to write your name. As long as you can show some glimmer of intelligence, Oxford's interested.'

You can be pregnant. She was probably thinking it. It was true, after all.

'I bet Oxford's still full of people who've had nannies and butlers and things from birth, though,' said Mel, still laughing. The phone outside in the hall began to join in with her.

On second thoughts, somehow it didn't sound as if it were laughing.

'I wonder who that can be,' said Larry, heading for the door. 'A neighbour asking after Mother, I imagine.'

While he was out in the hall, there was silence. He was listening, not talking.

Each of them looked at the others. Mel said it for them: 'Oh my God,' she whispered.

Larry reappeared. 'It was the hospital,' he said slowly. 'They are asking me to return. They say that Mother is not well. Not well.' His face was grey and sagging.

The person in overalls left the room. Laurence was glad. He needed no-one at this time, no-one but Dora. 'She looks so peaceful now,' he said, 'and more like Mother, with that dreadful mask off.'

'Yes. This is the way to think of her.'

The thought that was troubling him, could he voice it to her? Yes, he would. She would understand. 'Dora, do you believe in an afterlife?'

'I'm not sure what I believe, Larry. There are times – have been times – when I'd very much like to believe. But what did your mother believe?'

'Mother was a positivist, as was Father. According to her beliefs, she is now mud.' He reached out a finger and touched Mother's cheek. Did this feel like mud? Surely, it still felt like flesh, human flesh?

Oh Mother, are you here? Are you watching me? He looked up, into the four corners of the room in turn. Was she hovering here?

If she were, he could not sense her. He turned back to Mother's body and, with his right index finger, traced the furrows between Mother's nose and mouth, and the frown lines across her forehead. 'Is it possible that she is vanished, as absent as though she has never been?' he said. 'Or…perhaps she has gone on a journey. In which case I must act. There is something that I must do for her.' Yes, of course. He had studied the ancients, how could he be forgetting what they had believed?

He put his hand in his right trouser pocket and brought out a handkerchief, three screws, and a scrap of paper that might have been a receipt. His left trouser pocket, he knew without having to search, contained only the paint-tin lids. He felt in his jacket pockets: another handkerchief. 'I'm terribly sorry, Dora, but I appear to have come out without any money. I have to ask you for a coin. Do you have one? Anything will do – ten p, five p or even one p.'

She gave him a very generous ten p.

'This is Charon's fee,' he said. 'I must put it under Mother's tongue, or he won't ferry her across the Styx.' He tugged at Mother's lower jaw, but managed only to pull her head forward, not to open her mouth.

'Here, let me help,' said Dora. She held Mother's head steady, and at last he was able to put the coin in between her lips.

'Now she is on her way,' he said. 'She will pass by Cerberus and have an easy passage into the fields of Elysium.'

'Elysium... It sounds good. Tell me about Elysium.'

'Oh, Elysium is wonderful, a land without night or cold, where there are games and dancing for all eternity. But only the virtuous go there. Mother will certainly be admitted.'

'Do children go there? Small children, I mean, ones too young to have had a chance not to be virtuous. Babies.'

'Alas, no. They must remain on the far shore of Styx, wailing for their mothers. In death they attain the threshold of the underworld, merely, because in life they attained only the threshold of this world.'

'Oh. Oh well. Just a thought. I hope your mother enjoys Elysium, Larry.'

'I fear the dancing will exhaust her.'

'It sounds like the sort of place which ought to cater for all tastes. It ought to have a good library as well as a dance hall, at any rate.'

'Oh yes, what a good idea. I do hope it has a library.' Suddenly he found himself weeping. It was most extraordinary. One moment, he was perfectly lucid; the next, he couldn't speak.

He was aware of Dora's arm coming to rest on his shoulders. She understood, and did not condemn. He had no words to describe to himself how that felt.

*

Tom glanced at Dora's face as the full glare of the overhead light in the kitchen fell on it. Yes, he was right.

The three of them stayed sitting at the kitchen table, listening to the sound of Larry's feet plodding slowly up the stairs. Nobody seemed to want to move, although Dora and Mel must both be beyond tired, as Tom himself was. A door overhead closed. A grief-stricken man was now about to endure what remained of the night.

Mel blew her nose again. 'Do you think we ought to throw out those tulips before he comes down tomorrow?'

'No, leave them,' said Dora. 'They show you cared. I know that sounds cheesy, but right now it's all I can come up with.'

'OK… God, when I think of how I was gabbing on about the furniture earlier, and all the time his mother was dying.'

'Mel, you were fine, you couldn't have handled it better,' said Tom, taking her hand.

That face of Dora's. He was going to tell her. 'Up you go, Melly,' he said, as Mel yawned. He gave her hand a squeeze. 'You need your sleep.' Only one bathroom in this house, so no point in them all going upstairs at once to brush their teeth. But just now, that suited him.

As the sound of Mel's feet on the stairs died away, Dora closed her eyes for a moment. 'Do you know what gets to me most?' she said. 'Larry telling us we had to collect overnight things before coming back here. For God's sake, worrying about our toothbrushes and pyjamas at a time like this, "to make your stay more agreeable".'

'And insisting on making up the beds himself.'

'Yes,' she sighed. 'Can you imagine anyone but Larry…?'

'Dora, when you came out of that hospital room, you were in tears.'

She sat bolt upright. '*Was* I? No!' She wasn't loud, but she was emphatic enough to make the cat stir in his basket.

'You were. And you have the make-up streaks to prove it.'

'Bloody hell.' In three strides she was across the room and standing on her toes to peer into the mirror hanging underneath the clock.

'Christ, I look terrible. But it's one o'clock in the morning, I'd be streaky by now anyway.' She turned back to him, and for a moment she didn't say anything. But then she said, 'I feel as if you've caught me on the lavatory. Or masturbating.'

'Are you sorry I told you?'

Her eyes looked distant. 'Strange as it might sound, I don't know,' she said quietly. 'Well. Shall we wash up the cups and glasses and call it a day?'

He washed, she dried. Neither said anything that wasn't concerned with the job in hand, but that might only have been because there was too much to say – and little that could be said.

Upstairs in the main guest room, Mel was sitting up in an oak bed the size of a battleship. She was dressed in an oversized grey T-shirt with a cartoon sheep on the front. There was no question about who'd be sharing with whom in the main guest room on a night like this in a house like this, and who would be in the room next door.

'It'll be funny, sleeping under blankets rather than a duvet,' said Mel.

'Something to tell your grandchildren about,' said Dora, reaching for her overnight bag. 'First one down in the morning feeds the cat,' she went on, and headed for the bathroom.

Tom sat down on the bed beside Mel and put an arm around her. 'Good night, Mel,' he said, and kissed her cheek.

'Night, Tom,' she said. She returned his kiss, then quickly slid down in the bed.

Alone in the smaller guest room, Tom began to wriggle out of his clothes. The grandfather clock in the hallway downstairs struck the quarter hour. Anyone who had trouble sleeping this night would be hearing a lot of that clock.

He paused, letting his shirt hang from his fingers, as he heard Dora's feet coming back along the landing. She was about to get into the same bed as a girl with a baby inside her. He was right earlier; something had happened to Dora, and the tears at Mrs Wise's death must be part of it. It was as if a gear had shifted in her. Only it was impossible to tell whether she were going faster or slower. And therefore, impossible to keep pace with her.

Mel and Dora, both in the same bed. The image was one he didn't know what to do with. It was more disconcerting, somehow, than having them both in the same field of view, even thought he couldn't see them.

What was that?

The creaking sound stopped as soon as it had started. It must have been Dora getting into bed. Still, a house like this would be full of night-time creaks and other odd noises you couldn't put a name to.

He finished undressing and got into bed.

The clock downstairs struck the half hour, and then the three quarters, before Tom became aware he was lying there with one ear cocked: the ear that was nearer to the main guest room. Turning over didn't help; he heard two o'clock strike, and then a quarter past. He should have brought ear-plugs.

Next morning Tom arrived downstairs to find the cat fed and a schedule drawn up which required him merely to walk his body through the day. He and Mel would take Jenny and Jim skating – it was about time they had their Saturday treat – and Dora was going to spend the day comforting Larry, who wasn't down yet. At seven they were all going to meet up for supper at Syd's. Dora sounded bright, brisk, in charge. He stifled a yawn. 'Sleep well?' he ventured.

'Like babies,' said Mel.

Dora didn't seem to be disagreeing, but she was busy making coffee.

That day, Tom kept the yawns at bay with as much black coffee as he could get, but it was as well that he didn't have to do much talking over lunch with Jenny and Jim at their favourite pizza place. A passion for detail must run in Clayton genes: Jim and Jenny grilled Mel energetically about her life and her relations, particularly Carla, the trainee ski instructor sister – 'Wow!' – and Craig, the brother who managed a couple of up-and-coming rock bands – 'Wow, cool!' Sister Gemma, PA to a Jaguar dealer in Slough, and brother Scott, who was in business with their father, were of rather less interest, but their particulars were duly noted.

The evening at Syd's had all the signs of being a quiet one, in the circumstances. Even the children, playing on the floor in a corner with a yard-long pack of felt-tip pens and a stack of coloured paper, weren't pestering for attention. Larry, sitting very close to Dora, seemed to be finding their presence soothing, though, from the way he was turning around from time to time to look at them. Dora was being gentle and understanding, but every now and again, depending on how she was holding her head, Tom could see tautness in the muscles of her face.

The trouble with watching others is that you don't see the spotlight swinging your way until you're caught in its glare:

'Tom, if you were staying in Oxford, there might be a permanency going,' said Syd. 'I can tell you now, the Head would be arm-twisting you into applying.'

'I hope not, I'm not a judo expert,' said Tom. He took a sip of wine.

'Surely Linda Mason's coming back in September?' said Tommy.

'As of when I walked her to her car last thing yesterday, she's wondering a bit,' replied Syd. 'Her game plan is to carry on letting people assume she's coming back, but actually to see how it goes after the baby's born. Apparently her mother's having a hard job persuading her dad to move nearer Oxford so that they can be on hand to help out. But she doesn't want the Head knowing any of this yet, so forget what I've just said.'

Tom noticed Dora scratch her nose. Her face wasn't giving anything away, but she must be thinking *Baby talk, always and everywhere baby talk.*

'I do so wish Tom and Melanie were staying in Oxford,' said Larry.

'You'll have to come and see us,' said Mel, patting his hand.

'You'll have to come and see us,' repeated Larry. 'You'll have to come and see *us.*'

Would Dora welcome that? People with a baby could, of course, always find themselves too busy for visits. For a moment, a pit of sadness seemed to open up inside Tom, a deep, dark gulf.

He wriggled his shoulders. This was no time for imagining dark gulfs. This night, for the second night in succession, there was no question about who would be sleeping with whom: he and Mel would be here at Tommy's, and no sofa would be involved, as it had last time. Larry had insisted that they and Dora shouldn't put themselves out by staying another night with him. Tom had an inkling that Larry was steeling himself to learn to be alone in that vast house.

When Tom came back from the bathroom, Mel was sitting up in bed looking at some photographs. She was wearing the grey T-shirt nightdress. Which might mean no. Or it might mean maybe? He was going to have to take this step by very cautious step. But caution was something he was getting used to, wasn't it?

'I was wondering if Larry might have wanted Dora staying over tonight,' she said.

Ah. What should he say? 'Still rather soon after his mother's death,' he tried.

'Mm… And I think he's a bit sort-of old fashioned. In a

nice way, though. Maybe that's what was driving Dora crazy recently. You know, trying to work out if he was interested. But he is, obviously, you've only got to see the way he is with her.'

'I'm sure you're right, Mel.' This was what walking on eggs felt like. Change of subject needed:

'The baby?' he said, indicating the pictures she was flicking through. There was a look in her eyes that he hadn't seen before, not even the first night they went to bed together. That had been excitement mixed with wonder mixed with disbelief; this was something softer, deeper.

'Yes,' she said, pushing towards him half a dozen grey, grainy images of what looked like a tadpole. But which wasn't.

'Jesus, it's got a face,' he said. 'That's amazing.'

'Yeah, and can you see the brain, and the backbone? And that darkish smudge is the heart. That's the baby as of two days ago.'

So many functioning parts, already? He couldn't quite take this in. 'Mel, let me know the next time you go for an antenatal, OK? I'd quite like to be there if I can.'

'OK,' she murmured.

As he took off his bathrobe, she slid down in the bed. He left his shorts – his clean shorts – on, as he had the first time. As he had all his first times. All of them in single beds, some narrower than this one.

Four weekends ago now, that narrow single bed in Wales… *No, no. Go away!*

He pulled Mel into the hollow of his body. She didn't flinch away. Nor did she seem to mind when he kissed her, and having kissed her, kissed her again.

Oh Capella, let this work, let his body do what it was here for. Because from now on, there was one thing and one thing only that life required from him: he had to make Mel happy.

'Carla keeps going on about me putting Brunel first choice so she can play with the baby,' Mel murmured. 'I told her no way, she'll have to travel.'

'I'll pay for her petrol,' he said as he moved his arm down under the duvet and pulled up her T-shirt.

She was still wearing her knickers. As he put his fingers inside them, her quick indrawn breath sounded like a gasp. His hand came to rest on a small swelling, as if it were lying on a doll-sized pillow. She breathed out in a long, shuddering sigh, and he felt, thank God, his flesh begin to respond.

'Those pictures of the baby,' he said quietly. 'You know, there's something about the chin. But I'm not going to ask you again whether this baby's mine.'

'Good,' she said, equally quietly.

'What I am going to ask you is to let me teach her or him to say Dad.'

'Fine.'

A child, under that smooth skin of hers. A child with a face, a brain, a backbone, a heart – and he had it in his hand. What did you do with children this small? He knew about the older ones, the ones you could hold a conversation with. This one, what should he do with this one?

A movement under the duvet. Her hand, coming down to rest on his, stroking it as she turned her head and kissed him.

Whether it was the motion of her hand communicating itself to his, he couldn't tell, but his hand began to move, to caress the little mound beneath it. Was this what you did with a child this small? It wasn't a lot, when she was having to do so much. He'd better do it properly then, this thing that at least he could do.

He pulled the duvet back, but as he was leaning down and kissing the swelling, the narrow bed slid into his mind's eye again, the narrow bed in which he'd last kissed this part of a woman. *No, no, for God's sake!*

'Oh, Tom,' came Mel's whisper, 'oh, Tom.'

With fingers that trembled, he took off her knickers and pulled her T-shirt over her head. When it came to getting rid of his shorts, she murmured, 'My turn,' and that was the best thing she could have done. The touch of her fingers on his skin kept that flesh of his mercifully focussed on where it was, and who with.

As he took her in his arms and began to stroke the small breasts – the now surprisingly bigger breasts, but that must be because of the tide of hormones rising in her – she whimpered, as a puppy might.

As he put himself inside her, something seemed to click in his brain. He was going to be able to do this, it was going to be OK. 'Oh Melly, it's going to be good, it's going to be so good.' He wasn't much of a talker at these times. But that definitely sounded like his voice.

At the moment of her coming, the voice – his voice – said, 'I love you.'

'I love you,' she sobbed. She clung to him, weeping into his chest, while he stroked her hair.

He had to look after this girl until the day he died.

He held her until her breathing took on the slow, steady rhythm of the exhausted young in profound sleep. And then he carried on holding her. There wasn't an easier way to arrange themselves in the scant space this bed offered.

As he lay there, gazing into the darkness, a face appeared. It was pale and pinched and had make-up streaks under its eyes. As he watched, it began to fade and dissolve, until it was nothing but a whitish blur. When it disappeared, the darkness was profound. There wasn't a thing he could do to bring that face back. He couldn't reach out; his arms were full. He couldn't shout *come back* in case he woke the one his arms were full of.

Mel woke early, when the sky was just getting light. Anyway, there was enough light to see Tom by, and that was plenty of light for her. He looked as if he was going to be fast asleep for a while yet. So that meant she could just lie here and look at him. She leaned on one elbow, and traced with her eyes the curve of his right eyebrow, and then the curve of his left eyebrow, and then his nose, and then down each cheek to his chin. And then she did it all again.

It was all *right*. It was, it was, it was. The way she felt now, she could reach up to the sky and hug the sun as it came up.

Twenty-Three

The sound of an email coming in made Dora blink. Well, it wouldn't be Tom. He'd be taking a class right now, not sitting at a computer. Good of him to wangle the time to go to this funeral this afternoon, though. Good of Mel, too, to be coming up from Uxbridge early for it. What a lot of good people there were in the world.

Did she have to open this latest email? It wouldn't be from Larry, either. The likes of maintenance men didn't send or receive emails. There'd been something about the 'ping' this one had made, though: *this'll make you sit up.*

The message was from Steve: 'I went to the pub last week, as you suggested. You know I said I wasn't seeing anybody? Well, as of last night, it looks as if I might be. Just thought I'd let you know. And before you ask, it's not Jane, it's her sister Vicky. She works for a green energy company. I thought you'd be interested in that.'

Dora stared at the screen, trying to make out the words between the lines – if there were any words between the lines – until Susie came in. 'It's starting to tip down out there,' she said, shaking back her hair. 'Let's hope it stops before you go

293

to Larry's mum's funeral, but I can loan you a black umbrella if you want.'

'It's OK, thanks, I've got six,' said Dora.

Funeral at three this afternoon, then a tea party at Larry's, then a quiet pub supper with him and Tom and Mel. Over the weekend, more helping Larry with death-related paperwork. And how many moments in Jo's room? Not many. *Not enough.*

When Susie went out to make coffee, Dora turned back to her computer screen. *Were* there any words between the lines? Such as Steve had slept with Vicky-who-works-for-a-green-energy-company last night? Or was he saying it's not quite too late, but any day now it will be?

Look, never mind the words between the lines, just focus on the words you can see! 'Great news,' she typed, 'a green energy company, I'm really pleased. I've been meaning to put the house on the market for weeks, I'll do it right now.' As she clicked on 'send', her heart began to thump. *OK. Do it.*

She picked up the phone and this time she dialled the number on the Post-It note, which had been stuck to the side of her pen tub for days. The number rang. After three rings a sing-song voice told her how important her call was, and if she would please hold, someone would answer soon. While she was sitting there, Siobhan waltzed past the doorway, calling out 'Hi Dora, can you pop in?' Dora closed her eyes – *go away, Siobhan* – and then in her ear was a slightly breathless-sounding voice saying, 'Hello, sorry to keep you.'

'Hello,' said Dora. 'I wonder if you'd be interested in taking a look at my house.'

A minute was all it took for her to fix a date with an agent. And to turn her finger-joints white from gripping the phone hard enough to throttle it.

Next Friday evening. A week today. Now that she'd actually phoned them, why did they have to be so booked up? Why couldn't it be Monday? Still, Monday or Friday, it made no odds to what she was going to have to do over the weekend. Larry's paperwork or no, she was going to have to find time to kill the room.

The realisation took a while to sink in. She was still trying to fit it into her head when she came back from Siobhan's room to find another email from Steve waiting for her.

'What do you mean, put the house on the market?' said Steve's message. 'Something like that needs talking about, for God's sake.'

Dora typed, 'I've already done it, Steve. Over the weekend I'll get on with redecorating the room.' As she sent the message, Siobhan called out from next door, 'Oh Dora, I've just had a thought.' Dora took two deep breaths and got up.

That morning, more emails came piling in, and most of them were from Steve. She didn't open a single one.

About ten minutes before Dora was due to leave for Mother's funeral, it hit her: what if Steve took it into his head to try and stop her killing the room? He was enough of a bloke to think that painting and suchlike was for blokes. But she had to be the one to do it, this last wrecking job. If she wasn't the one to kill the room, the whole world would stop turning.

She picked up the phone. The third locksmith she tried could come at eight thirty tomorrow morning. Would that be early enough? It would have to be.

As she began to collect her things, she wondered what the locksmith would have said if she hadn't told him her keys had been nicked from her handbag in a pub last night, but that she wanted to keep her husband out of the house because she needed to commit a murder. Her shoulders started to shake. Which was crazy. If she now knew how to weep, why wasn't she weeping?

Tom couldn't have been seeing straight last Friday. It was late, they were all tired. And there'd been no tears since. That was the clincher, surely. It couldn't have been that she'd cried away all there was to cry, because once you breach a dam and empty the reservoir, the landscape is inundated, destroyed beyond all recognition. Whereas with her, there were so many landmarks still intact, whole forests of trees.

'Oh, are you off now, Dora?' said Siobhan's voice from the doorway. 'Hey, what's the joke?'

'Only a line my nephew told me last night,' said Dora. 'Knock knock.'

'Who's there,' sighed Siobhan.

'Boo.'

'Boo who?'

'No need to cry, it's only a joke.'

'Very funny,' sighed Siobhan.

The rain held off for the funeral, but it might as well have poured; the event could hardly have been more dismal. Just nine of them in the crematorium chapel: Dora, Larry, Tom, Mel, Larry's Aunt Anna, a near neighbour Mrs Shaw, Mrs Shaw's grandson Peter, an academic young enough to have a keen, bright-eyed look about him, Jock Stewart, and the retired former head of Larry's father's college. Ten, she supposed, counting the officiant, who by way of an address gabbled through some of the notes Larry had given him. When they came out, Larry was muttering, 'But he didn't mention her First.'

No, he hadn't. All he'd come out with was stuff about what an excellent wife to the late Professor Wise and mother to Laurence, etc, etc. Fool.

The retired head of Professor Wise's college mumbled something to Larry and slipped away. Not coming back for the wake, then.

The tea kicked off in the normal way for a funeral, everybody sitting stiff-backed, speaking in hushed tones about the weather. It had its less normal aspects, though, such as a pregnant schoolgirl presiding with the teapot.

Christ, the way the girl was standing with that pot as she went around topping up people's cups. The baby was showing. Aunt Anna, whose resemblance to a turkey was drawing Dora's gaze more than she could help, kept staring at Mel's middle – in between giving Larry looks that said, *You unsatisfactory boy, what have you ever achieved?*

No wonder he didn't like his mother's sister. By God, it wouldn't take much for her to push that face of Aunt Anna's down the woman's turkey throat. What would it look like, a face collapsing backwards? The eyes would meet together, they'd probably pop out—

Just in time, she turned the laugh into a sneeze, or at any rate something midway between a cough and a sneeze. Tom, while holding out his teacup to Mel, gave Dora a glance, then he turned back to Mel. Mel was radiant today, under that suitably sober dress. Things looked to be OK between her and Tom. More than OK.

Mel moved on with the teapot. Tiny mole-like Mrs Shaw, little paws clasped together, blinking behind her round North-Oxford specs, wanted 'a half-cup only, dear'. Jock Stewart took a full cup, looking as though he wanted something a bit stronger. Mrs Shaw's grandson Peter took a cup too, looking as if he'd like to be drinking something a lot stronger, preferably in his college senior common room.

'Dora?' said Mel, waving the pot. 'There's lots left.'

'Young woman,' said Aunt Anna, 'it is high time you sat down and allowed your friends to fend for themselves. In your *condition*—'

'Yes, Mel, let me,' said Tom, getting up quickly and reaching for the pot.

'Oh, I'm OK, no problem,' said Mel, her eyes darting glances at Larry.

Which left Mel and Tom each with their hands on the teapot. What were they going to do, wrestle for it?

297

Larry was looking puzzled. A frown was assembling itself, in slow motion, across his forehead, in time with the flush that was spreading over Mel's cheeks. 'Condition,' he said slowly, 'your "condition"… Are you not well, Melanie?'

'I'm fine, Larry,' she said, grinning brightly. 'Never better.'

Oh, bugger this. 'Mel's expecting a baby, Larry,' said Dora.

Tom closed his eyes. Mel's hand went up to her mouth. But it was Larry's face that was doing the really interesting things. That face, moulding and remoulding in front of Dora's eyes: shock, disbelief, horror even – what was she seeing take shape, all three? OK Larry, do it, then. Call Mel a Jezebel, turn her out of this house for desecrating it on such a day.

Well. Who would have expected this to be a good day for breaking things? Tom and Mel wouldn't be speaking to her after this. And look at the rest of them: Mrs Shaw rubbing her paws together and smiling too fixedly, Jock Stewart fighting with a frog in his throat and gazing into his tea cup, Peter Shaw looking so unwaveringly at the window that there must surely be a Dalek coming up the garden path. And Aunt Anna, doing an imitation of a turkey in full gobble.

Funny, the way people sometimes don't know what they're going to say until they open their big fat wrecking mouths. She'd done it this time. Really done it.

'Are you, Melanie,' said Larry, '*are* you expecting a baby?'

Tom answered for her. 'Yes, Larry,' he said quietly. 'It's due in September.'

'Due in September. In *September*.'

The room held its breath. Even the cat left off washing his face. Every living and non-living thing was waiting – waiting for a bad thing to be made much, much worse.

'In September!' Larry cried, jumping to his feet. 'In September, splendid, splendid!'

Oh? *Oh?*

Larry seized Mel's hand and – *Christ* – kissed it. Then he

bustled about the room pouring glasses of sweet dark sticky sherry for everyone. 'On the day on which we mark a death, there can be no greater privilege than to rejoice in a coming birth,' he pronounced, raising his glass. 'To Melanie, Tom and their baby.'

'Aye,' said Jock Stewart, 'good health to ye.' He took a swig of sherry – too quickly, judging by the cough that he did his best to stifle. The Shaws, grandmother and grandson, made appropriate congratulatory murmurs.

'Cheers,' said Dora, and took a tiny sip of sherry, all she could manage to force past the lump that had suddenly taken shape in her throat. She herself might be good at breaking things, but she ought to have remembered that Larry's job was fixing them.

Aunt Anna didn't say anything. For a moment she seemed to inflate, and her face went an impressive shade of vermilion. Then she swallowed two thirds of her sherry in one gulp.

'Thanks, Larry,' said Tom, sounding winded.

'Thanks,' said Mel, sounding choked. Then she landed Larry an emphatic kiss on the cheek.

So she hadn't 'done it' after all. Was she losing her touch?

Aunt Anna was first to leave. Larry saw her to the door. Dora tagged along – anything not to have to meet Mel's or Tom's eyes – and found herself standing next to Larry in the porch like the lord and lady of the manor. Larry thrust a hand at Aunt Anna as though he were giving it to her to take away, like a lucky bag at the end of a children's party. Aunt Anna looked at the hand for a moment, took it for half a second, said 'Goodbye, Laurence,' and dropped it. Dora had to stop herself from giving Aunt Anna's hand a slap.

Jock made himself scarce a few minutes later – 'One or two things to clear up back in the office, laddie' – and then there were six.

Larry surveyed the room. 'Aunt Anna is a shyster,' he said.

Mel giggled. So did Peter Shaw. Mrs Shaw gave a little 'hem' of a cough-cum-laugh, and took another sip of sherry. 'Melanie and Tom were just mentioning how busy they will be during the coming months,' she piped. 'Getting things ready for the baby – it's all so exciting!'

Exciting? That moment when you go into Boots and pick up a packet of first-sized nappies and can't get your head around the fact that it's you who's going to be using them: well, yes, that was 'exciting', Dora had to admit. Surreal, unbelievable, terrifying: all those, too.

Larry was looking at Mel as if he wanted to say it again, but hardly dared to. *I wish you were staying.* 'I look forward very much to meeting the baby when you visit Oxford,' he said, sounding suddenly shy.

'You won't be able to keep us away,' said Mel, touching his arm.

Tom gave Dora the quickest of glances, then he upended his sherry glass into his mouth. Which was a waste of time, because there was nothing left in it.

It's all right, Tom. When she does drag you back here, don't worry about me. I'll just hover in the background, ready with the odd gag about nappies and teething. I'll put my mind to thinking up some lines, it'll be something to do in the long winter evenings. They'll be safe lines, I promise. I doubt if I'll be up to anything that'll shock you.

She couldn't lose her touch yet, though, she had the room to see to. The room, Jo's room…

The talk fell to where Tom and Mel would be living and what they'd be doing, and Peter Shaw's ears began to prick up. If his grandmother resembled a mole, right now he looked like a bright, sleek, perky rabbit, a Peter Rabbit who'd just filched all the lettuces from under Mr McGregor's nose. 'Bristol, eh?' he said. He started asking all sorts of questions about her AS level scores and what she was expected to get at A-level. Mel rolled her eyes as she told him, but he was impressed. Maybe he hadn't snaffled all the lettuces after all, there was a fresh young one he seemed to have his eye on yet. 'Yeah, sure, I'm not surprised Bristol have agreed to a deferred offer to get you,' he was saying. 'We'd have done the same.'

'God, you don't have mums with young kids in *Oxford*, do you?' said Mel.

'Melanie, I've got one in my second year right now. She's on course for a First.'

'What? You're kidding,' said Mel.

'Absolutely not. Look, Melanie, why don't you get in touch when your results come out? You might want to reconsider your future. If you happened to decide to apply to us, I just might be able to give you an indication as to whether you stood a chance of getting in. You can get my contact details from the college website.' He gave her a wide rabbity smile, his whiskers twitching.

'Oh. OK, I'll think about it,' said Mel, still looking as if she didn't believe a word of what she was hearing.

'Oh yes, do, do,' said Larry.

Tom had been taking looks out of the window during these exchanges. Maybe the garden was suddenly full of rabbits. Dora could see only the side of his face: was he itching to go out and frolic with the bunnies, or was he wondering where he'd put his shotgun?

'Laurence, I'm afraid I must be going,' murmured Mrs Shaw, 'Proust will want feeding.'

Peter Rabbit seemed to take this as a cue. His ears pricked down and he became Peter Shaw again, helping his grandmother with her stick, taking her arm and leading her to the door.

'Bye Larry,' he said. 'I've still got that Cicero your mother gave me when I was fourteen, you know. I reckon I owe my Latin and Greek GCSEs to her.'

'Oh, indeed? She would be so very…' By the look in Larry's eyes, he too was thinking back to early lessons at Mother's knee.

And then there were four.

As they started the washing up, Dora braced herself for the questions that would surely begin the moment Larry disappeared upstairs to change out of the stiff-as-a-board three-piece suit – his father's – which he'd worn for the funeral. But what she got, from Mel, was: 'Hey, it was brilliant telling him like that. I was shitting bricks for a few seconds, then I thought, of course, you know Larry, you know what he's really like.'

Did she? Well, maybe she was beginning to.

Tom was running water into the sink. 'Yes. Great timing,' he said.

Well, if you say so, Tom. 'Do you think you'll contact Peter Shaw, Mel?' *Hell, why did she say that?*

'What, about the results?' said Mel. 'Yeah, yeah, in his dreams,' she laughed.

That evening in the pub they got to talking about babies' names. Mel had a sort of feeling it should be Faith if it was a girl. Tom wasn't sure they'd ruled out Martha.

'I think you'll soon find you have,' Dora told him.

'Faith… Such a pretty name,' said Larry.

Which of course clinched it.

'Hey, why don't you both come to the wedding next week?' said Mel, looking from Dora to Larry.

It was inevitable that Larry would look at Dora with eyes which said, *Oh please, do let's go,* and that she would answer for both of them. 'Thought you'd never ask.'

'Great,' said Tom. He buried his nose in his pint in a way that suggested the prospect of having her at his wedding was anything but great. Well, it wasn't as if she was itching to rush out and buy a hat.

*

At eight twenty-seven on Saturday morning, the locksmith was ringing Dora's doorbell. By nine, she had a new set of front and back door keys. By ten past nine she was out of the house and on her way to Larry's. It was funny: nothing she'd done in the last three years felt quite as final as this, locking her husband out of the house he half-owned. He *was* still her husband. Just.

Somehow that day Steve was more her husband than ever, as she helped Larry get ready for seeing the Probate people next week, and as she took him into what felt like every gift shop in the town which sold tasteful ornamental boxes and tins, in search of just the right receptacle for Mother when the crematorium was ready to release her ashes. And as she invited him back to her house for supper. And especially as she persuaded him that it would be quite all right for him to finish the topgallant masts on the *Principe de Asturias* while she went back and got on with the cooking.

That was one thing Steve had finally got into his head: she couldn't stand people hanging around in the kitchen in a matey way while she cooked. With those eyes of Larry's watching her, she couldn't even have opened a can of soup.

So. Another day of doing things with, for, to, and by Larry.

Not tomorrow, though. It had to be, *had* to be, tomorrow that she killed the room. Larry had to realise she had a life to get on with, just like Tom and Mel with their big noisy pre-wedding family meal out in Uxbridge tonight.

Finding something to cook was a challenge. Shopping hadn't featured hugely in her life of late. Eventually she put two chicken portions in the microwave to defrost – they probably hadn't been in the freezer longer than six months – scrubbed some not-too-shrivelled carrots, peeled the skins off a couple of onions, and began chopping.

No sign of Steve trying to get in today; no note through the letter box. She should have dusted the doorstep with a fine layer of flour before she went out. No, she should have stuck a strand of hair across the keyhole. No, no, she shouldn't have had the damn locks changed in the first place. Stupid thing to do. Bloody stupid.

As she was tackling the second onion, the doorbell rang. She'd told Larry seven thirty, and it couldn't be later than seven. The t'gallant masts must have been less fiddly than expected. Bugger.

She rinsed her hands. She went down the hallway still wiping them, and opened the door. And dropped the towel.

Steve picked it up and handed it to her. 'Can I come in?' He didn't wait for her to answer, he walked in past her and closed the door. 'Do I detect supper's under way?' he said, looking at her apron. 'For two, at a guess. Is he here?'

She shook her head. 'Not yet.' The words seemed to come out sideways, hardly making any impression on the air.

'Right, I won't take long,' he said, reaching into his trouser pocket. 'There's obviously no point in me having these.' He threw a set of keys onto the hall table. 'So, you're going to sell the house are you? And you're going to redecorate the room? Only you aren't, are you. He's going do it for you.'

'No he isn't, I'm going to do it on my own. I have to, can't you see?'

'No kidding, eh? Talented Dora Clayton just can't live without adding interior décor to her list of achievements? Doesn't it occur to you that Jo was my daughter too, and I might want to be the one to redecorate the room, seeing as I decorated it in the first place?' He sucked in a breath, dragging air into him in a way she hadn't seen him do, not even at the worst times. 'You know what? You are fucking *crazy*. You are beyond help. All right, decorate that room if you so much want to, do what you fucking like with it.' The words slapped her face, and there was nowhere to hide from their stinging

304

force. 'I came round here at ten this morning and I've wasted most of a perfectly good Saturday wondering what the hell you're up to. Well, I'm not going to waste any more of it.'

He pulled out his mobile. She watched his fingers as he pressed the buttons. 'Hi. Look, I'm free after all. Yeah, I can come round now, but we'll go out, don't feel you've got to – all right, if you're sure. I'm not going to twist your arm, I could do with staying in. In fact I'm positively gagging to stay in.' The one on the other end must be too, because Steve smiled, and then laughed. 'See you soon,' he said.

He switched off his phone. She couldn't take her eyes off his fingers. 'Right, I'm going,' he said. 'Enjoy your night in.' Seconds later the front door slammed.

She stood with the towel in her hand, listening while the sound of a car being driven away grew fainter and fainter, until all she could hear was silence. Then she turned, and her feet took her back down the hallway into the kitchen. Her hand picked up the knife. She looked at it for one, two, three seconds. She *was* fucking crazy. She was beyond help. She was –

The doorbell rang. She breathed in, breathed out, put the knife down and went to let Larry in.

The taxi driver dropped Dora right by the entrance to the DIY store. 'I'll only be a minute,' she said.

'Take as long as you like, love, you're paying,' he said, grinning. That was the thing about taxi drivers in this city, their sense of humour.

She grinned back, stifling the rising hysterical giggle. She couldn't have him seeing she was crazy. Crazy, crazy. Beyond help.

Inside the store, aisles and aisles of DIY stuff confronted her. Everywhere there were men in anoraks and sweaters who looked as if they knew what they were here for. Outside, the place had merely looked big. Inside, it seemed to stretch for miles. Along these aisles she was surely seeing the curvature of the earth.

Panic enveloped her, hot brain-melting blinding panic. She took a deep, too-shaky breath and then a breath she blew out slowly through pursed lips. She wanted paint and a couple of brushes that was all. Just paint and brushes. She grabbed a trolley.

Once she found the shelves of paints, it was ridiculously straightforward. The paint chose itself: Blue Babe. What else could she possibly have? She flagged down a man in an overall with the store's name on the front, asked how many cans for a smallish bedroom, and was promptly told a couple should do it.

She wheeled the trolley with its cargo of paint and two brushes, one wide, one narrow, to the checkout. So easy! Perhaps the whole thing was going to be easy, much easier than she'd thought. She wasn't beyond help. She was fine, fine, fine.

The taxi driver eyed the lids of the cans of paint. Well, the colour was a bit bright. But it was the only possible colour. It was the inevitable colour.

On the way out of the car park, it struck her that all she'd got was matt blue paint. She hadn't got any gloss for the woodwork, or white paint for the ceiling. Oh well, Blue Babe would have to do for everything. She'd create a baby blue box.

A spurt of giggle escaped. She covered it with a cough.

Back at the house, she stood the cans on the kitchen table, labels facing outwards. Then she swivelled them around so that the labels were facing inwards. They looked less something-or-other that way. Less what? Less frightening?

She contemplated them, massaging her shoulders. OK. You've got the paint. Now get on with it. Go upstairs. Clear the room.

She went up slowly. She went up as a small child would, lifting the second foot onto a stair before the first one had left it. She breathed in, breathed out, and pushed open the door of the room.

Well. First things first. She lifted the tin out of the cot and, hugging it tightly to her, took it into her room and stood it on the bedside table. Out of Jo's room, it looked too much like the tea caddy it actually was. When they left this house, she and Jo, would it be like moving a cat without any paws to butter, would Jo keep trying to go back to the only place she knew? Come to think of it, though, there was a place Jo knew which was going with them: her own body. What if she made Jo into tea? She could re-assimilate her. She'd be inside her mother again, back where it was safe.

Right. Now the rest. She went back to the room. The sun and the moon and the stars and the planets dangling over the cot looked particularly cheerful today. Poor things. Poor, poor things. She had to let them have one last dance. She pushed the button.

> *Twinkle twinkle little star*
> *How I wonder what you are*
> *Up above the world so high*
> *Like a diamond in the sky*

Could she save this mobile? No, no, not this, not even this, *most of all, not this*. It had to die. Along with everything else in here, she had to destroy it, as she'd destroyed its owner. She had to hack, smash and burn every single thing in this room. Oxfam might think differently, but to let these things go to other, unknown babies... No. It would be like giving Jo herself away. The mobile needn't go yet though. It could go last.

OK, then. So what now – take down the little-green-man-from-Mars clock? Ah, he was going again. He was telling her it was twenty five past seven, not a quarter past eleven or whatever the time now was, but he was ticking away all the same. Batteries did funny things at times, they started to live again when you thought they were dead.

She folded her arms tight across her chest. If only the little green man didn't have that happy smiling face. If only he were scowly and growly.

As if on cue, her stomach gave a growl. What could she expect, with no breakfast in it? If she went down and made coffee, had something to eat, maybe it would be easier. Maybe. Because it couldn't possibly be any harder.

Oh Capella.

She went down the stairs at a run. She picked up the phone and dialled a number she now knew as well as her own. Eating wasn't going to help, she had to get out of here, and there was only one place she could go, one place where nobody would ask any questions: 'Larry, I've finished the housework I had to do,' she said. Her voice was strange, it was coming out in gasps. Or sobs? 'Can I come round?'

Five minutes later she was on a bus.

Twenty-Four

The school library doors swung open. As thirty eleven- and twelve-year-olds began to shuffle and scuffle in, Tom had to bite back the words of an announcement: *Pay particular attention today, this is the last lesson I'll take as a single man.*

'OK, find somewhere to sit and settle down,' he called.

When they'd all got into some sort of order around the tables, he introduced himself: 'Hi, I'm Mr Ross, I'm standing in for Mrs Mason.'

'Hi, I'm Mr Stoddart. You can call me Jez,' said a boy at the back. A couple of girls giggled.

'Hello, Jez,' said Tom. Ah yes, that half-curious, half-challenging stare. This would be the class clown, there was always one. 'We'll have another word in a minute, Jez. Who's that next to you?'

It was Katie. And next to Katie was Beth, and next to Beth was Megan. One blonde, one red-head, one brunette, all with that other look on their faces, the sizing-up look. OK, nothing new there either, all male teachers under forty were subjected to that look. Half way round the group, a girl announced herself as Mel. She had that look, too. Pretty girl. In a few years she could be a hazard – to those who liked Nordic types. Provided she learned to look bright and interested...

At this age, how would Dora have seemed to a teacher? She would have disdained to give any male teacher the look – if there were any male teachers at her all-girls school. More likely, her teachers would have found themselves wondering if a bomb were going to go off when they least expected it.

Last Friday she made that announcement about Mel's pregnancy. What might she do tomorrow, the day of the wedding? Then again, perhaps it was himself he should be worrying about. To marry the one with the other watching: how many men could get through that? Oh Capella, if there could only be two of him, one for each...

Half a dozen names drifted past him before he realised he'd only half-heard them. Christ, he had to focus, focus, as he'd always been able to in class, no matter what was happening in the rest of his life.

The last child, Simon, the one right under his nose, was the one with the strongest specs and the pinkest cheeks. Class swot? Know-all? Or eager to learn what the boundless universe of books had to offer? Well, he had ways of finding out.

'OK, everybody, we're sitting here in a library. As you see it's a place with a lot of books in.' A ripple of titters. 'If I said, get up and take two minutes to choose one, any one, what would you do?'

Hands shot up. There'd be the predictable stampede for anything with spells and magic wands in it, but Jez would put on a blindfold, spin around three times, and take out the first book he laid hands on. More titters, the loudest from Katie and her two friends.

'Well, that's one way to do it,' said Tom. 'Feel free to try it in a minute, when I let everybody choose a book. But you might like to know you're going to be writing a page for me by

310

Thursday on what you thought of the book, and that goes for all of you. Simon? What about you?' The boy was sitting there, silent, arms folded, looking at him.

'Has it got to be fiction, Mr Ross?' said Simon.

'It can be non-fiction if you like, provided it's something that gets your imagination going. What are you interested in?'

'Astronomy. I've got my own telescope.'

'OK, Simon, you pick something about stars. And when you write about them, tell me why you like them.'

He kept an eye on them all as they milled about the library shelves, jostling and shoving. Simon and one or two others were soon out of the main melée, sitting on the floor in the science section, noses in books. Tom wandered across to them and looked over shoulders. A girl was gazing at pictures of glaciers, seemingly oblivious to him standing over her.

'This is great, Mr Ross,' said Simon, holding up his book. It was about the stellar year: what you can see month by month from your back garden if you look up on a clear night. 'The maps are really good. I'm going to show it to Mr Clayton after maths tomorrow. He runs the astronomical club.'

'I know, Simon. I went to one of his meetings earlier this term.'

'Did you? Do you know about the constellations, then?'

'Yes, I do. As a matter of fact, I discovered them when I was about your age.' Suddenly, he had a huge urge to tear the book out of the boy's hands. Reading material like this should be kept under lock and key, it could lead young minds astray. Then came cries of 'Gerroff, I saw it first!' and Tom trotted smartly across to the fiction section.

Tom drew back the curtains. The day had dawned, the Big Day. Was it going to be fine? There was cloud, but a watery sun seemed to be trying to burn its way through.

'Tom are you up?' came the voice of Tommy.

'Yes,' he called back.

'Good. Right, I'm off. I really wish I was coming, you know. Still, Year Two would run riot. I take it all back, by the way. I think it's going to work out.'

'Thanks,' called Tom. It was good of her to say so, and he was going to make damn sure that she was right to say so. But he didn't want to hear opinions on how healthy his marriage was going to be, he just wanted to get the business of the day over. 'I'll tell you all about it tonight.'

OK, time to shave. In less than an hour he had to be on his way. He knew what Larry was going to say, poor guy.

He was right:

'Oh,' said Larry, his smile fading. 'Oh. What a pity.'

'Well, in that office, a week never goes past without some kind of panic,' said Tom, ushering Larry into the car.

That text message from Dora last night: 'sry cnt do 2moro up 2 here w sbhn.' His first reaction, something that felt close to relief. But that was fifteen hours ago.

Was she in the middle of a work crisis? Or was she backing out because she couldn't face it? Either way, here was Larry, sitting beside him in the three-piece tweed suit he'd worn to his mother's funeral, massive hands folded in his lap, a white carnation in his buttonhole, staring ahead at a scene he wasn't seeing. He'd thought he was going to have a day out with Dora, and now look at him. Totally lost.

He'd bet that Larry wouldn't much want to chat. Well, it wasn't as if he himself did, either. The only problem was that he had an hour or so of driving ahead of him. What was he going to think about? He could think about Mel and what they were going to do today. He could think about Jez Stoddart's 'teacher walks into a bar' joke as the library class was finishing yesterday. Or about the fact that he hadn't lost the knack of laughing not too visibly when those characters tried to wind him up. The trouble was, too many of them were genuinely funny. If that boy could raise a smile this week from Mr Ross, he would go far.

He could think about Dora. Why did she text rather than phone last night? Did she think he'd try to browbeat her into coming? Oh hell, maybe she really did have a work crisis. Maybe her boss really had grounded her.

Or he could think about the driving.

'2 bd cu.' Dora gazed again at the text message from Tom. Maybe she should have come clean. Maybe she should have told Tom what she was going to do today instead of see him get married. She switched off the mobile and tossed it onto the bed. Looking at yesterday's text messages was not what she was going to do today.

She knelt down by the bedside table and gave a kiss to the midnight-blue tin covered in swirls of stars. Then she got to her feet and picked up the scissors, the heavy-duty kitchen scissors she'd brought upstairs just now, one slow step at a time. She went out of the bedroom and along the landing. 'cu', Tom had said. What would she rather have: 'cu' or 'fucking crazy'?

She opened the door of the room. She breathed in, and held her breath. She wasn't letting that breath out until she'd made the first cut.

She knelt down. She picked up the space rocket rug by its yellow nose cone, and sank the uppermost scissor blade into the bright fluffy pile. Her hand didn't shake. She began to close the blades.

And the breath fizzled out of her. The scissors wouldn't cut. *Shit.* Just when she'd brought herself to it, finally brought herself, the fucking scissors wouldn't work!

OK. OK. She had to stay calm. The scissors weren't up to it, the rug was too thick. Right, right, the garden shears, then, get the garden shears.

If she went out of here, though, if she allowed herself to go out through that door before starting the killing, would she ever force herself back through it? All right then, the clothes. Deal with the clothes.

She opened the cupboard. Ah, that lovely pile of jumpsuits, so neatly folded. All the colours of the rainbow: Richard Of York Gave Battle In Vain. Except that orange was missing, of course... Her hand reached out toward the topmost jumpsuit, the red one with yellow piping. It pulled out the suit and held it up, the sweet little arms and legs dangling. She opened the scissors.

And closed them again on air. Oh God, oh God.

All right. All right, all right, get the paint, start painting, do *something*.

But the paint was still downstairs...

Do it.

She ran out of the room and down the stairs, her breath coming fast. Ten o'clock already and she'd done nothing, nothing! If she could only get some paint on the walls. A brushful would do, then all the rest might be easier. Might be possible.

As she carried the two cans of paint upstairs, the brushes and a screwdriver for levering off the lids tucked under one arm, the tendons in her wrists stood out with the effort and the scar on her left wrist stretched livid across them. The other scar, the one across her abdomen, gave the sort of twinge she only ever had if a sneeze caught her out while lying flat. She hadn't brought up any old newspapers to put the paint cans on. Oh God, what did it matter, what did it matter! The floor might as well be blue too.

When she levered the lid off one of the cans, a pungent smell wafted up and filled her nose. She bent her head and sniffed deeply. Her head swam a little, but maybe that was because of last night, the sleep she hadn't had. But it wasn't hard to understand why people got addicted to this, people who wanted to escape from the world for a while.

Blue Babe. What a *perfect* colour.

She dipped the larger of the brushes in the paint. She wiped the surplus paint off on the edge of the tin. She advanced towards the wall. She touched the wall with the brush. She drew the brush down the wall, from eye level to hip level. She stood back.

A blue stripe. A surprisingly neat blue stripe, like a gash in the fabric of the universe. A gash which had trapped three of the spacemen.

Oh fuck.

She dipped her brush in the paint, didn't wipe off the surplus, and flung the paint at the wall. And again, and again, and again, until her breaths were coming in thick, hot gasps, her heart was racing, and she had a big Blue Babe abstract in front of her eyes. Then she stood back.

The spacemen were blown to smithereens. The universe had exploded.

Capella. Capella, Capella, Capella.

The brush dropped from her hand and she ran from the room. She all but fell downstairs, and in two minutes she was in Woodstock Road, walking fast. This was it now: walking, only walking, for as long as she had feet to walk with. She could never go back to that room. Never, never, never.

'Are you, Thomas Lachlan, free lawfully to marry Melanie Amber?' said the man in the municipal suit.

'I am,' said Tom. He gave another quick sideways glance at the girl he was standing next to, the girl in the dress which wasn't what girls apparently called a 'meringue' but which was special enough that he hadn't been allowed to see it until now. To look at her and continue looking at her was what he had to do: to let the sight of her keep his mind focussed.

315

'Are you, Melanie Amber, free lawfully to marry Thomas Lachlan?'

'I am,' said Mel straight away, loud and clear.

Before Thomas Lachlan drew breath again, or so it seemed, matching rings were on his and Melanie Amber's fingers and he was kissing her in front of this audience of theirs: her mother dabbing her eyes with a handkerchief; her father with arms folded, massive and impassive; the sisters and the brothers, laughing and joshing and busy with cameras; Larry, hunched awkwardly on his chair but beaming; Debbie Priday in tears but grinning; the cousins, aunts and uncles; and not least Grandma Battaglia, in eye-blitzing electric blue.

Tom held Mel's hand in his free hand while he signed the Register, and she held his hand in hers while she wrote, for the last time, 'Melanie Amber Baines'. 'Ross' it was going to be from now on, according to Mel, and despite the feminist protests of her friends. Larry signed and Debbie Priday signed, as witnesses, and he and Mel, still hand in hand, led them all out: all except Mel's brother Craig who was walking backwards in front of them with his state-of-the-art camcorder.

The next wedding party was already hanging around outside. Tom saw the groom's eyes look Mel up and down, felt the man's gaze swivel after her as they went down the red brick steps decorated with white splodges of bird-dropping and the odd bashed-in Stella can. The bride, chattering with a group of women, didn't seem to have noticed.

'Hi Mel,' he whispered.

'Hi Tom,' she whispered back. 'I was dead nervous, did it show?'

'You were brilliant.'

'By the way, it's your baby. Um, sorry for all that... you know.'

He stopped and looked at her, at her radiant face. 'Apology

accepted, Mel.' He took her into his arms, and kissed her, properly, to a chorus of cheers, whistles, 'Put her down!' from brother-in-law Craig and 'Hey, this a public place, mate!' from brother-in-law Scott.

In the general milling about as they all got into cars to go to the restaurant, he found a moment to tell Jackie Baines quietly that it was all right, she could cut back to ten a day from now on. 'You mind you treat her well or you'll hear from me,' she whispered, black eyes flashing.

Mel's grandmother seemed to have commandeered Larry – indeed was arm-in-arm with him, looking like a doll beside him, and even brighter blue out here than in the Register Office, if that were possible. With a little careful footwork, it proved possible to manoeuvre the comically mismatched couple into Tommy's car with himself and Mel.

'Hey, where's Dora?' said Mel as she got in. 'Didn't she come?'

'She couldn't get away. Something on at work. She sends her love.'

'Such a pity,' murmured Larry, 'but Dora has a very responsible job.'

'I just been telling Larry here, Mel gets her brains from me,' said Mrs Battaglia, as Tom started the car.

'She's lucky, Mrs B,' said Tom.

'Yes, and so're you. Congratulations, Tom, you got yourself a smashing girl.'

'I know,' he said.

'Oh Gran,' said Melanie.

'Now, Larry, we're going to have a bit of something to eat. And drink, if I know my daughter,' said Mrs Battaglia, as they pulled out into the road. 'You met Jackie yet?'

'Oh, yes, yes, I – I was introduced to Mrs Baines as we came in.'

'Good. You like champagne?'

'I – I'm very much afraid I can't remember, I –'

'Well, we'll get you a little glass to try. You stick with me, Larry.'

Thank you, Mrs Battaglia.

All through that long noisy lunch party, with bubbles being blown at him and Mel, and corks being popped, and cameras flashing like miniature explosions, whenever Tom looked at Larry there was Mrs Battaglia leaning towards him from one side and Mel's cheerful sister Carla leaning towards him from the other and a 'little glass' blowing bubbles at him from in front.

Larry was thinking, though. It was as evident as if his skull were transparent that he was thinking about Dora. Wishing so hard it were her beside him. With hindsight, maybe they'd been wrong to think a balance could be struck, as far as Larry was concerned. She couldn't just 'be nice' to him now and then fade out of his life. Did she realise that?

Hold on, Larry. This will end. Mel has to climb out of her wedding clothes in an hour or so and finish a German essay for handing in tomorrow.

They'd be back in Oxford by around eight, with pieces of cake for Dora, Tommy, Syd and the children in small white boxes. They could take Dora's to her straight away, but did he want to see her, with his mind still focussed on Mel? Larry would, though. He could just drop Larry, there were lessons to prepare for tomorrow. On the other hand, wouldn't that look casual...

Jesus, couldn't he even make a simple decision about her? What had she reduced him to?

Twenty-Five

'This box is only for the disposal of used syringes and needles,' said the notice stuck to the front of the tin box. 'It is emptied regularly.'

Dora pulled up her jeans, pulled the flush, and watched the lavatory paper swirl around the bowl and disappear. She let herself out of the cubicle and began to wash her hands. She watched the water spew from the taps, hit the side of the basin, and disappear down the plug hole: down, down, it went, gushing through the deep dark maze of pipework that was the Oxford sewage system. How would it be if you were an ant, say, and got washed down there...

Her hands were still dripping. There were blue patches on them, Blue Babe patches. They hadn't come off. For as long as she lived, she'd have Blue Babe hands.

Her hazy reflection stared back at her from the vandal-proof polished metal mirror. Was that how her ghost was going to look?

There was no one in here but herself. Out there was the world. And she had to go back out into it. But she couldn't. She couldn't.

Movement, sounds. Another hazy impression in the mirror. The world had come in to join her. It had brought something in with it that looked like a pushchair. Something that could only be a pushchair.

She didn't have to turn and look. All she had to do was stand here until the woman had done what she'd come here to do and taken the pushchair away.

The woman seemed to be searching in her bag. The mirror was showing Dora bleached-pale hair and a narrow face with black-ringed eyes, and what looked like a leather jacket pulled tight over a skinny torso. 'Shit shit shit – oh. Thank fuck,' came the mutter from behind her. There was no sign that the woman had noticed Dora, or if she had, that she cared whether Dora lived or died. She disappeared into a cubicle. Almost immediately, sounds came from the cubicle: rustlings, sighs, a groan.

So now it was just Dora herself and the pushchair.

She turned. Of course she turned. From the moment the pushchair arrived, she was always going to turn and fill her eyes with it.

It was parked between her and the way out, next to the Durex machine. It looked to be staying a while. The woman in the cubicle didn't seem to be in a hurry.

Dora walked over to the pushchair. As she was always going to. She looked in. As she was always going to. Why miss this opportunity to make a very bad thing infinitely worse?

Asleep. No more than two months old. Maybe as young as six weeks. Little snub nose, fingers clenched into tiny fists. Oh, the knuckles. Were knuckles ever that small.

It was a girl. Had to be.

More rustlings and sighings from the cubicle behind her. A sniff. Ah, was Mummy nearly finished shooting up, then?

A boiling in her head. *Do it. Do it.*

No, no, I've got to think –

Do it now, you haven't got time to think, do it now!

She grabbed the handles of the pushchair and pushed it out into Market Street. Oh Christ, where should she go, where, where? Left towards Cornmarket or right towards Turl Street? The thickest crowds were in Cornmarket. She had to go there, she had to lose herself in those lovely sheltering crowds, quick, quick!

She turned into Cornmarket, heart hammering, breath coming fast, so fast – too fast. She had to breathe slower, or people would see! Where now, for God's sake? Home, of course: home, home. The bus – no, no, a taxi, get a taxi.

She ploughed up Cornmarket, and as she went, the hindering treacle of nightmares surrounded her, knee-deep. Any moment, there would be yells, a hand on her shoulder. Any moment now. *Don't look back.* Her hands, still damp, felt cold.

She didn't look back as she turned the corner into George Street, and there were no yells. When she reached the taxi rank at Gloucester Green there was a line of taxis waiting. 'Wolvercote, please,' she said to the driver of the one at the front, trying not to gasp. It was a big black London-style taxi. She didn't have to take the baby out of the pushchair and collapse it, the driver lifted it on board for her. Oh, joy!

The taxi driver started the engine and they began to move out of Gloucester Green. Thank *God*. Hey, this was easy, so very easy, she was meant to find this baby. It was Capella's doing, this. Capella wanted her to have this baby. Capella wanted her to care for this baby as long as she lived.

Of course. Of course of course of course!

Soon they were heading north, picking up speed. As a police car, siren blaring, came up behind them her heart bucked and whinnied, but it passed them and raced on up the road. She leaned back against the seat and blew out a long breath. They'd be home soon. Everything was going to be all

321

right. Look at this baby, sleeping so peacefully. She knew it was all right, she knew she was going home.

Ah, those teeny tiny hands. Dora reached out a finger. She touched, very lightly, almost without touching, the back of the left hand. Oh God, the feel of it. She'd forgotten, she'd actually *forgotten* how hands like that felt.

So still. So quiet. *Was she alive?*

Be alive, oh please God be alive.

She put her finger under the nostrils. Was that an outbreath? Or was she imagining it, wanting and needing it to have been a breath? She slipped her hand inside the baby's sleeping bag. The chest was moving. Up, down, up, down. Thank God. Thank bloody God.

She sat back and closed her eyes. Then she sat up again, bolt upright, on the edge of the seat. She had to watch this child. Alive she might be, but it was up to her, Dora, to keep her alive. Never again could she close her eyes.

The streets out there. Was this Oxford? It looked so different. This could be a town in a foreign country, or on Mars. But it didn't matter. She – they – would be home soon. Home –

Wait a minute. She couldn't be dropped *there*. Stupid!

She tapped on the glass partition. 'You can drop me by the school, I'm not far.'

She kept her head down as she got out of the taxi. But there was nobody about, no mothers at the gate, no children in the playground. They'd be inside having lunch, trying to swap sandwiches made with wholemeal bread for crisps and Snickers.

Jo would have gone there. But why shouldn't her new baby go there? Yes, why shouldn't she, with her insulated spaceman lunch bag full of sandwiches made from Sainsbury's best granary, and her matching spaceman drinks bottle?

My new baby. *My* new baby.

Too soon for this, for thoughts like this. Get home, get home!

As she pushed the pushchair along the quiet streets, she still kept her head down. Let none of the neighbours see her. Then again, did it matter if they did? This was a cousin's illegitimate child, and she was adopting her.

The baby had to have a name. What was it going to be? Christina, to be known as Kit? Constance, to be known as Con? Catherine, to be known as Cat? Hm. Cat Clayton. It had something, it had a ring to it. Oh, it was such fun choosing names!

'Hello Cat,' she said to the back of the pushchair. 'How do you do, Cat.'

No-one was about when she turned the corner into her road. Nearly there, now. Nearly there.

A small brown dog, which was nosing about, looked up as she turned in at her gate, but Dora didn't stop until she was putting her key in the lock. She got the door open, manhandled the pushchair into the hall, and shut the door behind her.

She leaned against the wall. She slid slowly down it until she was crouched on the floor. Home. *Aah.* She bowed her head, let it drop onto her chest.

When her heart had shifted down a gear, she raised her head. A white splodge came into view. It was on the nearside front pushchair wheel. Birdshit? Chewing gum?

She had a strange pushchair in the house. A pushchair with some sort of mess stuck to one of its wheels. There was a baby it in. A baby. Which must be why she was shaking. Shaking from head to foot.

Ooh, Do'wa. What will dey say? A five-year-old boy said that, big-eyed, hands up to his mouth, gazing at the remains of the Wendy House. At Syd's feet, tiny plastic tea cups, cracked and buckled, lay here and there where she'd thrown them. The memory so clear, so crystal-clear.

323

A rustling noise. Faint, like a mouse. No, not a mouse. A baby.

She hauled herself up onto her knees, still shaking, and crawled across to the pushchair. The little hands were opening and closing. A pair of eyes was looking up at her, a pair of grey eyes, regarding her steadily. Oh, it was awake. Oh God. No, not it! She. Cat.

'Hello, Cat,' she said. Her voice sounded odd, as if she'd stolen it from someone. *Stolen* – no, no, this was *her* baby. She put out a finger and touched the back of Cat's hand, touched without touching, as she'd done in the taxi. The hand began to wave, to grope the air. Those fingers, those nails. Ah, those nails.

Cat yawned. Her little face screwed itself up. And she started to whimper.

Oh Capella, she's crying, help me, tell me what to do!

Now look. You know what to do, you've done it before. Stay calm. When they whimper they're bored, or wet, or dirty, or hungry.

Hungry. *Oh Christ I haven't got any milk. Oh bloody Christ.*

All the formula milk which she'd kept as a fall-back in case her breasts dried up was gone, of course. Steve binned it when she went into hospital after the wrist incident. But even if she'd still had it, it'd be way past its use-by date. Shit!

The whimper increased in pitch, became a wail. 'It's all right, it's all right,' she whispered. But it wasn't. And Cat knew it wasn't. She'd have to get her out of the pushchair, she'd have to try to soothe her.

Dora attacked the zip of the sleeping bag, but her hands were shaking so much that the zip caught in the fleece lining. The wail became a yell. Oh God, oh God.

She took a deep, long, shaky breath, freed the fabric from the zip, and unclipped the straps holding Cat in position. She slipped her left hand under the baby's bottom, her right hand around the shoulders and the back of the head – *always support the baby's head* – and lifted her out.

'Don't cry, don't cry,' she said, but maybe because she herself was whimpering, Cat shifted gear until she was crying steadily. As she cried, her face became red. The redder it became, the louder she cried. Louder, and louder, and—

Hey, the shopping tray. Christ, you stupid woman, try the shopping tray.

There was a Boots bag and a scuffed-looking rucksack in the shopping tray under the pushchair, and – oh, thank God – the rucksack had two made-up bottles in it, and some spare nappies, and there was a pack of formula in the Boots bag. With one hand she flipped the protective cap off one of the bottles, shook a few drops into the cap – *get the flow going before you put the bottle to the baby's mouth* – and put the teat to Cat's lips. Cat seized on it and began sucking. Ah. Thank God.

Inch by inch, Dora shuffled back to the wall and let it support her. She gazed down at the hungry Cat, felt the weight of her in her arms. This was what her arms were for. This was what she was for.

Oh Capella, thank you, thank you for showing me the way.

So obvious, so simple. And so unexpected, like all obvious and simple things.

Cat began patting the bottle. *At six seeks she waves her arms vigorously.* A laugh bubbled up inside Dora. But it was a quiet laugh, a happy laugh. Those other laughs, those mad, unstable, crazy laughs, they were gone for ever.

Cat finished the bottle, and Dora held her against her shoulder and winded her. How easily, effortlessly, it was all coming back now. Like riding a bike.

After you feed them, you change them. And Cat's nappy did need changing. Her rather grimy knitted all-in-one was dry, but under it the nappy felt solid. It must be soaked. Well,

Dora had the kit: the changing mat, nappies, bucket, lotion, cotton wool.

'Up we go,' she sang as she carried Cat upstairs, 'up the wooden hill.' To the Land of Nod. That was how it went on, didn't it? She'd have to get the books out of the loft. Just the nursery rhyme books first, the rest could wait until Cat was a bit older. Oh, it was going to be such fun!

She pushed open the door of the room, and stopped in her tracks. Christ, what was this? Blue daubs all over the wall, a paint brush flung down on the floor, spatters of paint on the rug… *She'd* done this.

No. No, she hadn't! Not her as she was now, not the self she'd now become. But this had been done, and would have to be undone, very soon. Not now, though. Now, she had to change Cat.

One-handed, in three trips, not putting Cat down for a moment, she took all the nappy changing equipment into her bedroom and spread it out on the floor. The cot would have to come in here too, there was no way Cat could sleep in that room. Even if it had been immaculate, there was no way Cat could sleep anywhere out of her sight.

She put Cat on the changing mat – *Cat, you're on the mat!* – undid the all-in-one and the towelling bodysuit under it, and eased the baby out. Ah, those dimpled knees, those feet! And the toe nails, the toe nails.

She peeled back the tapes at either side of the nappy and pulled the front flap open. And sat back on her heels.

Oh Christ. Oh Christ.

The baby peed. A neat arc of wetness from his tiny willy overshot the end of the changing mat and landed on the carpet.

Could this be? *Could* it?

She bent down and inspected the baby's face, studied it from every angle. This *had* to be a girl, surely. There was no beefy directness about the chin, none of that pigginess about the eyes that meant this child was going to beat up anybody at playgroup who had the toy he wanted.

The baby began to gurgle, then to kick. Those legs. He was going to make a Premier League footballer one day.

Oh my God. I've taken a baby. From a public lavatory.

She stood up, slowly. Then she sat down, slowly, on the edge of the bed.

The baby carried on kicking and gurgling. One-two one-two went those footballer legs, like pistons.

And then they slowed and stopped. The baby yawned, and began to whimper. He must be getting cold. Well, nothing lasted in this world. Nothing.

She pushed herself up. She had a choice. Go downstairs and fetch one of the baby's own nappies, or put the nappy on him that she'd brought into the bedroom. Jo's nappy. Going downstairs would mean she either had to pick him up, or leave him here for a minute. Only a minute.

She was halfway to the door when there was a louder whimper. She looked back at the baby. How small he looked lying there. How defenceless.

She went back to him, knelt down, and reached for Jo's nappy. With one hand she held his feet, with the other she slid the nappy under him – *up and under* – and in one fluid movement she let go of the feet and fastened the ties of the nappy around him.

Yet another thing she hadn't forgotten how to do. It was hard-wired in, all of it. She'd never forget. She'd never be able to forget. She eased the baby back into the bodysuit and then into the all-in-one.

Right. You feed them, you change them, the next thing is walkies.

She settled the baby back into the pushchair. She opened the front door and wheeled the pushchair through it. She wheeled it all the way down the Woodstock Road, through Cornmarket, and down St Aldates to the police station. She wheeled the now fast-asleep baby inside, and stopped when she got to what looked like a reception desk. A man in uniform was behind it, resting on his elbows.

'I took this baby,' she said. 'This morning. I took him. Arrest me.'

The man's jaw dropped. He leaned over the desk, looked at the pushchair, and said, 'My bloody Christ.' And then his face and everything else he was saying seemed to dissolve into a white-water hiss, and the world slipped sideways until Dora made contact with a hard surface that jarred her shoulder.

Blackness.

'A woman is being detained in connection with the abduction of two month-old Ryan Booth from a public lavatory in Market Street, Oxford, this morning,' said the radio announcer. 'The Thames Valley Police say that—'

Tom switched off the radio. He wasn't listening to news like that, not today.

'How dreadful,' murmured Larry. 'That anyone could do such a thing.'

'Some women are desperate,' said Tom. The lights of Headington were ahead. They were nearly there. 'Some even need medical help. I've heard of it happening when a woman can't get pregnant or has lost her baby, say in a miscarriage.'

Lost her baby. As he heard himself say those words, something began to stir in his brain.

Surely not. Surely not.

He wriggled his shoulders. Stupid thought. OK, when he dropped Larry at Dora's he'd stay, but only for ten minutes. Damn it, he *did* have lessons to prepare for tomorrow. And anyway, Tommy would be waiting to hear all about the wedding.

No lights were on in Dora's house, although the daylight was fading. There wasn't even a light on in the room. She couldn't be there. Nevertheless, Tom said nothing until Larry had tried the doorbell.

'Oh,' said Larry, after the third ring. 'Dora isn't home from work. She has to work *so* hard.'

Hm. She was at Sainsbury's, more like. Still, for Larry's benefit he'd better go through the motions and phone her office. Anyway, maybe she was still there.

He got a frazzled-sounding female voice that told him Dora hadn't been in the office all day, she'd gone to a wedding.

'Tell you what, Larry, we'll go round to Syd Clayton's,' he said. 'She'll be there.' She just might be. But whether she were there or not, his guts were telling him that, right now, he needed Syd.

Syd had no idea where Dora might be. 'Hasn't she been with you?' he said, his eyebrows lifting.

Tom kept his voice level as he gave Syd the 'work crisis' story. Syd's eyebrows lifted higher.

'We do so want to tell her about the day,' said Larry.

Syd was now chewing his lip. 'I think it might be an idea to pop back to her house,' he said, glancing at Larry, but addressing himself to Tom. 'She might have been in the shower. You wouldn't have seen the bathroom light on from the front. Tell you what, I'll come with you. I need to collect a printer I loaned her.'

As Tom began to drive them back to Dora's house, Syd said, 'Have you heard about that baby snatching in Oxford today? Apparently some woman walked into St Aldate's police station this afternoon and handed the kid over.'

'Did they say who she was?'

'No. All they said on the news was that she's being held for questioning.'

'Maybe she wasn't the one who took the baby. Maybe she rescued it, or found it abandoned.'

'Yeah. Maybe.'

'The poor child,' murmured Larry.

When Tom pulled into Dora's road, there still weren't any lights in the house. As they went up to her front door, he began to have the feeling that the house was sunk in forlornness, as if she'd left it and was never coming back. The feeling grew as Syd rang the bell.

'Bugger,' muttered Syd, after the fourth ring. 'OK, we'll go in anyway.' Tom tried to breathe slowly as Syd reached into a pocket, brought out a bunch of keys, and applied one to the lock. It wouldn't fit. 'Damn it, she's had the lock changed and not told me,' said Syd. He pushed against the door, as you do when you know there's no point but you do it anyway, while you try to think of what the hell you should be doing.

The door swung open. It wasn't properly shut, never mind locked.

They went in, into a house whose walls seemed to breathe out silence. Syd switched on the light in the hallway. 'Dozza?' he called, throwing open first the sitting room door, then the dining room door, and lastly the door into the kitchen.

'Ah, Dora has been doing some painting,' said Larry.

He was right. There was a faint but definite whiff of fresh paint coming from upstairs. Was that what she'd been doing today, decorating?

'Dozz?' Syd shouted up the stairs. No answer. 'Hang on,' he said, and ran up.

It took ten seconds, if that, for Syd to reappear at the top of the stairs. 'I think you'd better come up,' he said, sounding leaden.

Sweet Jesus, was she up there? *Was she—*

Tom must have got up the stairs in one bound, because he was standing beside Syd with his thought not finished.

Syd beckoned him into the dead baby's room. Dora wasn't lying senseless, or worse, on the floor, but she had been doing some painting. She had indeed been doing some painting.

'Oh,' said a voice from behind him. 'Oh, oh.'

Yes, Larry, there's more to Dora than you thought. Sorry.

There were one or two spots of blue paint on the rug, but apart from that – and the wall – nothing was spoiled. He had a huge urge to reach out and set the mobile going, to check that it was OK. Should he? Shouldn't he? Before he could decide, Syd said, 'Now come into the bedroom.'

The bedroom floor was like a scene from the baby equipment catalogue Mel had shown him at the weekend. In the bucket was a nappy. A used nappy, by the smell of it. *Get used to it,* said a voice in his head. Christ, not now!

There was a patch of dampness on the carpet by the changing mat. Syd went down on one knee, put a finger in it, and sniffed the finger. 'Baby pee,' he said. 'Takes me back. Jim was always doing this, the little tyke.'

'Oh,' said Larry, gazing at the carpet. 'Oh. Oh.'

Syd straightened up, reached into a pocket, and pulled out his mobile. He had the Thames Valley Police number programmed in. Well, he was a teacher.

So this was what a police station looked like from the inside. Tom had led a sheltered life, he now had to acknowledge.

'The doctors are with her now, sir,' the man in uniform was saying to Syd. 'I have to admit, first off we thought she was drunk, but—'

'Have you charged her?' said Syd.

The sergeant paused a moment. 'Not yet, sir. This is a difficult one… The baby's all right, I should say. Well cared for in fact, during the, er – period of time.' He cleared his throat.

'Period of time.' What a way with words these people had.

But he, Tom Ross, had a way with words too. 'cu': what

possessed him to text Dora that? He should have guessed that something was wrong and gone to her! 'Look, she's ill,' he began.

'The doctors will be establishing the, er, best course of action, sir,' said the sergeant.

'Can we see her?' he pressed.

'Please, please may we see her?' said Larry.

The sergeant looked from Tom, to Larry, to Syd. 'I'll see if this gentleman can go in,' he said, nodding in Syd's direction, 'as he's her brother. Hold on just a minute.' The man disappeared.

'Hold on,' murmured Larry, twisting the tuft of hair at the crown of his head. 'Hold on, hold on…'

She wasn't dead. There was that fact to hold on to, to hold fast to.

When the sergeant reappeared, he wasn't alone. A man and a woman, each in plain clothes, were following him, and following them were two men in paramedic uniform wheeling a pushchair-cum-stretcher contraption like the one in which Mrs Wise had been taken to hospital. Slumped in the contraption was the dried husk of a human being. Was *this* Dora, was this what she now was? Oh Jesus, could he have prevented this?

'I'm afraid matters have moved on, sirs, as you see,' said the sergeant.

'We think she needs to be in hospital at this point,' said the man in plain clothes in a low voice, 'for her own safety.'

'Oh,' said Larry. 'Oh. Oh.'

'Dozza?' said Syd, leaning close to her. 'It's me. Syd.'

Dora's eyelids flickered. 'Syd.' It wasn't a voice. This sound had as much in common with a normal human voice as a bird emerged from the egg had with the shattered shell left behind after the hatching.

Her lips moved again. Syd bent closer. 'I know,' he said, his voice breaking. 'It'll be all right, Dozz. Look, here's Tom and Larry.'

'Hello Dora,' said Tom, kneeling beside her.

A spasm seemed to begin to grip her face, then it faded. She said something, and like Syd, Tom had to bend close to hear what it was: 'How did it go?'

'Well,' he said. 'It went very well.'

'Good,' she whispered. Her gaze shifted to Larry. 'Hello,' said that broken shell of a voice.

At first the big man didn't move. Had he heard her? But then there was a sort of flurry of tweed and she was engulfed, and if anybody thought this was out of order they weren't saying. Dora might not be what Larry had taken her for, but that didn't seem to be making any difference.

'Oh Dora, Dora, Dora.' Larry was weeping.

Did all this happen because he was getting married today? Oh, Dora, Dora, Dora!

Twenty-Six

There were people here. They were watching her. They'd been here before, hadn't they? Maybe. Hard to be sure, too hard, too hard... Let them stay if they wanted, she'd just go back to sleep. All she had to do now was sleep. Sleep for ever...

Would death be like this? If it was, then...too hard, too hard, thinking was too hard. She didn't have to think any more. She didn't even have to remember her name.

People again. Two people, dressed in pale blue, lifting her, pulling back the bed covers, why? Now they were undressing her, why? Rolling something under her, something rough...a towel. Now saying things, to each other, but she needn't listen, it was no concern of hers... Water. Warm water, on her face, around her neck, over her body. Another towel, rough, over her face, over every part of her. Now they were dressing her again, and oh, how tired she was getting...

At last, they were covering her up. Now she could sleep. Sleep...

*

A smell. A smell she had smelled before, but where? They were sitting her up, shaking up the pillows behind her. Oh, the smell was food.

'Eat up, Dora. Lovely tomato soup today.'

A spoon held by a hand, moving towards her lips, a hand on the end of a pale blue arm. She opened her mouth and the spoon went in. It felt too large for her mouth, but she managed to swallow. She had tasted this before, but where, where? Too hard. Too hard. And she was so tired.

More spoonfuls of soup, and sips of water.

'Well done, dear.'

Then she was allowed to sleep, sleep, sleep.

The blackness was fading. From deepest ink, it was changing colour to shades of dark and then lighter grey. Now there was blue in it. Blue... There was light, somewhere above her. Was she in the sea? Up, up she was rising, faster and faster, and—

Ah. Her head was out of the water. Did she want to open her eyes? Not yet. She'd just lie here. The sea was so warm, she'd just float about for a bit. You wouldn't want to do a fast crawl in a sea like this.

What was that dream about?

'Morning Dora, wakey wakey,' said a voice.

She opened her eyes. There was someone here. No, two someones, in blue overalls. Two women.

What was that dream about? There hadn't been any people in it, only water.

Such an interesting ceiling in here. High, white, as horizontal as a ceiling should be. She could lie here forever just looking up at it.

'And who are you today?' said one of the women.

Who was she? Oh, no, no, the woman had said 'how', not 'who'. Funny accent. Why could she never place accents?

'Do you feel like getting up for a while?' said the other woman.

She opened her mouth. Would it work, would it produce words? 'I – don't – know.' What a rusty sound. Some seawater must have got in.

'Well, let's give it a try, shall we?' said the first woman. 'Just for an hour, while the doctor sees you. It'll give him a treat to see you awake and dressed for a change.'

She didn't know if she wanted them to take the covers off her, get her out of the bed and into the bathroom, and sit her on the lavatory. Then again, she didn't know if she didn't want them to. So she let them get on with it, if it made them happy. They waited while she peed. Then they stood while she washed, and combed her hair. And then they helped her into knickers, bra, a blue shirt and black trousers, socks, slippers. The clothes felt loose, but hadn't she seen them before? Were they hers? If so, how did they get here?

By the time they sat her in the chair beside the bed, her head was dizzy with the effort. A tray was put on a table beside her. On it were a cup with brown liquid in it, a saucer under the cup, a plate with toast on it, a bowl with flakes in it, a jug with white liquid in it, a plastic spoon, a plastic knife. Small plastic containers of butter and jam. The saucer had a tiny chip in it. Matching crockery, though. A sort of greyish-green.

As the women in blue began to strip the bed, she lifted the cup to her lips with both hands and took a sip of the brown liquid. It was coffee. What a fascinating earthy flavour it had. It was as if she'd never tasted it before. She poured some of the white liquid on the flakes and picked up the spoon. It was very light. Was that why they gave you plastic cutlery here, because the metal ones were too heavy for tired people to lift?

Was she hungry? She took a mouthful of the flakes, chewed, swallowed. Yes, she was hungry.

She was still eating when a man walked in and sat down in

336

another chair. She had a feeling she'd seen him before. How long had she been here?

'Ah, Dora, you're up and you've got an appetite today,' said the man. 'I'm very glad to see it.'

The women left, saying they'd come back later with the clean bedding. On their way out, one of them gave the window curtains a twitch. There was sky out there. Blue sky. Blue…

'Well, Dora,' said the man. He smiled, leaned back in the chair, swung one leg over the other. 'How are you feeling?'

How was she feeling? How *was* she feeling? 'It looks like a nice day outside,' she said. It was the only thing she could think of, and it sounded vaguely relevant.

'Yes, it's a lovely day outside,' said the man. 'The sun is shining, the birds are singing, there are all sorts of spring flowers out. Do you like tulips?'

'They're OK. I prefer daffodils. I had a daffodil once.'

'Oh? Was that a long time ago?'

'No, not long ago. It was very yellow, that daffodil. Very. Yellow.'

'Did someone give it to you? A friend?'

'The Angel Gabriel gave it to me.'

'Ah. Did he.' The man uncrossed his legs and leaned forward. 'Tell me about the Angel Gabriel, Dora.'

How long was the man going to be here? When would he go, and just let her watch the sky through that window? 'His name's Tom Ross. He's a teacher. He's just got married to a girl called Mel. What else do you want to know?' she said, yawning.

The man leaned back again. 'That's fine for now.' He smiled again. 'Dora, I'm going to ask you something. Take your time before you answer, there's no need to feel rushed. We have all the time in the world.' He was watching her face, seeming to want some kind of response, so she gave him a nod. She tried to focus on his face, but over his shoulder was the sky, the square of blue that was the sky.

'Dora, do you know why you're here?'

'I fell over. I couldn't do it any more.'

'"It"? Can you tell me what "it" is?'

'Well. Everything.'

'You came to a full stop?'

A full stop. A little black dot on a piece of paper. She'd come to something as small as that and couldn't go any further? 'Yes. I suppose so.'

'Do you remember what you were doing just before you fell over?'

'Police station… Taking a – a baby to the police station.'

'You remember that clearly?'

'Yes.' She yawned again.

'Just one or two more questions, Dora, and we'll finish for today. The staff'll be wanting to make up your bed.'

Bed. Oh bliss, to crawl back into bed.

'Do you remember why you took the baby to the police station, Dora?'

She shifted in her chair. It was impossible to get really comfortable in a chair, you had to be on a bed. 'It was the wrong one.'

He was still watching her. That sky, over his shoulder, how blue that sky was.

'Do you mean it wasn't your baby?'

Yes sir, that's my baby, no sir, don't mean maybe. Where did that come from? Some song or other?

'No, it wasn't mine.' She tried to stifle the next yawn, but it opened wide and seemed to swallow her up.

'I see,' he said. 'All right Dora, we'll leave it there for today,' he went on, getting up. 'We'll have another chat tomorrow if you're feeling up to it.'

As the man went out, the women came in with the clean

bedding. While they made up the bed, Dora kept her eyes on that blue, blue, sky through the window.

Not her baby. No, of course it wasn't. How could she ever have thought it was? Ah, that sky out there. She'd have to get them to leave the curtains open tonight. If she was very lucky, the stars might look at her as she slept.

'She's been a bit more awake today? That's good,' said Tom to the nurse on the other end of the phone line. 'Is it all right to look in again at the usual time?'

It was, it seemed. And her psychiatrist would be most probably reducing the dose of sedative from now on, if 'things carried on this way.' They still didn't think it would be a good idea for Mrs Ross to visit, though.

Up to now, Dora hadn't been awake enough to do more than stare blank faced at any visitors, including Tom himself. Larry would be ecstatic that she was coming out of her coma-like state of the past weeks; please let her remember how she'd been treating him when they visited later on. 'Complete depressive collapse,' the psychiatrist had said the second day or so. 'Possible acute psychotic episode triggered by stress,' a junior doctor had said a few days later. Words, words.

So, an awake Dora. Would she remember that he and Mel were married, that it was on his wedding day that everything had happened? Would that start her off again? Maybe he himself shouldn't be visiting. Oh Jesus, the focussing on Mel that he'd made himself do in these weeks, telling himself to stop all the 'but fors'! Marrying Mel was a necessary thing. Marrying Mel was more than that, he knew by now: it was a good thing. But Mel herself, when he told her about Dora, had amazed even him, who thought he knew what she was made of. 'Oh, poor Dora,' she'd said. 'Why didn't you tell me about her baby? Oh, I know – because you didn't want to upset me.' A kiss for him, another word of sympathy for Dora. A lot of girls – women – in the middle of a pregnancy wouldn't want to see Dora again, whatever the doctors were saying. But not Mel. Still, she didn't know about the room. And he wasn't going to tell her.

He'd have to tell her Dora was going to be charged with abducting the baby, though. According to Syd, the Crown Prosecution Service couldn't let her off, if only because other women in similar circumstances hadn't been. So Dora would have to go to court. She'd be stared at by a roomful of people: curious, contemptuous, hostile. The press would be interested. Not often you get a baby-snatching case in Oxford.

He seemed to have clenched his fists. In preparation for applying them to press people's jaws? He couldn't do much for Dora as things now stood, but he could damn well do that. He shook his head. Time to go, otherwise he'd be late picking up Mel from the bus station, then he'd be late getting to Dora's house to collect some more clothes and things for her, and then he'd be late getting to Larry's to pick him up. He had to leave enough time to drop Mel off at Tommy's before he went to Dora's. He wasn't having her go anywhere near that house.

It would have to be this evening that Mel's bus was twenty minutes late. Tom would never get Mel to Tommy's without wrecking the evening's schedule.

'OK, I'll go with you to pick up this stuff for Dora,' said Mel.

'All right,' said Tom. It would have looked silly to object. 'Steve said he'll have the things ready, so I won't be two seconds. You can wait in the car.'

'Oh, is he going to be there? Can't I come in and say hi?'

'It's not a social call, Mel.'

'Yes it is, sort of. I mean, just because he's got this new girlfriend and Dora's got Larry doesn't mean we can't be nice to the guy, does it?'

There was nothing he could say to that except, 'OK, fair enough.'

As they began driving north, Mel said, 'You know, I think the doctors are nuts. Dora isn't going to hurt me or Faith, she's just not the type.'

'They haven't said she necessarily would, Melly. They want to take things very slowly, that's all. If there's even the slightest chance that seeing you might upset her…well, it's a situation they want to avoid, in everybody's interests.'

'Mm,' she said. 'OK, Mr Ross.'

'Sorry, was I sounding like a teacher again?'

'Oh, I like you sounding like a teacher,' she said, grinning. She leaned across and kissed him on the cheek. Since the wedding, she seemed to have lost any small amount of remaining constraint with him – telling him the truth about the baby was proof of that. How long ago it seemed now, that day they went to the Register office, that day when so much changed.

His baby. He'd always known, but still, having her actually admit it… It was as if some balance within him had been changed, a balance he hadn't known was there. The fact that it was his made a difference to things. He had the feeling that he had yet to learn, fully learn, exactly what that difference was.

Steve Mitchell looked pale and tired, but even so he looked exactly the way Tom had pictured him: straightforward, solid. Was that why Dora had married him? 'Are you sure it's no trouble?' he said. The sound of a vacuum cleaner, which was coming from one of the rooms off the hallway, stopped. A tall blonde woman emerged, peeling off rubber gloves. Tom's impression was of bright, breezy cheerfulness. It wasn't lost on him that this woman looked nothing like Dora.

'Hi, I'm Vicky. We're doing a bit of spring cleaning,' she said.

Yes, the house felt different. But was the room still as it had been?

'Oh, when's it due?' Vicky went on, turning to Mel. 'Can I have a feel?'

Mel grinned. 'Middle of September,' she said. 'Yeah, go on, the baby likes it.'

As Vicky moved in on Mel, Tom noticed Steve's eyes widen a little. Thinking about lots of tall blond children? *So that he can buy them all dogs…*

In Steve's shoes he might be wondering if a re-awakened Dora might be such a new Dora that the marriage-wrecking project was now off. Who was Tom Ross to judge where another man's tipping point might be, though? If Vicky would be up for some nice uncomplicated baby-making, well…

'We're taking up your spring cleaning time,' he said. 'Are those the things?' There were three full plastic tote bags sitting in the hall.

'They are,' said Steve. 'Tell her I give in, that bag hoard of hers does have its uses.' He attempted a smile. 'I'll be up myself in a day or so, you can tell her that too.'

Vicky's smile didn't falter. Maybe she knew how to play the long game.

As they drove away, Mel suggested coming to the hospital to save time: she could easily sit outside in the car and get on with some revision. But Tom insisted on taking her to Tommy's before he picked up Larry. He wasn't leaving her alone, even in a car, outside the sort of hospital Dora was in. You never knew who might be about.

Dora greeted Tom and Larry with a smile. It was a tired smile, but it was a smile. 'Well,' she said, 'you two again. Good. I don't think I've said congratulations, have I, Tom. So, congratulations. Hey, Larry, have you finished the *Principe* yet?'

Larry was overjoyed enough to launch straight in to a

342

detailed account of gunports and so forth. He didn't seem to notice when she drifted off into sleep.

So, Dora remembered. She remembered she was being 'nice' to Larry, and she remembered Tom was married. She didn't seem unduly disturbed by that fact. He could almost say she'd taken it in her stride. Try as he would, he couldn't organise his feelings about that; there didn't seem to be a category he could put them into.

After Dora was fast asleep, he noticed strands of grey hair here and there among the black on her pillow and had to turn away for a moment to hide his tears.

Twenty-Seven

By the fourth day of getting dressed, sitting in chairs, walking from bed to bathroom – on her own – Dora was making decisions. Lasagne for lunch, not fish pie. Radio 4 in the bedside earphones, not Radio 2.

Radio. She never listened to the radio. But she did now. One afternoon there was a programme devoted to the history of the Isle of Wight. It was enthralling.

In the evenings, people came. They'd been coming all the time she'd been here, she'd seen them by the bed, but now she had the energy to have a proper conversation with them. She could tell them what she'd been listening to on the radio and what she'd had for supper. Her brother made jokes about Gardeners' Question Time. The big man with the untidy hair didn't make jokes, but he leaned close when she told him things, as if he'd never heard anything so interesting in his life, his eyes fixed on her. So blue, those eyes. So much blue in the world, and this man's eyes the bluest of anything. He was the one she was helping. Or was it him who was helping her? She should think about that some time.

The one with the face like an angel paid attention too – the

344

one who was married now. Should she mind that he was married? She had a feeling she might have, a long time ago. Somehow, she couldn't be bothered to mind now. Just couldn't be bothered. There was something different about the way that one listened, though. As if he were thinking and listening at the same time. Fancy people having the energy to do that. She might ask him what he was thinking about. If she could be bothered. Should she be bothered? One day, maybe.

Angel-face was good about curtains, she had to hand him that. When she said she wanted the curtains left open to that she could see the stars, he always pulled them back as far as they would go.

The man who used to call her Pet came once, too, with a huge bunch of flowers. He didn't stay long, which was just as well. She was a bit tired and couldn't do much more than smile at the flowers, which were cellophane-wrapped and had a big bow of ribbon tied around them. He'd seemed a bit awkward. Didn't he like hospital visiting? She ought to know, she'd been married to him.

Had been. Yes, he was with somebody else now. Yvonne, wasn't it? She'd have to get around to thinking about that, too.

There was one person who never seemed to come: the little girl with the baby inside her. She'd have to wonder why, some time when she had a bit more energy.

So much to think about. When she could get around to it.

Day by day, the doctor – Dr Finch – asked her more and more questions, but she yawned less and less while he was speaking.

'What were you thinking of while you walked towards the public lavatory, Dora?'

'That I needed a pee.'

'That was all? You hadn't been thinking about the painting job in Jo's room? Take your time, now.'

'I don't know. I suppose I must have been. In some

345

background way, not in detail. I mean, it was too big to think about… I'm not putting this very well, I'm afraid.'

He nodded, though. Her answer seemed to do. She looked down at her hands. Any blue marks on them? No. It had all come off.

These hands. Had they really done that, thrown paint at that wall?

That: then. This: now. How did they connect up? Did they connect up? Should they?

Too many questions. Any more, and she'd be yawning again.

But there came a day when she put some questions to the doctor:

'What's the date today?'

The answer made her sit up. It was the middle of May. She'd been here something like six weeks. 'I committed a crime. So when are things going to start happening? The legal things?'

He didn't answer straight away. He uncrossed and re-crossed his legs. Then he said, 'It's up to me to say when you're well enough.'

She took a deep breath. 'Am I?'

He leaned forward. 'I think you will be soon. But Dora, don't start worrying. The law isn't cruel to women like you.'

Women like her? What were women like her like? 'I'm going to plead guilty.'

'Don't decide anything until you've had legal advice.'

'I *have* to plead guilty. You do understand that?' After all she'd said to him, he had to understand. He was being paid a consultant psychiatrist's salary, for God's sake.

He bowed his head for a few moments. Then he looked up. 'Larry Wise mentioned last week that his family solicitor's firm is judged to be very competent on the criminal as well as the civil side.'

346

Judged to be very competent. She'd bet those were Larry's exact words.

So they'd already been getting on with things behind her back.

Whether it was the thought of things being got on with, or what, that evening she found herself with a surprising amount of energy. As Tom and Larry came in, she began to sing: 'Twinkle twinkle little star, how I wonder what you are.'

They looked at her.

'I need to give Jo's mobile a twirl, and I want you to be there. Take me there. Please.'

They carried on looking at her. Then they looked at one another.

'Please?' It was all she could say. If they wanted her to say why she wanted to do this, they'd have to wait until she herself knew why, which could be all night.

Tom reached for the buzzer. 'Let's see if Dr Finch is still in the building.'

'He will be. It's Friday,' she said.

He was, and he was willing to aid and abet the breaking of bail for an hour. But he wanted to go too, and he wanted her to travel in his car. As it happened, that evening Tom and Larry had come by bus so that Tommy could have the car to go to the supermarket, and so they all went in Fred Finch's car.

The inside of Dr Fred's car had a fragrant smell: orange peel mixed with chocolate wrappers. There were two child seats in the back, the larger one grey, the smaller one dark blue. Dr Fred took them out and put them in the boot so that Tom and Larry could get in. Dora's senses seemed alive, suddenly – more alive than alive. Was this what came of not being out in the world for six weeks?

'How's Mel, Tom?' she said. 'Up to here with revision, I suppose. Everything OK with the baby?'

Maybe it was those alive senses of hers working overtime,

347

but she sensed some stiffening going on around her. Fred Finch gave her a quick sideways glance.

'The baby's fine, Dora,' said Tom. 'And yes, Mel's busy with revision, but it's going well.'

'Great. Bring her in some time, I'd like to see her.'

Silence.

'Hello, hello? Anybody there?' she said. Then the penny not so much as dropped as fell with a mighty clang: 'Oh. Wait a minute. She doesn't want to see me.'

Oh, God. To Mel she was now some sort of she-devil. Still, could she blame the girl?

'Melanie does want to see you, Dora, she does, she does,' Larry burst out.

'Dora, I hadn't thought it was a good idea,' said Fred Finch at last.

'Why, for Christ's sake? Oh, hang on, I get it. You thought I'd throw a wobbly, make an exhibition of myself, right? Look, I want to see Mel, OK?'

'All right, Dora,' he said. 'You can see Melanie.'

She caught Tom's face in the mirror. He was thinking again. She'd never known a man so good at thinking. She'd have to ask him what he thought about, she really would.

As it turned out, Dora saw Mel a bit sooner than any of them bargained for. When they arrived at her house, sitting outside the gate was Tommy's orange Volkswagen, and there on the front lawn was Syd, pushing the lawnmower. The front door opened, and out came Tommy with a mug in her hand. 'Ah, I seem to have visitors,' said Dora.

'Do you want to leave it for today?' said Fred Finch.

She thought for perhaps half a second. 'No, I don't,' she said. 'Come on.'

'Dozz!' said Syd, when he realised who'd arrived. It turned out that he was taking a bit of garden-maintenance load off

Steve, and Tommy had just arrived with some lawn fertiliser he'd asked her to pick up at Sainsbury's. They were both bright, cheerful, with hugs all round, but they didn't seem to be asking what she was here for. They were darting a lot of looks at Fred Finch and the others, though.

'Er, Mel's inside,' said Tommy, looking meaningfully at Fred Finch. 'She came with me to Sainsbury's. She was just popping into the loo as I came out with Syd's coffee. We'll be off in a minute, we've got a boot-full to unload and I don't want the frozen stuff defrosting.' She was smiling, but judging from her pink cheeks and the way she couldn't take her eyes off Dr Fred she was embarrassed, God, was she embarrassed.

Mel was *here*. Dora had to go in this minute and say hello. 'It's all right, Tommy,' she said, 'I've got clearance to say hi to Mel.' Without waiting for anybody to say anything further, she marched into the house, calling 'Mel, it's Dora.' She'd hardly got the words out when out of the kitchen shot a small dark-haired girl.

'Dora!' Mel shrieked. Dora got such a hug that for a moment she could hardly breathe, but eventually she was able to stand back and have a proper look at this person she hadn't been allowed to see, in case she flipped and ran shrieking through the hospital like some inmate of Bedlam.

'Mel, you look great!' And she did. The skin, the hair: who needed cosmetics when they were in this condition? Not that anybody who didn't know what the situation was would readily suspect there was any living being under Mel's clothes apart from Mel herself. That floaty summery tunic she had on over her jeans would have something to do with it. 'Let me guess: twenty weeks?'

'Twenty-one. I had another scan last week. Everything's OK, and it is a girl.'

'Of course it is, Mel. Is she lively?'

'You bet – hey, there she goes again.'

'How extraordinary,' said Larry. He was gazing at Mel with a face full of wonder. Tom was watching them, her and Mel. What a man. He could watch and think as well as listen and think.

The room. How was she going to manage it with Mel here, and Tommy?

'Are they discharging you, Dora?' Mel was saying.

'No, Melanie, Dora isn't quite ready to leave us yet,' said Fred Finch. 'She's come to look at her house, that's all.'

'Oh, right. Well, great. And you've brought everybody with you, fantastic.' She smiled around at everyone, as if to say, 'and now I can join in too.'

Syd and Tommy were muttering together. Dora made out the words, 'home', and 'unpack'.

Right. Time to take charge. 'I'd love you to stay while I poke around, Mel,' she said, 'but the thing is, there's some stuff here you probably won't want to see.'

'That's right, Mel,' Tom said, 'I think it'd be best if you went back now with Tommy.'

Mel was looking mystified. 'Stuff?' she said. 'Sorry, what sort of stuff?'

Nothing for it now: 'Baby stuff,' said Dora.

For a moment, Mel looked more mystified still. Then her face slowly cleared. 'Oh, you've got some things of your baby's you want to look at? I think that's lovely. It won't bother me, honestly.'

'Melly, it's not just some things, it's the baby's entire room that Dora wants to look at,' said Tom. 'I didn't want you to know this' – he shot a look at Dora – 'but not only is the baby's room exactly as it was three years ago, her ashes are up there…'

Three years eight months and six days, Tom. And not exactly as it was, there'll be that nasty paint splash, that's new. But we won't split hairs.

Dora heard Tommy gasp, and there were more mutterings

between her and Syd. But Tommy was old enough to handle it. Mel was the issue here.

'That's right, Mel,' she said. 'Jo's ashes are in a tin with stars all over it.' There was a faint mew. Had a cat got in here? Ah, no. It was Larry.

Mel's expression hadn't changed. 'Jo,' she said. 'Jo... Nice name. Short for anything?'

'Josephine,' said Dora. 'Don't laugh.' But Mel wasn't laughing, nor did she look as if she was going to. 'God knows what made me agree to that. Steve's favourite granny's name, you see. I must have had a weak moment. Anyway, Jo was only ever going to be called Jo.'

Mel nodded. Then she said, 'You know what? I'd like to see Jo's room.'

'Mel –' began Tom.

'It's all right,' she said to him, 'really.' Her voice was gentle, encouraging, as if she were talking to a two-year-old.

'Are you sure?' said Dora. But she was only saying it for form's sake. This girl was sure, she had a steady, sure look in her eye.

'Yeah. If it's all right with you.'

'Come on up, then,' said Dora, making for the stairs. 'And the rest of you, form an orderly queue, please.'

When Dora opened the door of the room, there it all was: the spaceman rug, the green and grinning Thing From Outer Space, the panda, toppled onto its side, the man-from-Mars clock. No, there it all was minus one thing. 'Just a minute.' She retreated past the others, went into the bedroom, and picked up the tin from the bedside table. The swirly galaxy of stars seemed to sing, *Hi Mum, it's been a while, great to see you.*

Hello, Jo. And it's great to see you.

When she returned to the room, they were still huddled outside, waiting for her to go in first. 'Jo, everybody. Everybody, Jo,' she said, holding up the tin. Introductions had to be made properly.

She took a step into the room, and another step. That wall. What a *pity*. She traced a finger over the blue abstract shapes which her hands had taken it upon themselves to daub upon the wall that day which felt so long ago. The rug still had a splodge of blue paint on it, but not a large one. It could be cleaned off, with a bit of care. She opened the cupboard. There in neat piles were all the jumpsuits, all except the orange one. In the circumstances you'd think some fairy might have magicked it back here, but still, weren't most fairies shysters? She ran a finger around the edge of the nappy changing table. Hm, dust. Still, that wouldn't exactly be hard to remove.

Now to do what she'd come here for. She pushed the button, and the sun and the moon and the stars and the planets began to dance to the tinkly, twinkly music.

'So Steve hasn't done anything in here,' she said.

'I asked him not to,' said Fred Finch.

'Did you? Well, thanks. Who says you can't get decent treatment on the NHS.' For that matter, was the NHS paying for what she was getting, or was it somewhere like the Home Office? Hm. A detail she might not bother checking.

The star and planets came to a stop.

'Can I have a go?' said Mel.

Oh, Mel, thank you! 'Of course you can,' said Dora, striving to keep her voice level. She watched as Mel set the mobile going again. She wouldn't have dared pray for this, and now it had happened, just like that. She didn't look at Tom. If he was thinking, this was one time she was going to ignore him.

'Cute,' said Mel, smiling, as the stars and planets danced in their courses.

'Yes, isn't it.' And then out it came, what she hadn't known until this moment that she wanted to say: 'Look, I haven't given you a wedding present yet, so all this stuff, it's hardly used, take as much of it as you want. Take it all, I won't be needing it any more. There's more in the loft – pushchair, travel cot, toys, books, you name it. One thing, though – get a new cot mattress. It's never a good idea to use second-hand mattresses. And when you put Faith down for a nap, put her on her back. "Back-to-sleep." Got that? Sorry to sound like Old Mother Know-All.'

No-one spoke. Mel was looking at her, eyes wide. Had she gone too far, was Mel going to be superstitious? Oh well. Hardly surprising, was it?

'We'll have the lot,' said Mel, sounding choked. 'But what I really want most of all is this.' She pointed to the mobile.

'I hoped you'd say that. Have another go if you like.'

Mel pushed the button, and off they went again, the stars and planets, the sun and the moon. Soon they'd be dancing and singing for Faith.

'Right, that's it, folks,' said Dora, when the music stopped. 'I think I'll be off back to the hospital now.' The energy was evaporating, there was tiredness waiting to engulf her. 'Just one thing, though. I'd like to phone Steve.' Would he be at the flat?

He was. She was in luck tonight.

'Hi, I'm at the house,' she said to him.

'At the *house?* Are you on your own?'

'No, the whole world's here, including Dr Fred.'

'Fred…? Oh yes, Dr Finch.'

'The reason I'm phoning, Steve, is to tell you to feel free to decorate – I'll leave the colour scheme to you – and get on with selling the house. I hope somebody apologised to that estate agent, by the way. They'll have turned up on the Friday and wondered where the hell I was.'

Silence. Was Yvonne – no, no, it was Vicky, *Vicky* – with him? Hard to tell. Please be there, Vicky.

'Look, I'm sorry I said what I said,' he said at last. 'What kind of a man says things like that, for Christ's sake.'

What was he talking about? Oh, that. 'It's OK, Steve. Don't worry about it.'

'Well, still…'

Keep talking, Clayton. She explained about the baby equipment, and there was another moment or so of silence. 'OK then,' he said at last, 'when Tom and Melanie have had a chance to move the stuff out, I'll get on with things.'

'Good… Bye, then.'

'Bye, Dora.'

She looked at the phone for a moment, then put it back in the rest. Then she let out a long breath. Just for a moment there… But no, it was too late, too late. If she'd achieved anything recently, she'd achieved him and Vicky. Be there, Vicky. Be with him.

The others were discussing the logistics of moving the baby things. 'We'd better take it down to Uxbridge for now,' said Tom. 'Two trips might do it, more likely three.' He sounded odd, as if he were fighting a cold.

'Might I make a suggestion?' said Larry. 'I would be delighted if you were to store the equipment at my house. There is plenty of space, as you know, and it would be so much more convenient than transporting the things to Uxbridge, only to have to move them again in due course. You could bring it during the weekend.'

'Oh Larry, that would be great!' said Mel, kissing his cheek.

Which settled it, of course. Trust Larry, ace fixer. *Trust Larry…*

Outside in the street, Dora gave her house keys to Tom. He'd need them for the baby-gear moving operation. The tiredness was wrapping itself around her. Unless she sat down right now, she'd be falling asleep on this pavement. 'Use my car,' she said to Tom as she got into Dr Finch's. 'It works, Steve's been taking it around the block from time to time. The keys are on the peg in the kitchen. In fact hang on to it, I can't think why I haven't let you drive it before now.' She shut the car door before he could say anything.

Back in the hospital, she stood the star-covered tin on her bedside table. 'Well, thanks for the lift,' she said to Fred Finch, but looking at the tin. 'You'll be wanting to see what's cropped up while we've been out.'

'How do you feel?' he said, turning one of his gazes on her, the looks she'd been getting to know quite well in the past weeks.

'Fine,' she said, sitting on the bed, still looking at the tin. 'A tiny bit knackered, though,' she went on, yawning.

He carried on looking at her. 'Sleep well, Dora,' he said at last. He rested a hand on her shoulder for a moment before going out.

She didn't take her eyes from the tin. The 'JO' of silver stars twinkled in the light of the lamp over the bed.

JO. Poor Jo. Poor Jo. That was why she had to go home tonight, she couldn't leave Jo on her own any longer.

When the tears began, she didn't reach for a Kleenex, she just let them fall, like rain. When the shower was over, she lay back on the bed. She felt more washed than she'd ever been in her life. But for this overwhelming tiredness, she felt as if she could see forever.

There was some sort of obstruction in the middle of the view, though. It was Tom. She couldn't see around, past or through him.

Twenty-Eight

A s Tom carried box after box of baby things up Larry's
stairs to the big airy room at the top of the house, there
was one thing he was sure of. It wasn't any easier having Mel
and Dora in the same field of view post marriage, it was
harder. A new Dora, moreover, a Dora he ached to explore, to
see how much was really new and how much had been there
all the time and just needed a stimulus to come to the surface.
Was that why it was harder? That he was never alone with her
and it didn't look as if he ever would be again: was that, too,
why it was harder?

These baby items that had been Dora's, and were now his
and Mel's, they were lovely, and almost in shop condition,
you'd hardly know they'd been used at all. But the things
would mean he'd have Dora in his mind every time he picked
up his own baby. Wouldn't he rather have started from
scratch? Mel hadn't left him any opportunity to talk this over
first, but who would have expected him to have qualms, if the
young mother herself didn't? Yes, qualms: but the sort of
qualms he could never reveal. If he'd had the chance, though,
he could always have said he was having the more predictable

356

sort of qualm, the dead babies sort… Oh hell, the equipment was here now, he'd have to get used to it.

So. Cot base next, he supposed.

'Oh great, let's set it up,' said Mel, who was kneeling on the floor looking through the clothes when Tom lugged the cot base into the room.

'Is it worth it? We'll only have to take it down again when we move.'

'I want to put the mobile up. I think Faith likes it.'

So Tom assembled the cot. He fixed the mobile at one end, and Mel immediately set it going.

Twinkle twinkle little star…

Tom looked at each star and planet as it made its revolutions. For over three years, this mobile had been played with daily by a distraught woman. She'd breathed over it, saturating it with grief and guilt. But now, at this moment, if Mel were right, his baby was listening to it, enjoying it. *It was a toy, that was all. Just a toy.*

He hadn't wanted children. But now, everything was changed.

The mobile ran down. Mel pressed the button again and off went the stars and planets. Round and round they went, and round and round went his gaze after them. It struck him that what they were doing, very effectively, was leading him in circles.

He and Mel would be away from here soon enough. His field of view would be Mel-sized, only. But what was going to become of Dora? Her doctor had said the law would be lenient, but what about afterwards, would the years ahead be kind to her? He had a vision of a small figure standing at the entrance to a tunnel, huge and dark, and he shivered before he could stop himself.

'Cold?' said Mel.

'No – a bit, maybe. I thought I felt a draught.'

357

'Really? It's fine in here. Maybe you're getting something.'

'Touch of hay fever, that's all.' He blew his nose to add the appearance of truth.

By the morning Larry's solicitor came to see Dora, she'd had Tom in her mind quite a bit. He wasn't doing much, he was just hovering there. Maybe if she asked him what he was thinking about he'd stop hovering. Where would he go, though, where would he go? Still, for now, she had the law to think about. As soon as Dr Finch said she was fit enough, the law had started sending her pieces of paper: *You are summoned to appear... That you did without lawful authority or reasonable excuse remove Ryan Booth...* In two weeks she'd be up before the magistrates. When she tried to get her brain around that fact, all it would do was tell her to look out of the window, there was grass growing out there and she shouldn't miss it.

Monty Shuttleworth, the solicitor – the kind of man you'd pass in the street without a second look, but he seemed amiable enough – brought a hot-shot London barrister with him: Kate Ojo, six foot tall in a Chanel suit but with a friendly smile a mile wide.

Kate made no bones about Dora pleading guilty. 'There are all sorts of reasons why I think that's a great idea,' she said, 'but the clincher is this: the chief witness has done a runner.'

Apparently Rachel Booth had disappeared, vamoosed, scrammed. Two weeks ago, a neighbour saw her going into her mother's house with the baby about an hour before the mother got back from work, but the neighbour didn't think much of it. Not enough to notice when Rachel came out again empty-handed, anyway. When Mrs Booth got home there was the kid yelling the house down, and no Rachel.

'The fact that Ms Booth was on bail for drugs-related offences might possibly have something to do with it,' murmured Monty Shuttleworth. 'She vanished three days before she was due to appear in court. I should say also that the authorities have been asking questions about her care of the child. She – ahem – did leave the baby unattended in a public place, after all.'

'Oh.' Before Dora could fumble a Kleenex out of the box, tears were rising and spilling over. 'Poor baby, he'll have been hungry by the time his grandma got home. I hope there was a bottle made up. I really hope there was.'

'I hope so too,' said Kate. She took a glance at Jo's tin – not the first quick sideways slide of the gaze since she'd arrived. 'Tell you what, Dora, if the police ever catch up with Rachel Booth, it's not beyond the bounds of possibility that you could end up as a witness in a child neglect case.'

Oh? Well, anyway. Unlike Rachel Booth, she herself would not disappear, vanish, vamoose, scram, or even bugger off. She would keep her date with the justices.

Monty was leafing through a pile of papers. Was all that stuff really to do with her? It was only a very small baby she'd taken, for a very short length of time.

'I think we ought to get her sent to the Crown Court straight away,' Kate was saying to him. 'Arguably it's an either-way case but I don't reckon we ought to trouble the magistrates a minute longer than we have to. We get a PCMH asap, put in a guilty plea, then ask for an adjournment for reports, right?'

'And you will ask the Judge for an indication,' said Monty.

'You bet,' said Kate.

'Um… Excuse me?' said Dora.

Kate smiled. 'Sorry, Dora. What we were saying boils down to this: three hearings and only three, if we're lucky. Appearing in front of the magistrates'll be a formality, just to get the ball rolling. A couple of weeks later you'll go to the Crown Court and plead guilty – that's the Plea and Case Management Hearing – and at some point, when the judge has looked at the medical reports on you, you'll go back there for the sentence.'

'But you won't have to wait until the final hearing to know what the sentence is likely to be,' said Monty, 'Kate will have found out from the judge before you plead.'

'Oh. Just one thing – will the judge be wearing a wig?'

'It'll be the works, I'm afraid,' said Kate, 'but remember this. Under the fancy rig he's just a bloke. He goes to the toilet like anybody else.'

Dora evidently hadn't made herself clear to Kate. Wigs and rigs were all right. Admitting guilt to a man in a suit wouldn't have done. She had to stand up in front of someone dressed in the full regalia. The Works.

'Right, the priority now,' Kate went on, 'is to get the best possible reports on you.'

And that, it seemed, came down to not much more than Dora having to be seen to be just a *little* bit crazy. Not too much, in case the judge thought she'd need banging up in Broadmoor to keep the country's infants safe from her clutches, but not too little, in case he decided she'd been of perfectly sound mind when she snatched baby Ryan. The craziness had to be with her still, so that Dr Finch could say she'd need to carry on seeing him – but it had to be curable, given time.

'There's something to be said for getting her out of here sooner rather than later,' said Kate, looking thoughtful.

What? Out of here? But this was where she belonged, where she felt safe.

'Laurence Wise would help, I'm sure,' said Monty.

Oh? Oh? Did they mean move to *Larry's?*

'...and of course there is the fact of young Melanie Ross,' Monty went on. 'If it were to be seen that Dora is no threat...'

'Brilliant!' said Kate, snapping her fingers.

The lawyers knew more about Dora than she'd realised. They knew how a five-months-pregnant girl who often came to Oxford fitted into Dora's social equation. They'd evidently been talking to Larry.

So. Sorted. Apart from the little matter of getting the magistrates to agree to change the bail conditions, but Kate said there was no need to worry about that.

Dora felt suddenly breathless, as if she'd been pottering along what she thought was a country road in second gear, only to find herself on the slip road to a motorway.

She hadn't even begun to get her breath back after the lawyers had gone, before Larry turned up. It was on the tip of her tongue to mention what Monty Shuttleworth had said about her coming to stay with him, but after the excitement she'd just had, somehow the sight of those eyes lighting up would be too much. Those eyes would always be that bit too much. Best to look to one side, the way he did. Still, she seemed to be getting used to doing that. Which was funny, seeing how she'd always been hopeless at getting used to things. Was Larry so good at fixing things that he was even beginning to fix a tiny little part of her? Not the lot, no way. But something to be going on with, maybe.

'I'm steaming through the book, Larry,' she said. 'I've just finished chapter two.' She tried to stifle a yawn, and then the yawn broke through anyway. These yawns, they could still catch her out.

'Oh, I am so pleased to hear it, so pleased.'

'You know, I think I'll just slide under the covers for a while. I'm not supposed to while I'm dressed but I'll risk it.'

When she was under the blankets he tucked her in, like tucking up a baby. Another yawn escaped her, and it was mighty. The next one would devour her whole.

'Would you like to sleep now, Dora?' Larry leaned over her with one of his particularly solicitous looks.

'In a minute… Read to me for a bit.'

As he found the place in the book he'd loaned her, she

watched the sun's rays bounce off the stars on Jo's tin.

A clearing of throat. 'Chapter three,' he began, 'in which Pooh and Piglet go hunting and nearly catch a Woozle. The Piglet lived in a very grand house in the middle of a beech tree…'

A beech tree. Funny place for a piglet to live. Still, as long as he was happy.

Jo was listening too. It was the way her stars were twinkling in the sunlight. A mother could always tell these things.

Larry read on, a pleasant bit of rigmarole about Piglet's grandfather. After this, she'd tackle *The House at Pooh Corner*, and then all the other books Larry had said he still had from when he was a boy.

'… he happened to look up,' read Larry, 'and there was Winnie-the-Pooh. Pooh was walking round and round in a circle…'

The words began to float over and around her. They floated up, up, up, through the branches of Piglet's beech tree, and swirled round and round until they came to rest on the ceiling. She watched them bobbing gently up there like blue balloons.

Then one went pop.

How crazy was she? She didn't feel crazy. She felt less crazy than she'd ever felt in her life. Suppose she wasn't crazy enough for the judge, suppose she had to go to prison. Jo couldn't go too, she wouldn't be safe. Prisons were hell, and womens' prisons were hell squared. But who would look after her?

'…Oh, Pooh!' read Larry. 'Do you think it's a – a – a Woozle?'

She was being stupid. Larry would look after Jo. He could bring her in on visits.

Wait a minute. What if this new feeling of hers *was* craziness, a craziness so unfixeably crazy that it had flipped over into looking normal, but wasn't? Who could tell her? Not

Dr Fred. If she was fooling herself she could be fooling him, too. Could Tom tell her? Surely if anyone could, he could, who was so good at thinking. What if she asked him and he wouldn't tell her, though? Or what if he ran away?

Tom arrived back at Tommy's later than normal after a parents' evening to find Mel sitting in the kitchen, not only with Tommy but with Larry. Mel and Tommy were grinning all over their faces. Larry was beaming.

'Guess what,' said Mel, jumping up and putting her arms around Tom, 'Larry's said why don't we move in with him until I go to uni.'

'You'll have far more space there than here,' Tommy chipped in. 'No way am I chucking you out, but it makes a massive amount of sense. After all, Mel's going to be in Oxford as much as she can, A-levels and maternity hospital visits permitting.' Tommy smiled at Larry, whose beam now stretched from ear to ear.

'Are you sure, Larry? We wouldn't want to put you out,' said Tom, knowing what the answer would be, because it was evident that Mel, Tommy and Larry had already done the deal.

It turned out that not only had they done the deal, Larry wouldn't hear of taking any rent. They were going to move in the next day; Mel and Larry had it all worked out. They would have Larry's big guest room, the one Mel and Dora had slept in the night of Mrs Wise's death. Yes, it made sense, all right. It was good for him and Mel, and they'd be company for Larry. So why this feeling of stirring unease?

It wasn't many days later that Tom found out why. Dora was granted bail by the Magistrates Court. On condition that she, too, came to live at Larry's. *Jesus.*

Larry rushed straight out and bought the ingredients for a celebratory supper for all of them, Tommy and Syd included, and so that evening Tom found himself with the prospect of sitting at the same table as Dora in the North Oxford mansion.

The first thing Dora said when they went into the dining room was, 'Where's Trafalgar, Larry?'

'I have re-assembled it upstairs,' said Larry as he pulled out her chair for her. 'It's well enough where it is.' This was a different man from that sad shuffler Tom and Dora had intercepted in the street the day his mother fell ill. It wasn't hard to see who'd brought about the change. Because she'd helped him? No, it wasn't that, or not only that. It was because he was helping her.

'Welcome home, Dora,' said Tom as he sat down opposite her. Odd words. Not what he'd intended to say. But what was it he had intended to say?

Dora didn't seem to think what he'd said was odd, or at any rate, her slightly dazed smile didn't falter. How thin she looked. Her eyes were bigger than ever. She lifted her glass of wine, eyed it for a second or so, and took a tiny sip. 'So that's what it used to taste like,' she said.

Home. A place where you take out bin bags and do the washing up and go to Sainsbury's... He was doing all that here. Now, he'd be doing it under the same roof as her. He reached for his glass and took a mouthful of his own wine. But at least he wasn't cutting the grass. Larry was the one who cut the grass.

The cat was surveying them all from the doorway. He walked in, strolled the length of the room assessing each of them in turn, stopped next to Dora, and jumped up onto her lap.

'Hi, Prinz Eugen,' she said, stroking him. 'Larry, is this allowed? Cats in the dining room when we're about to eat?' Her eyes were sparkling. Because there were tears in them. The cat had accepted her again, just like that.

Larry's answer was yes. Tonight at any rate, the cat could stay as long as he wanted.

'Well, do you know what? I'm ravenous,' she said. 'I hope you've roasted a horse out there, Larry, because I could eat one, hooves and all.'

'There is no horse, I'm afraid, Dora,' said Larry, 'merely a joint of beef. But there is chocolate fudge cake to follow.'

'Chocolate! Syd, if I eat chocolate, it doesn't mean you're allowed any ciggies, OK?'

'Not even one?' said Syd.

'No!' cried Tommy.

'You heard the lady, Syd,' said Dora. 'Not even one.' She took another sip of wine. 'Well, guess what? You spend days building up to something and then you blink and it's over. Funny thing is, I've got no recollection whatsoever of what the court looked like. I can remember there were some people in suits, but that's about it.'

'That bit's over now, Dozz,' said Syd. 'You don't have to worry about it.'

'Mm… Just as well I had my name and address written down, though. I hope my brain doesn't fold up on me like that at the Crown Court.'

'Don't think about it,' said Tommy. 'It's ages away.'

Ages? A fortnight or so, they'd been told to expect. But it was time enough for Dora to get her name and address worked out, Tom supposed.

Hungry or not, Dora didn't make fast work of the beef when it appeared. God, how thin she was. Tom had a huge urge to get out of his chair and go round to her side of the table, to hold her fast and not let go. He found himself catching his breath. He covered the moment with a cough.

'Hey, there's that hay fever again,' said Mel, beside him. 'It's hereditary, isn't it? I hope Faith doesn't get it.'

'Hay fever?' said Tommy. 'Tom's never had hay fever.'

'It's nothing, Mel, just a tickle,' said Tom, applying himself to his beef. Dora was looking at him. He couldn't let himself meet her gaze.

Tom woke feeling certain that he'd heard something. It was still pitch dark. He lay there for a minute or so, rigid, ears straining for a sound, but there was only silence. He had heard something, though, he hadn't dreamed it. He eased himself out of bed, taking care not to disturb Mel, and opened the bedroom door a crack. There was nothing out there except a landing in darkness.

He slipped out of the bedroom, pulling the door closed behind him. He walked slowly along the landing, putting each foot down heel-first and rolling smoothly and steadily onto the toes. As he drew closer to the room at the end, the room where all the baby things were stored, he saw it: the thin frame of light around the door. The door was ajar, but it wasn't sufficiently open for him to be able to see around it. If he pushed it, just a fraction…

As his hand rose to make contact with the door, he heard the sound of tinkly music. *Twinkle Twinkle Little Star.*

Oh Jesus, he couldn't go in there. He swivelled on the balls of his feet and began to make his way back along the landing. Then he stopped. Unless he went in he might never find out. Find out what, though?

Oh hell. He retraced the few steps he'd taken. He pushed open the door, slipped into the room, and pulled the door to behind him.

Dora was standing by the head of the cot with her back to him. 'Hello Tom,' she said without looking around.

'Hello Dora,' he said, moving across the room to her. 'I heard you up. Are you OK?'

'Good question,' she said, not taking her eyes from the revolving mobile. 'I was hoping you might tell me the answer.'

'I? You thought I might know?' She couldn't have knocked him off-balance more effectively if she'd elbowed him in the solar plexus.

'I'll take that as a "no", then,' she said. 'Which is a pity… The thing is, I feel fine, so either I am fine, or I'm so not-fine that I'm meeting myself coming back, if you follow me. I'm in unknown territory, you might say.'

'Are you having second thoughts about handing over all these things? Because if you are—'

'No, no, absolutely not. I'm only in here having a… Giving you and Mel all this stuff, it's…' She shrugged. 'Sorry, not too good at words right now.'

She turned toward him. She must have seen his thoughts in his face, for she said, 'Are you fine, Tom?'

'Maybe we're about as fine as one another,' he said, trying to smile. 'Maybe we're about as fine as anyone can expect to be.'

'Oh. Can't we do better than that?' Her pinched, drawn face, those big eyes, looked up at him. He touched her hand, just for a second.

'I don't know, Dora. Capella only knows.'

'Capella again. Does it always come back to Capella?'

Did it? He was the one who'd brought Capella into this, though Capella only knew why. 'I'm in unknown territory too, Dora. With you, I always have been.'

Still those eyes looking at him, looking into him. Then she set the mobile going again. When it ran down, she gave a small, quiet sigh. 'Back to bed now, I think. What would Dr Fred say if he saw me up after *A Book at Bedtime*?'

Twenty-Nine

'OK, Your Honour Judge Barrington QC,' said Kate Ojo, reaching for the phone, 'be there.'

Dora stretched her legs out in front of her. She might as well sit back and look at the scenery: that bow tie of Monty Shuttleworth's, for instance. Green with yellow squiggles. What were they – butterflies, birds, bees? Hard to tell from this distance. They weren't wasps, anyway. She'd know a wasp from any distance.

Well. Quite an adventure today, catching a bus into town and coming to an office where serious people worked. But Larry was here with her, so that was all right.

The lawyers kept saying she had nothing to worry about. She did, though. After the other night, she had plenty. Tom was in unknown territory. Because of her.

'Oh hi Len, how's things?' said Kate.

Who was 'Len'? Was he Judge Barrington, Judge Barrington's clerk, the guy on the street door at the Court building, or the work-experience schoolboy who did the photocopying?

'I hope you've had all the papers by now?' Kate was saying. 'Oh, great. Right, I've got the draft bill here.'

'Bill of Indictment': it had a ring to it. It made you think of stern-faced men in big black hats without much of a sense of humour, the sort of chap Mel was swotting up for the A-level questions she was going to get on seventeenth century English history. 'Arraigned': that was another good word. Some day soon, she, Dora Clayton, was going to be arraigned. It sounded uncomfortable, as if thick ropes and iron spikes were going to be involved.

Did it really all come back to Capella? She wasn't sure either she or Tom were up to much astronomy at the moment.

'Of course, of course, definitely, no problem,' said Kate. Then: 'Uh-huh, uh-huh.'

Those squiggles on Monty's bow tie, *were* they wasps? If they were, Capella would be behind cloud for all nights to come. Could she lean a bit closer and check?

'Sure, that's understood,' said Kate. 'Right. Right. Bye. See you soon.' She put the phone down. 'Well,' she said, leaning on the desk, 'you haven't wasted your time coming in today, Dora. It's panning out the way I said. Barrington's no fool.'

'Excellent, excellent!' said Monty. 'There you are, Dora. Haven't we been saying repeatedly that a custodial sentence would be inconceivable in a case like this? Even a judge who was a fool could see that.'

'Oh Dora,' said Larry.

'Oh,' she said. 'Er, thanks, Kate, thanks, Monty.' She had to remember her manners, these people were busting a gut for her. She couldn't tell them that everything – everything important – could be down to a star they might never have seen. 'So what am I going to get, then, community service? Two hundred hours in a laundry which specialises in nappies? Five hundred hours of house-cleaning for knackered new parents?'

Kate and Monty laughed. Larry looked at her hard; he was weighing up these options. But if she lost a chance to crack a gag, where would she be? Especially now.

According to Kate, precisely what she was going to get would depend on these medical reports that kept cropping up in their conversations. It looked as if she was going to be seeing a fair expanse of white coat in the coming weeks and months, some of it on Court doctors.

'Isn't it great this Judge guy's come out and said he isn't going to send Dora to prison?' said Mel, rearranging the rumpled sheet around her. For a moment it looked to Tom as if she were going to disappear under it, leaving just a bump to betray her presence, a bump that had grown perceptibly during the night, unless his eyes were playing tricks.

'Yes, it is,' he said. He sat down on the bed and took her in his arms. 'Take it easy today, Mel, don't go out in this heat.'

'Under the trees in the garden's OK, isn't it?'

'Well…just about.'

'Actually, right now I think I might grab a bit more sleep.' She gave a wide yawn.

'Did the heat keep you awake?'

'It wasn't the heat, it was you. You were thrashing about all night.'

'Was I? Sorry, Mel. The heat gets to me. It comes of being a Scot.' He forced a smile.

As Tom let himself out of the house, the heat hit him like a hammer. Please, please let the temperature drop by ten degrees at least before Mel's exams started.

The North Oxford air seemed to suck energy from him as he walked along the quiet streets in the direction of school. He badly needed to get a grip. Keeping Mel awake was unforgiveable. It might help if he could stop this listening for sounds from the room next to theirs, the one he'd slept in the night Larry's mother died and which Dora was now occupying. It wasn't as if Dora had had any more small-hours excursions.

Night-time conversations. They stick with you longer than ones held in broad daylight, if that one the other night was anything to go by.

Capella only knows. Something to have engraved on his headstone, perhaps. Depending on how forthcoming Capella might be in the years he had left.

That day and the following ones were full to bursting. The exam season was getting underway, and the issues Tom had to deal with seemed to be the same at this school as at any other: candidates fell off bikes and broke their writing arms, and doctors had to be negotiated with for certificates; candidates had attacks of nerves, some of which needed hours of careful counselling. Meanwhile, the day of Mel's first exam, the German oral, was coming up fast. If only, if only, this weather would break.

Tom had given up the struggle to stop listening out for Dora at night, but at least he'd trained himself not to toss and turn. And there was an upside, of sorts. Dora was preparing him for months – years, maybe – of parenthood's broken nights.

The day before Mel's German oral, Tom got back to the house to find her lying on her side on the big sofa in the sitting room, Larry on his knees rubbing the small of her back, and Dora looking on with a supervisory air.

'Hey, what's up?' he said.

'It's all right,' said Dora, 'nothing to worry about, she hasn't got backache. We're just getting into practice for when she does.'

'*Das ist fantastisch,*' said Mel, '*richtig gut!*'

'Right, Larry, that's enough,' said Dora.

'*Der handballen,*' Larry was saying to himself, in time to the massaging, '*der handballen…*'

'They've been talking nothing but German all day,' said Dora. 'OK, Larry,' she went on, tapping Larry on the shoulder.

He looked up, blinking. 'You're doing a great job, but we can leave it for today.'

'Oh. Very well, Dora.'

'How was it today, frantic again?' said Mel as Tom helped her up into a sitting position. She could doubtless have sat up perfectly well on her own, but he had to do something, he had to involve himself if there was care of Mel in progress.

'Not too bad. They're getting into their stride now.'

'Good. Because we've had something in the post today, haven't we, Dora.'

'We certainly have,' said Dora. 'Come into the kitchen and we'll show you.'

'Thanks for – for what you're doing,' he murmured to Dora as they went through to the kitchen.

'My pleasure,' she replied quietly.

The something 'we' had had in the post was a summons requiring Dora to attend the Crown Court a week today for the Plea and Case Management Hearing. There it was again, the charge set out in terms that would make you think of transportation for life, but for the indication the lawyers had got from the Judge. 'Right, that's enough of that,' said Dora, taking it from him. 'Larry, can you file this behind the clock, please?' Her voice sounded bright and decisive. Out of sight, out of mind. Until this day week.

'Now let's show him the really interesting thing,' said Mel.

The 'really interesting' thing, which had arrived for Dora in the post that morning, was a moderate-sized cardboard box. She seemed hesitant about revealing what was in it. 'If they want any of you as character witnesses, don't breathe a word about this,' she said, hugging the box to her chest. 'The judge'll think I'm crazy beyond redemption.'

'Oh, no, no, Dora,' said Larry, frowning. 'Surely not?'

'Just joking, Larry,' she said, patting his hand. It struck Tom that she seemed to have settled down into an easy familiarity

372

with Larry that was quite unforced. Those touches of a hand, an arm, a shoulder weren't a pretence to keep Mel happy. What was more, there didn't seem to be any danger that Dora would back off and leave Larry stranded once he himself and Mel were away from here. Mel hadn't said any more about the lack of sex or even kissing in this relationship, but she might be putting it down to Dora's still being in a fragile state, as much as Larry's being 'old-fashioned'.. Anyway, it wasn't as if he and Mel went in for public displays of affection. Let him have a convincing response ready if the subject came up, though. Let there be no chink Mel would see through.

Mel took the box from Dora and opened it with a flourish under Tom's nose. In it was wool, ball upon ball of brightly-coloured knitting wool. What the…?

'I found it on the Internet last week,' said Dora. 'You wouldn't believe the number of websites there are entirely devoted to hand-knitting.'

He picked out a scarlet ball and squeezed it in his fingers, and then a ball the colour of new jeans.

'Very tactile, aren't they,' said Dora. 'And they smell nice too.' She picked out a ball the colour of pale gold and brought it up to her nose.

No, the wool wasn't gold, it was yellow. It was the colour of daffodils.

Scenes began to flash in front of Tom's mind's eye like a DVD on fast-forward. Before he could find the Stop button, he'd swung down into a gulley near a South Wales beach and stretched out his hand towards a daffodil. But the screen went dark before he could pick it.

'Dora's going to make Faith a coat,' said Mel, sounding excited.

'A wonderful coat of many colours,' added Larry, 'to keep her warm next winter.'

Well, well. 'So you knit, do you?' he said to Dora.

'I think I once made a string dishcloth at primary school,'

she said. 'Mel's convinced this coat's going to be the last word in chic, but I've been telling her not to get her hopes up too much. Still, either knitting's like riding a bike, in which case we're in business, or it isn't, and I'll have to teach myself.'

'You will master it,' said Larry. 'You will, you will.'

'It's going to be so cool!' said Mel, waving at Tom the knitting pattern which had come with the wool. 'I can't *wait* to take Faith out in it.'

'Hold your horses, Mel, she won't need it until at least next January, what with global warming,' said Dora. 'Which is just as well, given my likely rate of progress,' she went on, as she picked a ball the colour of green apples out of the box and sank her fingers into it.

He had to find something to say about this project. 'It's going to be very cool. I hope I can take Faith out in it too?' Knitting wool. Of all the utterly impossible things. Even for Dora.

'So what made you have the idea?' he said after supper as she painstakingly cast on the first row of stitches. She was beginning with an orange which looked as if it should smell of clementines at Christmas.

'I don't know,' she said, stroking the wool, her eyes unfocussed for a moment. Then she looked at him: a straight, direct stare. 'Maybe it was written in the stars.'

All he could do was finger the balls of wool.

Perhaps it was down to Capella. Dora couldn't think of any other reason why she should take it into her head to start knitting. Even so, she wouldn't in a million years have predicted it would turn into an addiction, but Faith's coat was with her from morning to night, including the bus rides to see Dr Finch. It wasn't easy, persuading Larry that she had to start going out alone again, and at first he insisted on seeing her to the bus stop. When she got back, there he was, hovering in the garden or by a window, looking out for her. A while ago, this much attention from him would have driven her nuts. Now, though, she really didn't mind. She might almost say she was glad of it. Just as she really didn't mind about Tom and Mel being married. In their case, though, she was definitely glad. Truly and definitely. Some constructive thoughts, by God. Where would it all end? No: as far as Tom was concerned, all she minded about was him being bothered about her. Such a pity. Such a waste of effort, when there were so many important things to think about, like what they were having for supper tonight.

Dr Finch wasn't too fazed about Faith's coat, but it was the string dishcloths at school which really seemed to interest him. Apparently he'd have expected her five-year old self to be doing messy experiments with bowls of water and things that sink or float, not knitting-one-purling-one. All she could do was shrug her shoulders and agree.

'Did your mother use the things you made?' he wanted to know.

She had to say she couldn't remember. Maybe her mother used them, or maybe it was a case of 'Very nice, dear,' and the items shoved to the back of a drawer and furtively thrown out a week or so later. That was the thing about a personality-lite mother, you couldn't recall a thing about her. Even when she was still, technically, alive.

The day before her Plea and Case Management Hearing, Dora arrived back at Larry's to find him and Mel at the kitchen table talking about something called the Long Parliament. No surprises there: Larry collected knowledge like some people collect stamps. Modern History? Light bedtime reading, for people who've been steeped in the Ancient sort, or at least for Larry it was. And of course the German he'd been talking with Mel would have been 'acquired informally during my doctoral work, in order to read the secondary literature,' how could it not have been? So, what with Tom taking care of Shakespeare and so forth, this girl was rather well prepared.

Next exam in two days' time. All well so far. Pity she herself couldn't do anything to help, except keep her fingers crossed.

She sat down with Larry and Mel and got out the knitting again. Stripes were pretty easy, when it came down to it. After this, what about a really ambitious project involving Fair Isle? A hat and scarf and legwarmers and mittens-on-a-string, perhaps? Maybe she should ask Tom's opinion.

On second thoughts, maybe not. It didn't look as if Capella was doing anything much for him at the moment. And with Mel in the throes of exams, this wasn't the time for Conversations. Afterwards, though, after the end of his term and his stand-in job, wouldn't he and Mel be off? Away from her, he'd get out of his unknown territory. But would she ever get out of hers? After all this, where in the world would she go?

Another day, another courtroom. And this one was a bit more like the ones on TV, what with His Honour Judge Barrington up there in that spiffy outfit. What did Mrs Judge Barrington think of him in it? Did he have lunch in it, and if he did, did he wear a bib to keep crumbs off it? A great big baby's bib, maybe. One of those rigid plastic ones with a sump at the bottom to catch dribbles...

She'd made her plea. Now she was just going to stand here and look at her hands until somebody told her she could go. It would be nice to sit down, though. Actually, it would be very nice. It was just possible that if she didn't sit down very soon, she was going to –

Hold on, hold on, you can't faint, not here! Think of that plastic bib. What's the design on it – leaping dolphins? Monkeys swinging through the trees? Perhaps he's wearing matching underpants –

Oh God. Could she prop herself up on the edge of the dock, or would that be contempt of court?

'Ms Clayton, are you not feeling well?'

Oh, somebody was speaking to her. Ah, it was the Judge. Oh Christ, how was it you were supposed to address these people, again?

'I – I, er…'

'Please sit if you would like to, Ms Clayton.'

'Oh. Er, thanks.'

A pair of hands appeared and guided her to a chair. Thank God. Bloody stupid situation to get herself into, though. It must be what came of not being able to eat any breakfast, in spite of Larry clucking over her. He'd have seen her come within an ace of passing out just then. The ushers must have had their work cut out to stop him from rushing to catch her. She'd better manage lunch after all this, otherwise she'd never hear the last of it.

Ridiculous. All this was just a formality, the lawyers had said so repeatedly.

It was warm in here. A cool drink would be nice.

A glass of water appeared beside her, put there by another pair of hands.

It was magic, this place. You only had to think a thought, and Hey Presto.

OK, let's try *Let this be over soon, please.*

But it was a good half-hour before the hands appeared again and guided her out.

A press photographer was waiting outside, but all he got was a picture of Larry, as he stepped between her and the camera. Then Kate Ojo shepherded them both into her car.

Adjourned for reports, just as Kate had predicted. Adjourned *sine die.* Which meant in her case probably three months or so, according to Kate.

She'd be meeting the Court doctors soon. Three months

of interviews, three months of more and more and more paper.

Still, there was another way of looking at this. A moment's mental firestorm a little more than two months ago had generated work for dozens, when you counted in the PA's of people like Dr Finch, Monty Shuttleworth and Kate Ojo, not forgetting the police, the hospital cleaners, the admin staff at the courts, the technicians who fixed computers and unjammed fax machines, and the guys like Larry who changed light bulbs.

Dora Clayton was a one-woman job-creation service. That certainly was one way of looking at all this.

Thirty

'Hello! Melanie and Tom, isn't it?' called the chubby-ish, young-ish man in a dark suit who was coming towards them.

Tom suppressed a sigh. Just when he'd managed to sink into a late-Friday-afternoon-in-summer state of mind after that walk in the Parks with Mel, talking about their future and forgetting, for once, the present, he had to make conversation. And with the neighbour's grandson from Mrs Wise's funeral.

'Hey, it's that bloke,' murmured Mel, 'you know, the one who was trying to sweet-talk me—'

She broke off. She had to, he was almost up with them.

'Hi,' the man said, and re-introduced himself, which was just as well as Tom had forgotten his name: Peter Shaw. But he hadn't forgotten Shaw's interest in Mel's university plans.

'Excuse the stupid suit,' said Shaw, red-faced from the heat, 'I didn't have time to change. I've just been invigilating the captain of our first eleven who broke his wrist – his *right* wrist – playing against Keble last week. Silly sod's ended up having to dictate his finals papers in a locked broom cupboard in College, with me in there breathing down his neck.'

'Oh, really?' said Mel. 'Poor guy.'

'You're too generous,' he said, wrinkling his nose. 'Are you staying with Larry Wise? I've spotted each of you in the distance a couple of times when I've been popping in to see Grandma.'

After the basic exchanges, Peter Shaw moved on rather quickly, Tom noticed, to how Mel's A-level papers were going, and he smiled when she said, with a grimace-cum-grin, 'Oh God, I'm surviving, just.'

He found himself catching Shaw's eye. Shaw knew as well as he did that it was what she would say. It was only the boys who said 'bloody brilliant, no probs.'

'I've got the Eng Lit closed text paper next Tuesday,' Mel went on, 'so we're going to be doing a whack of reading over the weekend, but then that's it.'

'Fantastic. Make sure you have a good time on Tuesday evening – not that you'll be getting smashed, I imagine…' For a second Shaw's gaze slid down to her bump, but when she was fully clothed it was still barely perceptible under the loose smock-style tops in which all girls seemed to be wafting around this summer. 'Everything going well on the baby front?'

'Oh sure, thanks, everything's fine.'

'Great, great. Well, musdash, Grandma's probably had the kettle on for the last half hour.' He smiled a good-bye sort of smile, then it wavered. 'Look, Melanie, I meant what I said about giving me a ring when the results come out. I'm not trying to twist your arm if you're really set on Bristol – it's a great place – but if you should happen to want to re-think…'

'Thanks,' said Mel, smiling. 'I mean, thanks for thinking of me.'

'It's myself I'm thinking of,' he replied. 'I'm a devious individual, always looking for ways of beefing up my intake. Hazard of the job, I'm afraid. Well, see you.' A farewell lift of the hand, and he was off, at an ungainly trot.

'He must be sweltering,' murmured Mel. 'Why do they have to wear suits here, why can't they wear normal clothes like everybody else?'

'It's formal academic dress, Melly. Exam invigilators at Oxford have to wear it. But at least he'd taken his gown and his white tie off.'

'White tie? You mean, as in white tie and tails? Christ.'

'Centuries of tradition, Mel. But day-to-day, he'll be dressing just as they do in Bristol or Keele or Cardiff or wherever. And I get the impression his brain is right here and now in the twenty-first century.'

'Hm... Hey, do you *want* me to give him a ring?'

'Of course not – I mean, all I was saying is don't judge him by what you saw just now.' His heart was suddenly racing. Christ, he'd praised Peter Shaw too much.

Mel laughed. Then a couple of blackbirds started squawking in the overgrown garden they were passing, and her head turned in their direction. Subject closed?

Apparently not. That evening over supper, Larry mentioned that Mrs Shaw's cat was out of sorts again. After a due amount of sympathetic clucking, Mel said, with a grin, 'That reminds me, we ran into her grandson. He still wants me to phone him, you know. His students must be really bad if he's gagging to take me on.'

'Well, if he's that keen on teaching you, he'd better move to a lecturership at Bristol,' said Dora, as she began another row of knitting. 'Hadn't he, Tom.'

'I don't think his grandmother would like that,' was all Tom could come up with.

Bristol, Bristol. It wouldn't be long now. After the end of term, he and Mel could start basing themselves in Uxbridge. She'd need to, what with the antenatal check-ups getting more frequent, and he had to take a hard look at his house contents and decide what he was keeping and what he was throwing out. That chore had to be got on with sooner rather than later. And the day Mel's results came out, he'd apply for any and every teaching job around Bristol and they'd start house-hunting.

A lot to do. A lot of change coming up. He should focus on that, let it fill his mind. He must focus on that.

The weather broke half an hour after Mel's last paper finished. Tom was waiting for her at his house – school gate hugs wouldn't have been quite the thing, in the circumstances – but if she'd been a minute later he'd have been racing down the road with an umbrella.

'Christ, just made it,' she said, panting, as he let her in. 'Did you see that lightning? It's going to piss down any minute.'

'Come here, Mel.'

She looked at him, and a great, big, jubilant grin began to light up her face. 'Yes, Mr Ross, whatever you say,' she said, moving toward him. 'Hey, I've done it,' she went on as he took her in his arms. 'I've done it!'

'You certainly have,' he said. As he held her close, Faith began to make her presence felt, kicking him with enough life force for ten.

'Do you think Faith's worried about the thunder?' he said.

'Stroke her and see if she calms down.'

As he put a hand on Mel's abdomen, an elbow came out to fend him off. Or was it a knee? Gently, very gently, he ran both hands up and down, up and down, over the burgeoning roundness. After a minute or so, the heavings and kickings began to subside.

'See? It works,' said Mel.

'Maybe she got tired. Or bored.'

'I don't think so,' she said. As she kissed his cheek, her mobile phone began to ring. It was her mother, wanting to know if the exam had gone OK. 'Yeah, it was all right, sort of,' said Mel. 'Yeah, yeah, we can come round right now... Champagne? No way, you and Tom'll have to... Oh, Gran's there, is she? OK, a tiny weeny drop then.'

'Well, according to the websites, a glass or so per week doesn't hurt,' she said, grinning, as she put the phone away, 'and that guy Peter Shaw did say to have a good time, didn't he.'

Did she still have Peter Shaw in her mind?

'Yes, I used to look at babies sometimes,' said Dora. 'On buses and so forth. I could hardly avoid it, there are a lot of them about.'

The woman across the desk from her pursed her lips. Those gold-rimmed glasses the woman was wearing said it all: she wasn't a Court-appointed psychiatrist, she was a Nazi. She was like one of those female characters in old films who turn out to be more dangerous than the men in jackboots.

'Did you think of taking one?' said the woman.

The light in here was glinting off the woman's specs in a ridiculously cod-interrogation-room way. One careless move on Dora's part and the woman would be calling the guards. What would they do to her, would it be the splinters under the nails? Or some sort of water torture?

'No,' said Dora, 'not in any conscious way. Of course, there were times when I—'

Shit. That wasn't the way to put it.

'Go on,' said the woman, picking up a pen.

Bugger. 'When I saw children being treated in a less than intelligent way by parents, but...' The sentence shouldn't need finishing. Judging by the woman's raised eyebrows, though, she'd better have a try. 'But I wouldn't actually have tried to take one, any more than the next woman would.'

Frau Himmler left her eyebrows where they were for a few seconds longer. Perhaps Mrs Average had a habit of being a lot more unpredictable than she looked. 'Tell me about your relationship with your husband,' she said, tapping her pen on the desk. 'I understand he is now involved with another woman.'

Fuck this. 'Steve's a great bloke, totally decent, and as far as I know, Yvonne – I mean Vicky – is exactly right for him. Can we leave him out of this. Please.'

Frau Himmler touched the pen to her nose for a moment. 'What was his view of the nursery you maintained?'

'He never went in there.'

'Did he want another child?'

'Yes.'

Frau Himmler stopped playing with her pen and began writing with it.

'Do you want another child?' she said, after a minute or so of scribbling. She didn't look up.

'At my age? You must be joking.'

The woman did now look up. That over-the-top-of-the-specs gaze: yes, this woman was a sadist, no doubt of that whatsoever.

'Women older than you have babies,' she said.

'Well, they can if they like but I won't be joining them.'

'It's a challenging undertaking in one's forties, it's true. And of course if there has been ambivalence in the past…'

Ambivalence? Who mentioned anything about sodding ambivalence? OK, Frau Himmler, cop this: 'The only baby I'm interested in now is the one my friends are having. I'm going to do as much for her as I possibly can, I'm going to be an honorary grannie and aunt rolled into one.' *If I ever see her.*

Frau Himmler didn't reply, but she started writing again, and as she wrote, an image took on extra definition in Dora's head, an image that had been sitting there in hazy embryonic form for days. Ah, embryos: could she still gestate them?

A vast semi-desert from a Clint Eastwood-style Western,

and a giant cactus in the foreground with a sign hanging from one of its arms. 'UNKNOWN TERRITORY,' said the sign. And she was standing right under it. There was nobody else around as far as the eye could see.

Roll on menopause. Never to gestate anything, ever again: that couldn't come too soon.

As Dora had predicted, when Tom's school term was over, he and Mel started spending time in Uxbridge. 'They've got a lot of things to do,' she had to explain to Larry, ten times or was it twelve. At any rate, every time he stood at the gate and watched the car – her car – disappear down the road. Tom still seemed to be willing to drive her Toyota. Or was it that giving it back would have been too stark, too obvious?

There didn't seem to be much she could say to him now. And yet it didn't feel as if everything had been said. Some days it felt as if nothing had been said, and it was all banked up, waiting to come crashing out.

Day after day, after Larry had asked her yet again would she be all right on her own and she'd said yes, fine, and sent him off to work, she lay on one of the sofas in the sitting room and knitted, with Radio 4 burbling away in the background. On days when the sign hanging from that cactus threatened to drop on her head, she'd look up towards the ceiling and allow the image of the stars and planets mobile to fill her mind's eye instead. But she didn't go up and set it going.

They took to passing quiet evenings in the kitchen after supper was cleared away, she and Larry. He sat at one end of the table carving animals for a Noah's Ark for Faith, she sat at the other, needles clicking. The cat bestowed himself on her lap or Larry's as the mood took him, and the radio sat in the middle of the table to keep them all company.

One such evening, it occurred to her that this was how the domestic scene must have been circa 1955. If her old team from Duckworth and Dunn could see her now. A vision flickered in her mind's eye for a moment, of her sitting at this table with white hair and gnarled hands, the knitting grown so long that it filled not only this room but the whole house, with enough left over to spill out into the street. Across the table was a great pile of carved toys, with just the tousled top of a mop of white hair to be seen behind them.

She gave her head a shake and the vision faded. 'Tea or cocoa, Larry?' she said.

One morning, the phone rang just after Larry had left for work. It was Mel.

'Oh, hi Mel,' said Dora. 'How's things?'

Things were fine, apparently. Mel was ringing to say that she and Tom wouldn't be appearing in Oxford next week because they were going up to Scotland for a quick holiday before the A-level results came out. Tom wanted to show her where he was from.

'Seeing relatives?' said Dora.

'Tom says not if he can help it,' said Mel, 'but Tommy says we ought to.'

'It wouldn't hurt to drop in and say hi. If they're awful you can always have a train to catch.'

'Yeah, I suppose so… Hey, Dora, I've been thinking.'

'Oh?'

'You went to Oxford University, didn't you. Supposing – only for the sake of argument, mind – I did contact that Peter Shaw guy. Be honest, how would somebody like me fit in? I mean, leaving Faith out of it for the minute.'

Ah. This was what Mel was really phoning about. Never mind dour Scottish relatives. Well. She could either lie, or answer the girl honestly. Where was Tom, though, was he listening?

'If "somebody like me" means bright people from State schools whose families haven't been steeped in higher education since the thirteenth century,' she said, 'you could walk through the main door of any college and you'd see them. They'd be coming back from lectures, going to lectures, coming to and from tutorials, hanging around waiting for the college bar to open, or just hanging around for no special reason. You'd recognise them because they looked like you. Get the idea?'

'Mm… You know, I've got a kind of feeling Tom'd like me to give it a go, but I wanted to get your angle while he's outside cutting the grass… God, I've just realised I'm bursting for a pee.'

'The fifth this morning?'

'And counting. See you, Dora.'

Dora fiddled with the phone cord as she put the handset back in the rest, twisting and untwisting it. Landlines with cords… Still, they went with mahogany and stair rods.

For God's sake, she should have told Mel just now not to mess Bristol about. What would Tom think if – when – Mel reported back on that conversation? 'Got a kind of feeling…' Oh Mel, wherever did you get that idea?

The next evening, Larry looked up from the giraffe he was carving and said, 'Dora, you appear rather pale. I wonder if a change of air would be beneficial. Would the authorities allow you a short holiday, do you think?'

'A holiday. There's a thought,' she said.

Why not? *Why bloody not?* Tom and Mel were having one. Even Frau Himmler had buggered off on a tour of gloomy castles, or wherever. Why shouldn't Dora Clayton have a change of scene too?

The lawyers thought it was a great idea. Judge Barrington didn't put up any objection in principle, but Larry had to undertake to keep an eye on her all the way to Grasmere and back – because of course, it was going to be Grasmere, staying at the B&B that he and Mother had patronised for years.

Larry also had to pretty well keep her on a lead on each and every Lakeland walk. Would he mind?

She had to smile when Monty relayed this back to her. She had to laugh, actually.

On the way there in the train, her nose pressed itself to the window like a five-year-old's. This coming week, she was going to take one bit of unknown territory, at least, and turn it into something known.

On fine days they went for walks, on wet days they went for bus rides. Every tea shop Larry had ever been in with Mother turned out to be still in business, most of them staffed by women in flowered aprons who remembered him.

'I like it here,' she found herself saying one afternoon, when the view through the tea shop window was of the car ferry chugging across Windermere.

He gave her such a look, a look filled with such joy, that she had to look away, on the pretext of reaching for another paper napkin from the basket at the side of the table. Still, all he seemed to want from her was her presence across the table, which was fine by her. She couldn't really see herself giving him much more, but she could give him that.. And as for what he might give her… well, there was a lot to be said for a friendly presence across a table. For a second, that vision she'd had at Larry's of two white-haired people sitting at the kitchen table flashed into her mind.

The day before they were due to go back to Oxford, they made their way to a small beach on the farther side of Grasmere, away from the tourist route to Dove Cottage. Dora sat down on a log and watched Larry take his shoes and socks off. He waited until another middle-aged couple had sauntered past, and when they were out of sight, he rolled up his trousers and went to the water's edge.

When he was in up to his knees, he held up a finger, boy scout-wise, to check the direction of the breeze, and opened the tin containing Mother. Then, with a great sweep of his arm, he cast Mother onto the waters.

As Dora watched Larry standing motionless in the water, head bowed, the lid of the empty tin flapping slightly, the wavelets lapping around him began to blur into one another. Then she realised she was seeing them through water of her own making. Salt water. She was getting really good at crying. After a lifetime of not doing it, who'd have thought it would be so easy?

Thirty-One

'Let me have a try,' said Tom as they were finishing their meal in the little restaurant overlooking the Firth. 'OK, I'm looking out of the window, and what do I see... I know. *La vista di l'isola da qui è bellissima.*'

'Not bad, any Italian would understand you,' said Mel, 'but it's actually "*dell'isola*", not "*di l'isola*".'

'Oh, right. Mel, I had no idea you were this fluent.' At this rate he'd be fluent himself by the time Faith was born.

'Comes of spending a lot of time with Gran when I was younger,' said Mel, spooning up the last of her ice cream. 'Mum's forgotten most of hers and Gemma and the others couldn't be bothered, but Gran was determined there'd be one of us who could speak Italian, so guess who that had to be. Still, it made Italian GCSE a doss, I can tell you.'

'I dare say. Well, that's one more thing I know about you.'

'Don't go too fast, I like being a bit mysterious.' She gave him a sly-looking grin.

During the meal, Tom had caught one or two appraising looks in their direction from other couples who couldn't see what Mel was concealing under the table. Man out with younger woman, cheating on the wife? *This is my wife,* he'd felt like announcing. *This, and no other.*

Was it easier, having Mel and only Mel in his field of view? It might be, but for the small lonely figure which was now a fixture in his mind's eye. In and out of focus Dora might drift, but absent she never was.

He looked out of the window again, and this time the feeling that had been growing in him throughout the meal was too strong to ignore. He had to go out there, he had to walk that path along the shore before they went back to London. There was only tonight left to do it. How would Mel react, would she want to come? Would she not want to come, but wonder why on earth he wanted to go for a walk as late as this?

When they were back at the B&B, he said, 'Do you mind if I take a stroll for half an hour? I'd like to get a bit more sea air while I've got the chance.'

'Yeah, sure,' she said. 'I'll go and have a long bath and watch Faith playing.'

'It's the sort of thing I do,' he said, catching her hand, 'I go for late walks. I promise it won't get in the way of looking after Faith.'

'Fine,' she said, smiling, and giving a shrug. 'I like long baths. I promise they won't get in the way of looking after Faith either.'

He kissed her hand before he let it go.

Out on the cliff path, there was the mildest of breezes blowing. The air was still warm, and it brought up to Tom the scent and sound of the sea. When he'd gone a couple of hundred metres he stopped and looked down. There was enough twilight, just, for him to make out the gently undulating line of white where the sea washed against the rocks not far below. There was no particular need for a head for heights here, narrow though the path was.

He shut his eyes and took a deep, long breath, a breath of sea mingled with green things and warm earth. Not so many months ago he'd been walking through Oxford and yearning to be here, needing this air to clear his head. That toy bear he'd stepped on that day, it must still be stuffed into a pocket of his heavy winter jacket.

Before he knew it, he'd looked down at his feet. Nothing was under them but the hard bare earth and embedded grit of the path. He walked on.

A clear head. A clean head. Would this walk bring him such a head?

A little further on, some massive dark shapes were moving slowly near a fence that separated the field they were in from the path. He heard the sounds of grass being torn up, and slow, rhythmic chewing. So cattle were still being grazed on that scrubby patch. 'Hello,' he said, and one or two of the heads swung in his direction for a moment or so, but there was no let-up in the serious business of processing sustenance. Did they have clear heads? He'd be willing to bet that they did. He was looking at one, two, three, four – no, five – examples of utter single-mindedness.

He took another deep, long breath, and walked on. It was getting darker now, and there was no moon. But the sky was clear, and the stars – ah, the stars – were everywhere. There was the Lyre, with Vega shining bright, and close by was the Swan, with Deneb at his tail. And there was Cassiopeia, reclining in her chair.

No Capella, though. It was no use looking for her, she was hidden from him by the lie of the land. He'd never seen Capella at this time of year from this path, only in the winter.

Twenty metres or so ahead was the point where the path wound between two large rocks. It was one of the few places along this path where you had to watch your step – another being the point about ten metres further on, where there was a ridge of tree root lying across the path, just jutting above the surface.

When was the last time he'd walked this path? And yet here it was in his mind, each and every step. That was good. He should be glad.

When he reached the tree root he all but caught his foot in it, indelible mental picture or no. Since he'd last been here this stretch of path had eroded slightly, leaving the root an inch or so above it in the air, all ready to trap an unsuspecting foot. He'd have to contact the local parish council about that, or there could be sprained ankles.

Tree roots. They catch you out.

'Oh God,' he said aloud. 'What am I going to do about her?' He couldn't do it, he couldn't just go to Bristol and wipe Dora out, like cleaning a blackboard at school. It wasn't because of the sex he'd had little of and would never have again. It wasn't even because of her vulnerability. If he had to try to put his finger on the one thing about Dora he couldn't do without, it was the conversations. Like games of ping pong, he'd thought that weekend in Wales, the weekend he'd remember every detail of for the rest of his life. Yes, the conversations: having to stay on his toes, never quite knowing what she'd come out with next…

He moved on, almost running now as the path opened up again. It was vital that he got a look at Capella. Wasn't there *some* point along here where there was a chink of clear view through to the north east? Winter would be too late, he needed to see Capella right now, now, now!

He kept going, straining his eyes for a glimpse, but there was nowhere with an open view to the north east, as of course he knew there wouldn't be.

At the point where the path began to climb up to the next headland, Tom turned and headed back. As he made his way to the B&B, the quiet streets of the little town seemed to have an apologetic air.

When he let himself into their room, Mel's bedside light was on but she was fast asleep, the book she'd been reading spreadeagled on the floor where it had fallen. He'd been out longer than he thought. He picked up the book. It was the new edition of *Macbeth* which the Oxford University Press had brought out earlier this year. Really? She'd said she wasn't going to let herself go to pot during this 'gap year', but this was impressive, by anybody's standards. For a moment, he found himself thinking of that Oxford academic, Peter Shaw.

He put the book down on Mel's bedside table, undressed, switched off the light, and slid into the bed. He lay there beside Mel, hands behind his head, staring into the darkness. The window was open, and from time to time he heard footsteps going down the street. People coming back from the pub, maybe. He'd met hardly any night walkers around here, ever, which was odd, considering that the locale was perfect for lone wandering. Maybe some had gone out but been disappointed, not finding what they were looking for. What would he have said to such people – keep trying? Up here, people didn't like being told what to do. They'd tell him that minding your own business should be enough of a job to keep any man busy.

He'd have to admit, they'd be right.

Mel's A-level scores beat the school record. Tom told himself that nobody deserved their results more than she did. But during the family's celebration at Grandma Battaglia's sheltered flat he sensed that she was thinking about something. He had a feeling he didn't need to ask what she was thinking about, and he was right:

'You know, I might just tell that guy Peter Shaw how I've done,' she said, as they were walking back to his house.

'Oh?'

'Well, you know, seeing as he was so interested.'

She sounded casual enough, but for a moment Tom saw in front of them not the road they were walking along but the motorway to Oxford. Which was where they were heading by midday the following day, after Mel had phoned Peter Shaw. Of course Shaw hadn't merely said well done and told her to have a nice time at Bristol, he'd said he'd really like to have a chat, and why didn't she drop in for coffee sometime soon? Like tomorrow at eleven?

Once they were on the M40, Mel got out her mobile. 'Hi, it's me again,' she said to Dora. 'Can you get the kettle on? We're coming back.'

'So, Mel, am I going to be looking for jobs around Oxford?' he said.

'I don't know,' she said, staring ahead of her out of the window, as if the answer to his question might depend on whether she could actually glimpse Oxford yet. 'Let's just see how this chat with Peter Shaw goes.'

When they were emerging from the Chiltern Gap, she said, 'This view really gets you, doesn't it.'

'Mm,' he said.

A few seconds silence. Then: 'Tom, do you think – I mean, I wonder if Dora and Larry – you know, when they were up in the Lake District.'

'Did they share a room, do you mean?'

'Er, yeah.'

'If you had to guess, what would you say?'

'Um… I'd say they had two rooms. It's that sort of relationship, isn't it. I mean, they need each other but they've both been through a lot and maybe sex would be too much… For now, anyway. What do you think?'

'I think you're right, Mel. What they've got's enough for now. Maybe enough full stop.' Would she come back on that last point? She didn't, and he let out a long and, he hoped, unobtrusive breath. Still, the idea that perhaps one day there might be more between Dora and Larry hadn't occurred to him. Should it have? Oh Capella, he had enough to occupy himself with today, didn't he? What point was there in getting sidetracked by what might happen some day in the future?

On that cliff path in Fife, he'd told himself he couldn't just wave goodbye to Dora. A dispassionate observer might say he should welcome the fact that this road he was on was heading straight for her. But he taught literature, he knew better. One man, two women, one dilemma. Or one woman, two men: either way, the story had filled an ocean of books. Same plot? Much of the time, it was. But as far as he was concerned, the ending was the point. He needed the one in which the character finally manages to broaden his field of view. How was he going to find it?

That evening, Tom discovered just how much Mel had been thinking about Oxford on the quiet:

'I had a bit of a look at the Oxford website before we went to Scotland,' she said when the four of them were half way through supper. 'I bet Peter Shaw's going to give me a trial interview. He's going to give me a passage to read and then ask me questions.'

'I wouldn't rule it out, Mel,' he said.

'Dora, tell me this college of his isn't one of the posh ones,' she went on.

'I've told you, there aren't any, not these days,' said Dora. 'And if you need to nip out to the loo, just go, Peter Shaw won't have conniptions.'

So Mel had talked to Dora about this already. Dora hadn't once looked in his direction since they'd been back. Not once.

During the clearing of the table, Larry went out to the garden to call the cat in and Mel had to 'nip out'. That left Tom and Dora alone.

'So, a change of plan,' she said, scraping a plate into the bin.

'Yes,' he said. 'Well, maybe… Who are the postcards on the dresser from?'

'*Weymouth By Night's* from Jim,' said Dora. She must mean the one that was entirely black, except for a pair of cartoon eyes. 'The one next to it's from Frau Himmler.'

'What, the two kittens?'

'It's from Jenny, actually. Just joking. You know me, I can't resist a line.'

She put the plate in the sink and turned and looked at him. Her great grey eyes were full of questions, if he still had any ability to read a face. For a second, his gaze locked with hers.

And then the cat shot in, carrying a mouse – very dead – in his mouth, followed by Larry, clucking that Prinz Eugen was growing decidedly skittish nowadays for an elderly cat.

It was obvious to Tom how Mel's session with Peter Shaw had gone when they were twenty yards away. Shaw was relaxed enough to be gesturing with his hands as he was talking to her. Walking her – slowly – to the College Lodge, evidently in no hurry to get rid of her. Yes, any passer-by who glanced in from the street would know how the session had gone.

'Ah, Tom, great to see you,' said Shaw, all smiles. 'My God, has Blackwell's got anything left in stock? Respect, respect!' Some might have thought that patronising, but Shaw was eyeing Tom's bags of new books with what looked like genuine respect. Maybe he had different ways of dealing with stress, like drink, cigarettes or casual sex.

You know me. You know me. Dora's words of yesterday evening, repeating themselves as regularly in his head as any mantra.

Peter Shaw and Mel had had a 'very stimulating' discussion, according to Shaw. The man seemed particularly anxious that Tom should know that. Of course Shaw couldn't commit himself or the college to anything; Mel would need to put in a new UCAS application this autumn. But if she were to, 'she would be a very strong applicant indeed.'

When they got back to the house, Dora was putting out a pile of newspapers for recycling. She stood up, looked at Mel's face, and said, 'You're in.'

'Christ, hang on a minute,' said Mel, 'I'd have to put in another sodding UCAS form, *and* the Oxford application form. I'm not decided yet.'

'Really? Oh, before I forget, Tom, Linda Mason phoned about half an hour ago.'

'Oh shit,' he said, hitting himself on the side of the head, 'I should have phoned her before now. Shit, shit.' Yes, he should by now have phoned the woman he'd been deputising for last term and asked after the A-level results of the people he'd been teaching, for God's sake. He should have shown some minute amount of interest.

'How's her baby?' said Mel.

'Jude's absolutely fine,' Dora said – a bit too quickly. Was there something wrong with Jude? Oh, God. 'I'm seeing her for coffee on Friday,' she went on.

'Oh great, can I come too?' said Mel. 'I'd love to see Jude.'

A slight pause. 'Of course. I'm sure Linda'll let you do a trial nappy change.'

'Fantastic! Right, I'm going you know where,' said Mel, making for the stairs.

'Before I phone Linda, what's the problem with Jude?' Tom said quietly.

'His feet haven't turned out,' said Dora, equally quietly.

'Is that serious?'

'Not as such, but it can be a nuisance to deal with. It might correct itself without the need for splints, but Linda says the doctors have told her it's a bit too early to say.'

'It sounds as if you had quite a talk with Linda.'

'I did. You'd better phone her now, she's got to go out at twenty-to.'

Linda Mason, it turned out, was far too concerned about Jude's feet for it to have crossed her mind that Tom was a day or so late in asking about the A-level results. And when they did get on to results, the ones she seemed to be interested in were Mel's. He mentioned that Oxford had now entered the equation – he could hardly gloss over it – whereupon Linda became even more animated. He soon found out why: 'I can now ask you what I've been gearing up to ask for several days,' she said. 'How would you feel about standing in for me next term as well? I just don't think Jude's going to be ready to be left by the beginning of term, not with this foot situation.'

Ah. Couldn't he have predicted something like this? He found himself having to stifle a giggle, of all things, by biting his lip. 'Sure, if Mel does decide to give Oxford a try, I'll do another term for you. Provided the Head agrees, that is.'

'Don't worry about Rex, he'll agree,' said Linda quickly. 'He rates you. But you don't need me to tell you that. Anyway, I'm going to tell him Danny Lawrence's B is down to you. I'd had that lad as heading for a C, if that.'

No, Tom didn't need to be told he'd fitted in rather well. Rex Philips had shaken his hand enough to detach it from his arm as he saw him out of the school gates on the last day of term.

He left it with Linda that he'd contact her as soon as Mel had made up her mind. That would have to be soon, very soon, because Mel couldn't keep Bristol dangling.

The smell of coffee drew him towards the kitchen. He found Dora sitting at the table, knitting. As he sat down opposite her, she put the knitting down, poured a large mug, and pushed it towards him.

'Mel must be having a rest after the excitements of the morning,' she said.

'Did Linda tell you she was going to ask me to stay another term?' he said.

She took a mouthful of coffee before she answered him. The cat, under the table, was snoring loudly, filling the silence but in a way which only emphasised it. 'Yes,' she said at last. She picked up her half-finished blue-and-red striped sock again. 'I dropped a stitch five rows ago,' she went on, peering at the knitting. 'Bugger.' She pulled the knitting off the needle and started to unravel it. 'I had a phone call from Monty Shuttleworth about ten minutes before Linda phoned,' she said. 'Frau Himmler wants to see you and Mel.'

'Us? Why?'

'To gain perspective, which could be helpful.' She smiled, but the smile didn't reach her eyes. 'I'm quoting Monty, you understand. Frau Himmler wants to ask you how well you know me, if you'd be happy to let me babysit, that sort of thing. By the way, do you know anything about cacti?'

Cacti? Of all the things she could come out with, that had to be one topic he'd never have predicted in a hundred years. But that was the point, wasn't it. *You know me...* 'Not much,' he said. 'They don't like being over-watered. Does Frau Himmler have them in her office? Or are you planning on taking up cacti growing?'

'Now you mention it, Frau H does have a few in pots, but I reckon cacti don't like captivity, they're best left to roam the range. I prefer knitting. And astronomy.' She seemed to leave the last word hanging in the air.

He had to say something. 'I tried to get a look at Capella when we were in Scotland.'

'Did you manage it?'

'No,' he said, into his coffee cup. 'No, I didn't.'

She looked at him for several seconds. 'That's a pity. In the circumstances.'

'Yes, it is... Well. I'd better phone Monty Shuttleworth.'

As Tom spoke, the kitchen door swung open. 'What's this about phoning Monty Shuttleworth?' said Mel.

As Dora fed the knitting back onto the needle, she told Mel about Frau Himmler's request.

'Oh sure,' said Mel, grabbing a biscuit from the tin, 'we'll tell her, won't we, Tom. If it's up to me' – she grinned – 'you'll be doing a hell of a lot of babysitting.' She looked from Dora to himself, and the grin widened.

'You've decided about Oxford,' he said.

'Yep. I'm going to give it a go.'

'Attagirl,' said Dora.

In the event, the only time when Frau Himmler could see Tom and Mel coincided with one of Mel's antenatals, so Tom went alone.

He supposed he could see why Dora called her Frau Himmler – the specs, the penetrating gaze – but this Dr Eastman didn't seem that bad. She was younger than he'd expected: thirty, thirty-five, maybe.

He let Dr Eastman make the running. That was evidently the way she was intending to play it; she wasn't expecting a power-point presentation from him on the phenomenon that was Dora. They chatted through how long he'd known Dora, how he'd met her, whether 'Mrs Ross' got on with her. Obvious enough questions, but it felt odd, talking about Dora like this, reducing her to a 'case'... Dr Eastman's PA came in at one point with a message, and Tom took a moment to study the potted cacti on the windowsill. Maybe they would have been happier in the open, under the baking sun and the vast cloudless skies of the American South West.

When the PA had gone out again, Dr Eastman said, 'Did it surprise you when Ms Clayton abducted a child?'

'It was a great shock.' Well, that was the truth. To follow

401

Syd into Dora's bedroom and see that nappy bucket… 'But she hadn't been planning it, I'm sure of that.'

Dr Eastman began scribbling on the notepad in front of her. While she wrote, he was back at Dora's house in Wolvercote, rushing upstairs. He was giving anything not to find her dead. *Anything.*

He closed his eyes, tight.

'Mr Ross? Are you all right?'

'I'm fine, just a bit tired. My wife's been restless the last few nights,' he said, uncrossing and re-crossing his legs.

'You said earlier that Ms Clayton has been supportive to your wife in her pregnancy. I take it that Ms Clayton has not been distressed or resentful about the pregnancy?'

'No, in no way.'

'Has any aspect of her friendship with your wife been unduly concerning, would you say?'

'Absolutely not.'

'Ms Clayton has taken no more interest than might be expected?'

'No. My wife would have objected if she had.'

'Your wife is very young, Mr Ross.'

'Melanie may be young but she is highly intelligent. She's a good judge of people, and more mature than many twice her age.'

He took a breath in and let it out, slowly. Maybe there was more of Frau Himmler about this woman than he'd given her credit for.

'Your wife would be happy to leave the baby in Ms Clayton's care?'

'Entirely happy. And I'm happy too.' Yes, he was, he realised. That, at least, wasn't a problem. Perhaps there was only so much one man could have on his mind.

Dr Eastman bent over the desk and began writing again. Then she put her pen down and looked up. 'Is there anything you would like to add, Mr Ross?'

He should have been prepared for this, the final question of any interview, but the remark that rose to the surface of his mind wasn't one he could make: *You're interested in perspectives, tell me how to widen mine.* When he got back to Larry's, he should check the dictionary definition of perspective; see if it could be stretched to include field of view. 'No, I think we've covered everything,' he said.

Thirty-Two

'Gone for a walk in the Parks. D.'
Dora left the note on the doormat, where Tom would see it as soon as he got back from being interrogated by Frau Himmler. Then she put a few chunks of stale bread into a bag and started out for the big pond in the University Parks. Tom knew that was where she'd go, to look at the ducks. Would he follow? Heads he would, tails he wouldn't. Only she wasn't actually going to throw a coin and find out. Sometimes it was better to stand the suspense.

Of course, there was her crystal ball. That had gone cloudy some while ago though.

When she got to the pond, the ducks were out in full force, clustering near the place where three small children were standing with two women: one young, and one who could be any age from thirty to fifty. She watched the kids chuck morsels at the waiting beaks, the youngest one squealing with delight when a duck snaffled one she'd thrown. In a couple of years that could be Faith. She tried to picture what a child of Tom's and Mel's might look like, and who might be with such a child, handing her pieces of bread to throw, but she had to

404

give up. Anybody whose crystal ball was full of swirling cumulo-nimbus was a fool to be bothering.

She held off dipping into her own bag of bread until the three children had been taken away. It would have been a pity to seduce the ducks over to her side of the pond too soon and spoil the kids' fun.

She was trying to throw pieces toward the small one on the outside of the group when he materialised beside her: Tom. One second he wasn't there, the next second, he was.

'My God, you gave me a fright,' she said.

'Sorry,' he said.

Dora put a hand into the bag and brought out another piece of bread. 'Don't just float there, barge those sods out of the way, for goodness' sake,' she said, aiming the bread at the little duck. The other ducks converged yet again before the runt could get a look in. 'Isn't nature ghastly,' she went on, taking a glance at Tom.

He was looking at the ducks. 'Let me try,' he said, holding out a hand.

'All right.' She gave him a piece of bread.

The other ducks were beginning to drift away, but the little one seemed to be hanging back: the first sign of common sense she'd shown. She snapped up Tom's piece and gobbled it down.

'Thank Christ for that,' said Dora. 'I wouldn't have put it past myself to fish her out and take her home.'

'You could have put her in the paddling pool. Next year, she could have played with Faith.'

'Duck shit's bad for small children,' said Dora. 'Trust me on this.' He'd actually mentioned the child's inflatable paddling pool, Mel's pool bought back in May for wallowing in on hot days in Larry's garden; the pool that hadn't had a lot of use over the summer, because the paddler it was for hadn't been around much. But it wasn't just that he'd mentioned it, it was how he'd mentioned it. As if he'd only just realised what a paddling pool was for.

'How was Frau Himmler?' she said.

'Oh…thorough. She writes fast.'

'I suppose you have to when you're capturing a lot of perspective. Well, shall we go? You'll have to push off soon and collect Mel.'

'Yes… Yes, I will.'

They headed off across the Parks. Dora couldn't get much from Tom on what had passed between him and Frau Himmler, and she didn't try very hard. In fact she couldn't get much from him full stop. Oh, he chatted – came out with remarks about dogs they passed looking like their owners, etc etc – but behind the chat she could see that he was thinking. He was thinking harder than she'd ever seen him think in the time she'd known him. It wasn't altogether easy, walking with someone who was thinking that hard. So much hinged on what came out at the end – like everything. She hadn't expected him to rev up the thinking like this, not now. By the time they got back to Larry's house, she was all-but holding her breath.

In the days that followed, Dora rather got into the habit of breath holding – or if not quite that, at least breathing at the shallowest level necessary to support life. But all of them were doing the same, she sensed. The baby's birth was getting close. Mel's ante-natals were going fine, but the hospital did wonder if she ought to be spending quite so much time away. Or, if she needed to be in Oxford, maybe her maternity care ought to be transferred there?

'Well, I don't fancy just hanging about in Uxbridge all day,' said Mel, after getting back from the appointment when she'd been told this. 'Everything's happening here now. I want to carry on going to the Bodleian as long as I can, I mean Peter Shaw did go out of his way to blag me that reader's ticket. And what with Tom and me staying put for a bit, thanks to Larry, and Tom's term starting soon…'

It was a no-brainer. As Larry's suggestion had been, that Tom and Mel should stay on in the house at least until Christmas, when Mel ought to know whether she'd got an Oxford place. Tom had smiled and said great, fine, thanks. He even sounded as if he might mean it, and went with Mel and Larry to look at washing machines 'in case the latest models might have advantages' when it came to slogging through piles of used baby clothes. On for five minutes, then covered in puke or poo… Ah well, they'd find out soon enough.

And she, where was she herself going to live? Larry hadn't asked her to stay on. That could be because he'd already forgotten she'd lived anywhere but here. Yet again, that vision she'd had of two white-haired people sitting at the kitchen table came into her mind. Could she see herself staying if he got around to asking her? She might, of course, be residing somewhere at Her Majesty's expense. After the perspective Frau Himmler had got from Tom, the conscientious doctor might put in such a blockbuster of a report about her that the Judge would have to re-think.

Tom. It always came back to Tom. She kept catching him looking at things as if he'd never seen them before. Stupid, ordinary things, like the dish mop. Once, she came out of her room to see him going into the nursery, as well he might, now that it was going to be Faith's nursery for a few months at least. He didn't see her.

She didn't hear him playing the mobile, though. If he only would. It mattered.

Dora was shaking muesli into a bowl when the postman arrived, about ten minutes after Tom had left for his first day back at school. 'The guy's early,' said Mel as Larry went to fetch the letters. 'Still, it'll only be junk, it always is.'

'Blimey,' said Dora as Larry placed the largest envelope in front of her, 'that doesn't look like junk, Mel. Three guesses as to who it's from, both of you.' But nobody needed to guess. Dora pushed her muesli aside. Suddenly, she didn't seem to want it. Larry and Mel were looking at her with anxious eyes.

Well, the contents of this envelope weren't going to leap out onto the table of their own accord. Dora reached for a knife, slit the envelope open, and pulled out what was inside.

In the middle of all the court verbiage, one thing stood out:

'They want me there for sentencing on the twelfth,' she said.

'Oh Dora,' murmured Larry.

Frau H. had evidently done the business. Judge Barrington must have decided he knew all he needed to.

'It'll be fine, Dora,' said Mel. 'Piece of cake.' But even she seemed to be making an effort to smile. Still, full marks to her for trying, given the load she was carrying by now.

The twelfth: little more than a week away. Practically the day Faith was due. Just as well Mel was steaming ahead with drafting her application for Oxford. And that her hospital bag was packed, right down to the spare batteries for the camera and enough change to feed the hospital parking meters, and every mobile phone in the house was charged up.

Please let Faith not arrive when Dora was in the dock. It mattered. These days, so much mattered.

The following Saturday morning, Tom found himself contending with the sort of weather he didn't like, as high summer returned in a burst of almost stifling heat, which sent Mel into the hammock Larry had rigged up for her in the garden and the rest of them into deckchairs close enough at hand to bring her drinks and help her up to pee the drinks out again. The birth was close now. Was that the reason why life – amazingly – had seemed very simple this last day or so? He, Dora and Larry had one thing to do, and one thing only: look after Mel. When Larry, who'd been keeping the wasps off her since she'd fallen into a doze, went in to fetch more orange juice, Tom moved his chair closer to her.

'I'll take care of the wasps,' said Dora. 'You get that marking finished.'

'OK,' said Tom, picking up his pen again. She didn't need to spell it out to him to get his marking done while he could, he knew what she meant.

'Sod it, there's another of the buggers,' she said. She was right: it was buzzing like a chain saw. She batted at it a few times, and after a particularly loud, sulky buzz it flew off across the garden. 'A lot of them about today,' she went on. 'Still, soon be winter.' A flurry of chirping from the blue tits in the hawthorn tree across the garden made him jump. 'Hey, keep the noise down,' she called, 'you'll wake the baby.'

But it was too late, Mel was stirring. 'You won't believe this,' she said, yawning, 'but I need another pee. Like right now.'

Tom slid an arm under Mel from the left, and Dora slid an arm under her from the right, and together they manhandled her down onto the ground. Off she went at a lumbering trot that made his heart constrict for her.

'Oh, the feeling of having that load bounce up and down when you're trying to get there in time yet again,' said Dora. 'She has got every last thing packed, hasn't she? Has she got the wet wipes and the Evian water spray?'

'Yes, Dora. For the third, or is it the fourth, time.' It was so easy now, talking to her. Because there was only one thing to talk about?

'Just checking,' she said with a grin.

They were on the point of sitting down again when Larry appeared in the kitchen doorway waving his arms. 'Tom, Dora, could you please come!'

They looked at one another. And ran.

Mel's waters had broken all over the kitchen floor. Twenty minutes later they were at the hospital, with Tom holding Mel's hand while a midwife checked her over. An hour after that they were back at Larry's again.

'They say labour hasn't started yet,' he said to Dora and Larry as he helped Mel out of the car. Once inside the house, he collapsed into a chair. But it wasn't the heat that had exhausted him, it was the anti-climax, like a slap in the face.

'I feel really hacked off,' said Mel, flopping onto a sofa. 'I feel like a kid who's had her birthday cake whipped away because the icing's not set.'

'Why couldn't they just have kept her in?' he said.

'Look, they wouldn't be letting her out unless everything was fine,' said Dora. 'Have they said when to bring her back?'

'Tomorrow morning. Unless of course things start happening sooner.'

'Well, tomorrow will come. Trust me.'

He looked at her for a moment. She meant it. 'All right, Dora,' he said, and he tried to smile.

Mel said, 'Well, folks, what shall we do this afternoon, go and see a film?'

'Oh, Melanie, don't you think that would be a little…bold?' said Larry.

'It's OK, Larry, she's only joking,' said Dora.

'Oh? Oh…. OK. OK, OK…'

'What she'd settle for is going back into the garden and maybe doing a few laps of the rose beds, just to jog things along,' said Dora. 'Right, Mel?'

'Sounds good,' said Mel. Her eyes were bright, but she was tying her arms into a knot.

Oh, Mel, if I could only do this for you!

Dora laid a hand on Mel's arm for a second. The look Mel

410

gave her wasn't hard to read: *I'm glad you're here.*

So was he, he realised. *So was he.*

By nine o'clock that evening, Dora had had to calm Tom down twice when he'd been on the verge of grabbing the car keys and sprinting for the front door. The first time, Mel had had what she called 'a couple of vague aches,' about twenty minutes apart, but then nothing happened for an hour or so, when she had 'a twinge.' Each time, the hospital said just to keep an eye on things and encourage Mel to get some sleep.

Mel herself seemed fine as she hauled herself – gingerly – upstairs to go to bed. It was Tom who was looking as if he could do with a shot of something – whiskey? Valium?

'How in hell do babies ever manage to get out?' he muttered as they got on with the washing up after a sketchy and interrupted supper.

'They've been managing it for millions of years,' said Dora.

'Sorry. Statement of the bleeding obvious.'

'Hm. Right now, I'll take statements of the obvious, clichés, you name it.'

'All right, how about this: not long now.'

'Not long now,' he repeated. 'Not long now.'

Just then, Larry came into the kitchen. 'Not long now, not long now,' he said, giving Tom one of his concerned looks. Was there anybody who could do concern as well as Larry?

Not long now. At ten to five on Sunday morning there was a hammering on Dora's door that shot her out of bed almost before she was awake. She heard the 'Ah, ah!' from next door before she flung open her door. Tom was standing there in boxer shorts, looking frantic. 'Dora, I've just phoned for an ambulance. The baby's coming, it's coming!'

Dora was in Tom's and Mel's room before he'd stopped speaking. It couldn't surely be happening? Not this quickly, a first birth?

411

Mel was half-propped up against the pillows, panting, her eyes huge in a white face and her legs apart but covered by the sheet. 'Oh Dora,' she wailed.

'Contractions?'

Mel nodded. 'Yeah,' she gasped. 'Couple of hours, on and off. I thought it was just those aches like earlier, and then – Oh God, here's another one. Shit, I want to push!'

Christ, it looked as if it was happening. What should she do, what should she *do?*

Oh pull yourself together, woman. You've looked at a dozen websites on emergency delivery, get on with it.

'OK Mel, try not to push, just blow, like they told you in the classes. Like this.' Dora gave a series of short breaths through pursed lips, willing Mel to blow with her, and thank God, she did. 'That's it, good girl,' said Dora, when the contraction had passed. 'It's going to be all right,' she went on, stroking Mel's hands. 'You're going to be fine. Mind if I have a look?'

'Go ahead,' gasped Mel.

Dora had a look. No sign of the head yet. But it was happening, it was certainly happening. It looked as if Faith was going to be delivered in this room by the ambulance people. If she waited that long.

She became aware of Tom, looking over her shoulder. Behind him was Larry, his blue eyes wide with amazement and his mouth open. 'Tom, come over here and support Mel's shoulders, and Larry, could you bring about half a dozen big towels or blankets. Oh, and boil the kettle.' What was it they had to do with the hot water, again? Oh God, let the ambulance get here soon.

Ah. Another contraction. Mel's face was screwing up with the effort. 'Breathe, Mel,' she said, and once again she blew, and so did Tom, and Mel blew with them.

'Oh God, oh God,' sobbed Mel when it had passed, and Tom held her, tight.

'I love you Melly.' The words came out of him in a panting gasp.

'I love you too,' said Mel in a tiny squeak. 'I just want this thing out – *now!*'

Dora had another look. This time, unless her eyes were deceiving her, there was something, a small circle of something dark that could only be a baby's head.

OK. Gradually, gradually, that's what the websites said. Let the head come out gradually. Time for a morale boost, though. 'Hey, I can see Faith,' she said.

'Can you? Oh my God,' sobbed Mel.

There was no holding Mel back with breathing exercises then. A herd of elephants couldn't have stopped her pushing.

Support the head, don't let it pop out.

Right. Right. Dora held her hands against Faith's head through the next five contractions, as the small circle became a bigger circle, then a decidedly big circle.

And then the doorbell rang. Thank God. No, no, thank Capella!

Two women in paramedics' green overalls appeared, and with them Larry, carrying a huge pile of towels. 'Over to you,' said Dora and slid off the bed. 'OK Larry, let's go and find the camera, shall we? Give us a shout when you need it, Tom.'

'I – I was not sure whether to bring the kettle upstairs,' said Larry. 'It has boiled, but…'

'Tell you what, let's make a big pot of tea,' she said.

The tea was made and some of it even drunk, by Dora and Larry. What was left was by no means cold by the time they ran upstairs with the camera. It wasn't Tom who'd given them a shout, but Faith.

Tom sat there, gazing down at the sleeping human being in his arms. Ah, the *lightness*. And at the same time, the *weight*. He hadn't really taken in anything that had been said to him for

413

hours, all he'd been able to take in was this: Faith, his daughter. That is, if anyone could call what he was doing 'taking in', this amazed breathless contemplation. 'A perfect little girl,' he'd been told. But it was going to take a while for Faith's perfection fully to sink in. A long while. The rest of his life, perhaps.

At last, the house was quiet, the to-ings and fro-ings of people in uniform had finished, Mel as well as Faith had been checked over and cleaned up, and it was just the four of them here – no, *five* – in the early light of what looked to be another fine day.

'OK, that's the lot for the moment,' said Dora, switching off the phone she'd been holding in front of Tom's mouth while he told the people who needed to be told: Jackie Baines, Tommy, his father, who said little more than 'Ah, aye,' and not forgetting Syd Clayton. Dora took over when Syd's children came on the line and Tom was beginning to trip over his tongue.

Larry, sitting beside Tom, said, 'Wonderful…wonderful.' It was what he'd been saying from the moment Faith was born.

Tom bent his head and touched his lips to Faith's forehead. It was like kissing gossamer. 'Your turn,' he said, placing Faith in Larry's arms. Dora picked up the camera and took what had to be the hundredth picture of the day so far.

After a minute or so there was a whimper, and a pair of eyes opened. Blue eyes, but apparently that could change. 'Oh, oh, little one,' said Larry.

Time to go to Mum for another breakfast? Tom took Faith from Larry and gave her to Mel, who was sitting up in bed looking like a queen.

Yes: blue eyes, for the moment, at least, and hair that was fair rather than dark. 'She's a little angel,' Dora had said when she first held Faith, with that trust-me-I-know-what-I'm-talking-about tone in her voice. He'd taken the picture then.

The look she gave Faith, stroking her with her eyes, as you might use a feather to stroke the dust from a priceless ornament, would stay with him. The look she gave him would stay with him too. *It's all right now. Isn't it?*

Insofar as he could think at this moment, it did seem all right. Something had happened to his perspective. His field of view was suddenly wider, like a film screen from the days of wide screen epics, and there was a baby in it. And there was a young woman who'd never looked lovelier, even with those circles under her eyes. There seemed, astonishingly, plenty of room left over for an older woman who had a way both with words and with friendship.

When Faith was imminent, he'd gone to Dora without a second thought. At that moment, no-one else would have done.

'Right, people, seeing Faith there having a snack suggests to me that it's time for a little something,' said Dora.

'Oh yes, shall we make breakfast, Dora?' said Larry.

Tom was sitting on the bed, an arm around Mel as she fed Faith, when Dora reappeared with a tray, Larry coming behind her with a pot of coffee. 'OK guys, it's only toast and the trimmings but it's hot,' she said, keeping the loaded tray carefully balanced. She was biting her lip with concentration, and for the most fleeting of moments his heart seemed to miss a beat.

Tom's heart was beating at its normal rate by the time Dora put the tray down, but it occurred to him that there was one whose opinion he'd have to consult before he could be sure about the all-rightness of things. Capella.

She was rising in the sky day by day, now that the year was wearing on. Some night soon, he – they – would have to look at Capella.

Thirty-Three

Tights again, a skirt again. A stomach full of butterflies again. The day when the Judge would tell the waiting world whether, in his opinion, and taking due consideration of the views of the experts, parents of infants could sleep soundly in their beds without fear of Dora Clayton. He had to be nice to her. She'd as near as dammit delivered a baby, hadn't she?

Let me not faint this time. Please.

Judge Barrington was clearing his throat.

OK, breathe. In, out, in, out. Blow if you have to, the way you did with Mel.

Let me get through this. Let me hold Faith tonight.

'Ms Clayton,' began the Judge, and then Dora was struck by something. He had a mole, just where that paramedic, Jo's paramedic, had had one, and it was bobbing up and down as he talked. How hadn't she noticed that before? Oh God, what was he saying, what was he *saying*, what – probation? Had she heard that right, was he actually talking about probation?

A year's probation. And continued care from her psychiatrist. Dear God, was that it, was that all? He must have got her mixed up with someone else, probably the next case. Should she say something?

But Kate Ojo was grinning all over her face.

There was a hand on her arm. She looked up, at the folds of a black gown. 'You are free to go now, Ms Clayton,' said the usher.

Free to go. *Free.* All right, she'd go then.

Larry was waiting for her by the door. She saw him see her, and then his face crumpled. The next moment, she was seized and held, her nose pressing into an expanse of jacket.

'Let's go home,' she said when he relaxed his grip sufficiently that she could move her jaws. To think she'd ever thought of herself as the one who was helping him.

It got into the *Oxford Mail*, just a couple of paragraphs. The main story interest wasn't in Dora at all. Rachel Booth was still missing, apparently, and baby Ryan was in care because his grandmother couldn't cope with both him and Rachel's two younger brothers, each of whom had behavioural and learning difficulties. The older one had had an ASBO slapped on him for letting down car tyres.

'They can't punctuate nowadays, these journalists,' she said. '"The baby who has a heart condition is now living with foster parents," this says. It should be: "The baby comma who has a heart condition comma," shouldn't it. I know that, and I was only a scientist.' A heart condition. Oh God. Please let her not have made it any worse.

Nobody said anything as she refolded the paper and tossed it onto the kitchen table. Faith didn't even give a whimper, but then she was in the middle of breakfast, snuffling and snorting away there at Mel's right breast. Mel was looking at Dora. She could guess what Mel was thinking. *Poor little sod, he'd have been miles better off with you.*

Ah well.

'Ow!' said Mel, laughing. 'If she's like this now, what's it going to be like when her teeth start coming through?'

Can't tell you, Mel, sorry. Never got that far. For a moment, Dora's nipples tingled as if electric sparks were streaming from them. But only for a moment.

Oh, it would go on happening, of course it would. Especially when she herself held Faith and the baby rooted for a nipple, as she did to anybody and everybody when she was hungry. But she'd cope. With Faith, things were all right.

The phone in the hallway began to ring. 'I'll get it,' she said.

It was Syd. 'Yes, yes, OK, *OK*,' he said. Then: 'Sorry, Dozz, the kids are right here. They've got me in an armlock, so to speak. They're insisting I tell you astronomical club's happening tonight, and they'd really, really like Faith to come. I've told them there isn't a bat's chance in hell, but my life wouldn't be worth living if I hadn't at least mentioned it.'

'Remind them they're coming here on Sunday to coo at her.'

'I have. Hey, get off, Jim!'

Down the phone came mutterings and scufflings, and then: 'Hi, Dozz!'

'Hello, Jim,' she said, holding the phone slightly away from her ear.

'We wanna see Faife!'

No mention from him about how her court case had gone. Good. But then, he and Jenny weren't aware that she knew all about the court system now. Syd had never been in the habit of telling them every last thing she got up to. Dozz had had a spell in hospital, just like a few years ago, because people did when they weren't feeling well, that was all. And now she was all right again.

What if Jim and Jenny did find out, though? At school, say. Somebody's mum or dad might see the *Oxford Mail* piece and recall aloud that Dora Clayton was that woman who used to live around the corner until a few months ago, wasn't she? Small ears might be flapping. There could be playground talk.

Oh shit, she'd deal with it when it happened.

As she was trying to tell Jim that Faith was a bit young to look at stars yet, Mel and Faith appeared in the hallway: time for the post-feed nappy change. Mel cocked an eyebrow. 'Just a minute, Jim,' said Dora, at which moment Tom appeared too. He didn't want to be left out of the fun of nappy-changing. He was getting so predictable.

It was all right now with him, too. Wasn't it?

Mel said why shouldn't they all look in at the astronomical club for a little while? It wasn't cold, and Faith would be wrapped up anyway. And it wasn't as if she had a bed-time yet to be up later than.

Tom seemed to need to think about the proposition. At any rate, for a moment his eyes had a faraway focus, as if he were looking beyond Mel and Dora rather than at them. Then he was back with them. 'Yes, all right. I can carry her inside my jacket.'

Hm. Tom with Faith strapped to his chest in the baby sling? The women club members would go home afterwards and re-evaluate their lives and find them so horribly wanting.

So. She'd be looking at stars again, with him. Would Capella be visible? Better be, actually. Bloody well better be. It was time.

That afternoon they had a flying visit from Jackie Baines, in cropped trousers and big sunglasses, looking not a day over thirty-five. On the face of it, Jackie was bringing yet another armload of presents for Faith, from what seemed like an unending supply of relatives. What she was really doing was checking out – again – this weird house-share her daughter had got herself into.

Dora didn't dare catch anybody's eye when Larry, presiding

over tea in the garden, offered 'Darjeeling or Lapsang?' But she could relate to Jackie, there was a sort of restless ferocity in her. Daughter of Italian war refugees; five kids; married to a builder; office manager for a firm of estate agents. Maybe when she knew Jackie better she'd find out what all that stacked up to.

'If you're going to want me to mind the baby when you're doing these university interviews,' said Jackie to Mel, 'you better give me plenty of notice, right?'

'I've told you, Mum, we're going to manage,' said Mel.

'That's right, Jackie,' said Dora. 'I'm between jobs, I'll be glad to look after Faith whenever Mel wants.' Between jobs: that was a good one, on the spur of the moment.

Nice of Siobhan to keep her job open, though. One of these days she might get around to wondering if she was ever going back, but not now, not yet.

'Melanie will have every support from both Dora and myself,' pronounced Larry. 'We will be delighted to help.'

Jackie looked from Dora to Larry and back. She didn't seem to know quite what to say to that. Tom leaned towards her and said, 'Don't worry about the babysitting, Jackie, let's talk about the real issue. Which is what Faith's going to call you, right?'

'Not Gran, I'm not being Gran,' she sparked. Jackie obviously got on better with her son-in-law than she was letting herself admit. No surprises there.

What about another career shift? Maybe she ought to sacrifice those regular high spots in front of the University Offices photocopier and become a hospital cleaner, or something useful like that. Probably not in a maternity unit though, she might have trouble getting the references. Perhaps the stars tonight would tell her.

She found she was still looking at Tom. She looked away.

As Larry bustled about, pouring tea, offering scones, there came a sound she hadn't heard in a while. 'Nh, nh, nh-h-h-h-nh.' She couldn't help smiling.

Just before nine, Dora went upstairs to fetch a jacket. 'I'm off out for an hour or so, Jo,' she said. 'If you need anything the cat'll be downstairs, but remember he's not as young as he was so don't play him up more than you can help, will you.' The tin's stars twinkled cheekily at her from the table beside her bed.

Dr Fred Finch wasn't going to cure her of this. He wasn't even going to try, if he knew what was good for him.

At the astronomical club, stars were forgotten when people realised what Tom and Mel had with them. There were cries of 'Lovely,' 'Fantastic,' and 'Well done!' Some man with a particularly icky approach to life murmured something about a new star shining tonight.

'Jen, Jen, I've just realised, we've got a new cousin!' trilled Jim.

'No we haven't, *stoopid*,' said Jenny. 'Just 'cos Dozza's living with Faith doesn't mean she's a *cousin.*'

'It's OK, Jenny,' said Mel, 'Faith can be your honorary cousin. She'll like that.'

Dora glanced around for Syd, and saw him standing next to Tommy. No surprises there. One of these days, Jim might just turn out to be more right than Jenny on the subject of cousins.

Larry was commandeered by Mel to tell some constellation stories, and he soon gathered a small crowd, including Tommy. Syd wandered over to join Dora.

'So, Dozz,' he said quietly.

'So, Syd,' she replied.

They stood for a moment, not speaking, gazing up at the streak of spilt milk that was the countless millions of stars at the centre of the Galaxy.

'You know what?' he went on, 'I've got a bet on with Tommy. You'll all be staying put at Larry's and living happily ever after.'

'Oh, come on.' He'd seen what she was teetering on the brink of seeing but didn't quite want to look at full-on, in case it didn't happen.

'Well, you all get on fine, don't you?' said Syd. 'By Christmas Larry'll be putting in extra bathrooms and talking about making you co-owners. As a matter of fact I wouldn't put it past him to turn each floor into a separate flat. He'd be in DIY heaven.'

'But Mel hasn't got into Oxford yet. And Tom's job is for this term only.' Was she being superstitious? Maybe. Sure as anything, she didn't have enough fingers on her hands to cross for something like this.

'Mel will walk it. And a little bird tells me that Tom will be hogging the best chair in the staff room a bit longer than this term. Not a word yet, not even to Tom, but Linda's decided to get pregnant again.'

'Oh?'

'Yup. Of course, the permanency will have to be advertised, but…'

'Of course. As a matter of interest, which of you is betting what?'

'I was lying,' said Syd. 'We're not betting anything. We're in total agreement. Look, Dozz, think about it, won't you?' A serious tone had crept into his voice. 'If it came off, I think it would be good for you.'

'I'll think about it, Syd. Honestly. By the way, Mel and I have got a bet on about you and Tommy. She says a Christmas wedding, I say next spring.'

'What? Well, you cheeky – ' Just then, someone on Syd's other side made a remark to him, something to do with servicing one of the telescopes. As Syd turned away to answer, she heard, from her other side, 'Hi, Dora.'

Tom. A second ago, he surely hadn't been there? How *did* he do it?

'Hi,' she said. She looked up at the Milky Way again. He was looking up too, she knew that without having to turn her head. 'Mind-boggling, isn't it,' she said. 'I mean, they're so far away, and yet you could almost reach up and touch them. Sorry, was that a cliché or a statement of the obvious?'

He didn't reply straightaway. 'I'm not sure,' he said at last, 'but don't worry, I'm still OK with either.' He adjusted the level of his gaze to a point lower down in the sky. 'Can you touch that one?' he said.

Her turn not to reply straight away. The one he meant, it wasn't the brightest star on offer tonight, but it had something about it. She'd noticed that star the moment she set foot in this field.

She lifted her left arm and stretched out her index finger until its tip covered the point of light. 'Do you think she felt that?'

'If you felt it, she'll have felt it.'

'Ha. Ask a silly question. OK, you try it.' Her finger was tingling, very slightly. But stretching sometimes did that to fingers. Must be something to do with the circulation.

For a moment, she thought he wasn't going to play – after all, he did have both arms encircling Faith. Then he lifted one arm and stretched out a finger. 'From now on she'll rise a little higher each night,' he said. 'She'll be a little easier to see.'

'Only until February. Then she'll start dropping down again.'

'She'll be back, though.'

'You can't always predict the future by looking at how things have panned out in the past.'

A second passed. She felt him look at her. 'Very true. But in Capella's case it's a risk I'm prepared to take.'

'OK, I will if you will.'

'Right, then,' he said. 'Anyway, have you considered that she might see us even when we're not seeing her?'

'No… But I might allow the possibility to cross my mind. Do you think she likes what she sees?'

'Oh, I think she's pretty happy with it, actually.' As he spoke there came a tiny whimper from inside his jacket, and then a louder whimper.

'Ah, time for a snack,' she said. 'We'd better find Mel.'

'She can feed in the car,' he said. 'Then I think we'd better round up Larry and head for home.'

Tom settled Faith down in the cot and then sat down on the bed and gazed at her – his side of the bed. Not the conventional place to put the cot, perhaps, but to hell with convention. There was more room on his side of the bed. And this way, he could be involved in every feed: picking up Faith when she woke, handing her to Mel, doing the nappy change afterwards. He'd never have believed it, but you could feel great on only a few hours' sleep. Not that Faith was difficult or fretful. So far, they were lucky. Bloody lucky, even. Yes, he could take not sleeping through the night. The only night when Dora as parent had slept soundly, look what had happened. *Christ, man, don't.*

But this was it from now on, wasn't it? Fighting such thoughts, praying until the end of your days that someone else would outlive you?

He closed his eyes and took a breath, a long shaky breath. Then he opened his eyes again. OK, he'd have to deal with it. People did. Just as he'd have to deal with those stray times when just for half a second his heart would shift gear when Dora came into view, or when one of those conversations batted back and forth between them. Such as last night, when they were touching Capella.

Ah, Capella, Capella.

His hand, without any hesitation, reached out. It touched the start button of the cot mobile. The stars and planets began to revolve to the tune he'd had running at the back of his mind for weeks, months, and at last he could acknowledge that fact.

> *Twinkle twinkle little star*
> *How I wonder what you are*
> *Up above the world so high*
> *Like a diamond in the sky*

There was a sound behind him. He turned. Dora was standing in the doorway, smiling.

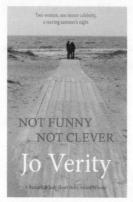

Bells

Jack has fun playing away – not with loose women, but as part of a Morris dancing team. But when a gig is cancelled and he falls for the young woman behind the desk at The Welcome Stranger, he is launched into a world of love-struck subterfuge.

"Excellent" The Bookseller

978 1870206 877 £6.99

Everything in the Garden

When Anna and Tom Wren join together with three other couples to buy a rambling farmhouse in Wales, the intention is to grow old with the support of tried and trusted friends. But life turns out not to be the bed of roses Anna had imagined.

9781870206709 £6.99

BETHAN DARWIN

Back Home

Ellie is broken hearted and so decamps home. Tea and sympathy from granddad Trevor helps, as does the distracting and hunky Gabriel, then a visitor turns Trevor's world upside down...

"A modern woman's romantic confession, alongside a cleverly unfolding story of long-buried family secrets" Abigail Bosanko

9781906784034 £7.99

Two Times Twenty

Anna's got a significant birthday coming up when she spots Jane, catering queen and all-round good egg, dallying on the doorstep of a man who isn't her husband. To tell or not to tell? Confronting her best friend with her infidelity probably means the canapés are headed for the bin...

"Chatty, frank and witty and you won't have any trouble turning the pages" Western Mail

9781906784232 £8.99

M STANFORD-SMITH

The Great Lie: A Nick Talbot Adventure

Kit Marlowe – England's finest poet – has been killed in a tavern brawl, his talent lost to the nation. Nick Talbot is an unproven youth, torn between a life on the stage and following in his military father's footsteps. Together they bring about a daring conspiracy...

"A tremendous ride through the swirl and bustle of Elizabethan life" New Welsh Review

9781906784164 £8.99

Sea of Troubles: A Nick Talbot Adventure

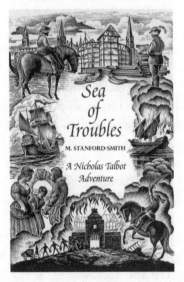

Tucked away in Verona, Kit Marlowe – according to history a dead man – continues to write his wondrous plays, now performed at the Globe in the name of Will Shakespeare. Nick Talbot has responsibilities to many, including Marlowe and his ability to seek out trouble is unerring...

9781906784270 £8.99

Hector's Talent for Miracles
by Kitty Harri

Hector, his mother and grandmother live quietly in a small Spanish town but when Mair arrives on a mission to find her lost grandfather their meeting has explosive results, and all their lives are revealed as fragile constructions forged in the fire of a vicious conflict...

"An intelligent and sympathetic exploration of the lasting damage done to survivors of war" Planet Magazine

9781870206815 £6.99

Salt Blue
by Gillian Morgan

Life is made of memories, sweet and sour: Stella's journey from seaside Wales to upstate New York, from child to woman, set in the late fifties. A novel of tangible sensual pleasures, Salt Blue paints a striking picture of life in a largely forgotten era...

9781906784157 £8.99

About Elin
by Jackie Davies

A haunting novel of love and loss.
Elin Pritchard, ex-firebrand, is back home for her brother's funeral. Returning brings all sorts of emotions to the fore, memories good and bad, her own and those of the community she left behind.

9781870206891 £6.99

Flint
by Margaret Redfern

On the long march from the Fens to north Wales, commandeered to build Edward I's new castle ditch-digger Will and his mute brother Ned find their loyalties divided.

"Utterly unforgettable…lyrical and haunting and beautiful"
www.thebookbag.co.uk

9781906784043 £6.99

The War Before Mine
by Caroline Ross

A brief wartime romance leaves Rosie heartbroken and pregnant, not knowing if Philip – on a suicide mission designed to stop the Nazi invasion – is alive or dead.

"A versatile and senstive chronicler of the world at war"
Sunday Telegraph
"Complex and engaging"
Western Mail

9781870206976 £6.99

HONNO CLASSICS

...is a unique series that brings books by women writers from Wales, long since out of print, to a new generation of readers.

Honno selects texts which are not only of literary merit but which remain readable and appealing to a contemporary audience. Each title includes an introduction, setting the text in its historical context and suggesting ways of approaching and understanding the work from the viewpoint of women's experience today. These classics help us to understand our own situations better, as well as provide, in a variety of different genres – novels, short stories, poetry, autobiography and prose pieces – a fresh and entertaining store of fascinating reading matter.

Professor Jane Aaron, Editor, Honno Classics

Queen of the Rushes by Allen Raine,
Introduction by Katie Gramich
A tale of the Welsh revival of 1904.
"[Raine] at the height of her powers as a novelist"
Sally Roberts Jones
9781870206297 £7.95

The Very Salt of Life
Welsh Women's Political Writings from Chartism to Suffrage
– edited and introduced by Jane Aaron and Ursula Masson
9781870206907 £8.99

Betsy Cadwaladr, A Balaclava Nurse
Introduction by Deirdre Beddoe, edited by Jane Williams. An autobiography of Elizabeth Davis the Welsh ladies' maid who gained fame as a nurse during the Crimean War.
9781870206914 £8.99

ABOUT HONNO

Honno Welsh Women's Press was set up in 1986 by a group of women who felt strongly that women in Wales needed wider opportunities to see their writing in print and to become involved in the publishing process. Our aim is to develop the writing talents of women in Wales, give them new and exciting opportunities to see their work published and often to give them their first 'break' as a writer.

Honno is registered as a community co-operative. Any profit that Honno makes is invested in the publishing programme. Women from Wales and around the world have expressed their support for Honno by buying shares. Supporters' liability is limited to the amount invested and each supporter has a vote at the Annual General Meeting.

To buy shares or to receive further information about forthcoming publications, please write to Honno at the address below, or visit our website: www.honno.co.uk.

Honno
Unit 14, Creative Units
Aberystwyth Arts Centre
Penglais Campus
Aberystwyth
Ceredigion
SY23 3GL